The Last Train
(To Brackley Central)

An Inspector Vignoles Mystery

Stephen Done

The Vignoles Press

British Library Cataloguing in Publication Data:
A catalogue record for this book is available from the British Library
ISBN 978-1-9164010-1-3

1st published The Vignoles Press 2019
Originally published by The Hastings Press 2011

The Vignoles Press
Stephen.done@gmail.com
FB: The Vignoles Press
www.inspectorvignoles.ukwriters.net

Set in Garamond
Cover design & layout: Bill Citrine
Photographs: Stephen Done and as credited
Printed in Poland by booksfactory.co.uk

The Last Train (To Brackley Central)

Author's Note

The Great Central Railway ran between London Marylebone, Leicester Central, Nottingham Victoria and onwards to Hull, Manchester and Birkenhead. Tragically, Britain's newest main line was gone by 1966–67, axed by the Labour Transport Minister, Barbara Castle.

Two sections of the Great Central have been preserved and one day will be reconnected. Readers are encouraged to travel on Britain's only preserved mainline double-tracked railway. Vignoles books purchased at the Great Central Rly shop at Loughborough Central will help support the railway's operations.

I am grateful to the Sefton-Smith family for the photographs taken in the desert campaign in Egypt, and to Mrs Ivy Clarke for the wonderful photograph of herself near Staverton Viaduct as a J39 Class locomotive passes, taken in 1949 by the late Harry Clarke. There is no connection between Mrs Clarke and any characters or events in this book.

A number of books have helped provide background, in particular Austerity Britain 1945–51 by David Kynaston (Bloomsbury, 2007); The Great Central: Then and Now by Mac Hawkins (David & Charles, 1991); the glorious photographic books by Colin Walker, of which Great Central Twilight (Pendyke Publications, 1986); and Mainline Lament: The Final Years of the Great Central route to London (OPC, 1973) proved useful. 'Steaming into Northamptonshire' by Richard Coleman and Joe Rajczonek was invaluable.

The excerpt from 'A Dream In the Desert' by Eliot Crawshay-Williams is used with special thanks to Miss Sylvia Crawshay.

There was never a railway detective department, and considerable liberties have been taken with reality to create this work of fiction. Any similarity to persons living or dead is unintentional.

For Adrian and Rosemary

Chapter One

Egypt
July 1882

The line of camels plodded slowly but sure-footedly through the white sand, the sapphire blue sky broken only by a line of palm trees shimmering on the horizon, marking the place where the single-track railway crossed their path. A locomotive smoked below the palms at the head of a short line of cream-coloured coaches swimming in the heat haze whilst it took on water at the pretty little station at El Alamein.

The heat seemed to soak up sound like a dry sponge takes on water, rendering the scene almost a silent mirage, and those travelling with the caravan could hear only the small and intimate sounds of their own progress; the heavy plod of the seven camels on the undulating ground, the creak of saddles and the straps and stays of the packs slung across their flanks, the occasional snort or grunt from the beasts and the gentle clink of bridle metal. The brightest sound was the tinkle made by the jewellery of Anoukh El Ali as she swayed, rhythmically, to the steady tread of her beast.

She was dressed in all the finery of a Nubian woman of considerable wealth and status, wearing a closely-fitting tunic of white cloth relieved by two emerald green and scarlet stripes, the deep cuffs of which were woven with designs in the same scarlet and green and shot through with yellow. Her pantaloon trousers revealed thick ankle-bands of gold above bare feet, whilst her long and voluminous head dress hung in great pale billows about her body and flowed elegantly down the back of the camel's hump. Anoukh's upper arms were gripped by chunky bracelets and half-moons of gold swung from her ear lobes, whilst about her neck hung necklaces made of finely-cast bronze discs and squares of gold which clinked gently against the twin mounds of her heavy breasts, sending darts of light into the eyes of Mustafa, her man servant, whenever he looked back to see if she needed water.

His lady was troubled. Her face an impassive mask that resembled the gigantic statues of long-dead ancestors carved in black stone standing in the temples beside the Nile and staring into unblinking infinity. Her almond shaped eyes had black pupils, like polished beads, her young skin a flawlessly smooth cocoa brown and her generous lips elegantly sculpted as if from obsidian. She looked far ahead with an enigmatic expression that betrayed no emotion, masking her inner turmoil and sense of loss. Mustafa turned away and made a clucking sound with his tongue to urge the haughty camel forwards, concentrating on maintaining a perfect straight line to the caravan.

Anoukh sighed, silently, but no less long and deep, seeking a release from the great press of sadness swelling inside. She had left in such a hurry, with hardly time to even think of what she was doing, but there was now time enough to appreciate the dreadful reality unfolding before her. She had been dragged away, tears streaming down her face and forbidden to even see the body of her husband; just bundled onto the waiting camel and told to adorn herself as if it were her wedding day, with her most precious jewellery, and what she could not wear, she must keep close to hand, for it was time to flee with anything of value that it was possible to take whilst perched upon a camel.

A shell fired from a British naval gun had killed her husband instantly. It was impossible to see his mutilated body, she had been told, impossible to kiss his cold lips one last time and say goodbye.

The bombardment of Alexandria had been sudden and terrible; a terrifying day filled by great detonations that rocked the ground and sent shockwaves of heat rolling along the streets and physically pushed people aside like a stubborn camel will sometimes body-charge its keeper. Fires had raged unstoppably and the acrid smoke and stench had been held low upon the houses by the immense heat of the day rendering it almost impossible to breathe, choking everyone on the poisonous fumes. Confusion and panic had spread faster than the flames as the warships pounded the fortified walls of the ancient city, and soon the hysterical talk was of an imminent invasion, and of the terrible, unspeakable things that these Imperial marauders would do to the Egyptian women.

Her servants had begged and pleaded with her. She must escape the city until things calmed down and order was restored. It had been but a matter of hours before they trudged out of the burning city and headed west. They had taken tents and clothes and just some of the smaller and more valuable of her possessions.

Anoukh cast her eyes down to a small pouch slung over the pommel of the saddle and slipped a long-fingered hand inside, removing a small square box of dark wood decorated with patterns of inlaid brass and ivory. She opened the lid and carefully lifted the ring from the velvet lining.

It was an object of rare beauty. A simple gold band supporting a large solitaire diamond. Holding the ring between thumb and forefinger, she lifted it, so the late afternoon sunlight pierced the stone. Even an untrained eye could tell this was no ordinary gem.

The light flashed and burned inside, appearing to smoulder like the embers of a fire, and whilst the outer edges of this intense light were of the purest white, deep in the heart of the stone it appeared tinged with yellow.

'Almost pure white and completely free of occlusion, of any imperfections, all except for one tiny and surprising detail. There is a stain of yellow, no more than a pinprick of colour, and the jeweller has used this imperfection to his advantage, placing it at the heart of the stone, where all the light collects and reflects in a masterstroke of his art. The effect is like looking into a cobra's eye!' That's what her husband had said when he presented it to her, his face alight with an almost fanatical excitement. 'Look, Nushka, it transfixes you, just as a cobra does with his eyes when poised ready to strike!'

Anoukh, although thrilled by the obvious quality and beauty of the ring, had been less enthusiastic about the analogy. An angry cobra was something to fear, not love, and as the days and weeks had passed and she had repeatedly gazed into the depths of this truly remarkable diamond, she could not shake off the feeling that it held nothing less than a drop of deadly venom that rolled and pooled deep inside the heart of the stone. It was a ridiculous notion, and she had tactfully remained silent on the matter, but his insistence that henceforward the diamond be known as the Cobra's Eye had done nothing to quell her unsettled feelings about it. He had written the name on a slip of paper in his elegant cursive script and pasted it to the base of the box, 'so you will never forget the name, dear Anushka!' The truth was, she preferred not to be reminded.

As Anoukh now turned the ring and felt the brief darts of blinding

3

refracted light prick her eyes, she was filled with a mixture of profound sadness and creeping fear. Since Muhammad had bought the Cobra's Eye, nothing had gone right for them. Her husband had paid a considerable sum for it, of that she was sure, but soon afterwards his thriving trade in antiquities had unexpectedly taken a painful loss when a once-loyal customer swindled him cruelly. Their finances had been put under a terrible strain as a consequence. They had also started to bicker and argue in a way they had never done before in the two years since their marriage, and Anoukh's mood was not improved when her dog was struck down by a heavy cart in the street outside and died in agony. And now, Muhammad himself was dead. Blown to pieces amidst the ruins of his shop in a stroke of unpleasant irony, by a shell from a British warship. The valuable stock he had traded with wealthy British tourists on their 'Grand Tour', was now probably burned, mangled or looted. Anoukh was not sure if a ring could carry bad luck, but it certainly felt that way.

Was it coincidence that she had forgotten to wear it the very morning the shelling had commenced? Had this curious oversight somehow spared her life? It was an unsettling idea, but there was no denying that she and her loyal servants were now safe in the desert, and if she sold the cursed ring she could raise more than enough money to live comfortably for a very long time. When things quietened down, she would travel to Cairo and rid herself of the bad influence she was increasingly sure this odd stone had brought into her life.

She closed her eyes for a few moments, holding back tears. But this was the last thing her dead Muhammad had given her, and his hand had written the label pasted to the base. Could she really part with it?

Anoukh placed the ring back in the box and closed the lid, lifting her eyes to the horizon. She watched as the train pulled away from the station with little black puffs of smoke that hung in the sky like the explosions from the warships sitting off Alexandria, the sound of the chuffing finally reaching her ears, delayed by the distance and out of synchronisation with the appearance of each cloud from the chimney. As she watched, she felt for the opening of the pouch and let the little box slip inside, her mind already made up to sell the diamond at the earliest opportunity.

But she made a mistake. Her fingers had slipped between the pouch and the soft blanket thrown over the saddle, fooling her into thinking the box would drop safely to join the other pieces of antique jewellery and a clutch of gold coins that lay inside the pouch. Instead, it tumbled silently to the ground, unseen and unheard, to be immediately pressed into the sand by the hind leg of her camel.

Chapter Two

Egypt
4th July 1942

'Bugger me, I'm parched!' Private Raymond Coulson of the 7th Armoured Division spoke aloud and to no one in particular as he threw his dusty bedroll onto the ground and dropped his pack beside it. Unscrewing the top of his water bottle, he drank heartily to clear the cloying dust from his throat, enjoying the sound of the water glug-glugging from the constricted opening and at that moment, tasting better than a pint of the elderflowery Hopcroft & Norris IPA in the Red Lion.

Driving a Humber Mk II armoured car across a scorching desert was hot and dusty work. His clothes were damp and in places stained white with sweated salt, his neck and forearms burned pink from the sun and his eyes dry from staring into the heat haze, trying to detect Rommel's Afrika Korps, who were lying dangerously close; coiled like so many angry cobras in the sand and ready to spring and bite, in their desire to halt the allied push west towards distant Tobruk.

Coulson and his crewmates had just finished lashing up a makeshift canopy of sun-bleached canvas to one side of their vehicle and were now selecting a billet spot for the night. The others had chosen to bed down beneath the awning in what would be a crowded huddle, but Coulson needed more space.

Squeezed into the pint-sized vehicle all day, smelling the sweat and fear of the crew, their arms and legs continually pressed close to each other with no room to stretch or change position, he now needed space to breathe freely. He wanted to lie on his back and stare at the stars during the bitterly cold desert night and feel his body cool after roasting in that Tommy-cooker of a Humber, and gratefully inhale fresh air, seeking to eradicate the constant stink of exhaust fumes, cordite, sweat and motor oil.

Loosening his blouson jacket, he flopped onto the bedroll to remove his boots. Stuffing his noxious socks into the boot openings to prevent scorpions climbing inside, he wriggled his toes and already felt more comfortable. He pulled a packet of Camel cigarettes from his top pocket, extracted one and rested it on his cracked lips. Catching the eye of 'Bounder' Baker leaning against a stack of water cans, he raised the packet in a gesture of silent invitation. Bounder grinned, and Coulson expertly flipped the cigarette across the divide in a spinning Catherine wheel flight.

He lit his own cigarette and lay down, preparing for a few minutes of luxury with his legs stretched out fully for the first time that day. He wriggled his back, trying to get comfortable, but then sat up, patting the bedroll and feeling for the lump jabbing into his spine. Stones were always the impediment to a good night's sleep when off the deeper and softer dunes. The land near El Alamein was flat, and the sand only partially masked the rocky terrain below. This made it easier for their vehicles to traverse but was a right pain in the backside when bedding down. He noted the many stones on either side of his bedroll and decided against trying another spot, so instead, he knelt down and peeled the top corner back to reach underneath and explore with his fingers.

He was surprised at the neat and regular shape he encountered and the sharply-defined corner standing proud of the sand. This was not a stone.

Coulson peered around the bedroll and saw a small ornamental box poking out of the sand at an acute angle. He immediately felt a tingle of anticipation. Palming it in one of his big hands, he made a play of throwing away the two flat stones between which the box had been trapped, then patted his mattress flat.

Checking no one had noticed his discovery he lay down again, but this time on his side with his back to the Humber and his crewmates. Placing the box close to his body, he opened the lid.

He dragged heavily on his cigarette to mask the involuntary inhalation of breath he was forced to take. The Cobra's Eye sprang alive as the evening sun filled it with light for the first time since Anoukh El Ali had inadvertently dropped it so many years before. Coulson stared in wonderment at the yellow fire inside the perfectly cut diamond, marvelling at how it almost appeared alive as he slowly turned the ring, making the stone glint and sparkle. He knew nothing of gemstones, but he knew quality and beauty when he saw it. This was special. It was bewitching.

This was a ring any woman would love to wear, and now he,

Private Ray Coulson, a garage mechanic from a small market town in Northamptonshire, was going to be the man who gave this to his darling Betty Boo. It would be the perfect engagement ring, and he felt a rush of excitement course through his veins as he imagined Betty's face when she saw it. If he could just get through this next campaign and ship home on leave... He just had to avoid those deadly long-range 88mm guns all the Tommies feared. He closed his eyes and offered a silent prayer.

He swiftly kissed the cold stone, thanking the Lord for this extraordinary piece of good fortune then closed his fist, hiding it from view. Hauling his pack towards him with his free hand and puffing on the fag wedged between his cracked lips, he stuffed the empty box into the bottom and rummaged about until he located his emergency sewing kit.

The red ball of the sun slipped towards the distant sea and sent impossibly long shadows reaching across the undulating desert, burnishing the outline of a wrecked locomotive and a line of damaged railway wagons in a siding beside the distant station. Coulson carefully sewed the precious ring into the bottom of one of the pocket liners of his shorts, answering the curious enquiry from Bounder that he was 'just mending a hole'.

It would be safe from loss or detection sewn there, and yet would remain with him at all times. If the Humber took a hit and they had to bail out, his pack might be lost or burnt, and they often shed their jackets and undershirts in the terrible heat of the day, tying them onto the outside of the turret, but assuming he could stay alive, he would always be in his trusty, if rather voluminous, army-issue shorts.

Chapter Three

Helmdon
20th September 1942

It was hot, and the air was standing Sunday-still above the land with just a trace of breeze to rustle the long grasses and set bobbing the many wild flowers on the lush embankment. The sun beat down upon the broad vale, and Helmdon village, glimpsed between the arches of the Great Central Railway viaduct, was shimmering in the haze as it straggled up the valley side in a succession of picturesque cottages, built from a pale ironstone and topped by thatched or stone-slabbed roofs.

A tank engine and two grubby coaches looked like a toy in the sleepy station built by the long-forgotten Northampton & Banbury Junction Railway. It now cowered, as though overawed and humbled, below the dominating presence of the newer grand trunk line that spanned the valley on a giant construction of blue brick carrying the main line to London. A skylark climbed, its trilling, burbling song tumbling towards the land like the sound of tiny bells, the complex melody counterpointed by a flock of noisy jackdaws wheeling and cawing about a stand of beeches, in the shade of which, clustered cows contentedly chewing the cud.

Betty Askew was seated on a tartan blanket, her legs stretched out before her, glad she had chosen to wear cycling shorts, so the sun could warm her legs to just above the knees. She was leaning back upon her elbows, head tilted up to soak in the delicious warmth of the day and helping her feel relaxed and at ease, despite being completely alone with Ray for what was really the first time. She had been nervous and self-conscious as they had taken the short train journey north from Brackley Central to Helmdon.

Until today she had always met Ray in the company of others, only allowing him to accompany her alone on the short, late-evening walk along the broad main street back to her parents' house, where they enjoyed a few stolen moments in the moonlight at the gate, during which his arms encircled her waist as he tentatively sought a goodnight kiss. He had looked so eager when he'd asked her out, his eyes like that of a sad dog, and she could not refuse.

'What a day! It's a real Indian summer.' She closed her eyes for a moment, seeing red as the light passed through her eyelids. 'Gosh, but never mind India, is it hot like this in North Africa?'

'More! Far hotter than you could ever believe. At midday we couldn't be outside like this.' Raymond Coulson grinned at Betty, enjoying the look of incredulity on her face as she tried to imagine the desert sun and its terrible heat.

He was lying on his side, propped up on one arm with a long blade of grass in the corner of his mouth, enjoying the bitter green taste as he chewed the end whilst making the seed heads flick like a pony's tail at the other. He had just used another precious frame of film in his Box Brownie camera to capture the image of Betty with the viaduct behind her, but now he gently rubbed the side of his thigh, massaging the ache he still felt from the deep shrapnel wound that had sent him home to recuperate.

'Goodness, I don't think I could stomach that.' Betty brushed a damp lock of hair back from her forehead and felt a drop of perspiration trickle between her shoulder blades, hoping she did not look an overheated mess in the photograph when it came back from Boots the Chemist. 'How do you manage inside your armoured car? It must be stifling.'

'It's bad. Terrible at times, what with the sun beating down, and then there's the engine and exhaust right next to you. You almost can't breathe, and the metal is so hot it burns your hands to touch; but at least we're under cover; you would fry like a piece of bacon in the sun.'

Betty gave him another look of disbelief.

'The lads joke that if we rubbed lard on our skin we'd make a perfect Sunday roast by the end of the day!'

They both laughed, as so many did these days when trying to make light of something deadly serious; seeking to ease the burden of the dangerous and frightening reality that continually preyed on their minds and haunted their dreams; looking to find a twist of black humour in a war that could kill either of them in a moment.

'You're still as brown as a gypsy boy.' Betty gave an admiring glance at his wiry frame covered by his open-necked shirt and light flannel trousers.

Chapter Three

Coulson inspected his forearms, bared by his rolled-up shirtsleeves. 'It's faded. I was browner than a cobnut at one time.' He looked up, his face now serious. 'But it must be just as hard for you on those steam engines in this weather.'

'Not that bad.' Betty gave him a gentle smile, 'Though it can get jolly hot when I'm crawling between the motion whilst the firebox is roaring, and the boiler is making steam above my head. Oh, Ray, we must look such a frightful sight! What with the grease and the oil and coal smudges all over my face, and then there's the lovely perfume of the engine shed in my clothes that's so hard to wash out. I've got through more packs of "Frisky" soap powder than you can imagine.' She wrinkled her nose, accompanied by a cheeky grin. 'I do hope my hair doesn't still smell of that darned shed.'

'Not a bit of it, Betty. But I think you girls are not so different from us "Desert Rats". Coulson smiled sympathetically and they both laughed. 'That's what Jerry calls us. We're the "Tobruk Rats". It was supposed to be an insult, but we like the name and have adopted the title. It's become a sort of badge of honour, being a Desert Rat.'

'I know what you mean.' She paused, trying to decide whether to carry on. 'We call ourselves the "Dirty Girls Brigade." It's a scandalous title, but that's Mary Barrett for you. She's our boss - more like our ringleader - and quite a character. The name was her idea, of course.'

Coulson raised an eyebrow but grinned encouragingly.

'We're such a sight, what with our uniform of blue overalls, bright headscarves and heavy boots, and we like to sing all the time when we're cleaning the locomotives, to keep our spirits up.'

'I can believe you'd need something to help. It must be a rotten old job...'

'Oh no; I really love the work. Most of the time, anyway.' She paused and wrinkled her nose. 'In the winter it can be jolly hard, especially at 5am when the alarm wakes me...' Her voice brightened as she continued, 'but it makes one feel like one's doing something important. Helping to make a difference.'

As if to illustrate her point, their attention was drawn to the sound of yet another train approaching; one of a never-ending succession that had passed in both directions across the viaduct since they had laid their rug on

11

the grassy slope. Askew shaded her eyes with a hand and ran an expert eye over the filthy black engine with prominent dribbles of white staining the boiler barrel like spilt distemper, and an ugly scar of livid orange burnt into the base of the smokebox door at the front.

'A V2. They're jolly good engines, Ray. They'll go forever and can take a heck of a beating.' She spoke with the confidence of someone who knew about locomotives.

'Yeah?' He squinted at the unprepossessing looking beast as it slowly huffed and panted towards them, hauling an immensely long train of box vans that rattled and clattered past for what felt like an age. He looked unimpressed. 'Let's just hope this blessed war is soon over and you can do something more suitable.'

'What do you mean, "more suitable"?'

'It's no job for a woman, is it? Cleaning engines. I mean, it's all right as an emergency measure, I suppose, but...'

Betty flashed her eyes and drew herself up into a seated position, with legs crossed. 'Well, I love it. It makes me feel completely alive and happy, in a funny sort of way. I'd hate to be stuck in a boring office filing papers all day, or to be some mousey shop girl.' Her voice took on a contemptuous tone. 'In fact, Raymond Coulson, I'm really not so very different from you!' She gave him a defiant look, with a glint in her eye. 'I like to get my hands dirty and mend things. I enjoy getting everything running sweet, because sometimes, when we're short-handed, I'm allowed to help a fitter fixing up an engine. Only simple tasks of course, but still, it's satisfying to help get them up and running again.'

Ray Coulson was grinning at her mischievously.

'Well? What's so funny? You love your cars and lorries and mending engines and gearboxes and whatnot, and in the same way I like to prepare these wonderful iron horses.' She looked across at the brake van bringing up the rear of the goods train and the smoky trail left by the engine that was now dipping behind a stand of Scots pines, her eyes taking on a wistful look. 'I just wish I could drive them. The Soviet women do!' She gave him a look that defied him to argue against this fact.

He laughed and looked at her with admiration, eyes twinkling. The truth was, he liked her tomboy qualities, even if some men might consider her unladylike. She certainly looked woman enough now, with those thick, auburn curls touching her shoulders, a flatteringly thin, close-fitted summer shirt and shorts that revealed a tantalising hint of soft thigh.

She was right about him as well: he was a mechanic at heart - the son of a garage owner - and could imagine no other life. Not for him a life of books or numbers or whatever it was people did in offices, nor the relentless toil of the factory floor, working like automatons and just waiting for the hooter to signal the end of shift. He liked nothing better than tinkering with a car in the garage trying to solve a ticklish mechanical problem, or even puzzling how to effect an emergency repair to their armoured car in the middle of a barren, burning desert. Yes, a woman like Betty would suit him very well, and he felt they understood each other. He could imagine she would approve of his wish to carry on his father's motor garage business when the time came.

Another train rumbled over the viaduct, this time hauled by two heavy freight locomotives in tandem, both working hard as they pulled a line of wagons bearing a load tightly wrapped in brown tarpaulins with white letters declaring 'WD' upon them, strong chains securing the secret loads on wagons constructed from immense pieces of riveted steel. Although the cargo was concealed, it was obvious this was war equipment, and judging by the distinctive shape and bulk of the wrapped packages, they were probably tanks.

They both watched in mute silence as the monstrous train rumbled on its way, the engines barking and throwing dirty clouds of smoke into the sky as they dug into the incline. This unavoidable reminder of the war jolted them both back into harsh reality, and the effect of the soothing sunshine and the cheerful skylark were forgotten.

'When do you return? Have you heard?' Betty Askew bit the inside of her lip, not trusting herself to speak more without betraying emotion.

'I have.' He blurted it out. 'I didn't have the heart to say until now.' He gave a nervous cough and could feel the official letter folded tightly into his rear trouser pocket, pressed close to the little wooden box. 'I leave for the coast tomorrow.' His voice sounded clipped and dry, and he tried to soften the sound by swallowing saliva and easing a sudden dryness that was constricting his throat. 'My leg is mended and will strengthen on the voyage over. I'll be fully fit by the time I reach Alex. As good as new!' He tried to sound thrilled at the prospect.

They looked at each other in silence for a few moments, the laboured panting of the two engines echoing across the vale was like their own gulped breaths and pounding heartbeats. Betty eventually spoke, her gaze fell onto the tartan pattern of the rug.

'Tomorrow?' The word held so much meaning, rendered more heart wrenching for the slight break in her voice. 'So sudden.'

'That's why I begged you to come here today. I was desperate to have an hour or so with you away from everyone. Just the two of us, alone.' He felt a grip of nerves in his chest and a pounding in his ears.

Betty threw him a glance, but hurriedly looked away, using the shrill whistle of the tank locomotive in the valley floor as an excuse to do so, her vision suddenly blurred by a stinging in her eyes, and the little train swam past as though it were under water. She unconsciously touched the metal cap badge she had been wearing as a brooch since Ray had returned to Brackley as war wounded.

'I wanted to... be with you, like this. Because I, er...'

He stopped. He'd rehearsed this speech a thousand times during the last few weeks, endlessly practising the lines in his head, trying to imagine how Cary Grant or Spencer Tracy might handle it, but now it came to the moment he found his tongue felt too big for his mouth and the words failed him, just as his nerve had repeatedly failed the whole time he had been back in England. He had not once managed to pluck up the courage to broach the subject that filled almost every waking hour since that fateful discovery near El Alamein. Well, this was it. It was now or never.

Betty managed to surreptitiously wipe the moisture from her eyes and force a smile, suddenly pushing all scruples aside and reaching out to lightly touch the back of his hand with her finger tips, by way of encouragement. She could not trust herself to speak but knew her gesture would stand in for any number of fumbled words.

Ray placed his free hand upon hers and gave it a squeeze. 'I leave at seven tomorrow. I don't know exactly when I shall return. Perhaps I won't...'

'Don't say that!'

'But it's true. We both know that's how it is. And something I do know for certain is that I need a reason to return. I need something, er, someone, to keep me hoping and praying as I drive that blessed cooking pot on wheels towards the Boche, and that reason is you. My darling Betty Boo.' He could see her eyes fill with tears and felt her nails dig into his hand.

He gently released her grip to allow him to sit upright and delve into his back pocket. Now facing her, he brought his balled fist around into the space between them and slowly opened his fingers.

'W—what is that?' Betty allowed tears to run freely down her cheeks as she felt her heart miss a beat. Such a small and beautiful box could surely hold only one thing...

'Open it!'

'I—I can't... my hands are shaking too much!' She was not fibbing. Her hands trembled as she tried to open the ornately-decorated lid. 'Gosh, but is this really what I think it is? Oh, my giddy aunt...'

Ray grinned and nodded, 'Look inside. It's yours if...' He tailed off and watched with anxious anticipation.

'Oh, dear Lord!' She took a deep intake of air. 'It's so beautiful, so... I can't find the words to say just how beautiful.' Her eyes opened wide and her face glowed with excitement as she gazed at the single diamond glinting with its potent inner fire in the velvet lined box between them. 'Oh, Ray! Does this mean that we...' She bit her lip.

'...are engaged? Of course!' His eyes flashed. 'I want to see it on your finger...if you agree, that is.'

She nodded quickly, her lower lip held gently between her teeth, and she watched as he took her left hand and slipped the ring onto her finger. It fitted perfectly, as if made for her.

'With this ring I ask you to marry me.' He rushed the words out before he could change his mind or allow his nerves to fail him again. 'When the war is over, when we've both made it to the other side, we will marry.'

Betty held her hands over her heart for a moment, her breasts rising and falling as she took in what he'd said. 'We're engaged? Such a surprise, a bit of a shock. Oh, sorry, what I mean is of course, yes! Yes!' She leant forward and kissed him once, twice, then pulled back and with one hand on his shoulder, she held her left hand between them, twisting and turning her wrist to allow the sunlight to strike into the heart of the stone.

'My goodness, Ray, this is simply the most beautiful thing I have ever seen. The colours are incredible. Nobody would ever think it's not a real diamond. And I just love it so very, very much.'

'But it is, silly! This is not paste. It's real.'

'W—what? How? I mean...it's impossible — on army pay?'

He told her the story of the box under his bedroll. 'It was meant to be. I know it was. It was a gift from above, for us. Who knows who lost it or how long ago?' He gave a boyish grin, his face relaxed now he had heard her accept his proposal. 'See here,' he flipped the little box over to reveal a little paper label pasted to the base. 'I got one of the wogs in camp to translate what it says, and it's quite odd. It's called the Cobra's Eye, would you believe?'

'Ooh! How thrilling!'

'I know. I didn't let on to the man that there had been a ring inside, of course, just that I'd found the box, but he was intrigued, and he wanted to buy just the empty box!' He suddenly looked serious. 'But it wasn't stealing; it really was lost. Just buried in sand right in the middle of nowhere.'

'My goodness, what a story. And you immediately thought of me?' Betty blushed.

'Of course! I even had it looked over in London when I was shipped home, just as soon as I could get around on my crutches. The jeweller said it was of the very highest quality.' They exchanged excited looks. 'It's awfully valuable.'

She swallowed and sat in silence for a moment trying to take everything in. 'And you would give this to me?'

'If you agree to marry me.'

'I do, I do, I do!'

They kissed again, and she allowed herself to be gently laid back onto the warm blanket and feel his arms enfold her and hold her tight as they both admired the stone against the cobalt blue of the cloudless sky, the strange yellow fire inside mesmerising them. Betty stretched her fingers straight, making the sunlight flash in their eyes in pulses as she altered the angle of the diamond.

'Like a signal lamp,' Ray observed. 'We sign to each other across the desert with handlamps. They wink like eyes in the night.' He felt a sudden cold flush run through his veins, chilling him to the marrow as he recalled being on the Front, his burning desire to caress his best girl as she lay in his hands, body now trembling with excitement and her usual reserve apparently diminishing as she pressed herself close to him, was quelled in a moment as if he'd been plunged into an icy pool. Now he felt only a need to hold her close and press her hair to his face and breathe in the scent of her hot skin, whilst images of the vast desert night sky scored by incandescent rocket-tails, searing burning traces made by high velocity bullets and the great thunder flashes of explosions crowded into his mind.

She sensed the change, and also lay still, her mind a turmoil of acute excitement and the deadening weight of sadness that pressed onto her like a sack of potatoes, making her insides ache. She gripped one of his arms as she silently stared first into the sky and then into the indestructible solitaire diamond that she once again held aloft on her outstretched hand, praying that their love, now declared and sealed by this ring, would prove as enduring.

A solitary Spitfire droned overheard. It was flying slow and low and the pilot had left the canopy open, perhaps to better enjoy the day. Betty could clearly see the leather flying helmet and sheepskin-collared jacket of the figure inside. The pilot appeared to be in a happy and unhurried mood, for the aircraft described a gentle arc across the sky to allow him a clear view of Askew and Coulson embracing on the rectangle of tartan blanket below. The green-and-brown plane with the big red-and-blue roundel on the side, having completing a wide circle was now even closer to the ground as it passed over them again in a throaty roar, and Betty then realised that the pilot was a woman — part of the Air Auxiliary delivering a new or repaired plane — and she now raised a gloved hand above the cockpit side and waved. Betty smiled and returned the gesture, showing off her engagement ring. The airplane waggled its wings before rapidly accelerating away, the Merlin engine throbbing and crackling as it gained both height and speed until it looked as small as one of the many crows gliding and swooping over the Northamptonshire hills.

Chapter Four

Woodford Halse
23rd September 1942

The massive buildings of Woodford Halse Locomotive Depot completely dominated the northern end of what was really no more than a large village. It was an unexpected sight to a visitor not forewarned of its sprawling and brooding presence in the midst of one of the remotest parts of rural Northamptonshire.

There it lay, forever smouldering and never completely at rest. Even in the darkest dogwatch of the coldest morning there was at least one sooty figure slinking between the dark flanks of the great metal beasts stabled in tidy ranks; moving between icy engines with a shovel of oily wadding and broken kindling ready to set a fire; or quietly turning a valve or shutting a damper on one or other of the dripping, creaking, ticking machines that still held a fire within its belly; nursing them through the night until clocking-on time, when the fifty or more engines were stoked and prodded, watered and fed back into roaring life. And then this railway metropolis hooted and clanked and rumbled, punctuated by frequent bursts of noise like short landslides from the tall 'Cenotaph' coaling tower, whilst acrid smoke rolled across the gently dipping fields and verdant copses that should only be animated by the occasional chattering jay and rattle of pheasant, the sough of wind in the leaves, the bark of a farmyard dog or the clink of a horse harness at the farrow.

The running shed of the 'loco' was large, spanning six parallel tracks and topped by a forest of ventilation chimneys that attempted to remove the thick smoke belching from the stabled engines within although when the day was as windless and hot as it was now, with little draught to draw it upwards and out, the interior soon became blue-grey with a pungent, eye-stinging haze that made those working inside hack with dry, tickly coughs. When the sun shone it forced its way through filthy side-windows to create bright, delineated diagonals of light that scythed through the viscous smoggy gloom, vividly highlighting the crowded engines that were all so filthy that they looked monochromatic in their subtle hues of greys, dusty fawns and oily purple-browns, each engine standing over a black inspection pit between the rails and worked on by figures slowly turning just as devilishly dark with the all-pervading filth.

But today as the bell of St Mary's sounded, the midday sun was doing its best to bring some cheer, illuminating a welcome splash of scarlet on the front buffer-beam of an ungainly freight engine that Betty Askew and some of her fellow 'Dirty Girls' had been attending to that morning.

Betty had scrubbed the front end almost clean, appreciating that the red warning colour might alert a railway worker to the engine's approach and so help save their life. She now sat upon the front of the footplate of the 'O2' class freight engine, one steel toe-capped boot on the massive coupling hook, the other swinging free past the big, gold-blocked number 3839 painted on the buffer beam. Her hair was wrapped inside a turban of orange cloth with a silvery metal regimental badge pinned to one side that was glinting as her head bobbed in and out of the dust-laden sunbeam. Her friends were gathered about in a loose semicircle, all gripped with eager suspense.

Like Betty, most of them were wearing boiler suits faded to varying shades of pale blue and coated in grime and oil, with leather belts cinched at their waists to help improve the fit of these shapeless garments. They had further enlivened their dour uniform with coloured scarves tied at their throats and turbans or headscarves that offered glimpses of surprisingly glossy and perfectly arranged curls or rolls of hair, whilst bright lipstick completed the look. It was considered a woman's duty to keep her spirits up and to demonstrate through these little details that she was not beaten or cowed by Hitler, despite the acute wartime restrictions. However, despite their brave attempts at femininity, they were terribly grubby and wearing heavy work boots or rough clogs. As they urged Betty to 'get on with it and put us out of our misery', some of them were also removing an odd assortment of thick gloves or leather gauntlets, and these, once cast off retained much of their shape due to being impregnated by gunge and grease, making them appear like so many severed hands lying on the locomotive footplate.

'You can't keep us in suspense a moment longer.' Rosalind Dale looked almost in pain, such was her anticipation, her pencil-thin eyebrows forming two narrow lines of copper red against her freckly skin.

'Don't go coy on us, we need to see that blummin' ring; whip it out girl!' Rosie McMahon was one of the wilder members of the gang, seen by many as more 'forward' and outspoken that some of the others. She was lighting a cigarette perched on her bright scarlet lips as she spoke and winking in an exaggerated manner.

'Patience.' Askew grinned, her expression a mixture of glowing pride and embarrassment. 'I won't wear it on my finger at work for fear of damaging it, so I've decided to keep it on this...' She now worked her fingers beneath an orange and white scarf at her neck and pulled at a thin silver chain, carefully easing it free of her blouse to bring the ring into view.

'Ray won't mind - he'll be wanting a peek down there all the time!' Mary Bennett rolled her eyes suggestively whilst accepting a fag from the packet being proffered by McMahon. 'Good excuse! Might have to try that trick myself. Ha ha!'

'He'll love getting his hands down there!' Pearl Cooper laughed like a drain whilst somehow managing to keep a cigarette in place on her lower lip, expelling puffs of blue smoke in rhythm with her laughter. The others joined in. 'Good excuse for a fondle, eh?'

'Don't be silly,' Askew looked shocked. 'This is just whilst I'm at work.' However, her eyes gleamed with excitement. She now held the ring between thumb and forefinger for all to see.

'Oh, look at that. Just look at that diamond!' Susan Gibson clapped her hands together like a seal. 'It's unbelievable.'

The joking had stopped instantly, replaced by sighs and coos of admiration, turning into a breathless and hushed wonderment as Askew turned the ring in the light. McMahon pulled on her cigarette thoughtfully, Bennett just held her unlit cigarette still, frozen in the act of lighting it as if caught in a snapshot. The loudspeaker hanging in the roof space crackled into life as someone switched the radio on for Worker's Playtime, and the words of Al Bowlly singing 'That's a plenty' seemed to strike an appropriate chord.

'Dear God, I've never seen anything so perfect,' Bennett spoke in little above a whisper.

'It must be worth a King's ransom!' Dale was shaking her head in disbelief.

'I think it might, actually.' Askew clapped her free hand over her mouth and opened her eyes wide. 'I don't exactly know, of course. It doesn't matter. It's not ever going for sale.'

'Of course not.' Gibson nodded solemnly. 'Doesn't matter what the price tag is.' She was the one woman not wearing overalls, just a short-sleeved floral print shirt over a thin green vest, both damp with perspiration, beneath a pair of dungarees with the bib folded down and the braces tied around her slim waist. A little enamelled 'V' shaped brooch in red white and blue was pinned to her shirt collar. She was still breathing hard from having rushed across at the appointed hour from the neighbouring wagon repair works where she was a rivet hotter, assisting in the sweltering task of heating steel rivets on a forge until red hot, then holding them in place with tongs whilst the riveter turned the ends over with blows from an immensely heavy hammer, and so hold the massive components together on the wagons they repaired. She considered it not unlike assembling an oversized Meccano construction kit.

Gibson had been caressing her own wedding band, as if reassuring herself it was still there, but now mopped her glistening brow with the back of a hand, making a grey smudge of ash on the centre of her forehead as though she had just returned from the altar rail on Ash Wednesday. 'There's nothing more precious. Especially at a time like this.'

'When did he propose?' Bennett's eyes were wide with excitement. 'You kept that little secret quiet, you minx.'

'It's not a secret, Mary. It's just that...' Askew gave a thoughtful half-smile. 'You'll think I'm just being a silly goose, but it was all a bit of a shock. A nice one, but I needed time to take it in; to adjust to the idea that one day I shall be Mrs Betty Coulson.' She laughed, 'Gosh, it sounds awfully funny saying it out aloud.'

'Lucky you!' Dale grinned.

'Better start getting used to it, my duck.' McMahon leant forward to get a closer look at the diamond.

'I'm sure I will. Assuming Ray will... you know, be OK.' Her smile faded. 'He left straight afterwards. He was shipped out again, back to the front. We had no time to take it in properly. He was gone at the crack of dawn the next morning.'

'Woke you up did he?' Cooper gave her a wink and elbowed Askew's knee suggestively.

'No, he did not, Pear Cooper!' She carefully stressed the name in the same way her own mother used to do when she was being admonished. Askew's eyes flashed with indignant outrage, but she still laughed along with the others, hinting that Cooper was not completely wide of the mark. 'I suppose my emotions have just taken a bit of a shaking up,' she continued, her eyes turning glassy and voice cracking as she hurriedly ended the sentence.

Gibson, who had joined Askew sitting on the front of the footplate, put a consoling, if slightly damp, arm around her shoulders. 'That's normal, Betty. We all know how you feel. You've just won yourself a wonderfully generous, kind man and you want to start dreaming of your future together; but now he's back to that beastly war.'

Askew nodded quickly. 'It's not that I'm unhappy, and I know I mustn't be glum.' She took a sharp intake of breath. 'It's just...' she slowly turned the ring with everyone's eyes fixed upon its cold fire deep inside. 'I don't know how to say it right, but since Ray gave me the ring, since everything became so serious between us, I just can't shake off the most awful feeling of dread. There's a black cloud hanging over me and I just can't stop worrying about what's going to happen to us. I've not really felt like celebrating, or even talking about it. Is that beastly of me?'

They all fell silent, allowing the sounds of the engine shed to encroach. The soft hiss of steam, the rhythmic clang of a hammer on metal, a distant telephone started to ring, and an engine 'peeped' its whistle outside the shed.

'Ray will be back before you know it, just you see!' Margi Dickinson, who was a late arrival at the gathering, gave Askew a friendly pat on the hand.

''Course he will! He'll be back in no time,' McMahon tried to sound bullish.

Dale dropped her eyes to the oily concrete floor and looked thoughtful. 'Every night I cry myself to sleep praying my Derek will return home safe.

When our bombers are buzzing overhead my heart leaps and I look up and wonder if he is onboard and if he's looking down to earth to see me looking back, giving me the thumbs up that all's well. Until I get his telephone call from the base, I live in a state of nervous suspense. I can't know what ops he's flying, nor even when he's in the air, so I just survive each of the long nights, hoping and praying, and I'm only ever released from the burden during those few precious hours following his call. Then it starts all over again.'

Askew nodded sadly. 'It must be so hard. Gosh, and here I am acting like I'm the only girl in the world with a man in the war. I'm sorry; I must buck myself up and not be defeatist. He's still on a ship sailing to Africa, so I really shouldn't be worrying, not yet, anyway.'

'That's the spirit!' Bennett smiled.

'And it is the biggest rock, ever!' Cooper grinned, eager to dispel the sense of gloom circling about them like unsettling ravens threatening to pitch them all into a slough of depression. 'Hell's bells, Betty,' she adopted something approximating an American accent, 'you just got yourself set up for life with this little baby!', slapping her thigh and giving an extravagant stage wink.

They all laughed. As Askew looked up, her attention was drawn along the line of locomotives and the rows of cast iron roof supports, to the open front of the shed and towards a solitary plump magpie hopping confidently amidst the ash and clinker near an engine resting in the noonday heat. She wiped her eyes dry and tried in vain to catch sight of its mate.

One for sorrow...

Chapter Five

Brackley
1ˢᵗ September 1950

'Hoy, over here Digger!' Adrian Turvey called his dog. Digger wagged his tail to acknowledge but kept his eager nose to the ground whilst he weaved from side to side, moving from a clump of grass to a small bush and then on to another, as if vacuuming around them. Digger's amber coloured eyes furtively monitored Turvey's progress along the narrow path beside the Great Ouse until he judged it was time to bound across to his master, brush past his legs, then surge forward to buy himself some more quality sniffing time.

Turvey was walking in steady treads along the narrow path beside the meandering river, away from the pretty village of Turweston. He would soon cross the river on a rickety wooden bridge and pass Brackley mill, the roof of which, he could see nestling below the railway viaduct amidst a clump of trees. He would then cut up past St Peter's and climb up Church Lane, before having a couple of jars of the local brew whilst soaking in the last rays of sun on the bench outside The Greyhound.

It was a perfect evening, the day still firmly clinging to summer. The air was warm though a trace of coolness was creeping in after the intense heat of earlier, releasing a damp smell of loam and an aromatic perfume from the cow parsley florets that swished against Turvey as he walked. A waft of scented blue wood smoke hung in the air, curling lazily in circles and bleaching white when caught in the sunlight, whilst clouds of tiny insects danced above the path, back-lit against the tea brown of the sluggish water. A metallic dragonfly darted above the river in a flash of jewelled green. The bricks of the enormous viaduct were darkening to the colour of the ripening blackberries as the sun slipped behind the tree-topped hill to the right, leaving just the upper courses and coping stones to be set aflame by the fiery orange light. The massive edifice appeared almost insubstantial, softened around the edges by the haze lifting from the valley bottom.

As they neared the base of the viaduct pillars, the path became noticeably less clogged by the verdant vegetation, and Turvey looked up at the steep and regular slope of close-cropped grassy railway embankment studded with dandelion clocks and daisies in a riotous profusion of colour against the cloudless sky above. A few dense bushes huddled at the base of one the massive supporting walls of the viaduct that sank into the slopes like the ramparts of a castle.

Digger bounded up the nearest bank without noticing the incline, happily nosing around a few straggly hawthorns whilst Turvey stopped and rested on his stick and watched as a smart blue express locomotive trundled across the viaduct. He narrowed his eyes and could just read the name 'Victor Wild' on the brass nameplate. It was hauling a long train of teak-built coaches that were every hue from golden brown to that of tea without milk and even a lifeless grey, although he observed that one had a fresh coat of creamy white and bloody red that sparkled in the sunlight. Turvey recalled reading in the paper that this was to be the latest livery for passenger coaches and wondered how long it would take them to repaint the many thousands across the system. It sounded like it would be an awfully long process.

He could just hear the brakes squealing as it slowed to a halt in Brackley Central, a sound not unlike that made by the many swifts swooping and racing under the viaduct arches before describing a spectacular U-turn and hurtling back, flying low with deft twists and turns that made Turvey's head spin if he tried to follow one on its flight. The clock of St Peter's chimed seven and Turvey decided it was time for that pint and walked below the towering vault spanning river and path, enjoyed the echo of his footsteps as he did so, before stopping abruptly as his dog clattered down the embankment and almost knocked him over.

'Steady boy! Now what you got there?'

Digger wagged his tail furiously.

'Come on, give!' Turvey carefully took the little bone from his dog's mouth. Digger sat on his haunches and looked up, expectantly. 'What you've found, eh?' He turned the delicate bone in his fingers and puzzled over it for a moment. 'Where did you find this? Show me!'

His hound needed no more encouragement, bounding back up the bank, eager to show how clever he was, and recommenced sniffing around the base of a thick bush with gusto. Turvey stayed where he was and tilted his head to watch. After a few moments, Digger pushed his snout into the tall grass below the bush and then lifted his head, proudly holding something in his mouth, his tail working even more frantically. Without waiting to be called, Digger dashed headlong down the slope and skidded to a stop, just inches from the riverbank.

'Another one?' Turvey held the two slim bones in his palm, the most recent still glistening with saliva. Both were picked clean but in otherwise perfect condition. 'They don't look like sheep bones. No, Digger, they're no use to you. They'll be sharp on your mouth.' Digger looked crestfallen for a few seconds, then lost interest in this emotion and walked off, cocking his leg against a suitable fence post.

Turvey was about to toss the bones in the river, when he stopped. Was it the many swifts whirling close by? Or a trick in the way sound carried from the distant station? It had to be something like that, but whatever the reason, he could have sworn a sad, and almost inaudible, feminine voice had just whispered in his ear.

"Find me." It was a tiny sound borne on a breeze, little more than a breathy sensation inside his ear, as though someone had placed a speaking tube there and whispered down it as softly as they could.

"Find me".

He looked about but was alone. Was it the voice of a child playing somewhere? Or had he imagined it. Whatever the explanation, it startled him and he felt an odd sensation of discomfort crawl over his skin, making the hairs stand up on his forearms. As he watched the wheeling swifts and his lovable old dog fussing around beneath a bush and the sunlight on the sluggish river he started to feel calmer and tried to brush this odd experience aside.

He took another look at the little bones and chewed the inside of his mouth in a contemplative manner. What animal were these from? A badger? He was not convinced, and looked back up the embankment and thought it an unlikely location for an animal corpse.

Turvey stood lost in thought a moment longer, then shrugged his shoulders and slipped the bones in the top pocket of his threadbare jacket and deciding to ask his friend Geoffrey what he made of them. Geoffrey

Chapter Five

Austin was the town's head librarian, but he also fancied himself as both amateur naturalist and archaeologist and was thought to be 'good on bones', having famously once discovered and identified part of a Roman skeleton in a local dig before the start of the last war.

Whistling his dog to heel, they walked into the town, Turvey's thoughts already turning towards that well-deserved pint of 'Brackley Bitter'.

Chapter Six

Woodford Halse
3rd September 1950

'Nearly done!' Violet Trinder was holding a pair of long wooden tongs that hinged using a strip of curved metal at one end, and was using these to prod the steaming mass of white napkins inside the zinc tub on top of the stove, swirling the hot soapy water and lifting and turning those on the bottom to the top, releasing a pungent, chemical smell in a cloud of steam as she did so. Once satisfied, she clamped the lid back on and rested the tongs on top, cut off the gas flame and turned to Anna Vignoles, who was seated on the far side of the big wooden kitchen table, idly reading the back of a brightly coloured soap box.

'I'll let them stew a few minutes longer whilst we finish our tea. I can rinse and wring out later.'

'I'll help you, it'll take half the time, and if Robbie wakes you can look after him.'

'You really don't need to. I can manage.'

'As you manage every day. I'm perfectly happy to help, and the sooner we get them on the line in this lovely weather, the quicker they'll be dry.' Anna smiled. 'Do you find this Omo good?' she asked suddenly.

'I love washing dried in the sun and fresh air. It's the mangle that takes all the time when you're on your own.' Violet looked out into the sun-drenched yard as she was speaking. 'Sorry, what were you asking? Oh, the powder... Yes, I think it does a splendid job - one of those pesky door-to-door salesmen got me onto it. I normally have nothing to do with them, but he offered a free sample and I've stuck with it since. I always used Oxydol or Reckitt's Blue before.' She pulled the lid off a circular metal biscuit time with an image of the King and Queen on it. 'Have a flapjack - they're made with local honey - but they're a little overdone on the sides.'

'I like them like that,' Anna deliberately chose one with a darkened edge. 'Crunchy on the edges and soft in the inside!' She raised her finely plucked eyebrows and took a bite.

'You're too kind. I left them in too long because Robbie needed me at just the wrong moment.' Violet looked across at the shiny cream and black pram with its four large wheels and upswept pushing handle, and at the tiny pink-faced bundle lying inside, breathing softly beneath a white crocheted blanket. 'He's having a good sleep. If he could just wait until we get the washing on the line, that would be perfect.'

Robert Trinder was just three months old. His father was detective sergeant John Trinder of the British Railways Detective Department, based in Leicester Central station, where he worked for Anna's husband, detective inspector Charles Vignoles. However, for the last year, Trinder had taken over a tiny cubby hole of an office in Woodford Halse station two days a week in an arrangement that allowed the department better cover along the lower reaches of the Eastern Region's run into London Marylebone. It also meant that he could also keep a watching brief over the cross-country lines that intersected at Woodford Halse.

Apart from these operational advantages, it meant that Violet and he could continue to live in the rooms above her rented shop, and which could not be much closer to the railway. The shop was at the end of a terrace that sat in the shadow of the embankment and bridge that carried the railway across the village at the bottom of Station Road, which formed the main drag of the village. Although little more than a long row of typically Victorian red brick two-storied shops with sun-bleached awnings sagging above the windows, it was the centre of village life away from the dominating presence of the railway and its vast clanking marshalling yards and smoking locomotive depot.

The two women had become friends, and were long accustomed to the stresses and strains, odd hours and unpredictable happenings their husbands encountered in their work and had even become embroiled in some startling incidents themselves.

Violet had first met her future husband during one especially unpleasant incident involving her grown-up daughter, Jenny (born out of wedlock following a single night of ill-advised passion, when Violet was just 17). A gang of desperate men on the run had kidnapped Jenny, and it had turned into a dangerous and dramatic chase to liberate her. Violet and Anna had taken to each other immediately in the aftermath of this incident, and a close bond soon developed, a friendship also fuelled by a mutual love of fashion and nice fabrics.

In Violet's case, this was also a professional interest, running her own dressmaking business that retained her maiden name of 'McIntyre'. Anna was of English birth but Italian parentage, and had apparently inherited the Italian woman's innate love for stylish clothes, aided by a figure and looks that turned heads - she had famously stopped D.I.Vignoles in his tracks walking along the platforms of Leicester Central station in 1942, and the poor man had been rendered unable to think of much else until they were married in an austere service the following year. And whilst their wedding may have been much affected by wartime restrictions, Anna had worn a simple but perfectly fitted dress that only accentuated her natural beauty. Years later, when Violet saw the wedding photographs for the first time, she immediately spotted Anna's potential and encouraged her friend to wear some of her own creations or skilful adaptations of life-expired garments, appreciating that Anna was the prefect mannequin and could only help encourage others to commission or buy more of her work.

Their conversation that morning had already touched on the latest dress patterns, and they had agreed the design for an elegant evening gown for Anna. With a long billowing skirt and a tightly-fitted bodice, it required a zip down the back, and both women had become quite animated about the delivery Violet had just taken of a box of fifty brand new zip fasteners; the first of these precious items since 1941. Until now Violet had to be satisfied with re-using salvaged (and usually malfunctioning) examples.

'I shall ration these carefully as I can't be sure of getting more. Demand is going to be crazy. But don't worry, one of these is reserved for you. I can't wait to get started. You'll look an absolute dream, Anna.'

'I hope so. Or at least I hope Charles thinks so, as he's paying, bless him. It should be perfect for the autumn season.'

'You couldn't ask for a better birthday present: a gorgeous dress you'll love to wear and which he'll love you wearing!' They both laughed.

'Talking of perfect presents, I've not had time to show you before, but he also bought me something else...' Anna reached for her handbag and extracted a small leather-bound book with gold lettering blocked onto the spine and an embossed design on the front. A narrow ribbon dangled from between the pages. 'I was saying to Charles only a while ago how I wanted to learn more about the legends and folk stories of the area, and he managed to find this.'

'What a lovely book.' Violet admired the cover and the marbled end papers that swirled in complex fluid shapes of blues and greens. 'The History and Antiquities of Charnwood Forest,' she read aloud. 'Looks interesting, is it very old?'

'1842.'

'But it looks almost as good as new.'

'It's a remarkable survivor and in almost perfect condition. I like the woodcuts and engravings inside...'

Violet turned the pages as Anna was speaking, noticing their eggshell smoothness and creamy colour supporting highly detailed engravings on full-page plates protected by sheets of translucent tissue paper, and the elegant woodcuts used on the chapter headings. 'I like this one of a fox running through the fields. It captures the landscape around here so well and evokes something romantic inside me about England.'

'Doesn't it just?' They both admired a large plate showing a loose formation of ducks flying low above a river thick with bull rushes and reeds, the plate entitled, "The Seven Whistlers".

'I've only read a few chapters, but it reminds me how very old this country is. It reveals the layers of tradition and beliefs that lurk almost anywhere you choose to look. There seems to be a mystery around every turn and embedded in the very names of the villages and wells and the woods. But I'm especially taken with the chapter on the supernatural!' Anna widened her eyes as she looked at Violet.

'Ooh, really? I do adore a tale of the supernatural - although, preferably in company and on a sunny day!' The warm soapy smell in the air overlaying the scent of a Woolton Pie baking in the oven was suitably comforting and helped banish any fears of unwelcome hauntings.

'It's just silly superstition and old wives tales of course, but I can't resist them, and I do quite like the thrill. Part of me wants these to be true.'

'I'm never quite sure what to make of ghosts. I wonder if there's not a grain of truth behind the stories?' Violet shrugged her shoulders 'I've not actually seen one of course - but there's always a first time.'

'According to this book, we could get a chance to do so closer to home than I dared imagine!'

'What do you mean?' Violet sat upright, her voice slightly less confident.

'Let me find it - if I may?' Anna took the book back and flipped it open at the place marked by the ribbon. 'It's about the so-called 'Shag-dog of Birstall" She rolled her eyes melodramatically. 'A huge, black shaggy dog-like creature with a chain around its neck that it drags upon the ground, and with eyes that burn like coals. Woo-ooh!' She rolled her eyes in mock horror. 'But guess what? This beast prowls a lane between Belgrave and Birstall. Just yards from our house!'

'Oh goodness. Don't say that, I'll be petrified to visit you, especially now with Robbie.' Violet instinctively placed a hand on the handle of the perambulator and gave it a gentle rock.

'Ah, but according to the legend it protects vulnerable people especially women – and I'm quite sure small babies would be included too - so we have nothing to fear.' Anna had now found the place in the book. 'Apparently an elderly woman told the author that, "there is a shag-dog that lives in shag-dog pit. Sometimes I've heard him rattling his chain when I've been along the lane. They say he goes down to the Soar to drink."' Anna glanced up at Violet who now looked the very picture of alarm.

'She then tells of a young woman called Katie who was being followed one night down the lane by a drunken man whom she feared had sinister intentions, when; "Suddenly she heard a deep, strange bark. The dog came bounding down the slope from the shag-dog pit; huge and black and wild, his open jaws luminous, like dying coals, his eyes wide and staring and glowing with unearthly light, padding silently behind young Katie." The man was chased off by this beast leaving Katie to continue home, quite safely. The man was found drowned in the river the next morning.'

'What a curious tale. It could just be a mastiff or some such dog, and the girl elaborated it into something more, to make a good story.'

'I imagine so. The funny thing is Vi, there really is an old lady living in Belgrave who reckons the shag-dog helped her once, just like in the tale. Charles met her one time and she was so eager to tell him all about it, saying it was better than having a bobby walking the lane at night to keep her safe.'

'I'd be scared out of my wits if that great slavering thing was behind me. Give me a detective sergeant anytime!' Violet laughed.

Anna agreed. 'Charles thinks the shag-dog pit was landscaped into a bunker when they made the golf course, so the beast might have moved on by now.'

'That's a relief!' Violet looked thoughtful. 'You know, it's funny you've brought this up, because John came home the other evening with a strange tale. He'd been down to Brackley Central on a small matter, something trivial that makes no odds, and he was taking a cup of tea whilst waiting for his train home when a couple of the men working there got talking about some odd goings on. He said they were quite shaken up. 'Spooked' was the word he used. All on edge about strange apparitions seen around the station.'

Anna bit her lower lip in mock alarm. 'What sort of thing?'

'They talked of omens and warnings. Something about haunting whistling sounds in the night sky.'

'Not a very convincing argument on a railway station, as they're full of engines and guards whistling all the time!'

'I know, so you can imagine what John thought of that idea!' Violet laughed. 'What it all boiled down to, was a few birds flying overhead and a "woman in white," who had been spotted on the line on a number of occasions, pointing, as if indicating something beside the track. As though she was alerting them to something. The signalman raised the alarm and some of the men racing down the tracks to remove her from the running line, but she had vanished without a trace. Not a sight nor sound of her anywhere, and they found nothing by the line either.'

'This could easily be explained away...'

'Exactly what John told them. She was obviously a local who knew a short cut - a dangerous one of course - and no doubt she away melted into the fields and copses during the cover of darkness before the men could see where she'd gone. But John said the men were not convinced.'

'And that was it?'

'No. She has been seen at least one more time. One of the men was returning from trimming the wick on the lamp of a distant signal, when he saw this woman all in white standing on the line. He called to her, and she turned towards him for a moment. She raised her arms as if in alarm, but as soon as he hailed her she slipped down the embankment and disappeared. The thing is,' and Violet leant closer, 'he reckoned that she had no hands...'

'Get away!'

'It was dark and turning misty and he said she had a long coat on that might have been too long for her arms. A simple case of someone letting their imagination run riot.'

Anna took a sharp intake of breath, her eyes sparkling with excitement. 'A variation on the classic tale of the headless woman. They are nearly always dressed in white according to this book,' Anna tapped it with her manicured nails.

'Well there you go, and as far as these men are concerned, a woman in white – perhaps without hands - is stalking the line near Brackley viaduct!

Chapter Seven

London Marylebone
3rd September 1950

'Your ticket please, sir.'

'I have it here... er, somewhere.' Richard Irons put his holdall on the ground and fumbled in his baggy corduroy trousers, checking first one pocket, then the next, a look of consternation developing on his face as he withdrew a grubby handkerchief and a couple of coins, but no ticket. 'I only bought it a few minutes ago. Where on earth did I put it?' He patted his jacket wildly, an action that was unlikely to help find the tiny rectangle of printed cardboard.

The ticket inspector took a deep breath but looked at Irons indulgently; he was amused rather than irritated by the young man's actions. It was late, and there were only a few passengers beneath the echoing roofs of Marylebone station, so he was far from being rushed. He also had a fresh mug of tea steaming on the wooden shelf of his little booth at the barrier, whilst the warmth of the glorious "Indian summer" of a day London had just enjoyed, still lingered, so he was content to watch this young man's growing sense of alarm whilst aware that help was close at hand.

'Ah hum!' Someone cleared his throat.

'I really do have it.' Irons was flustered, not helped by the mocking raised eyebrow on the ticket inspector's face.

'This wot yer lookin' for, mate? You left it on top of yer blummin' trunk!' It was the voice of a young porter who had approached the barrier hauling a flat-bedded four-wheeled trolley laden with a couple of mail bags, a few interesting looking parcels wrapped in brown paper and tied with string, and a large trunk with a label boldly declaring:

Richard Irons Esq.
Magdalen College Grammar School for Boys,
Brackley.

'How silly of me! Thanks awfully.' Irons gratefully took the ticket from the porter, who winked and laughed. The ticket inspector barely glanced at the ticket before waving him through, an action accompanied by a slight shake of the head, despairing at the young men of today.

'I presume that's my train, old chap?' Irons nodded towards the short line of four coaches with a smooth flanked tank engine coupled to the front and hissing quietly to itself in the otherwise deserted station.

'That's correct, sir. The last train to Brackley Central. Stops there and comes straight back, so if you happen to fall asleep, you won't miss your stop, as they'll turn you out.' The inspector winked at Irons, and judging from the young man's slightly dishevelled appearance, sallow complexion and the redness around his eyes, had probably enjoyed a riotous weekend and was now feeling the effects.

Irons had indeed caroused long into the night. If that was not enough, he'd then been waylaid and encouraged just a few hours ago to have 'a hair of the dog,' by two of his more riotous chums in the Marylebone station bar. The weekend had cost him deep in the pocket and left him worse for wear, and to top it all, he'd managed to miss the train he'd planned to take earlier that evening. Thank goodness for this late one. He really needed the journey to sober up and make himself more presentable before he arrived at Brackley.

However, Irons had no regrets, because he had something to celebrate. He was heading out of London to start a new job - in fact, summer vacation work and teaching practice excepted - this was to be his very first job.

Teaching mathematics to fourteen and fifteen-year olds in a grammar school 'in the sticks'. Heaven knows what it was going to be like, and he was more than a little apprehensive about the days ahead, but he'd been impressed by the surprisingly ancient and authentically 'collegiate' look of the place, and the headmaster, Mr Stonehouse, whilst probably a bit of a tyrant and a dusty old cove dressed in his black cape, seemed a decent enough cove.

Another incentive, and one that was appearing ever more attractive at this moment, was that the school had overnight boarders, and he was to get his own (small and Spartan) room on site, with meals included, at a modest cost stopped from his salary. This was going to prove a lifesaver, as he'd already mentally calculated the cost of his weekend celebrations. Money was to be on strict rations until he repaired the deficit - and it was not as if his salary was generous.

He walked along the platform towards the waiting train, the young porter on his heels, the rumble of the metal trolley wheels and the lad's jaunty whistling of an infectiously catchy tune, the only accompaniment. Irons suddenly felt very weary and mumbled a few words of thanks as the porter hefted his trunk into the guard's compartment, whilst he stepped through an already opened door into the coach vestibule. Irons wondered if he should have tipped the lad, but it was already too late, and besides, he was never sure what was the correct amount to give. It didn't help that he was low on coins, just one half crown and a measly farthing in his trouser pocket, and he thought he ought to hang on to both of these.

He flopped onto the creaky moquette of the bench seat in an empty compartment, in what sounded like an equally empty coach, and rested his now throbbing head against the cool glass of the window and closed his eyes. Almost immediately he felt himself drifting into a semi-conscious state, comforted by the familiar sounds of the train hissing and panting; of a drowsy fly buzzing and bumping along the window ledge; the slam of a door and the porter's softly whistled melody that he recognised as being from "The Third Man," which had gripped cinema goers for many months recently. There was an echoing call across a far platform and the short blast of the guard's whistle close by, followed by the jolt and clatter of the starting train.

It was warm in the compartment, and he was lulled into a deeper sleep, by the rhythm of the train clickity-clacking across the rail joints. The neatly compact 'L1' tank engine at the front of the train settled down into a faintly asthmatic huff-huff-huff as it trundled north through long tunnels and beneath bridges, threading its apologetic way between the salubrious north-west London suburbs, concealed in cuttings and hunched behind retaining walls as if embarrassed to disturb the middle-managers and aspirational office-wallahs from their evening radio show or quiet smoke in their handkerchief-sized yards. The train marked its progress with little iridescent clouds that tumbled and disintegrated on fences clothed in sweet-scented honeysuckle or broke like waves on sturdy brick back walls.

He was not sure for how long he had slept, but the sound of someone entering the compartment awakened him. He parted the fingers on the hand covering his face and peered blearily though sandy eyes that refused to focus. A young woman was sitting diagonally opposite, close to the sliding door opening into the corridor.

It struck him as faintly surprising that she had chosen a compartment already occupied, and especially by a young man. He closed his eyes again, not wishing to startle or unnerve her, but he was intrigued, and his mind started whirring.

The woman must have observed he was asleep and if she was travelling only a short distance to the next stop, had taken the risk of sharing the compartment. Or had the train had suddenly filled up, and this was the only space left? But he would have been disturbed by the sound of many voices, the clumping of feet in the corridor and the sliding and slamming of doors if that were so. He had been awakened by just the faintest of sounds as she had crept, like a church mouse, into his compartment.

Well, it was she who had made the decision to join him, and now he needed to adjust his aching neck and sit upright. He did so slowly, not wanting to startle her, whilst glancing across to take a better look.

'Hullo!' He feigned surprise at seeing her there.

'Sorry, I did not mean to wake you.' Her voice was low, a whisper, like someone speaking in a library.

'I was just dozing.' Irons looked at the floor, staring stupidly into space, the alcohol and the short nap dulling his mind like a strong head cold. Irons felt self-conscious, aware that his hair was a dreadful mess and he must look dishevelled. He wiped a hand over his face then blinked a few times to try and buck himself up. He risked another look in her direction and offered a pathetic smile. 'It was quite a long weekend. A few late nights...'

'You're tired. Please don't mind me.' It was a gentle voice, and yet one filled with sadness. World-weary was how Irons was later to describe it.

'I am a little. But nothing a cup of tea followed by a good night's sleep won't fix!' Whilst Irons was speaking, he was struck by her appearance. Her eyes were like pools of green water glazed by a cold, silvery light, though this was likely to be the effect of the dreadfully poor bulb in the compartment ceiling that appeared to be dimming even lower.

She was gazing at the empty seat opposite, but he was sure she saw little of her surroundings, appearing preoccupied by something troubling her. Her skin was pale; so much so, he thought it without colour, and she sat upright, virtually immobile save for an anxious movement of her hands and looking the very picture of dejection.

'Excuse me, but are you all right?' Irons asked. 'Sorry, I don't mean to be inquisitive, but you seem rather blue...' He tailed off, aware that he was indeed being intrusive.

'Fine, thank you.' She hesitated. 'I need to rest. I'm weary of this endless travelling.' She twisted the fingers of her right hand around the ring finger of her left, in an anxious, nervous motion that was the only spark of animation about her. Her anxious demeanour did not suggest she was about to be successful in achieving her desire for rest.

'I know the feeling! Weekends are never long enough, are they?' He tried a touch of levity, but her unhappy countenance made him look away. He found it oddly disturbing in someone so young. She was about eighteen or so, although her sallow skin, the dark rings beneath her doe-like eyes that were watery as if on the verge of tears, put some years on her.

'Sleep evades me,' she added.

'Sorry to hear that. It can be jolly miserable not sleeping well. I was like that in the days leading up to my interview - I just couldn't get a wink, and as I lay there in the night, it preyed on my mind that I would be too tired to make a good impression. Although I must confess, it's an affliction I rarely suffer from; normally I can sleep anywhere, just like on this train – I went out like a light...' He stopped himself short and winced. What an unfeeling ass he was. He was not used to this sort of conversation with a young woman and was babbling on like an idiot.

'You are lucky. Untroubled sleep is something to crave.'

'I suppose I am.' Irons was puzzled by the strange turn the conversation had taken. How on earth was he discussing sleep, and all the implications of the bedroom this brought to mind, with a young woman? He felt safer adopting a more serious tone. 'Can a doctor not help? With a sleeping pill, perhaps? The National Health Service is jolly good these days and I'm sure they could do something.'

She looked momentarily puzzled, a slight frown appearing as if she had not understood, her fingers still worrying away at her ring finger. 'I have nothing to do with doctors. I don't trust them.' She narrowed her eyes. 'They're dangerous men, wielding power as they see fit.' She had become quite animated.

'I see.' Irons did not see but ploughed on regardless. 'I can't profess to much experience of doctors, not unless you count the rather brutal army doctor who decided that I had fallen arches and declared I couldn't do National Service. I cannot say I was mortified. Got me out of two years of yard bashing – I could have hugged the man! But seriously, they can't really be so bad? They're here to do us good.'

'It pays to be wary of men who have the power of life and death over us.' Her voice carried a note of anger, though still barely a whisper.

Irons was not sure how to respond. Her vehement reaction had momentarily floored him. He wanted to ask her why she held such a strong opinion, but realised that if she was speaking from experience, then he would be straying again into dangerously personal territory and so chose to tactfully withdraw. He offered a lame nod of the head and a smile he hoped would appear sympathetic. She fell silent and returned to contemplating the seat opposite. He took this opportunity to take a good look at his curious companion.

If she did her hair in a more modern style and got into the sunshine to relieve the pastiness of her skin, plus an extra ration of bacon and butter for a few weeks to feed her up, she would look a whole lot better. She was slim and trim, almost underfed - but who was not, these days? - And whilst no pin up, she had a face he was sure someone could easily enjoy waking up to each morning. He noticed that the light summer dress she was wearing was made from a fabric that clung close to her body and hinted, quite generously, at what lay beneath.

He turned away from fixating upon her small and intriguingly pointed breasts and stared out of the window into the impenetrable night and the faint reflection of the girl, now rendered insubstantial in the grubby glass, a little surprised by these carnal thoughts. He could not deny that this close proximity to a young woman was thrilling, and he felt a stab of sympathy towards her, wishing he could gallantly do something to relieve her obvious sadness.

Chapter Seven

Pure foolishness on his part of course. Her boyfriend was most probably the cause of her upset, and in no time at all they would make up and she would smile and laugh again. They'd had a lover's tiff over the weekend and she was regretting not resolving this before parting. It was none of his business, and she didn't need him interfering.

He felt a strong shiver and realised the compartment had turned surprisingly cold. The train heating was turned off and the little window wide open, but until now he had been thankful for the cool air it allowed into what had felt like a hot and muggy compartment, but now there was an icy draught. Perhaps the effect of the drink wearing off.

'Are you cold? I think the night has cooled quite noticeably.'

'I don't feel it. But do as you wish.' She gave him a strange look, her eyes almost making him melt.

Irons stood and closed the window before slipping his brown corduroy jacket on and sitting back down. He was now shivering uncontrollably and he shrugged his shoulders as icy fingers ran down his spine, a surprising reaction that had started the moment she held his gaze.

He extracted a slim book from his holdall on the seat beside him, and idly flipped it open. He was not in the mood to swat up the algebra questions he might set his new students, and the dreadful lighting that appeared to be on the verge of failing, made it impossible to read, but the book would offer him a refuge for his wandering eyes. He was becoming increasingly fascinated by this woman and must restrain himself from openly staring at her. There really was something oddly compelling, and perhaps even a little unsettling, about her. If only she would not look so darned unhappy.

'That looks serious.'

'It is rather dry, but I need to think about the week ahead and what to give my new charges. I'm a teacher, you see. I'm starting a new job tomorrow. It might be useful to run over a few ideas for my first lessons at the front of the classroom.' He gave a little nervous laugh.

She gave him a slight smile in response. 'Where is the school?'

'Brackley. Magdalen College Grammar for Boys. Do you know of it?'

'Oh!' She gave a slight start, as if hearing the name had surprised her. 'I know the place very well. I was born in Brackley. I lived there until...'

'I say, what a small world!' Irons interrupted her in his excitement.

'You're travelling there? What a coincidence.'

'It's been a long time, now.' Her answer was ambiguous. She took a deep breath as if steadying herself, then gave him a look that for the first time held a spark of animation. 'It is considered a good school. You'll be happy there, I'm sure.'

Irons however, felt another wave of powerful shivers course through his body and wondered if he was catching a chill. That was all he needed; to be laid up in bed at the start of his first week in work. He closed his eyes and rested his head against the cushions as he answered. 'I'm glad to hear that. Please forgive me closing my eyes... awfully rude of me...' his voice was slow and heavy, the book abandoned on his lap. 'I might be going down with something. I just need to... to rest my eyes for a moment...'

He desperately wanted to prolong the conversation but was powerless to prevent waves of intense drowsiness wash over him, and despite the coldness of the compartment he immediately drifted in and out of sleep, always aware that she was there - although she made no sound - but equally unable to open his eyes and talk with her.

After he knew not how long, he was jolted wide awake by a particularly noisy and aggressive application of the brakes, and when he opened his eyes in surprise, he saw that she was standing up. It was probably because he muddled real life with a vivid dream about an exotically beautiful Egyptian girl with big brown eyes leading a camel into the guard's van whilst another woman he could not see, sobbed relentlessly and called his name, but he sensed that she had been standing there for some time, studying him whilst he slept. It was an unnerving sensation.

The moment he looked at her, she turned to leave the compartment, glancing back for just a moment and he heard her clearly say, 'Brackley Central. This is your station,' before slipping down the corridor and out of sight.

He rubbed his eyes. The train was shuddering gently as it slowed, and he heard another compartment door open further along the coach and someone shuffling their feet on the floor as they gathered their things together. He was now hot, almost sweaty, and uncomfortable. It was dreadfully stuffy in the compartment and far too warm. Why on earth had he felt the need to close the window, and why had he turned the carriage heating full on?

He stood up, removed his jacket and loosened his tie. Looking in the small oval mirror on the compartment wall, he grimaced at the reflection and ran clammy fingers through his limp hair, then wedged his hat on top of the untidy result. Laying his jacket across the top of the holdall, he left the train, eager to say goodbye to the young woman.

He stepped onto the platform and took a deep draught of cool air and immediately felt more awake than he had during the whole journey. The guard was standing on the platform overseeing the unloading of his trunk, along with a bicycle, and two baskets of cooing pigeons, by a porter. Irons nodded to the guard, indicating that he had seen his trunk was being dealt with, then took in his surroundings.

The station was small, but the island platform was long and quite wide with an open and airy feel about it, although it was now so dark he gained only a sense of vast remoteness all about, as though the station were a little ship becalmed on a black sea. He remembered from his previous visit for his job interview that Brackley Central was set right on the northern edge of the little market town, nestling in the lee of a hill topped by Scots pines, with both hill and trees serving to mask any sense of habitation close by, and this now added to the atmosphere of quiet isolation.

An elderly woman with a stick was plodding towards the stairwell that would take her up to the short bridge spanning one of the railway tracks and so to the tiny booking hall that commanded an elevated position on the crest of the hill. There was a thin man with a bushy moustache, wearing herringbone pattern tweeds and a matching deerstalker, hefting what looked like hunting guns in canvas bags onto his shoulder, whilst two young lads in blazers – quite possibly Magdalen pupils - were sharing a joke as they hurried towards the exit. But of the sad young woman, she was nowhere to be seen.

Irons presumed she must have moved along the train and stepped out directly opposite the exit stairs to make a swift departure. He could not blame her for wanting to hurry home, but still felt a pang of disappointment. It was as if she'd deliberately made the decision to leave the train quickly so as to avoid him. That was a slap in the face. He was sure he'd not acted in a manner that could be considered 'fresh'. If anything, he'd stupidly fallen asleep and ignored her for much of the journey. Women really were the most perplexing of creatures.

He watched his trunk being expertly propelled along the platform on a little two-wheel trolley, the handles of which reached to the porter's shoulders leaving only the lad's face and cap peeking over the top in a comical manner. Irons also started to walk towards the exit, and as he did so, he hit upon an explanation for the woman's swift disappearance.

Her father would be meeting her, and so she had not wanted to walk alongside Irons through this little station, as surely, they must, without deliberately ignoring each other, only then to have the embarrassment of trying to explain to a suspicious father whom this strange man was - and the nature of their relationship.

Clearly, there was no 'relationship' to explain, as Irons reminded himself, and they didn't even know each other's names, so it would be an unnecessarily awkward encounter, added to which, she was feeling a bit down in the dumps. When he considered this scenario, he realised she had displayed a delicate touch of sensitivity that was appealing.

Well, she was a Brackley gal, she'd said as much, and whilst he could not recall if she still lived there or not, he felt sure he would have other opportunities to meet her in what was a small town. It was time now to push such thoughts aside and concentrate on more pressing matters.

Irons arranged for his trunk to be held at the station overnight and forwarded on to the school early the following morning on Bob Phillip's brand new 'Mechanical Horse,' a vehicle that, he was advised with much barely concealed excitement by the head porter, was 'speshly reserved for such duties'. Irons then dipped into the Gents and splashed cold water on his face, rubbed fresh Brylcreem into his hair and combed it into place, neatened up his shirt and re-knotted his croqueted woollen tie and shrugged on his jacket. He used his handkerchief to give his shoes a quick shine before making a readjustment to his hat. Not brilliant, but it was late, and dark, and he would not make too ghastly an impression when he rolled up at the school.

Suddenly feeling decidedly more chipper through a mixture of nervous excitement about his new life ahead and a promise to meet the young woman again, he whistled the infectiously melodic 'Third Man Theme'

Chapter Seven

the Marylebone porter had imprinted in his brain, whilst he strolled down the long and wide tree-lined avenue that formed the spine of the town. He walked past a little park filled with big dark trees and the towering majesty of Winchester House public school that looked like something King Charles might have lived in, and as he did so, he imagined himself to be like Joseph Cotton arriving in Vienna for the first time, soon to encounter the beautiful, if beautifully sad and tearful, Alida Valli.

Chapter Eight

Leicester Central
5th September 1950

Detective Constable Simon Howerth was seated on one side of a large wooden desk in the main office of the British Railways Detective Department in Leicester Central station. The desk was one of a pair, dating from the opening of the line in 1899 and was rubbed smooth in places from countless uniform sleeves polishing and burnishing it to a deeply smooth patina. The chair he was perched on was equally old and creaked alarmingly as he tipped it back on the rear legs, and indeed the majority of the office fittings had not changed much since the end of the 19th Century. The walls had been distempered a year or two ago and there were now electric bulbs in enamelled shades hanging from the ceiling in place of the original gas mantles, but apart from the telephones on the desks and a copying machine that only the WPC's seemed to know how to use and which exuded a noxious smell of solvent, there were few concessions to modernity. In truth, it was a dour, grubby place, crammed with old filing cabinets, heaps of case files bound together with red string, loose papers in untidy mounds on the desks, an assortment of ill-matching chairs and a lethal looking electric fire on the end of a brown cord ominously frayed in a number of places. But compared with the conditions Simon had previously known in the locomotive sheds, it was sheer luxury, made all the more so in that he had a big enamelled mug of tea close to hand and even a Garibaldi biscuit, courtesy of Mrs Green, the detective inspectors' slightly fearsome secretary.

He was leaning as far back as he dared in his chair with his nose in a magazine, whilst DC Blencowe seated opposite was hammering out a report on the massive typewriter that occupied the greater part of his side of the desk, hunched over the machine with a look of intense concentration on his face. He was no typist, even after many years of practice and used just forefingers and thumbs to strike the keys and had been belting away at what was only a short document for some considerable time.

Blencowe slammed the typewriter carriage across for the last time, making the little bell ting and wound the sheets of paper and the blue carbon paper out of the machine with the air of man who'd completed a tiresome chore. He sat back and stretched his arms above his head, groaning a little as he eased his shoulders. He then took a sip of his tea and stood up to stretch his legs.

'Working hard eh lad?' He gave the young constable the benefit of a raised eyebrow. 'What's so interesting in that rag of yours?' Blencowe walked to the end of the desk, the better to deflect some of the warmth from the little fire onto the back of his legs.

Simon hurriedly tried to pretend he had not been reading, although it was obviously a futile action. 'It's actually about police work...'

'I bet. "True Crime Magazine"?' Blencowe spoke the words with a mocking tone. 'Complete rubbish. Come on then, let's have a gander.'

He took the magazine from Simon. It was printed on thin paper, the ink smelling strongly and instantly smudging under his fingers with a lurid cover painting showing a glamorous blond with an impressively curvaceous body squeezed into a revealing red evening dress, all long legs and cleavage. She was lifting one arm in self-defence, her full red lips opened in a cry of distress as a dark figure of a man in a long black coat and Fedora approached her up a flight of steps with a gun in hand, his face screwed into an expression of pure malice, the scene illuminated by a strong side light that threw dramatic shadows. Blencowe smiled.

'Hmm...I can see what the attraction was. Most instructive,' and he gave Simon a stern look. 'Let's hope what's inside is more mature.'

'Actually, some of the articles are jolly interesting! Real life cases where they explain exactly how the villains were caught...'

'Hoping to pick up some tips?'

'It can't do any harm. There's an awful lot I need to know about this job and anything that helps has to be good.'

'You're not wrong there.' Blencowe paused and pulled a puzzled face at a page for a moment, then continued skimming through. 'My way of looking at it is that proper detective work is built around hard graft and paying attention to the correct procedures, in chasing up every tiny little point of detail - and not rescuing scantily clad damsels.'

'The cover is a bit misleading. Though Eddie and I were once in a van spinning about on that frozen reservoir once! And then there was that man found buried in the coal...'

Blencowe laughed and had to concede the point. There was no denying that Simon and his best friend Eddie Earnshaw over the last four years had somehow managed to worm themselves into more than their fair share of extraordinary scrapes and even helped crack some of the more dramatic and dangerous cases the department had been called on to investigate. Hard though it was to believe, two young lads working their way up the ladder to be loco crew from sleepy little Woodford Halse had been slap bang in the middle of some seriously challenging crimes.

It was this meddling in things they really shouldn't that had resulted in Simon Howerth now working for the detective department. A strange turn of events in the eyes of some, but D.I. Vignoles had seen in him a restless desire to solve problems, and whilst still too impetuous and ill-disciplined in his approach at times, the freckly carrot-topped young man had an apparently innate ability to sniff out when something was not quite right. He had, according to Vignoles, "a detective's nose for a crime".

Simon's nose had certainly got him dangerously involved in an especially nasty situation the year before, but then he had made a creditable effort to extricate himself and see justice done - at no little risk. True, he had broken the law along the way and the railway authorities had little choice but to dismiss him from his job as a trainee fireman, but Vignoles had taken a punt. He'd stuck his neck out and brought the lad into the fold 'where I can keep an eye on him.' Initially, Blencowe had been sceptical, but was cautiously starting to think that Vignoles was correct in his belief that the young DC one day just might make a detective.

'"The Startling Case of the Lady in Red". What rot! The rubbish they write...' Blencowe flipped more pages, shaking his head.

'Look at the article on unsolved crimes near the back. That's what's got me hooked.' Simon was trying to recover some kudos. 'The writing is more serious, and they look at crimes still puzzling the police - including two on the railways.'

'Righty-o. Let's see what they say.' He read for a few moments, occasionally sipping on his tea. He nodded once or twice as if agreeing with what he read. 'I remember that one. The mail theft in '38, up Sheffield

Darnell way. They've still not got the vicious bugger who shot the guard. How can anyone even think to kill a man for a few piddling postal orders, it beggar's belief.'

'I said it was good reading...'

'Now that's odd. I don't recall that.' Blencowe was the department's 'Mr. Detail,' a man with a memory almost photographic and a penchant for lists, charts, maps and teasing out scraps of information from almost any source. Whilst not the quickest thinker, and certainly not the best at handling interviews, he was a highly prized asset to the team.

'Which one?'

'They call it "The Broad Street Trunk Mystery" Yuck.' Blencowe looked disgusted. 'That's horrible. Now why have I not come across this before?'

'Shocking, isn't it?' Simon looked more excited than horrified however. 'You have to wonder how they never found out who left it there. It's really got me thinking about how to track down the killer, there just has to be a way!'

'Oh yes? Reckon you can crack the mystery better than those older and with more experience?'

'No...Maybe. Seeing as it was a railway crime or at least, the trunk was found in a station luggage office so that makes it as good as a railway crime, I thought perhaps...'

'Now listen up, you young pup. You do exactly what the sergeant tells you to do, and nothing else. Right? You don't decide what gets investigated and you'd do well to not forget that! Keep your nose out of stuff that's none of your business.'

'Or course.' Simon looked contrite.

'I'm still a bit miffed we never heard of this.' Blencowe was shaking his head slightly. 'May 1945, they made the discovery. I suppose we were too busy thinking about VE day? It was quite a time, mind, painting the town red and then of course there were the drunk and disorderly everywhere plus our own hangovers to nurse.' He still looked puzzled however. 'I might have a word with some of the chaps down that neck of the woods.'

'So, does that mean we are looking into it?' Simon instantly cheered up.

'No, we are not! I'm just curious, that's all. Now get this report onto the Inspector's desk, then take the post into town and when you're back I want these files putting away.'

Yes sir, of course sir, three bags full sir! Simon remained silent however, and despite railing at being put in his place, he smiled to himself as he saw Blencowe sit behind his side of the desk still staring intently at the magazine.

Chapter Nine

Brackley & London
17th September 1950

Irons was kept busy over the following two weeks trying to settle into his new job and establish a rapport with both the other masters and his classes of young boys. He worked hard just to remember the names of his pupils, let alone understand their many foibles and tricks or begin to impart any serious mathematical understanding in their young minds.

Teaching was proving to be harder in reality than during his training practice when he'd had the safety net of a seasoned practitioner looking over his shoulder, and he often sat up deep into the night planning lessons in the hope that these would run more satisfactorily than he'd managed so far.

With it being the start of both a new term and a new school year, the whole place felt to Irons like a shapeless muddle and confusion; it was what Timmy Bunyan the Latin master, called 'the annual organised chaos', and to Irons it was a ceaseless series of misunderstandings by a succession of bewildered young lads looking for classrooms, and frazzled teachers searching for books and pencils and other equipment that had mysteriously vanished over the summer 'vac', followed by lessons that never seemed to settle down until they were already halfway through their allotted time and ended with a mutual feeling of dissatisfaction.

Irons also had to learn to adjust to the relentless life of the school, including taking his share of being 'duty master,' a task that involved being on call throughout the night for when one or more of the boarders felt genuinely ill, suffered homesickness or simply caused trouble through excessively high jinx in the dorms. As the newest and youngest on the staff, his turn on nights seemed to come around more frequently than it did for the senior masters, and the lack of sleep it invariably caused did nothing to help his teaching.

All this meant that he had little time to explore the town let alone a decent opportunity to chance upon the woman from the train, although he still harboured the idea and in odd quiet moments imagined what he might say when they met on the street, or perhaps in the Oak Cottage Cafe on the edge of the market square.

However, his first thirteen days had largely been circumscribed by his room, the refectory (a chilly noisy place), and walking each morning to the school's very own 12th century chapel that was almost the size of a small parish church for morning assembly then skirting the pocket-sized quad with its square of grass edged by pungent box hedges to his classroom that lay inside the venerable main building.

He liked this classroom however and was starting to enjoy trying to stamp his personality upon it. He liked its great dusty blackboard with its shelf of coloured chalks and the dust that soon coated his clothes. There was the heavy desk and bottle-green Anglepoise lamp and the mechanical pencil sharpener screwed to one edge, the tall cupboard built into the wall filled with life-expired books and which smelt of musty paper, erasers and rubber bands, and the ancient windows with leaded glass that looked onto the market square with the robust Victorian-era iron radiator below that would be most welcome come winter. At times, when the boys were finally bent to a task in their workbooks, he allowed his eyes to stray out of this window in the hope he might catch a passing glimpse of the young woman, but so far had seen her not once, and felt a nagging twinge of sadness that this were so.

Occasionally, he was required to walk along the edge of the Waynfleet playing fields at the back of the school to one of the more obscure classrooms located in a large shed that had been erected for Civil Defence use in 1939.

It was a draughty wooden construction, but it smelt pleasantly of pine impregnated by pungent malt and hops from the Hopcroft & Norris brewery that backed on to the school. The walk there gave Irons time to take in the sight of the boys playing cricket in the fields that stepped down in broad terraces, and he found this pleasing to his eye, with cricket whites against the green of the close mown grass offset by the almost Golden Syrup coloured walls of the buildings; for both school and chapel were constructed from the same local ironstone that defined much of the town's architecture, and were of considerable antiquity. Parts of the building were survivors of the original Hospital of St. James and St. John built in 1150 by the Earl of Leicester. The newer additions dated from 1548 when it was converted to a school, and so the walls were thick and pierced by heavily mullioned windows, the oaken doors worn smooth with the rub of hands over hundreds of years, the roofs formed of stone slabs punctuated by tall elegant chimneys; the whole ensemble clearly betraying a close allegiance to the great Oxford college with which it shared both name and origin.

One day, whilst he was attempting to explain long division to his youthful charges, he thought he caught a glimpse of a slim woman in a green sundress carrying a pale mackintosh across one arm. She was walking the steep 'barrel run' railway siding that lay to one side of the wooden classroom, down which short trains of wagons filled with firkins of freshly brewed ale backed cautiously, with considerable noise from the little tank engine tasked with this Herculean job as they dropped towards the Midland Region's Brackley Town station.

The 'bottom station' lay on the sleepy branch line that ran between Banbury and the lonely outpost of Verney Junction, and the regular beer trains were one of the few moments of intense activity between the occasional arrival and departure of the otherwise almost empty passenger services.

Irons did not get a good view because the verdant hedgerow and many trunks of the trees that lined the barrel run incline repeatedly concealed her, but his heart still leaped as he was sure it was the woman from the train and wearing what looked to be the same dress.

He caused considerable surprise and much sniggering by dashing out of the classroom and sprinting the short distance to a gap in the hedge used as a short cut into the playing fields. But he had been mistaken; the steep incline with track buried deep in limestone gravel with the odd yellow flowering weed, was completely empty and he was forced to invent a story about catching sight of a rare bird to pacify the incredulous boys.

This incident was a rare thrill, as his walks to and from the wooden classroom were usually moments of relative calm amidst the constant chatter and clamour of the boys, the carefully weighted conversations with senior staff, and the need for Irons to remain constantly vigilant for the unwelcome appearance by the ascetically severe headmaster, who prowled the school in his mortar board and black cape like a giant malevolent raven. The headmaster was proving to be a bit of a tyrant and prone to walking unannounced into a lesson and commence poking at the blackboard or flipping open a book on a desk with the end of his thin cane whilst firing questions about what was being taught, or challenging a terrified boy into dividing 203 by 7, or some other puzzle designed only to fluster and humiliate the startled lad.

Irons found this most wearying. He knew that given time he would become accustomed to this way of life, but as his first Sunday completely free of any duty approached, he needed respite.

Having been practically confined to school since the night he arrived, he had spent little of his meagre salary, which was a bonus, and so Irons had been able to justify purchasing a return ticket to London, travelling up on an early train out of Brackley Central to meet with one of his friends in the city, though with no intention of 'pushing the boat out' on this visit.

The weather had remained glorious and he had enjoyed strolling around the Euston Road with Algie Meredith, and window-shopping for goods neither could afford (even if it had not all been destined for export), followed by a liquid lunch and a bag of greasy fish and chips seated on a bench. They took a walk through Regent's Park, weaving their way between the endless ranks of allotments that now replaced the acres of grass that had once grown there before the war, marvelling at the profusion of vegetables, countless ramshackle sheds, the wooden wheelbarrows and lines of bean canes, laden fruit bushes and plump late lettuces of all hues of green, and the diligently Londoners picking, pruning, hoeing or barrowing in the constant drive to feed their families. When they tired of all this market gardening, they stopped to lean over a cast iron footbridge and look at the boats quietly passing below on the Regent's canal, soaking up the sun on their backs.

Irons said farewell to Algie at four and made his way to the station and could have been back in Brackley by early evening, with time to run his eyes over the lessons for the following day and an early night. And yet, flying against all logic and reason, he deliberately lingered and chose to take a later train.

He loitered at Marylebone Station, seated on one bench or another inside the cavernous hall with a paperback copy of Scenes from Provincial Life that he'd splashed out on when he first learnt about secured the post at Magdalen. The book was open but he'd hardly read a page. Instead, in an act of unsubtle espionage, he was observing the people coming and going across the top of his book, or when he wearied of this, stood idly browsing the lines of emaciated magazines on the W H Smith bookstall until the proprietor ceased throwing him suspicious looks and growled that he 'stop reading it all for free and bugger off!'

Irons moved across to the deliciously scented flower stall just inside the stone arched entrance, examining each zinc bucket filled with freshly cut flowers in an exotic profusion of colours, debating at length whether to be reckless and buy a bunch. He resisted doing so as they were prohibitively expensive, and it was a foolish notion to even consider that a bouquet of flowers would be well received, or indeed that the opportunity would arise to offer them.

He constantly checked the hands on the station clock as they inched their way around the dial, creeping sluggishly towards the departure time of first one, and then a second train that could have carried him back to his new home.

Why was he doing this? He knew the answer, but formulating the equation in his head was faintly embarrassing. He was waiting to see if that same young woman would board one of these train so he could engineer a second meeting. Irons was of the opinion she had actually joined the train further along the line, but without knowing at which stop, all he could do was survey the crowds milling about at the starting point for every train north whilst holding on to the hope she might appear. In a profoundly illogical piece of thinking, he was actually marking time until the departure of the very last train to Brackley Central, intending to recreate the same journey on the same day of the week, in the pathetic hope that she might be doing likewise.

Was he going nuts? Or just a single man tired of the unrelenting company of men and boys, with nothing pressing to do that evening and having spent a refreshing day with his best friend, was now in the mood to meet a member of the fairer sex - and perhaps tentatively explore the idea they could strike up an acquaintance. There was little to lose, and he need not confess to anyone he had spent the greater part of Sunday evening mooching about in a booming London terminus.

Of course, she would be back with her beau by now and their lover's tiff would be forgotten. He was prepared for that eventuality - and would take it on the chin like a man. He just needed to see that she had cheered up, that was all.

The trouble was, over the last thirteen days as soon as he stopped concentrating on his school duties, her face had a habit of appearing in his mind and he could easily recall her soft, sad voice. These were foolish daydreams, but at times the images were surprisingly vivid, and he'd convinced himself that she was calling to him like the Lorelei sitting half naked as they combed their long hair on the rocks in the Rhine. And sometimes he found himself remembering her thinly veiled body and imagined her, also half naked beside a river on a warm summer's day... No. This was not helping.

As he sat on yet another uncomfortable wooden bench with the carved letters 'GCR' impressing themselves in his back, he forced himself to consider a less highly-charged scenario, that of sitting on the more comfortable seats of the train and her waking him from a pleasant snooze to announce they had arrived at their stop. But this time, he would immediately follow her out of the compartment and not waste time staring in the mirror and flattening his hair until she had gone.

He drained the last cold dregs of a mug of tea in an impatient gesture, suddenly annoyed with this foolishness that was making him act like an imbecile. He returned the heavy china mug to the Women's Voluntary Service attendant behind her mobile tea trolley, then strode purposefully towards the ticket barrier. As he showed his ticket to the inspector he realised that he was the same man as the last time.

'You arrived in good time, sir. Been here for hours!'

'Yes... I, um, didn't want to risk missing my train.'

'Gor blimey, not 'arf! But you've missed two since I noticed you 'ere.' He gave Irons a questioning look.

Irons reddened. 'I like stations... the atmosphere, and er, the trains.' He shrugged and gave an innocent smile.

'Most people prefer to stand at the platform end to collect the numbers, sir.' He nodded in the direction of three youths seated on a trolley part way up one of the empty platforms, little notebooks on their laps, each sucking or biting the ends of their pencils and flipping through small reference books to compare their 'cops', a tall bottle of fizzy pop near to hand. 'You get a better view of the engines on the platforms, if you catch my drift. But each to their own, eh?' The inspector winked, but his eyes lacked the sparkle of mirth. 'We don't want nobody to think you're loitering with intent.'

'Good Heavens, can't a man sit at a station?' But Irons was not really listening, for he was already watching a short train backing into the platform from out of the indigo light of the dying day, stirring a chattering flock of starlings into looping about the lofty train shed like dog-fighting aircraft. He was feeling curiously excited that everything was an exact rerun of his previous journey.

He strode up the empty platform and once the train had come to a halt he walked the length of the four coaches as far as the big tank engine at the front that gleamed in a sparkling coat of glossy black paint. He should at least appear to be interested, to appease the ticket inspector. The engine was adorned on the side with a painted stylized lion balancing precariously on what looked like a wheel and big cream numerals declaring it to be number 69800. He paused for a moment, finding the sequence of numbers appealing to his eye, momentarily tempted to see what his mathematical brain could make of this as a mental puzzle, but this was a needless distraction and he turned his back on the locomotive.

Irons had checked each coach was empty as he walked the platform and now stepped aboard and worked his way back, making a second sweep to be doubly sure the train was empty, until finally settling in the same compartment as before. This time, he was determined to stay alert and sat upright, pensively looking across both compartment and the narrow corridor and out onto the platform. Nobody could pass or step board without him seeing.

He heard the guard talking outside the luggage compartment and watched as a handful of people walked past, none of whom bore any resemblance to the young woman. He recognised the old lady with the stick making her slow progress along the platform and a red-faced vicar in a dog collar who shuffled towards his compartment holding a pencil and notebook opened at a page covered with lines of locomotive numbers. The vicar hesitated momentarily at the door as though about to enter, but Irons looked away and tried to give off unwelcoming and decidedly un-Christian thought waves, which proved successful, for the cleric moved on. A few others boarded the train, but the sad girl was not amongst them.

Once the train was in motion, it again started to dull his senses, lulling him with its gentle rattles and squeaks, the rhythmic beat of the sturdy engine at the front and the hypnotic rhythm on the tracks combined with the equally regular looping of the telegraph wires like Arabic calligraphy in the sky, serving to make his eyelids grow heavy. He could feel the pleasant effect of being in the sun all day and the weariness from the walking and the beer. Oh, it was so hard to resist closing his eyes...

He instantly sat bolt upright, aware he had dozed off and cursing aloud as he did so. He stared at a station running-in board sailing past the window in the gloom of the night and just had time to read 'Amersham'. The train was accelerating smartly.

Damn! How many stations had he missed? Irons stared angrily at the indistinct moving silhouettes of trees and house roofs etched against the final thin stain of pale light below a starry sky and wondered how he had managed to fall asleep at the most critical moment of his hair-brained plan.

His frustration was short lived however, for moments later he saw the blurred and slightly fuzzy image of a slim woman reflected in the dirty window glass. He froze and held his breath, an action accompanied by an odd thrill - that now familiar sensation of icy fingers running down his body that made him involuntarily shiver. It was the same young woman, and she was entering the compartment!

Irons dared not move, watching her reflection eagerly as, to his amazement, she chose to sit on the middle of the three seats opposite, their legs almost touching. He allowed himself to breathe and silently reminded himself to take it easy and not do anything daft.

'Hello again.' Her voice was just as soft, and just as sad.

He turned and smiled. 'Hullo! What a pleasant surprise.'

She offered a hesitant smile. 'I wondered if you might be on this train.'

His heart leapt. 'Really? Actually, I thought the same. That is, as we both travel to Brackley I wondered if we might bump into each other.'

'You travel this line often?'

'Yes. No. That's to say I like to visit London - to see my friends as often as time allows. I shall take this train whenever I return to Brackley,' he added pointedly. Even as he was speaking, Irons was mentally reviewing the cost of a return ticket and recklessly convincing himself he could afford to repeat the journey the moment he had another evening free. 'But only when I can get time away from my school duties, of course. You may recall that I started at Magdalen College Grammar?'

She gave a movement of her head that indicated she had. 'I also find it necessary to make this journey frequently.'

'You work in Amersham?' He nodded his head towards the window. 'I noticed the station name.'

She frowned, and her eyes became glassier, the odd cold glint in them more intense. She stared at the floor for a moment, her hands starting the same nervous wringing motion as before, worrying away at her empty ring finger. 'I am compelled to go there.'

Irons thought this an odd turn of phrase, but his attention was immediately distracted by a train passing on the opposite track, thundering close to the window with a sudden slam and a whoosh of exhaust followed by the noisy chattering and booming of empty metal-bodied wagons, the sound making them start.

'Always gets me when they do that!' He wafted some smoke away with his hand, aware that a faint haze of locomotive exhaust now filled the compartment and made his view of her blurred and indistinct despite their proximity. Even through the hazy gloom, it was obvious she was unhappy. She had not repaired relations with her boyfriend then? However, the little glow of encouragement this offered was offset by the fact he was starting to feel decidedly chilly once again and cursed the rotten old train which clearly suffered terribly from draughts. He was trying to resist rubbing his hands together to warm them as he felt the first tremble of a shiver.

'I take it you're not exactly enjoying your work? It can be a rotten bore having to do something you don't like and commuting, on top,' Irons tried to keep his voice light and prevent his teeth chattering.

'You are right,' she replied. 'But there's little point complaining.'

'Indeed! Look, I say, we really ought to get the introductions out of the way'. He extended a hand, 'Richard, Richard Irons, fledgling junior math's master!'

She did not unclasp her hands to return the handshake but did lift her head and look him in the eye. 'Elizabeth Askew. But absolutely everyone calls me Betty. Locomotive cleaner.' She managed a smile that appeased Irons, who now slowly withdrew his hand and consoled himself with the thought that she was of a more reserved disposition than he had imagined, although this seemed strangely out of kilter with her decision to take a seat close to himself in an act that almost suggested intimacy. Indeed, it was she who had opened the exchange by greeting him. Gosh, she really was a puzzle, though a delightfully intriguing one.

'A locomotive cleaner? But I thought all the women had left the railways? What with the men coming home and all that.'

She gave him a puzzled look. 'Not a bit of it! There's a whole gang of us. They'd never manage without our help, I can tell you that for nothing.'

Irons winced. 'I wasn't trying to suggest you didn't work hard and do a decent job, only...'

Askew sighed. 'We are still working hard.' She frowned and added, sotto voce, as though to herself and not Irons, 'at least they were the last time I was at Woodford.' She now looked him squarely in the eye and adopted a livelier and almost confrontational tone. 'We're doing our bit. But we've got used to men doubting our abilities, so you're not alone. It's nothing. It's forgotten.' She looked down at her hands clasped together in her lap.

'Oh cripes, what a blundering oaf I am. I didn't mean it come out that way. Please forgive me, Miss Askew. It's just that I don't know the first thing about railways and clearly have my facts completely wrong.' He smiled. 'I'd love to hear about what you do.'

'You're just pretending, when really you think the work dull and menial - and unsuitable work for a woman.'

'Not a bit of it.' He smiled. 'Please, I really would like you to put me straight about this. Do tell me about your work.'

And to his surprise she did, talking about the 'loco' and prompting Irons to smile at her charmingly out of date notion she should 'not say exactly where it was, as one cannot be sure who might be listening,' this said whilst tapping her nose and adding, 'spies!'

Well, old habits die hard, and he just laughed this off, though he was sure she had already let slip the name 'Woodford' a moment earlier, although if she meant Woodford Halse then this was nowhere near Amersham, and so why was she travelling this part of the line? This was a little confusing and on top of that, there was something about her story that did not quite add up, but these thoughts were soon brushed aside, because he was more than content to just look and listen whilst she talked of 'The Dirty Girls Brigade'.

'The engines steam and sigh like stabled beasts in the smoky shed. Just like racehorses back from the gallops and in their stalls. I swear they are alive! As alive as any beast in the fields.' She became more animated as she got into her stride, telling of how she and the other girls would 'clamber over these magnificent machines like proper tomboys', scraping at layers of caked muck and grease, washing and scrubbing or raking clinker and barrowing away the contents of the ash pans and smoke boxes.

'In winter, the engines without fires in them for a night or more turn so bone-chillingly cold your fingers stick to the metal because the frost is like a strong glue! It can hurt you. They look quite magical though, rimed white all over, the hoare frost touching each rivet head, the wheel spokes and motion, everything picked out in white as if by an artist's brush. It is like those photographs you see in the paper that are too dark and they've painted in the highlights with white.'

Irons was captivated. Her air of sadness evaporated as she lost herself in recounting tales of the jokes, songs and the laugher the girls shared during their work. Her eyes regained some of their sparkle, and he could see they were actually blue, like a summer sky. And then, just once, she laughed heartily with a light trilling sound free of constraint. It was like music to his ears, and yet she seemed to surprise herself, and this broke the spell. She stopped abruptly, frowned and withdrew again, as if annoyed she had allowed an uncontrolled expression of pleasure.

An uncomfortable silence ensued, the easy communion between them lost just as quickly as it had started, like a soap bubble expanding into a large and glorious shape described by swirling vibrant colours, only for it to suddenly burst in a tiny flurry of tears. The guard sauntered along the corridor and looked in at their compartment without slowing his pace, his eyes meeting those of Irons for a moment, until he passed out of sight.

Irons bit the inside of his lip, wondering at the curious contradictions of Miss Askew. He was sure she had confessed how she disliked her work and yet had looked positively excited when in full flow about life working in the loco shed. It only served to compound his theory that women were delightfully perplexing.

However, there was a more important question that had been nagging away at him since their first meeting, and he decided to chance his arm and risk asking it, knowing that he must hear her answer even if it was not to his liking.

'I can't help noticing that you are always holding your ring finger, as if perhaps you -' He faltered, then plunged in, '- you once wore a ring and are missing it?'

She darted a look towards him, then dropped her eyes to her hands that were indeed twisting and turning again around the finger in question, caressing the place where a wedding or engagement ring would lie. 'I do? I suppose I must, now you mention it.' She shook her head, sadly. 'I do miss it - more than I can say. And yet I sometimes wonder if it is for the best that it's gone. It brought me no luck.'

'I am hazarding a guess you were once married?' Irons held his breath. This was dangerous ground.

She nodded. Hands now still. Her chest heaved as she took a deep breath, 'Engaged. To the most wonderful man. We had such dreams and hopes for the future; for when the war...' She fell silent as if the effort of completing the sentence was too much.

'I'm sorry.' Irons considered this revelation for a moment, struck by the realisation that she must be older than her appearance suggested if she had become engaged during wartime. He then mentally slapped himself on the forehead for being so slow. She obviously meant the Korean war that had started but a matter of weeks ago. Crikey, then no wonder she was feeling desperate. Her fiancé must have died recently. Perhaps she'd just received the news the first time they had met? It made complete sense. Crikey, he'd better show some sensitivity.

'I take it he was killed? Ouch, that sounds so beastly. I'm sorry, but I can't think how else to put the question.'

'Beastly, but true.' She gave a rueful shake of the head. 'I saw the letter they sent his parents. It said that Ray had been "lost in action whilst engaged with an enemy aircraft on the front line." He was not lost. They knew perfectly well where he was. He was killed, like you said. Why didn't they just say so? Killed in his armoured car near - well, it does not matter where. Of course, it was a successful push for our boys, so I suppose it was not in vain. I should feel proud of what he did. I am proud, of course. But all the same...' She let the sentence hang unfinished and briefly stopped wringing her right had around the fingers of her left to touch a regimental cap badge she was wearing in her lapel that occasionally caught some of the sickly light in the compartment.

'I'm dreadfully sorry.' He sat upright and leant towards her, one hand on his knee in dangerously close proximity to hers, trying desperately to resist the temptation to give her leg a friendly squeeze.

She looked up in response to the movement. 'Thank you. You are kind. I think you are a good man.'

'I don't know about that! But I would have to be made of stone not be touched by your story.' He felt a flush of guilt for harbouring private thoughts that were less honourable than she imagined, although he did feel genuine concern for her.

'Betty...sorry, Miss Askew, you're still so young... and as time passes the pain will fade and eventually you can start to look towards the future again. There's still so much life ahead for you.'

She looked perplexed, just as she had once before, as though what he said made no sense. 'There is nothing ahead for me. Nothing at all.'

'Oh goodness, but is life really that bleak?'

Her eyes filled with tears.

'And now I've upset you. I really am a blundering, insensitive clod.'

She shook her head and dabbed her eyes with a small handkerchief. 'No. You haven't - truly. Don't feel bad.'

'Miss Askew, are you in some kind of trouble? Aside from your dreadful loss, that is? Can I help?'

She looked at him through liquid eyes and he felt his heart melt, before releasing him by dropping her gaze and giving a little nod of her head. 'There is something, I need help to right a dreadful wrong. I must lay something to rest and can only do so by seeking a form of...redress. But it will not be easy.'

'Say it, and I'll do it! Whatever it is, I will do it - and gladly.'

'Don't be too hasty to agree.'

'Just tell me how I can help!' Irons felt a surge of excitement.

'It's my engagement ring. I no longer have it, but it meant so much. I want someone to help me... Oh, gosh!' She suddenly looked agitated, urgently turning her head to peer at the blackness beyond the window, her demeanour now one of extreme anxiety. 'We're nearly at Brackley. We'll soon cross the viaduct!'

'We will? I say, you must know this line awfully well, as I can't see a darned thing out there!' Irons had instantly cupped his hands around his face and peered out of the window into the night, but all he could see was a poor reflection of his own eyes and a few indeterminate shapes of trees moving against a black sky. 'How on earth can you tell? It's pitchy black.'

'I must go. We shall talk more another time, I promise.'

'But you've not told me how I can help?'

He judged she was about to stand up and so he did the same, and they found themselves close together within the narrow well between the facing bench seats, both swaying to the rhythm of the train. Irons however was shivering, desperately fighting to control the strong physical tremors gripping him; it was in complete contrast to the delicious frisson he received looking at this young and lithe woman just inches away.

'Please don't be so downhearted, things will surely look up!' He could not resist any longer and reached for her hand, wanting to clasp it for a brief moment.

Askew's eyes widened and she pulled back as if stung, trying to avoid his touch.

Did she scream? Or was it the sustained pull on the train whistle that wailed through the night and which reverberated inside his head and bounced around the small compartment?

Irons was unclear about what happened next, but later could recall seeing her rush out of the open compartment door in a flash of summer dress and bundle of pale coat, hair tumbling onto her neck and he heard her call over her shoulder, 'next time!' whilst he tumbled face first onto the opposite seat, aided by the momentum of the slowing train.

He now leant on his hands that sunk into the soft cushions, feeling the old springs groaning beneath the horsehair stuffing, his nose pressed hard into the faded jazzy plush that smelt of old books and soot, and feeling thoroughly foolish.

That was a dumb move. He'd pushed things too quickly, and screwed his eyes closed for a moment, praying that he'd not ruined everything. But as he hauled himself upright, patted his clothes back into line and adjusted his hat, he was also shaking his head, not in self-rebuke, but puzzlement.

He had reached out just a couple of inches towards her, and in those brief moments had drunk in the sight of her light brown hair and the smooth porcelain paleness of her skin, seeing it all with the startling clarity such intimacy offered, and yet he'd become unbalanced and fallen over without even so much as glancing against her or feeling her clothes touch his. He had reached for her but felt nothing; there was no resistance as he tried to grasp her delicate hand, and the shock and surprise of this failure to connect with flesh and blood had tipped him beyond the point of recovery. In wild desperation he'd actually flung his arms around Betty, intending to steady them both - and (if he was quite frank) steal a moment with his face pressed to hers. But he'd missed her completely!

How the heck had he managed that? There had been the most peculiar sensation of falling through her, as though she were nothing but a mirage. She had been as insubstantial as a cloud of steam. It was as though she were a ... No, no, this was the way to madness. Quite impossible. Irrational. Maths teachers did not dabble with the irrational

'Idiot, idiot, idiot!' Irons cursed aloud. He stopped, his attention now drawn to a tiny, but carefully folded piece of paper lying on the seat. It was white and distinct against the mellow greens of the seat fabric and he was sure it had not been there before. It was startlingly bright and he could not have missed it before. Betty Askew must have dropped it when she left in such a hurry.

There was no time to think about what it contained now, so he stuffed it into one of his trouser pockets whilst hurrying out of the compartment, eager that she did not leave the station without him a second time and without him at least apologising for his appalling behaviour.

He wiped his face with one hand, again feeling hot and flushed and not in the least bit shivery and stepped onto the platform where he encountered the guard looking along the length of the train. Irons did the same, urgently seeking for Miss Askew, painfully aware that this was indeed turning into a slightly nightmarish rerun of his previous experience.

'Can I help, sir? You look like you've lost someone.'

'I'm looking for a young woman; slim, with auburn hair wearing a pale green sun dress and carrying a pale mac - did you see her?'

'She's meeting you?'

'No, she was with me on the train. You must have seen her in the compartment with me. Did you see where she went to?'

'I cannot rightly say that I did, sir. I don't recall anyone of that description even boarding this train, let alone step off.' The guard looked perplexed. 'As you will know yourself, it's a very lightly loaded train, and so I know exactly who got on and who...'

'Then she must be still on board! It's all right, thanks. I'll just walk along inside and look for her.'

'Not so fast, please. We terminate the train here, so I'd rather you did not, as we shall draw the empty stock out of the station in a few minutes before reversing back into the opposite platform for the return journey.' The guard took a couple of steps towards the open carriage door, subtly blocking Irons from re-entering. 'Now, about this young woman you managed to lose. Is everything all right between you?' He gave Irons a steady look that challenged him to reply.

Irons removed his hat and ran fingers through his hair, feeling thoroughly exasperated. He stared along the gas-lit platform at a country gentleman hefting what looked like a fishing tackle bag onto his shoulder, and at the elderly lady with the stick being assisted by a porter and wondered where the young woman could have gone. Surely no more than a few seconds had passed before he had raced onto the platform? She just had to be on the train.

'Everything is quite OK.'

The Guard was not convinced and held his look, forcing Irons to continue.

'We had a – minor misunderstanding. It was nothing,' Irons added. 'She left the compartment just as we came to a stop and now I can't find her.' Irons gave a brief smile that he hoped would appease the guard.

'I see. Well, this is what I'll do lad.' He spoke slowly and ponderously as if carefully weighing each word in a manner that was intensely irritating to Irons. 'I shall take a walk along the train to try and find this young lady whom you appear to have misplaced, and meanwhile I suggest you wait along there by the exit steps in case she tries to make a run for it.' It sounded like a joke, but the guard was not smiling, and neither of them laughed. 'I should warn you, young man, I take a very hard line on any funny business on my train - is that understood?'

'Funny business? Look here, that's a darned cheek!' But Irons lacked conviction, aware that he'd tried to throw his arms around Miss Askew and quite possibly prompting her to run because of this rash action. Rather than argue the point, he smartly turned about on his heels and walked towards the station buildings, peering in at the carriage windows as he did so.

A minute or so later the guard joined him on the platform together with the stationmaster in his formal tail coat and glossy top hat. It was clear that the stationmaster had observed the scene unfolding, with professional curiosity.

'Is there anything amiss?' The Stationmaster reminded Irons of the headmaster and this immediately put him on edge.

'This young fellow claims he's lost his girl. Though there's absolutely no sign of her on the train - nor indeed did I see her at any point along the way.' The Guard slammed the door of a carriage closed and nodded at the fireman standing in the cab of the hissing tank engine a few feet away. 'All clear! When you're ready, mate!' He turned to Irons. 'She's not on board, of that I'm quite certain.'

'But she must be!'

'The train is quite empty.'

'A missing person?' The stationmaster looked concerned, glancing from one to the other. 'That's most worrying, and a young lady, did you say?'

'I don't suppose she's missing...' Irons felt embarrassed. 'Not in that sense. You really don't need to be alarmed, it is just odd how she managed to be off the train so quickly and gone, that's all.'

The stationmaster furrowed his brow and stroked his thick beard. 'I too am perplexed. I saw no young ladies, lost or otherwise, on the station. Are you quite sure? Could she not have got off at an earlier stop?'

'Like I said, I never saw someone meeting with her description board the train, nor step off at any station along the way. At no point did I check her ticket, neither. So how do you explain that?' The guard spoke in a ponderous, pedantic voice with more than a hint of scepticism.

'She was in the compartment with me the whole time, as close as you are to me now! You must have seen her when you walked past? Are you saying you don't believe me?'

'You boarded at Marylebone. You were alone, if I recall correctly?'

'Yes, that's correct.'

'I thought so, as I checked your ticket shortly after we departed. At what station did your lady friend join you?'

'Amersham. I'm sorry but this is just wasting time, I must go after her...'

'Brown hair, green dress you said?' The guard was looking perplexed. 'No one meeting that description boarded at Amersham. We did have two middle-aged gentlemen, both bound for Calvert, and there was Colonel Bradshaw - the gentleman with the fishing rods you will have seen on the platform. But there was nobody...'

'What on earth is all this?' The stationmaster was glancing between Irons and the guard with a look of growing impatience. 'Is a young woman missing, or not? One of you claims she was on the train, the other denies she ever got onboard. Gentlemen, kindly explain yourselves!'

'She must have just darted off the train in double-quick time and evaded us all. Don't think anything more about it. I'll go after her as she can't have gone far,' and without waiting for their response, Irons hared up the long flight of creaking wooden stairs, and between his pounding footsteps he caught a snatch of an exchange between the stationmaster and guard.

'What a curious affair? Could she be a fare dodger?'

'I can't see how I missed seeing her getting on and off. It just makes no sense to me.'

Chapter Ten

On the "London Extension"
17th September 1950

Edward Earnshaw was worried about the rapidly falling steam pressure and what the gauge glasses were telling him. He could see that water was sloshing about the glasses with the rocking and rolling motion of their rough-riding K3 type locomotive, giving the impression there was plenty left in the boiler, but he knew that once they settled into a smoother ride, the water would do likewise and show it to be dangerously low. He needed to get the steam injectors on, but this would just pump gallons of cold water into the boiler and further depress the failing steam pressure, and if it went much lower they'd be out of puff. It was a tricky situation, and he needed to deal with it.

He glanced nervously across at his driver half leaning out of the cab, his grizzled weather-beaten face staring into the night, one arm stretched across the boiler back head to rest on the regulator handle, the other crooked beneath his body over the narrow cab side.

Driver Boswell had been holding this position for the last twenty minutes or so, peering into the banks of mist rising from the fields and collecting in the gentle folds of the Buckinghamshire countryside, concentrating hard so as not to miss a signal light winking through these opaque clouds that indiscriminately spanned the twin tracks on their run north.

It was not raw, but the night still had an edge, sharpened by their forward movement, and Eddie reckoned Boswell must be pretty near frozen down one side and mightily sick of being pelted by the bits of char and burning cinders that bounced off his face and grease top cap like a shower of tiny stones. But the old pro remained stoical, silent, intent on the job in hand, the glow of the fire illuminating his profile in brilliant orange when the fire doors were opened, at other times just a faintly etched shape against the indigo night and the moving backdrop of smoke.

Eddie felt guilty for letting him down, but the fire just would not burn properly and had not done so since they left Cricklewood. Now he was in danger of committing one of the cardinal sins of an aspiring fireman; not providing enough steam for the job. This would be a humiliating embarrassment and invite a barrage of derision and leg pulling at the loco in the days to follow. As a cleaner with aspirations to making the next grade following an exam booked the following month, it was not going to look good if he ran out of steam. Even worse, if he caused the boiler to run dry and drop the fusible plug, so releasing the remaining water in the boiler onto the fire to douse it. That would cause both damage to the engine and block the line until they could be rescued.

His predicament was made worse because this was the return leg of the first day on what he'd been promised was to be his roster for at least two weeks; working a long and fast trip to London and back. It was a significant step up from the usual grind of shunting around the yards at Woodford Halse or the short runs up to Leicester North Yard that was his usual fare. It had filled him with pride that morning when shed master Saunders had chalked his name on the board beside this run, but now the thrill had evaporated, rather like his steam, and he felt a sinking inside as he realised he was going to blow it – rather than blow the safety valves.

'Damn this dirty rotten stuff! It's bloody useless!' Eddie gave a rare curse and dug his shovel into the mound of poor coal and prodded and probed for something decent to feed the flames. Rivers of dust and tiny pieces of slack cascaded out of the tender front flowing over the shovel and onto the wooden floor adding to the many pieces crunching beneath his booted feet.

'What you doing with that fire? I need steam!' Driver Boswell had responded by glancing into the cab and his experienced eye needed only moments to register the situation.

'It's the coal - it won't burn!' He had to shout to be heard over the roar of the engine and the rattle of the unfitted freight coupled behind.

'Looks like coal to me,' Driver Boswell's voice was sarcastic. He gave the steam gauge another sharp glance and pulled a face. 'That's no use. Put your back in it, lad!' and he returned to staring into the night air. 'And get some water in the boiler!'

Eddie whacked the fire doors open and flipped his shovel over to deflect the worst of the fierce heat and bright light that made his eyes water as he peered into the roaring pit, searching for the reason he was losing steam. He groaned. Instead of the evenly spread incandescent bed of merrily burning coals, he could see a great mass to one side, sitting like an ugly dead weight licked by small blue and purple flames. Over half his fire was not burning properly and he could see clinker forming on the fire bars. It needed drastic action.

Taking a deep breath, he turned the water supply on and worked the steam injector until he heard the distinctive rushing sound as it engaged. He kicked the damper lever on the floor to open it wide, turning the blower on full before throwing a quick four rounds of coal onto the healthier side of the conflagration. He slammed the doors closed with an impatient clang and leant out of his side of the cab to watch the chimney. The smoke was not turning a filthy black as it should, despite being lifted clear of the boiler by the rush of air from the blower.

He ducked back and rattled the fire irons on the tender top as he tried to find the 'long pricker'. These irons were long bars, some up to twelve foot, with big looped handles at one end and various shapes at the other. Eddie thought they looked like giant sardine can keys made for Gulliver. He found them hard to manoeuvre so that the far end - which was a sharpened point bent over at ninety degrees - faced the firebox, whilst being careful to not let it poke out of the cab and risk striking a bridge or signal post. Fortunately, his engine was a type known to the men as a Ragtimer, probably because of their distinctive syncopated beat and unsteady gait, and these had a very open cab and tender that was useless for keeping the bad weather out but did facilitate swinging the fire irons around.

Eddie started to riddle the lump of poorly burning coal and chip at the clinker gripping the fire bars. His arms were soon aching with the effort and the pricker refused to go quite where he wanted it. After taking too long in this task, he carefully eased the now red-hot iron out of the fire, concentrating with justified nervousness on the glowing tip as he swung it away from the driver, his eyes burning with great bobs of coloured light that swam in a disorienting manner, the engine was swinging with its Scott Joplin-esque rhythm beneath his feet and rendering him unsteady. He gave it a mighty shove, intending to launch the long pricker onto the mound of coal behind, but stared in horrified disbelief as it bounced once with a metallic twang, and then flew off the side and onto the line.

Oh heck! I don't believe it! He closed his eyes for a moment hoping this would somehow undo that he'd seen. He had to pray it had not landed across the rails of the other line. Should he alert his driver, so they could stop and recover it? Eddie's stomach churned with apprehension that he might now be the cause of an accident.

'Ach, it's no good. We're out of puff. We're stuffed!' Driver Boswell turned to face Eddie at that same moment, giving him an inscrutable look as though challenging him to speak, but Eddie's nerves failed, and he said nothing. The driver eased the regulator back a touch. 'I'll limp her along as far as Brackley then see what can be done. Sunday evening and all! Worst bloody luck.'

'It's the coal. And this blasted engine.'

'What about the blasted fireman?' Boswell took a deep breath as if about to lay into Eddie but seemed to change his mind. 'Keep your eyes on the road and holler the moment you see a signal.' Driver Boswell stood up and stretched his back for a moment, indicating that Eddie should take his place with a nod of his head. 'Let's see what a pig's ear you've made in here...'

Eddie stepped over to the driver's side and leant out to look ahead along the line. Despite feeling sick at his shoddy performance, he got an instant frisson of excitement taking control of the train, even if it was wheezing like a sick coal miner and coasting down a slight incline at no great speed.

The driver took his turn peering into the fire, rattling the remaining fire irons for a moment before expertly swinging one into place as though it weighed nothing and was but a few feet in length. It was soon put back in another deft move, and he started to hurl heaped shovels of coal onto the fire in smooth, almost lazy movements. Eddie glanced across and marvelled at the ease and confidence he displayed.

'Keep yer eye on the bloody road!'

Eddie quickly looked back along the engine boiler and at the plume of dark grey smoke, a rich flash of red occasionally licking at the rim of the chimney.

'Distant! All clear!' Eddie shouted as he spotted the black and yellow board pointing skywards.

'Uh huh,' grunted Driver Boswell, who banged the fire doors shut and squinted at the gauges. 'That'll be Brackley down distant. We'll make the station, any road.' He nodded his head to indicate that Eddie should now move out of the way. 'Bloody useless!'

Eddie cringed.

'Tubes are clogged; the fire arch dropped and the big end's knocking like billy-o. Can you hear that clunking? She's leaking steam like a sieve.'

The young fireman nodded assent, but stayed quiet, staring mournfully at the steam pressure gauge. The fall plate he was standing upon occasionally banged against the tender as the tired engine swayed and rolled, whilst he listened out for the other, more ominous, knocking sound the driver had identified.

'When we get to Woodford, I'll sign her off failed. Remember the number - 61835 and avoid it like the plague! A friggin' disgrace giving us this, the buggers. Sixty-one, eight three flippin' five!' Driver Boswell shook his head in disbelief, but then suddenly stood upright in a movement that jolted Eddie out of his blue reverie. Boswell slammed the regulator shut with a loud curse, then rapidly started winding the engine back into neutral, whilst his other hand applied the brakes in a series of short, sharp applications, at no time taking his eyes of the road ahead.

'Woman on line!' His shout was harsh and cut through the noise of the footplate, the fear audible in his voice.

The train was moving not much over fifteen miles an hour, but with a string of loaded box vans behind and on a falling grade, it was going to take time to stop. Worse still, driver Boswell needed to be careful not to cause a ripple down the train as each four-wheeled wagon collided with the next, creating a dangerous tidal wave of energy that could seriously injure the poor guard in his van at the tail and even breaking coupling chains along the way.

Boswell continued to work the brakes, expertly slowing the train, winding the valve gear into reverse and both men feeling the jarring and banging of their complaining train behind, sensing the great weight of the vans pressing against them as a barely controllable force. Making a rapid stop, even at this modest speed was to experience a sickening sense of helplessness as the momentum carried them relentlessly forwards aided by rails rendered greasy by the cooling night.

'Is she crazy?' Boswell held the whistle cord and gave a series of long and angry blasts. If an engine could adopt the emotions of a living being, then this one was furious.

Eddie looked over the driver's shoulder and could just make out the slight figure of a young woman in a dress partially covered by what might be a pale mackintosh. He could discern few details other than the equally pale oval of her face turned towards them and he thought one of her arms pointed to the side as if indicating something. He bit his lower lip and winced at the sound of squealing brakes and gripped the tender side.

Fortunately, she responded to the screaming whistle and stepped off the track and Eddie felt the tightness around his chest release. The woman ran towards the wooden fencing that protected the line in a fluid movement that made her appear little more than a shadow flowing smoothly and soundlessly across the land. Eddie felt a prickle of perspiration form on his brow and a tremor of nerves as she paused to look back at them one last time, before dropping down the embankment.

'Stupid cow!' Boswell thumped the cab side with a balled fist. 'We could have killed her.' Despite his rage, the driver's voice held more than a trace of genuine relief, and as the train finally came to a stand and Eddie wound the hand brake down to hold it steady, Boswell took a moment to mop his brow with a grubby blue neckerchief pulled from his overalls.

'Golly, that was close.' Eddie realised he was shaking.

'Not half. Look out for Bob at the back, I'm going to see what's she's playing at.' Boswell swung himself out of the cab and dropped on to the ballast whilst Eddie remained standing at the cab side. Now the danger was over, and his initial alarm quietened, it seemed an anti-climax looking at the empty track.

Eddie liked this approach to Brackley, which in the 'down' direction was signposted by first passing through a deep cutting and dipping under the distinctively skewed Buckingham Road Bridge. He looked back along the train and could see they had cleared the black outline of this bridge and that the cutting was falling away on either side leaving the locomotive exposed on top of the falling embankment that lead onto the long curving viaduct. The town was just a distant sprinkle of lights across a hill to his left, and Eddie could make out the belfry on the town hall. The Ouse valley however was a mass of formless dark, pierced by a few dimly illuminated windows peeking through a sheet of mist that had collected at the bottom. How the driver thought he was going to find the girl in all that, he was not sure.

The hand lamp of Bob Goodless the guard was now flashing as he made his way forward alongside the train. At least he was OK, and no doubt coming down to enquire what they were playing at by slamming the brakes on with little warning.

Eddie peered at the fire and saw it was burning slightly better and the needle was at least steady, if not climbing across the pressure gauge. He dropped down onto the ground to meet the guard.

'What's up? That were a nasty surprise.'

'There was someone on the line.'

The guard pulled a face and rubbed his shoulder. 'Did we strike them?'

'No.'

'Thank God. Damn nearly ripped my ruddy arms out.' Goodless winced as he touched a sore point. 'I felt summat was not right and when I heard the warning sounds coming down the train, I bloody well knew what to expect.' He rubbed an elbow. 'I held onto the brake pillar for dear life, but no real harm done, all things considered.'

'We'd have run her down, but she stepped off the line at the last minute.'

The guard gingerly flexed a shoulder. 'Aye, well... Where's the driver?'

'He went looking for her. She was just standing right in the middle of the track!'

'Not again? She's becoming a bloody nuisance.'

'You mean she's done this before?' Eddie was incredulous.

'Oh aye. Last night and a few before that. It's been the talk of all the lads around here this month past.'

'Then someone had better keep a look out and arrest her. She's a menace! She needs locking up!' Boswell reappeared at the front of the K3, chuntering loudly and with a face like thunder. 'She's going to have a short life playing daft games like that. Jesus, Mary and Joseph...' He bent down and peered at a drift of steam softly issuing from somewhere between the wheels. 'She must be doolally.' His voice softened as he straightened up again, having vented his rage. 'You alright, Bob?'

'As well as can be expected. I'll be bruised blue by tomorrow though. No sight of her?'

'Nah. Too dark down the bank to see anything. It's all trees and bushes.'

The guard made a face and shook his head, 'It's a strange business that's for sure. Right, I'd best check the couplings are sound. I'll signal from my van when it's OK to move off.'

'I'll ease us into Brackley; we need to lay over for a bit of a blow up. Soft lad here made a right hump in the fire,' Boswell grinned at Eddie. It was as though he wanted to lighten the mood with a bit of joshing, and help dispel any residual shock.

'Goodless winked at Eddie. 'Thought it was a slow run.' He laughed and then winced as doing so agitated ribs now sore from being thrust against the brake pillar. 'We're protected here - the signalman's dropped the distant peg and can no doubt see us from the box, so we won't get shunted from behind at least. Give me a few minutes to check the train over before you ask the box to call us on.' And with that, Bob Goodless stumped off, shining his lamp beam between the wagons.

Boswell pulled out a metal tobacco tin with Craven A on the lid and opened it. 'Smoke?' He handed a hand-rolled cigarette to Eddie without waiting for a reply then selected a second from the collection pre-assembled in the tin.

They stood in companionable silence for a few moments, the sound of Boswell's lighter flipping open and the rasp of the flint the only communication between them. Their engine hissed and dripped quietly, the metal occasionally ticking and creaking, the injector gurgling, but otherwise all was still. A sickly green moon slid behind a thin veil of cirrus minor as a growling lorry on the climb through town missed a gear before settling back into a low murmur.

They both pricked their ears up at a series of strange, clear and yet breathy, piping sounds, not unlike numerous children's toys being squeezed in rapid succession from somewhere high above.

Whee-oh, whee-oh, wheep...

Driver Boswell cocked his head to one side, his brow furrowing as he took a long lungful of smoke and held it inside. 'That explains it,' he exclaimed, smoke streaming from his nostrils. He surprised Eddie by crossing himself.

Wheep, whee-oh, wheep.

The plaintive sounds moved across the sky. They were soft, yet surprisingly audible, a complex series of high whistles and calls.

'Explains what?'

'All that's gone wrong tonight. Them whistlers warn of trouble. They know when there's something bad going to happen. A warning, and not a curse just as long as there's only the six of them!' Boswell made a rueful expression. 'Mebbe that's why she cleared off the line?' He looked troubled, tossing his cigarette to the ground as if he'd lost the taste for it and stared into the ragged clouds now stained green and silver by moonlight. Eddie thought he was trying to count the calls.

'They're widgeon. A bit early though.' Eddie's voice was light. 'I'd expect them to come in next month.' He was born and bred in the village of Woodford Halse and despite the overpowering presence of the locomotive shed and wagon works and the vast sprawling acres of sidings, it was surrounded for miles in each direction by open farmland, by woods, coppices and meandering streams and so like any country lad, he could tell a widgeon from a teal or a mallard.

'Widgeon? That's what you think they are?' Boswell shook his head deliberately in an ominous motion, the whites of his eyes shining in the moonlight. 'Listen to 'em!' His voice was a hoarse whisper. 'They're soul birds, that's what. They send shivers down your spine.'

The strange thin piping calls wheeled across the sky, and Eddie sensed a growing unease. It was indeed an odd sound, especially when disembodied from the birds that he could not locate amidst the clouds. He'd never thought the sound haunting before, but as the ducks wheeled above sending their piping calls from first one direction then another, he could appreciate why his driver found it so. They were just ducks, strangely late on the wing and looking for water to roost upon for the night - but seeing this tough, experienced, railway man acting so fearful, was unnerving. If his grandmother was talking like this, he would just laugh at her silly superstitions and humour her, but coming from Boswell, it made him question what was really happening.

'Look there - against the moon!' Eddie pointed, and they both tracked the unmistakable silhouettes of the waterfowl flying in a loose formation as the clouds ripped apart to create a silver fringed gap. 'Could they be teal?' He asked the question in an attempt to break the acute tension palpable between them.

'Six... can you see the seventh?' Boswell was staring into the sky as if his life depended on it, his skin drained of all colour by the cold light. 'Lord help us we don't find another,' he muttered under his breath. 'There's a death when seven come.'

'I think just six.'

'Just a warning then. Perhaps we've used up our bad luck for tonight.'

'I hope so...' Eddie fiddled with his cigarette.

'We'd have killed her if the seventh had whistled.'

Eddie remained silent. The piping was growing fainter, but he was nervous. He wanted to be away from here.

Driver Boswell gave Eddie a hard look. 'That was a warning of a death if we don't retrieve the missing iron! We were being told. She was pointing. The girl was pointing at something beside the track, did you not see? And then the whistlers came. It makes sense.'

'Er, yes, I suppose so.' Eddie tried to swallow, but his mouth was dry and bitter with the hard tobacco smoke. Again, he felt unsettled by his driver's surprisingly deep-rooted belief in something that sounded like silly superstition. But Boswell had a point, he'd not only rumbled the fire iron falling onto the track, but there was no doubting it had the potential to cause an accident.

'Were you going to speak up or just hope I didn't notice?'

'I-I was. Honest! But then there was the emergency stop and the girl on the line, and then checking on Bob at the back....'

'Yeah?' Boswell shrugged this away. 'Well, now we've got time on our hands, you can advise the signalman at Brackley about what you did. Clumsy oaf. He'll have to send a man to walk the line and retrieve it, you realise that? One long walk for some poor bugger. Let's just hope that's what they're whistling for and we forestall an accident.'

Eddie felt an involuntary shiver down his body. A sensation his mother said happened when someone walked over your grave. The thin reedy piping came again across the night air, but now far quieter.

'What are they? These soul birds?'

Driver Boswell fixed his beady eyes on Eddie for a moment as if trying to formulate a satisfactory answer. 'The Seven Whistlers. Some folk claim they're the lost souls of unbaptised children who died young and are doomed to wander the skies forever. I've always believed they are the undying dead. Unhappy and tormented souls of murdered folk who's bodies have never been found and properly laid to rest.' His voice was low and earnest.

Eddie's eyes opened wide like saucers. 'Really?'

'You might scoff but you ignore their warning at your peril!' Boswell pointed his finger to reinforce his point.

Eddie could think of nothing to say in reply to this, and hurriedly clambered back into the warm cab muttering something about checking his fire and busied himself with practicalities, trying to clear his mind of this strange talk by concentrating on earthly matters of coal, fire and water.

Chapter Eleven

Brackley
17th September 1950

It made no sense to Irons either. He was standing at the open door of the booking hall, panting with his recent exertions on the stairs, looking out onto the short semi-circular service road that turned off the A43 and which was empty save for a blue and black Austin taxi. The driver of this vehicle was leaning on the bonnet with one foot nonchalantly resting on a broad mudguard whilst he hand-rolled a cigarette, a cap pushed to the back of his head allowing the lamplight to shine on slicked hair furrowed with comb lines.

'You the last out?'

'It looks that way.' Irons ran a hand over his face. 'I say, did you see which direction the young lady went? She was the one in green.'

'Sorry, no young women went past here in any colour dress – more's the pity. Except Mrs Mathers of course, but as she can't be a day short of 80, I can't think you mean her!' The taxi driver grinned. 'What's up, mate?'

Irons puffed his cheeks full of air then slowly exhaled, trying to release some of the tension building in his chest. 'Most odd? Is there another way out of the station?'

'This is both entrance and exit, that's why I'm here. Well, saying that, I suppose you could always walk up the goods road. Bit of a drag and very dark at this time of night.' He wrinkled his nose.

'Where does that come out?'

The driver pointed with his thumb towards town, 'over that way behind the trees; it drops down pretty steep to the side of the station. She done a runner on you?' His voice was laughing, the little cigarette bouncing on his lip as he spoke and sending a cloud of smoke around his face.

'It rather looks that way.' Irons tried to keep the same jocular tone but stopped from saying more. He had no right to be telling just anyone about his meeting with Miss Askew and reminded himself that this was a small town where word could soon spread. It would not do for a new teacher to get a reputation for being some kind of tearaway. 'She must have gone that way. That explains it. Thanks!' He made to start walking.

'Hop in!' The driver stood up and opened the front passenger door. 'I'll get no more fares tonight.'

'It's all right, thanks. It's not far to Magdalen College.'

'On the house. Gratis. I'm off home and since I'm going your way, we can look for your missing girlfriend on the drive down. The name's Hancock. Dennis Hancock.'

'Richard Irons. Pleased to meet you.'

He gratefully accepted the lift. He rarely got the opportunity to ride in a car and the comfortable leather seat was a rare indulgence even if only for a few minutes. On top of that, the taxi driver appeared a friendly face and more worldly-wise than either the guard or stationmaster. Added to which, he might prove useful.

As the Austin grumbled into life and pulled out onto the deserted main road, both men kept a watchful eye for the walking figure of Miss Askew as they passed the white-painted gate and dark blue enamelled sign that indicated that the inclined road leading towards 'British Railways Brackley Central Goods Yard'.

'So what part of town is your girl from?'

'She's not exactly my girl to be honest. We've only recently become acquainted. We've not discussed where she lives, not yet, anyway.'

The driver glanced across at Irons, the fag still dangling from his mouth, and gave a throaty chortle that was heavy with suggestion. 'Good priorities, mate. You don't want to be wasting time on the domestic side of things when you can just go straight for the nooky. Ha ha!'

'Good Heavens. We're not much more than acquaintances at the moment. Botheration, I can't see her anywhere...' Irons was leaning forward in his seat looking out at the empty town with a feeling of disappointment building inside.

'She could have gone down any one of these side roads, that's your problem. What's her name? I know about every family in town. I know which girls are lookers!' He gave Irons a conspiratorial wink. 'Pays to keep an eye on the pretty ones.'

They had pulled to a stop at traffic lights protecting a junction, the sound of music and laughter spilling through the open door of 'The Plough' and into the taxi as the dark presence of Magdalen College chapel loomed ahead to their left, framed in a gap between a long avenue of dark trees that had been disfigured by years of pollarding.

I bet you do! But Irons felt his spirits lift. The man might know her and offer some inside information that could prove handy. 'Her name is Betty. Betty Askew.'

The taxi driver misjudged letting out the clutch and stalled the Austin. He gave an angry puff on his cigarette, gunned the ignition and pulled away, making the vehicle express his impatience. 'She's not from around here, you said?'

'Oh yes, she told me she was born in Brackley and lives here. Do you know her? She must be about eighteen or nineteen. Brown hair, blue eyes and an athletic figure.'

The driver frowned and swung the taxi to the left, turning off the broad thoroughfare and down the separate access road that ran parallel that gave access to the front of the school and the market place. He stopped the taxi under the overreaching arms of a tree that rustled with drying leaves, hinting at the coming autumn. 'Magdalen you said? I'll drop you here.' His chirpy demeanour had shifted in these brief moments to something darker.

'Perfect. Thanks awfully!'

'Are you quite sure about her name? It sounds to me like you two don't know much about each other, so you could have heard it wrong.' The driver looked puzzled.

'Elizabeth Askew. I'm quite sure I've got it right. She also told me about the town, this school, about how she works up at the loco sheds at Woodford.' He laughed for no particular reason, now feeling confident and he abandoned his reserve about opening up to a stranger. 'She's one of a gang of girls that work there and...' Irons stopped.

The driver was now staring at him with a look like thunder, the stub of his 'rollie' twitching in the corner of his mouth, a pulsing vein prominent on his neck. 'Listen chum, I don't know what your game is, and I've nothing against a feller chasing the local girls; but you're an out-of-towner, up from the big smoke if I'm any judge of accent, so you listen to me. Be careful what you go around saying, yeah? You might think it clever or some kind of joke, but there are plenty of folk around here who could take exception to what you're doing. Decent people, who could be very hurt. So, cut it out and get out of my cab!'

'I don't understand? What have I said?'

'Are you a reporter?' He jabbed an accusatory finger towards Irons.

'No! I'm a math's teacher.'

'A teacher?' The taxi driver cut him off and spat a piece of tobacco from the corner of his mouth through the opened door window. 'Know what I think? I think you're here in the hope of stirring up a story to flog to the papers.'

'This is ridiculous!'

'Do you know about what happened?'

'I really don't know what you're talking about. I just wanted to meet her again and take her out to the pictures!'

'You're sick in the head. Now listen, take some sound advice. Let it rest. I'm telling you as clearly as I can; forget about the Askew's and leave those folk in peace - or else I'll personally come looking for you.' He scowled menacingly. 'Now hop it!'

'You've got this wrong,' Irons looked at the taxi driver imploringly, 'I meant no harm. I don't understand what I've said to upset you...'

Irons was now standing on the pavement with the trees dropping leaves about him as a gust of wind rattled the stunted branches above. He looked lost and bewildered. The taxi driver stared at him for a few moments, and then along the polished bonnet of his car that reflected the gas lamps on their tall standards and the backlit dial of the town hall clock. When he finally spoke, it was without anger but no less clear and forceful for being quieter and controlled.

'Betty Askew is dead.' He let the clutch out and started to pull away. 'A long time dead. Poor kid.'

Irons stood at the gates to the school, the big harvest moon casting moving shadows on the ground through the stumpy limbs of the tree. An owl screeched from somewhere beyond the school playing fields and he heard the urgent, insistent whistling of a distant train. He should have heeded its warning.

Chapter Twelve

Amersham
18th September 1950

'There's not a breath of wind and yet those blessed French doors still managed to slam and crack a pane of glass. It's the limit, it really is. That must be the third time it's happened,' Isabella Liney looked pale with annoyance. 'I've been telling you to fit hooks and eyes to keep them open for I don't know how long.'

'Again?' Jocelyn Liney shook his head in frustration. 'And I keep telling you that wind or no wind, a through draft can cause doors to slam. Oh, very well, I shall call Parkers later and get them to come and replace the glass – and fit some hooks.' He looked at a ridge of ominous cloud boiling up in the distance, rising above the tall mature trees that surrounded their garden. 'There's a storm coming, so its best you keep the doors closed for now.'

Isabella Liney shivered, despite the strong sun and the humidity building in the air. She shrugged her shoulders as if trying to rid herself of a bad memory. 'It's still odd how the draft is only ever in the dining room and nowhere else, the rest of the house is quite free of this problem.' She pursed her lips for a moment as she composed herself. 'It's always cold, have you not noticed?'

'Exactly my point about the doors...' Liney mopped his brow. 'Gosh it's getting close. A hot day for digging.'

'I can never get that room warm, even on a day like this!' Mrs Liney continued her theme, worrying away at it. 'I have Doris keep a fire in there every day, but to absolutely no effect. If you get too hot with your digging, just go and sit in the dining room for five minutes! But mind you take your dirty shoes off first.' She still managed to get a warning in despite her distracted thoughts. 'I'm sorry to say it's my least favourite room in the house. There's plenty of light and such a lovely view onto the garden and yet I always feel ill at ease in there. Sounds silly, but that's the truth of it.'

'I thought that room was one of the reasons we bought this place?'

'I know,' Isabella Liney looked uncomfortable. 'But then I hadn't expected it to be as cold as a grave.' She shivered, despite the heat and the close atmosphere.

'That's a bit strong, old girl!' Liney gave her a funny look, sensing that his wife was not joking. He turned back to the herbaceous border he was standing amidst and changed the subject. 'Never mind that now, what I'm thinking, is why we can't get someone in to do this? Amersham must be full of willing tradesmen who would have it cleared in half the time it'll take me. I could arrange it at the same time I instruct Parkers to get the glass mended?' Liney ended on an optimistic, questioning note that he knew would be futile.

'I'm sure there are, Jocelyn, but that's absolutely not the point. You know they'll only prevaricate and find all manner of reasons to delay, and the next thing, it'll end up being weeks before its finished – mark my words,' his wife made a thin line with her mouth. 'It's a perfect summer's day, at the moment at least, and we must crack on. I've been dreaming of a Gertrude Jekyll style border since the day we moved in - and that was goodness knows how many years ago.'

'Don't I know it...' Jocelyn Liney muttered under his breath. 'Seven years, I think you'll find.'

'' if we can get all this horrid stuff cleared out, you can have a bonfire this evening and the a well-earned G and T!' Isabella Liney gave her husband one of her arch looks that brooked no dissent and put a well-manicured hand upon her hip. 'And besides, the exercise will do us the power of good.'

'Hah!' Her husband looked at the long border running down one edge of their garden, thick with matted fronds of ground elder and studded with a motley selection of unhealthy hydrangeas that faded to an unpleasant grey-pink, like bruised flesh. A large stone bird bath sat in the middle of the border on a plinth, a thick mat of ivy clinging around the base. He grimaced. 'We? I take it you are referring to myself, in the singular? I can't see you digging this lot out, dearest.'

'It would completely ruin my manicure; but I'll put my gardening gloves on later and lend a hand making the bonfire - when I return from the nursery, that is.'

'Now that really takes the biscuit; you're swanning off choosing plants whilst I break my back digging this dammed border!'

'Language!' She gave a petulant frown. 'Someone has to choose the plants. It's a fine art making a border that manages to look perfectly wild and carefree and not just a ragged mess. I have not had my nose in this...' She held up a well-thumbed copy of Gertrude Jekyll's Colour in the Flower Garden, 'for nothing. You wouldn't know what to buy. And besides; it's your waistline that needs the most working on. I don't know what they feed you on at the bank, but it must be off-ration, as its expanding your waistline in line with your bonuses! Whilst the latter are to be welcomed, the former, somewhat less so.'

Jocelyn Liney glanced down at his rotund stomach and the waistband of his trousers that dipped alarmingly low below this soft overhang. 'One simply has to have lunch, and in a style that befits our company. It goes with the nature of our work at Cazenova's.' He stood upright and made an unsuccessful attempt suck his flabby belly in. 'Actually, we do a lot of exceedingly good business over a bottle of claret and some fine dining.' He looked wistful, as if already dreaming about the substantial and leisurely meals awaiting him in the week ahead. His wife however was already walking towards their large arts and crafts styled detached house.

'It'll be the Devil's own job, digging this out,' he called after her, waving an unseen hand at the border.

'Then the sooner you make a start, the quicker you can relax,' she tossed over her shoulder.

'I'm not moving that blasted bird bath!'

'I didn't ask you to. Just clear around it, and I'll see what I think when the plants are in. I'll be a couple of hours, so I'm sure you'll be all done by time I'm back!' She gave him a flash of smile. 'I'll tell cook to make us some nice lamb chops for dinner...'

'All done a couple of hours!' Liney pulled a sour face and shook his head, but his complaint was lost on his wife who was out of earshot. He was resigned to the task ahead. His wife insisted that the garden was a job they must to do themselves and absolutely forbade him employing a gardener, even though he could easily afford one, or even two, for that matter.

After staring sadly at the mass of green leaves and wiry fronds a while longer, he looked around as if checking that no one was watching whilst he demeaned himself with manual labour, though this was highly unlikely, as the garden was protected by a high brick wall draped in sweet-smelling ivy, now alive with bees. He picked up the garden fork and jabbed it into the nearest matt of foliage.

Twenty minutes later he had already made a reasonable pile of grubbed out elder on an old blanket spread out for that purpose on the lawn. He was now perspiring heavily and could feel his back and legs complaining, whilst his hands that usually wielded little more than an expensive fountain pen, were rubbing raw. He'd been worrying away constantly at the many roots that seemed to lie like sinuous rat tails through the soil and which would not give up their purchase in the earth unless he put his not inconsiderable weight behind pulling on them. After one especially hard wrestling match, he now found himself suddenly sitting down with a bump, on the grass with a clump of earth in his hand stuffed with broken roots sticking out like so many severed electrical cables, having unexpectedly snapped free.

'Stupid bloody weeds!'

He was about to toss this aside, when his eye was drawn to something entwined within the twisted roots. Easing it out and rubbing most of the loose soil off, he saw that it was a woman's bracelet.

It was cheap, made from some kind of plastic in garish orange and ochre. Liney wrinkled his nose at the poor workmanship and thanked the Lord that his wife did not have to wear such end-of-the-pier trinkets.

He tossed it onto the blanket without a second thought and got back to work, but soon stopped again and leant on the fork handle, breathing hard and taking the opportunity for a rest as he contemplated what he had just exposed. A bold robin skipped across the freshly dug earth and cocked its head as if also inspecting the find.

Liney stretched down and released a piece of green material that showed signs of having been extensively burnt before being buried. Despite this combustion, there was still a sizable portion left.

'How did that get there?' he muttered under his breath, glancing towards the robin as if seeking its opinion.

He stood upright and turned the cloth over in his hands for a moment or two as he considered this discovery, privately cursing the sluttish behaviour of some people who could litter their own gardens in this manner. It looked like the remains of a dress, as part of the neckline and the opening of one shoulder could still be identified. He threw this onto the blanket in disgust, and as he did so, noticed that Isabella was fast approaching across their manicured lawn.

'You're back early, checking on me?'

'Not a bit of it. I forgot my purse, that's all. What a nuisance; I'd driven all the way there and only realised when I arrived. Oh, what's that?'

'It looks like a piece of someone's dress.'

Isabella walked closer and took a closer look. 'It's been burnt.'

'Very observant.'

'Is that not odd?'

'It's on a pile of stuff that we're going to burn. People are forever burning waste in their gardens, so I don't see anything strange about it.'

'I suppose not.' Isabella did not look convinced.

'There's a horrid bracelet as well. Here...'

'A young woman's, and inexpensive.'

'You mean cheap.'

'Do you think the dress and bracelet were owned by the same person?'

Jocelyn Liney pushed out his lower lip and made an unconvinced expression. 'Possibly.'

'Look, what's that?' Isabella Liney bent down and eased out of the disturbed earth where the dress fragment had lain, a metal buckle with a short piece of leather strap still threaded through. 'From a handbag, I'd say. Gosh the little squander bugs - they must have burnt a dress and leather handbag and during strict clothes rationing? Absolutely unforgivable!' The robin flew onto the top of the wall and started to sing, as though broadcasting her sense of outrage.

'We can't know that. It could have lain here for absolutely years and years, and besides, this is just a fragment of strap. Perhaps the rest of the bag was re-used for something?' Liney looked dismissive. 'Not that we ever had to stoop to that ghastly make do and mend malarkey.' He sniffed in a self-satisfied manner and exchanged a knowing look with his wife. 'The same goes for the dress - most of it could have been cut up for re-use and they were just burning the bits left over. I certainly wouldn't blame anyone for using that for rags!' He gave a contemptuous laugh. 'What I do know is that its turning into a ruddy waste heap around here! No wonder the plants look sickly.'

'I suppose you're right, but I still don't like it.' Isabella Liney pulled her thin beige cardigan a little tighter around her body. 'I find it unsettling, though I'm not quite sure why. Just old rubbish.' She wrinkled her nose up at the belt buckle. 'Do you think we should alert the authorities?'

'Call the police in over a few scraps from a bonfire? Absolute rot! The chap's wife was having a clear out, that's all. Besides, it would be scandalous if word got out we'd been wasting everyone's time over a bit of junk. I'd never live it down.' He closed his eyes for a moment as he imagined stepping into his regular compartment for the short electric train ride into the city and meeting the looks of self-righteous indignation he would receive from his fellow bowler hatted companions, each pointedly shaking their newspapers in disapproval before returning to studying the share prices.

His was a closed and highly ordered world where everything was expected to run smoothly and without either fuss or bother. A chap soon learned not to rock the boat by attracting undue attention, especially when it concerned his private life.

'Keep a lid on it, Liney, and maintain the dignity and quiet professionalism of the business at all costs. Do that, and you could go far.' That was the advice he'd been given when he first started at the merchant bank, and he was not about to blow it now over some rotten old rubbish.

'As long as you think it's nothing,' and Mrs Liney tossed the buckle on top of the scrap of dress. 'But didn't you say we bought the place from a retired doctor?'

'What's that to do with anything?'

'He was a confirmed bachelor. I distinctly recall you said he was "a solitary old bird rattling around in this big house," or words to that effect.'

'Did I?' Liney laughed. 'Such men can still have lady friends, Isabella.' He raised a knowing eyebrow.

She gave him a disapproving look. 'That's as maybe, but do they burn their young floozy's clothing in the garden?'

'I wouldn't know.' He felt the first tickle of doubt on the back of his neck. 'We must be careful not to let our imaginations run riot. I'll burn all this later - and do it properly this time – and we can forget about it. Now, I must get on if you want me to finish before that thunder storm brews up.'

Chapter Thirteen

Brackley
18th September 1950

Askew dead. What was the man thinking? Of course, she wasn't dead! He'd sat talking with her during two train journeys so that cocky cabbie was badly misinformed. Typical cabbies, they like to think they know everything - and not just the name of each road in their town - but about the comings and goings of the townspeople to boot. Well, he was spectacularly wrong on this occasion.

But despite his confident assertion, Irons was still dogged by the memory of that unsettling moment when he'd heard the man state so emphatically that Betty was dead. He was finding it hard to erase the sickening sensation it induced. He'd slept barely a wink in his narrow and lumpy bed in Magdalen that night, and when he finally succumbed to a short and fitful sleep, his dreams had been unpleasantly vivid and upsetting, taking the form of a long and exhausting journey that felt more like a chase, although it was far from clear if he were pursuer or pursued.

He was following Miss Askew who was always just ahead of him, sometimes close, sometimes far off, but always out of touching distance. She was hurrying, though occasionally stopping and turning, as though checking he was behind, her face tense and nervous. Was she scared, or was there something more ambiguous about her expression? Whatever her emotion, she urged him on. Were they trying to escape from someone? He really had no idea but certainly, he had a horrible sensation of dread. But no matter how hard he tried he could never catch her up and when he repeatedly called for her to 'stop and wait!' it was in nothing more than a hoarse croak.

A sinister taxi cab, without any visible driver was parked close by, on a driveway or at the side of the road they were running along, and each fresh sighting of the car induced a sense of extreme panic inside Irons. Sometimes it's long nose could be seen pulling slowly into view around a street corner in a menacing manner, the windscreen reflecting the light in such a way that he could not see inside. He knew it was malevolent, or at least it's unseen driver, was, and each time it appeared, it forced him to slow down or duck into a doorway and lose ground on Betty until such time as the taxi silently moved away - only to reappear somewhere else. Finally, after all manner of twists and turns, he found her standing at the top of a steep grassy bank whilst Irons slipped and slid in a frantic attempt to climb up to join her.

As he made wild attempts to reach the crest of the hill he was forced to watch in horror as she frantically beat her arms like windmills whilst a flock of angry owls swooped, flapped and pecked around her head and hands, catching in her hair with their sharp talons, tearing at her flesh with claw and beak, her mackintosh coloured with bright red streams of blood, her screams piercing like a locomotive releasing steam from a safety valve...

Irons woke up sweating and a hand tangled in the bedclothes and with the sensation that it was his own voice that had jolted him out of the nightmare. He lay staring at the ceiling breathing in short gulping breaths, his mind seared by the dreadful images. As he regained some composure, he realised there was an insistent little tapping on his window, as though someone wanted to attract his attention.

Tap tap tap; gentle yet hard, like a finger on the glass.

Tap tap tap.

Could there really be someone outside? But his room was on the first floor. The sound persisted, with three more strikes on the glass, inviting him to pull back the curtains. He suddenly had the craziest idea that Miss Askew had managed to track him down and come to seek his help and like the high jinks of a 1st year fresher, she'd clambered up a drainpipe and was perched precariously on the ledge.

He leaped out of bed, rubbed his hands across his face to get the blood flowing and with a nervous sense of anticipation, eased a curtain aside.

It was nothing more than a little bird pecking at the metal frame. A blue tit that now fixed him for a moment with one beady eye before darting away in a flash of blue and yellow when it saw Iron's bleary face. He smiled at his foolishness and went the bathroom at the end of the corridor to wash away any lingering memories of his nightmare.

Irons had to face Monday morning exhausted and in a disturbed frame of mind despite his best efforts at washing away what was nothing more than a bad dream. His inability to fully concentrate on the job caused him to retreat into demanding long periods of silent study or rote learning from books, and any lad foolish enough to break these enforced silences was rudely punished by a surprising eagerness to cane their opened palms, and threats of worse hanging over the bowed heads of the startled pupils.

Irons needed time to make sense of everything that happened last night. The taxi driver's outburst was the easiest to resolve; it was a regrettable coincidence that two young women with identical names came from the same town, and especially tragic that one had met an untimely end. Irons could forgive the man for reacting so emotionally if he was not aware of Miss Askew's doppelganger, for despite claiming to know every girl in town he was clearly fallible. Hearing Betty's name would have caught him off guard and triggered his alarming response.

One lesson Irons had learnt from this was about discretion. It would be wise to keep his interest in the living Betty Askew to himself. Whilst part of him wanted to make further enquiries and clarify this misunderstanding, he decided it might be wiser to play a more cautious innings henceforth. Only if his fledgling relationship with Miss Askew managed to stand on firmer ground would he confess it to anyone.

The detail about the sad story of the other unfortunate Miss Askew could wait. If 'the poor kid,' as the taxi driver had called her, really was dead, then she was past help - unlike his Betty Askew, who not only looked to be in some distress, but had actually asked for his help. Indeed, it appeared she had even left him a clue in the compartment after her sudden exit, although this curious document raised more questions than it answered and did nothing to suggest how he could help her.

On numerous occasions during that tiresome day whilst his pupils were bent to their studies, Irons would lay the tiny slip of paper picked from the carriage seat on his desk or hold it surreptitiously in the palm of his hand out of sight and re-read the few words it bore, in the hope he could make sense of them.

'The Cobra's Eye'
RC to BA forever.
20th September 1942

It was written with a neat hand in black ink on a tiny square of heavy cream paper not more than an inch square and slightly discoloured at the edges with a spot of foxing on the back. It looked as though it had been left in the sun and was certainly not freshly written.

But what was the Cobra's Eye when it was a home? He thought perhaps a restaurant or a place name and the location of the lover's tryst between one RC and a BA. That must be Betty Askew? It appeared to refer to her engagement and the ring that was now lost.

And what to make of the date? This was the strangest part in some ways. An engagement, eight years ago almost to the day. Yet he judged Betty to be only nineteen, no more than twenty-one at a push? She would have been very a young girl in 1942, so something was not adding up.

She had talked of her beau being killed in the war, but she must have been referring to the present Korean conflict? And yet 1942 placed this engagement firmly during the Hitler war. Had Betty Askew really become engaged whilst still a child? Irons felt slightly nauseous and his head swam if he allowed himself to imagine this scenario.

It was possible, Betty had dropped the note accidentally and he was not supposed to solve this riddle, but he believed it had been a deliberate act and part of her attempt to secure his help, so he persevered in trying to make sense of it, but to no avail.

As the day wore on his mood became increasingly fractious, as did that of many others in the school. The air pressure was dropping like a stone and the sky that for so many days had been dotted with a collection of white fluffy clouds grazing like sheep across a benign field of blue, was now turning dark and deeply oppressive. An ominous wall of slate grey turning a livid purplish-black like a vicious bruise, was now creeping up from the horizon as though a heavy awning was being slowly winched over their heads. Great towering thunderheads brilliantly illuminated by the last high beams of sunlight stood tall above this deadening blanket, leering over the rooftops and chimneys like vast outriders driving the slow rolling storm clouds forward.

The electrical charge was palpable, as was the increasing humidity that made the air hot like that from a furnace and shortened tempers, made sweaty collars stick to hot necks and sharp prickles of perspiration erupt beneath damp hair on pink foreheads. The boys were abandoning their caps despite warnings to the contrary, whilst both master and pupil were surreptitiously loosening ties. Everyone repeatedly looked out of the ancient mullioned windows at the premature darkness descending on the town in advance of the gas lamps being lit, rendering the market square almost dark due to the ominous presence above. The patient shoppers standing in the bread and meat queues that reached far out of the row of shops looked upwards with fretful expressions, praying they could collect their ration and be home before the floodgates opened.

The shoppers had their prayers answered. The storm sat overhead and stewed a while longer, and as evening drew in and the shops locked up, everyone became desperate for the rain to break and the electrical storm to vent its pent-up energy and release the town from its brooding grip. The ceiling of dense cloud was weighing heavy in all directions without relief, stretching as far as the horizon, animated occasionally by distant flickering and low grumbles that reminded many of the blitz nights when a distant town received a hammering.

The evening meal at Magdalen was over, and everyone released from the stifling humidity in the refectory and from the smell of boiled cabbage and braised meat that had challenged even the hungriest to consume the food set before them. All anyone wanted was flop in saggy common room chairs or lie on beds, too frazzled to pretend to look at their homework. The masters were desperate for the chance to finally shed their sweltering black gowns and mortar boards and have a restoring cup of tea or a cigarette leaning against an outside door in the hope of some fresher air.

After a day of deliberation, Irons knew what he must do to break his own mental storm. He was no closer to solving the riddle of the note, but he knew he must find Betty that night. He sensed she was in some kind of danger and delay was impossible. As he was excused from monitor duty until later that evening, he seized his chance.

After idling away an hour or so in desultory conversation with an eye always on his watch, he finally told Jim Duggan the biology teacher he was 'going for a fag and a pint before last orders,' and promptly rushed off before the flame-haired Scotsman could suggest he join him. With little thought of the rain that was surely to come, Irons raced straight out of the school gates without even a hat and just his jacket tucked under an arm that became instantly clammy in the humidity.

He strode purposefully up the high street and past The Plough, although not without considering that a swift pint was the more sensible option. He pushed this idea aside and continued towards Brackley Central. The trees in the park were rustling anxiously and leaves skittered and circled across the broad pavements in wild dances, this gathering wind suggesting the storm was preparing to unleash its venom any time soon. The Scots pines in front of the little red brick station building sighed in the dark, relieved only by the light of a solitary gas lamp above the entrance. Irons found the sound of the wind eerie, like that of soft female voices whispering in the branches above, and fought to reassure himself it was just wind, wood and needle at play.

He had pulled up short in his approach to the station and stepped between two of these creaking trunks, heart pounding, for there was the unmistakable shape of the Austin taxi guarding the station entrance. To his unsettled mind it was reminiscent of his terrifying dream. He could not see if the driver was inside because the windscreen was a sheet of reflections, exactly as in his nightmare. Why was he feeling scared? He'd been only too pleased to take the cabbie into his confidence, and yet now he was skulking behind trees feeling apprehensive of meeting the man again. Even worse, he realised he was acting suspiciously and surely inviting a bad reaction, if not from Hancock the cabbie, then from anyone who might see him.

At that moment there was a series of brilliant flashes that starkly illuminated the interior of the vehicle, confirming it was empty, followed by an ear-spitting bang that struck Irons physically to the core. The rain came moments later, pouring down in heavy drops like a silver curtain that blurred his vision of both car and station, splashing noisily on the ground like so much gravel tipped down a metal chute. It was torrential and instantly soaking; a rain that demanded he took cover.

Mr. Hancock and one of the station staff appeared at the doorway and peered out at the sudden and noisy downpour, their faces momentarily bleached by another lightning flash, eye sockets black pools of shadow rendering their faces like skulls. They ducked back inside, and Irons saw a door open and both enter what looked like an office.

Holding his jacket high and head bowed against the heavy rain, Irons sprinted across the divide, his shoes sodden and trouser turn ups darkened with water in the short moments it took for him to enter the booking hall. He did not slow or risk a look as he passed the ticket window, and continued across the bridge that lay directly ahead, his feet loud on the wooden boarding and pounding down the stairs onto the platform below.

He stood panting to catch his breath, the rain still falling in torrents and beating on the glass canopy in a tremendous roar before gushing noisily through the down pipes. Everywhere was the sound of water, drumming, running, splashing and gurgling. The sky was being ripped apart repeatedly by sustained strikes of lightning followed immediately by a series of deafening cracks of thunder like a bombing raid. The lightning flashes allowing him brief glimpses of a rain lashed tank engine crawling over the viaduct hauling its short train of coaches, the steam from the chimney beaten down to one side like a soggy white pennant.

The last train. He was just in time.

A porter was leaning on a doorframe, a shadow thrown across the platform by the light from the office. A distant bell tinkled, barely audible through the noise of the storm, but otherwise, the station appeared deserted. It was battened down like a ship in a storm.

The smart Thompson L1 tank engine hissed and fizzed noisily as it clanked to a halt close to Irons. Its gay apple green livery was slicked and glossy as a dance band crooner's hair, reflecting the string of lamps under the canopy as the rain bounced off the cab roof, from under which two pairs of eyes looked out from the darkness within.

The fireman stepped briskly onto the platform with a friendly nod towards Irons and after a momentary pause to steel himself for the task ahead, he trotted out from under the cover of the canopy and across to the curved metal arm jutting from below the tall cylindrical water tower on the platform end. Doubled over against the rain, he pulled on a chain to swing the arm and its dangling rubber hose like an elephant's trunk, across to the side of the engine. He clambered on the slippery side tank, getting drenched whilst doing so and had the water filler lid open and the end of the hose in place in a matter of moments, holding it steady with one hand and keeping his cap firmly wedged on his head with the other, waiting for the driver to now run out and turn the metal wheel at the base of the water tower that opened the water valve.

The hose expanded and bucked as it filled, and the fireman adjusted the angle of its entry into the tank until he was happy it was secure, then leaped back down onto the platform whilst the driver stepped back into the cab and fiddled with something that made a steamy hissing sound from near the wheels.

Irons meanwhile, was keeping his eyes fixed on the length of the train, carefully observing the few passengers getting out.

'What a night, eh? I'm flippin' soaked!' The fireman beat at his overall legs and flapped his sodden jacket to shake the worst off as he addressed Iron. 'Jesus, it could have held off a few more minutes!'

'It's been brewing all day.' Irons was keeping his eyes on the passengers now hurrying along the platform and on the porter half-heartedly loitering beside his little two-wheeled trolley, although it was clear he expected no work tonight. 'It was giving me a headache, so I'm glad it's broken.'

Irons watched two middle-aged women carrying wicker shopping baskets and wearing impractical hats fall out of a carriage with an unfurling of umbrellas, giggling and screaming in mock anguish as they tottered on their heels through the rain. They were followed by a sober-looking businessman with a leather attaché case, an elderly gent and his wife, and four senior schoolboys, each wearing prefect's badges on the lapels of their Winchester House School blazers, reminding Irons that he must soon return to his own school-masterly duties. But there was no Betty Askew.

Botheration! Where is she? He cursed under his breath, a feeling of intense disappointment flooding over him that was far worse than the drenching he had already endured.

The young porter sauntered across and exchanged greetings with the fireman before addressing Irons. 'Are you travelling tonight, sir?'

'Er...no' Irons was taken off guard. 'I was just looking. Taking the number...' He pointed at the numerals on the side of the L1 tank. 'I'm developing an interest in trains...'

'And I'm developing an intense dislike for 'em on a filthy night like this!' the fireman laughed heartily, the porter joining in. There was a rueful smile from the driver inside the cab.

'Did you see her? On the way in?' the porter tossed the fag end of his cigarette over the side of the platform and looked up at the tall fireman.

'Not a dicky bird. All silly nonsense, if you ask me.'

'Thank the Lord. We'd have no chance of seeing her until too late.' The driver added, an oily cloth in one gloved hand, the other resting on one of locomotive cab handrails. 'I know she's supposed to be crazy, but even she'd think twice about being out on a night like this.'

'Who said she were crazy?' The young porter had his hands in his trouser pockets and was hopping from one leg to another with nervous energy whilst glancing at Irons to see if he was catching his attention. 'There's some as say she's not natural. More Super-natural, if catch my drift?' He gave Irons a look laden with barely concealed meaning.

'Poppycock!' The fireman flipped the porter's cap upwards with a swift movement of his hand, sending it tumbling down his back. The young man reacted with surprising speed, twisting himself around and managing to catch it before it hit the ground in a move that suggested this was not the first time he'd been so treated.

'Oy! Give over, that's my best cap!' He tried to make his young, fresh face look suitably grave, but just succeeded in looking more like a naughty schoolboy. 'It's true. I swear it!'

'Get away. I don't hold with all that nonsense.' The driver stepped back into the gloom of the cab and did something so the engine changed the note of its constant hissing yet again.

'She's nuts. No more to be said,' added the fireman.

The porter was readjusting his hat with an unnecessary level of concentration, like a cat caught losing its footing and then preening with exaggerated fastidiousness to cover its embarrassment. 'I've seen her! And she looked just like a spook to me.' His face flickered in the blue light of another lightning flash, head nodding with the weight of this revelation, and this time he caught Iron's eye. 'She proper gave me the shivers!'

The fireman's response was lost by another thundering boom, but he was laughing, and looked unmoved. Irons however, was staring at the porter.

'Hey, watch the water!' The young porter pointed over the fireman's shoulder and laughed raucously, clutching at his stomach with exaggerated glee.

The fireman sprang into action as water cascaded from the tank filler in great white streams that splashed, together with the torrential rain, over the edge of the platform in a foaming torrent. 'That's your fault talking such tosh, you monkey!' He shut off the water and sprang back aboard the locomotive to free the hose.

'Give over! I was just telling you what I know.'

Irons had been listening to the exchange with interest. 'Excuse me, who are you talking about? It sounds most intriguing.'

'You not heard about the girl in white? Now there's a story for a stormy night...'

'Don't listen to him, he's full of rubbish.' The driver grinned.

'No, seriously guv, she stands on the tracks making the trains stop and then just vanishes into the night! Spooo-ky...' He rolled his eyes dramatically in an expression rendered all the more grotesque by another flash of electrical charge.

'Where does she do this?' asked Irons.

'Here! Near the viaduct. Far side usually, but some say she walks around here when it's locked up at night. What do you make of that? A real ghost prowling our station!'

The fireman had a half smile on his face, shaking his head in mild disbelief as he walked back to the cab of his engine.

'How very odd?' Irons looked back along the now deserted and rain-sluiced platform, the air still muggy, though rapidly cooling to a more pleasant temperature. 'What does she look like?'

'Thinnish, youngish and wrapped in a white death shroud.' The porter waved his hands in an action aimed at suggesting a ghost. 'I thought it looked more like a coat with a dress underneath, but the scariest thing of all is that she just stands and stares, pointing at... Oo er, I'd better jump to it or I'll get a flea in me ear!' The porter straightened himself up and nodded towards the open door where the top hatted stationmaster was standing, thumbs hooked into his waistcoat pockets and looking like a sombre funeral director 'Gotta dash!' and with that, he stepped smartly away with a cheery parting salute.

The fireman, having completed the watering of the engine, hopped back onboard, looked along the train from out of the cab, his cap peak instantly collecting a string of clear beads of water as he waited for the flash of the hand lamp from the guard. A signal clonked into place giving them the road, and the driver offered a short toot on the whistle to acknowledge he'd seen it.

'We're reversing back onto the other side in few moments, then we run around ready for the return leg,' the fireman offered helpfully, sensing that Irons was new to trainspotting.

'Righty-o. Thanks.' Irons glanced at the station clock and decided he could wait until they'd completed this movement, the fireman's advice lending this idea legitimacy. Would Betty turn up to catch the return service? Though he thought it unlikely she would be travelling south at this time. Indeed, it looked unlikely there would be any passengers, as the station was now just an empty expanse, fizzing with curtains of rain.

He paced the up and down under the shelter of the awning, watching as the short train was propelled into the opposite side of the platform, the guard leaning out of the leading coach, guiding them slowly into place. The locomotive uncoupled, backed off and trundled off into the unwelcoming night, ready to run through the station and reappear on the front end.

It was growing steadily chillier and Irons now put his damp jacket on and stood gloomily watching this flurry of activity, wondering what on earth he was doing risking catching a cold loitering on some God-forsaken station. He looked in one of the waiting room windows and saw a cheery fire in the corner, a padded leather bench and a table with brochures and a newspaper laid out, and immediately stepped inside and stood before the warming blaze, trying to dry himself. It was a futile gesture, for he was going to be soaked again by the time he walked back to Magdalen, but the smell of burning coal and leather seats was suddenly appealing in a homely sort of way. He now felt dog tired, and as he stood with his back to the fire he closed his eyes for a few moments, wishing he were snoozing in the saggy armchair in his room. The adrenaline rush of the day had evaporated and the desperate belief that he must meet Betty had gone as well. He felt foolish and embarrassed. If he left soon and got back briskly, he might be able to hide this idiotic escapade from his peers and forget all about it and push any thoughts of that Askew woman away at the same time. He was acting like a fool.

Another series of lightning flashes crackled outside, so intense that his eyelids were no defence, blazing a bright orange and yellow. He opened his eyes in surprise and as he did so, he caught the last dying moments of the brilliant sheet of light and was startled to see a pale figure passing one of the rain-soaked windows. Even with just that fleeting glimpse he was sure it was Betty.

Irons dashed to the door and saw someone stepping into one of the coaches. It was just a glimpse of leg, a swirl of coat and an arm swinging the door closed behind.

He ran to the nearest coach and climbed aboard, moving along the corridor looking into a succession of empty compartments. It must have been her! But where was she? Why was she so darned elusive? He heard footsteps ahead and continued, but the corridor was empty. A toilet door swung slowly open, but there was no one inside. He walked forwards, trying to keep his footsteps silent, edging up to each compartment and peering inside.

There was a short toot on the locomotive whistle, followed by a shudder, a groan and the train started into motion.

'Oh heck!' Irons stared in horror as a Brackley Central nameboard glided past the window, the pair of gas lamps that illuminated the sign, distorted and refracted into many broken fragments of colour through the rain and soot streaked carriage window. He had no ticket, and still worse, had to be back in Magdalen in the next quarter of an hour. Deserting his night monitor duties without explanation or warning was going to land him in serious hot water when he finally rolled up - but when would that be?

There was nothing to do until they reached the next station. He would have to make the best of it, but until then he may as well find Betty and recover something out of this mess. Surely, she was on the train? He could not have made a mistake. He silently prayed he would at least have that satisfaction and moved into the next carriage.

*　　*　　*　　*

Adrian Turvey was sitting on one side of the old kitchen table in his snug back kitchen, with Geoffrey Austin, the silver haired head librarian seated opposite. A double spread of the Weekly Dispatch was opened between the two men, upon which a series of small bones were carefully laid out. Austin was still making a few final tweaks to the arrangement, his curved brier pipe releasing an aromatic curl of smoke, adding to the scent of wood smoke from Turvey's little black range. The solitary bulb in the overhead light suspended on a brown cord from one of the low wooden beams was not bright, so Turvey had lit a large brass oil lamp that looked as though it belonged on a boat, and the glass bowl protecting the burning wick now threw interesting shadows across the table.

Neither man had spoken for the last fifteen minutes. Austin just making the odd grunt or a contemplative sort of noise whilst sucking on his pipe as he worked, with Digger resting the tip of his nose on the edge of the table and sniffing, as if his sense of smell would help resolve the developing mystery, his tail constantly beating time.

Turvey had been supping at a pint of flat home-brewed ale, hoping this would fend off a sickening feeling of dread forming in the pit of his stomach. His friend had hardly touched his glass, concentrating instead on the clutch of little bones they had collected earlier that day and placed in a cardboard box that had once held Rutland Stove Lining.

Austin was trying out various positions for these delicate objects on the newspaper, sometimes lifting and turning one to improve the fit as though he were assembling a jigsaw puzzle, but instead of a helpful box illustration to guide him, he just had the image of a man cheerfully trowelling stove cement into place on box artwork. Turvey found himself staring at this cartoon-like illustration and wished they could talk about the glowing range that he had successfully repaired last spring using the contents of the box, or how low the Ouse was running these last days, and that it would benefit from this downpour, or the price of beer; in fact anything other than think about the horror of what now lay on the table between them, unpleasantly juxtaposed against the newspaper's grainy monochrome images of British and American troops hunkered down under North Korean attack, south of Seoul.

'There's no doubting it. None at all, I'm sorry to say.' Austin sat back in his chair and waved his pipe towards the table. 'Some bones are missing. I dare say other creatures had them away or we didn't look hard enough, but no matter. It's definitely a human hand.'

'Oh.' Turvey ran a hand across his face. 'Are the bones very old?' Turvey knew they were not but was trying to stave off the awful reality a moment longer.

'I'm afraid not. Not archaeologically old, if you take my meaning. That would be quite impossible, finding it on the side of an embankment that's been there just a touch over fifty years.'

'I suppose so.'

'I'm a rank amateur, and better at dating Roman or even pre-Roman remains, but I'd hazard it's been there for anything between one and ten years. No longer.' Austin sucked on his pipe and shrouded his face in blue smoke, his lined and creased face impassive, but his eyes betraying something between professional excitement and acute apprehension.

'Just lying in the bushes? I don't understand why the bones would be there.' Turvey stared at Austin, one hand now stroking the ears of Digger who nuzzled close to his master's grubby brown trousers.

'A puzzle indeed. And then we have to ask, who's hand is it?'

Lightning flashed behind the heavy curtains and the little cottage shook with the following clap of thunder. They sat in silence and glumly stared at the bones as the storm further dampened their spirits. 'To add an unwelcome touch of the macabre, one could also ask if the owner is still missing it now?'

'Or past caring?' Turvey swallowed some beer hurriedly. 'If they are dead...' He tailed off. Both men understood exactly.

'It's quite small, so I'd suggest it could be a woman's or that of a youth.'

Turvey groaned. 'It's illogical, but somehow knowing that makes it worse.'

'Making it even less likely to be the remains of an accident to a railway worker. Not a very credible idea, I know, but perhaps the least unpleasant hypothesis and one that would not have quite such portentous implications.'

Turvey nodded grimly. 'I'd better call the police straight away. There's a telephone in the Greyhound. Look, I don't know about you, but this glass of home brew is losing appeal with that in the room. What say we place the call, then cheer ourselves in the snug by the fire with a couple of proper pints?'

'Yes... yes, I rather think that might help steady the nerves. Going out in that -' Austin paused, and they listened to the relentless splashing of rain hitting the road, 'is going to be jolly unpleasant, but I still think it better than sitting here staring at this little box of tricks!'

*   *   *   *

The train was cold. Freezing actually. If felt like too many windows had been left open allowing the wet air in, which was very unwelcome in sodden clothes. He hurried along the dingy swaying corridors past the stinking toilet with the banging door and across the noisy divide between coaches, chasing a shadow, a fleeting sensation of the woman in white.

Suddenly Irons stopped. There she was! Sitting alone in an unlit compartment. The bulb must have blown, rendering it nearly pitch black, so he was fortunate to even catch a glimpse of her pale face in the smoky blackness within. It was strange to choose such a sad, gloomy location when there was a train of empty, but fully illuminated, compartments close to hand.

He stepped through the compartment doorway and greeted her. She looked up, and he thought she might have smiled although it was hard to make out anything other than the rough outline of her features, her face rendered as little more than a series of dark hollows and shapes that emphasised the delicate outline of her skull.

'May I join you?'

'Of course.'

It was as though she had been expecting him. 'Gosh, it's awfully dark in here!'

'I like it like this. I can see outside better. Your eyes soon get accustomed. Its preferable to having those great heavy blackout curtains drawn across and being permanently worried about showing a light, and besides, I think they make the compartment so stuffy.'

'Quite!' Irons was momentarily puzzled by the reference to blackout curtains. They had been taken down years ago, but this was a small detail and his obvious delight in seeing her immediately pushed this point aside, although the icy cold now enveloping him made him silently yearn for a stuffier and overheated compartment.

He could now see her a little clearer, aided by a flat flicker of distant sheet lightning. She looked gaunt and drawn and her naturally pale skin was rendered the purest white.

She leant forward, not flinching from his gaze and her voice was more urgent than he had heard before. 'We don't have much time because we will soon be in Finmere, where you really should get out and hope to flag someone down for a lift into town.'

Irons was surprised by both her directness and her appreciation of his situation. 'Heck, yes! I'm going to be in awful trouble – no ticket, and it won't be easy to get home at this time of night and in this weather. But never mind that. You don't seem surprised to see me?'

'Nor you, in finding me.'

'True.' He gave her a wry smile. 'I must confess I was rather hoping you would be on the last train from Amersham, or even at the station. I nearly left when you didn't step off when it arrived.'

'You said last time you would try to help me?' She looked at him earnestly, the urgency back.

'Of course! But you left in such a hurry. You simply vanished, or at least so it seemed, and you never told me what I can do.' He sounded breathless and eager. 'Look, would it be dashed impertinent to exchange addresses? Or a telephone number where I could reach you? I know that sounds awfully forward, but...'

'I'm sorry if I appear a little strange and...unconventional,' she interrupted him. 'There are severe constraints on my time, and on my liberty. I have so little time, so we must "cut to the chase," as the American airmen like to say.'

'Then tell me how I can help.'

'I need you to recover my engagement ring.' They both looked at her left hand, a pale shape in the intense gloom. 'It's called the Cobra's Eye. A funny name isn't it. It's a solitaire diamond set on a gold band, and a thing of rare beauty - and great value.'

Irons nodded, he had started to suspect something along this line, although a diamond was an interesting development.

'I know who has it. He stole it from me. He took it by force and menace and...well, let's just say he acted in a most brutish and evil manner.' Her face betrayed a painful memory. 'He covets it. I'm sure he gloats over it in secret, but I also know it holds a sort of spell over him. That's because of how he took it from me - it will always have the potential to destroy him. He can never tell anyone about the diamond, never confess how he came to own it - and so it remains his guilty secret, knawing away at his soul.'

'Then we must go to the police at once. This is an absolute outrage!'

'It is not as simple as that. There are complications.' She spoke with the same sad voice, but with an authority that made Irons listen intently. She had stopped fiddling with her ring finger, her hands folded in her lap. 'I cannot say more, because to do so will confuse and alarm you, perhaps even frighten you off.'

'You must tell me; I want to understand. Nothing will shake my resolve.'

'It is inadvisable, and besides, I do not have the time. But please believe me when I say the police will not help. This man knows many influential people; judges, politicians, aristocrats. They are in his debt and so will go to great lengths to keep him free of scandal. That makes it my word against his, and nobody is going to believe the word of a poor railway cleaner.'

Irons pulled a face as he felt the injustice like a sting to his heart, but he could see her point. 'What do you need me to do?' He wished he had some water. His tongue was sticking to the roof of his mouth.

'I need you to enter his house and find it. He lives alone and is an elderly man - far older in body and spirit than actual years. I can at least derive some satisfaction in knowing that he has already aged as a result of his guilty secret. But you must not confront him! Don't challenge him or do anything to give your identity away – be silent and stealthy and just take the ring and be gone!'

'Break in? Oh. You want me to steal it from his house?'

'Hardly stealing when he took it from me with such - violence.'

'Violence? Oh gosh, I see...' Irons gulped. 'He was so awful?'

Askew nodded. 'He was.'

'That's an absolute outrage. I could punch him right now! Or worse.'

Irons was angry, but this soon changed into something more ambiguous. 'A tooth for a tooth, an eye for an eye?' He ran a hand through his hair. 'I-I don't know, this is all rather...on the edge. I'm not sure this is the proper way to deal with a matter like this. The law is there to bring justice and it is not for us to act like vigilantes. Surely the rule of law is the only right and proper way?'

'That is impossible.'

'Golly, this is all a surprise - and there is my position at school to consider.'

'It will be a far lesser crime than that he inflicted on me. Think of it as helping right a wrong. If you are careful, nobody will ever know, trust me. You found the note I left?'

'On the seat? Yes, I have it in my wallet.'

'Good. I need you to leave that in the place of the Cobra's Eye. A straight swap. This is very important. You must exchange them.'

'Why would you want me to do that?'

'It is the name of the diamond. The name is also written in Egyptian and English on the base of the little box it comes in, so the doctor is quite familiar with the name. He will understand the significance of the initials and the date of our engagement when he sees it in place of the missing ring.'

'You want him to make the connection with yourself? But surely you are just inviting immediate retribution if he is as unpleasant as you suggest? Would it not be better to take the ring as surreptitiously as possible and leave it at that? No trace, no clue.'

She shook her head. 'It is important that you remain anonymous in this affair, but I need him to understand that I am behind it. He cannot reach me. I am quite beyond being hurt any worse than I have already suffered at his hands. That little note will complete my revenge in a most elegant manner.'

'Revenge?' Irons stared at the pale shape of her face, indistinct and blurred despite being so close. He felt a cold sweat of dread on his skin, a slightly nauseous feeling that he was being drawn into something dangerous and disturbing. And yet he could also feel the adrenaline coursing around his body, and the unmistakable urge of attraction and desire that made him unable to stand up and walk away.

Askew leant closer towards Irons, 'Once he realises that note is about Raymond and me the shock is likely to be too much for him to bear.' She gave a little smile, 'Death by natural causes. A heart attack, and impossible that any blame could be attached to a cat burglar who crept in a few hours, or days, previously. Perhaps a few weeks will pass, depending on when he discovers the exchange and how strong his constitution is? And remember, nobody knows he has the ring, so when there is an inquest into the "good doctor's" demise, it will not be mentioned. The note will be a puzzle, but an enigmatic one, and quite impossible to connect with yourself.'

Irons stared at her, his emotions on a stomach-turning fairground ride that mixed acute horror with intense excitement. This was so bizarre and unexpected. It was like something out of a film. She was a real-life femme fatal! What a delicious thrill. He could almost hear zither music twanging in the background as they sat swaying and rocking in the colourless compartment, the scene inky black except for their faces that were illuminated from the side by hard flashes of lightning, their skin streaked by the shadows of the rain streaming down the window. It was pure Film Noir. Betty was now transformed from engine cleaner into someone more like the strangely alluring Marlene Dietrich, asking him to kill a man by proxy as the rain hammered on the roof and the thunder ripped the sky asunder...

'Please do this for me. He lives in Ivy Cottage - they only have names on their houses in Turweston, no numbers. You must make it a neat job and wear gloves not to leave prints. I could not bear it if you were held accountable. You could be in and out in no time. I know he keeps the ring in a locked drawer of his desk in the study at the back of the house.'

'But how do you know this?'

'No matter; just make the switch – and take some of his considerable ill-gotten wealth whilst you are there. He collects gold sovereigns – take some as your reward - then vanish into the night! He will never report the burglary once he realises the Cobra's Eye has been exchanged for that potent little note. It will gnaw away at him, rot him from the core.'

Irons rubbed his face with both hands and exhaled long and slow. There was something dreadful and yet utterly compelling about this extraordinary story.

'Nobody but the doctor, yourself and I, will ever know what happened.'

She then smiled and took a deep breath as if steeling herself to make a great effort. With lungs filled and the air held inside, she clenched her fists for a moment, then reached forward with both hands and clasped one of his between them. They were as cold as ice and her fingers felt almost brittle as if they could be snapped like frozen twigs.

'You're so cold, Betty! You must be catching a chill from the rain.' Irons was reeling from what she had asked of him, but the thrill of excitement like an electrical charge that accompanied this contact between them pushed aside any lingering reservations. He edged a little closer, his knee now gently pressing against hers and wondering if he dare risk a kiss.

'Do it tomorrow evening.'

'So soon?'

'The longer you wait, the more likely your resolve will fail.' Her face was close and her voice a soft but urgent whisper that enveloped his senses. 'Strike whilst the iron is hot!'

He laughed. 'How appropriate - Irons is my surname!'

She smiled indulgently. 'It must be tomorrow night.' She held his look, her liquid eyes silvery. 'When you have the ring, come to the church yard of St Peter's and place it beneath the little pot of flowers on the grave of private Raymond Coulson.'

'R.C.? The same as on the note.'

'The same.'

'Raymond Coulson and Betty Askew. But I don't understand the date. In 1942? How can that be?'

She appeared to ignore his question. 'The stone is fresh and clean – although the grave below is empty.' She bit her lip and paused. 'We do not have his body, and perhaps never shall. It lies in a simple grave in Egypt. A hard twist of cruel fate we both to share not to lie together.' Her hands clasped around his a little harder, the look on her face implying that even this simple act was taking great effort on her part. 'I will be close but hidden and watching for you. But we cannot meet. You must leave the ring and go. Leave it and then go far away and get on with your life. And forget all about me.'

'Never! That's impossible, Betty. Look, when this is over and done, I wonder if you and I... that's to say, we will have shared something important.'

He looked at her face, seeking encouragement. 'We might become friends, or...?' He could see her expression was immovable. Despite their close proximity he was finding it hard to keep her face sharp and in focus. The lightning had ceased, and the darkness was rendering her more and more insubstantial. She was little more than a fuzzy charcoal drawing. 'Is there no possibility we could meet again?'

'I'm sorry, truly. But where I must to go it is impossible for you to follow. I will be long gone. Things are changing and cannot be stopped. And I am glad. In time, you may understand.'

'But how will you know when I am there? I cannot be sure what time I can get to the church yard.'

'I will be there. I will wait for as long as needed. I will wait every night if necessary. Now, the train is slowing, and I can hear the guard approaching.' She suddenly gave Irons a kiss on the mouth, her lips imparting more of a sensation of intense cold than flesh meeting flesh, a shocking touch of an ice cube not warm womanly flesh. 'Please do this! I'm sorry.' She looked pained and continued with what looked like an intense effort of will on her part, 'I cannot give you what you want,' and freeing her hands from his, she stood up. 'Don't follow me. Thank you - and goodbye!'

Then she was gone, somehow fading soundlessly into the dark, replaced immediately by the bulk of the guard standing in the doorway.

'I don't believe you have a ticket, young man?'

Chapter Fourteen

Brackley
18th September 1950

PC Ian Dowd was young and inexperienced and with that sort of face that looked as though it has been scrubbed raw with cold water and carbolic soap; his pimply skin was a dough white colour irregularly blotched with pink, and whilst the light golden down on his chin and upper lip had made a valiant attempt to grow during his long day on duty, it was unlikely to resolve into a beard or moustache even if he were not to shave for a few months.

His uniform was new and fitted imperfectly, the jacket hanging loose across his narrow chest with the sleeves a touch too short, whilst his starched shirt collar looked tight, the whole effect making him self-conscious as he stood and listened. His stoutly-made shoes (a definite perk of joining the constabulary) squeaking quietly in the way only new leather can whilst he rocked backwards and forwards in what he thought was an appropriate movement, aping the style of Jack Warner in 'The Blue Lamp', but only making him look like he urgently needed to use the outside privy.

His limited police training had not given him any guidelines about what to do when called to a house late on a stormy night to look at a bunch of old bones described as those of a woman's hand. He couldn't rightly say if they were or not. They did look a bit like a human hand, but there again he was no expert and could not claim to have seen any part of a human skeleton until now.

And the two men had quite obviously had a pint, or two. Both were quite animated, even a little over excitable and he reminded himself to be careful not to get drawn in by their nervous energy and jump to hasty conclusions. He should try to maintain an air of caution. Their talk was a confusing muddle, all about Romans and field excavations, and how these bones were too recent to be ancient, and yet nothing to do with a railway accident, (he was not aware there had been an accident on the railway at Brackley) and then they talked about how the land was relatively new on the embankment, so it could not be from an ancient burial, although there were some fascinating and ancient sites in the area including the remains of Brackley castle, and how someone called Digger had dug them up, or was that the dog who'd sniffed them out, or... Oh heck, what on earth was he to make of it all?

His notebook was wet and his feet were aching, and he was supposed to be clocking off and getting home to rest a while before turning in. He was looking forward to loosening his shirt collar that was rubbing his neck raw, not aided by the dampness from the rain, and relaxing with a nice mug of cocoa that his mother knew how to make to perfection whilst seated in front of the fire. The longer he tried to make notes of their jumbled explanations, the more confused he seemed to become. And besides, the bones were obviously quite old. This hand had belonged to someone long dead. Did the older of the men, the one with the smelly pipe, say something about Romans? Then the Romans could jolly well wait until tomorrow. It hardly felt like an emergency. Did they really have to drag him out to tramp all the way up town on a night like this? What was wrong with tomorrow morning?

Anyway, they seemed pleased enough that he was taking the bones away in a box wrapped in newspaper and secured with string, and after (somewhat reluctantly) refusing a glass of whiskey 'for the road', he donned his heavy rain sodden cape and with head bent down against the rain and the package tucked under one arm, he trudged gloomily back to the police station.

Tired, wet and lacking the enthusiasm to log the box of bones in the ledger that night, he placed the package out of sight under his desk, deciding that he could do the paper work tomorrow when he felt more in the mood. He turned off the office light and locked up, and promptly pushed all thoughts of this annoying diversion to the back of his mind.

Chapter Fifteen

Near Turweston
19th September 1950

He ran as fast as he could, heart beating so hard it hurt in his chest, lungs gulping air in rasping breaths punctuated by the leaden thud of his officially recognised flat feet in their brogues pounding on the road, arms pumping as he drove himself forward. His whole body was screaming 'stop!', but fear and adrenaline drove him on with little thought to where he was going and what he would do when he got there.

Irons just wanted to be as far away as possible and to put behind him the terrible reality of what had just happened. If he could just run and run forever and lose himself in the one thought of how to keep his legs moving and fight the burning in his muscles; if he could just shut everything out and become a running man, free of all responsibility, free of reason - and free from the retribution that was coming his way as surely as dawn was creeping towards the horizon.

He must be about half a mile out of Turweston and thankfully had encountered no one along the way. It was a sleepy village, populated by the well-to-do or older types exactly like Dr Melcombe, who could be expected to take to their beds not long after closing time at The Stratton Arms. It would be unusual if Irons met anyone in the early hours. In that respect Betty had been correct, arguing that he had a good chance of being in and out of Ivy Cottage without being observed.

The problem was, Dr Melcombe was a light and fitful sleeper, often given to waking and reading in bed at odd times in an attempt to induce sleep to return. On these occasions he used a weak reading lamp that gave no visible clue from the outside that he was awake. The thick curtains across his bedroom window, a legacy of the blackout, allowed not a chink of light to escape and the pencil thin line of yellow beneath his bedroom door was so narrow and dim it gave no warning.

And Irons was no stealthy cat burglar. Though he had come well prepared, armed with a pocket torch and a long and seriously hefty screwdriver lifted from the toolbox of Magdalen's handy man (a misdemeanour that had given Irons a pang of guilt, but he'd reminded himself this was only for the night and would be returned the following day). He wanted this in case he needed to prize a casement open or to work on the locked drawers of the doctor's desk.

The back door of Ivy Cottage was locked, but it took Irons only a minute of hunting around to find the spare key under a plant pot. He'd suspected that Turweston's inhabitants were the trusting type. However, even with a key, it was alarming just how much noise the lock made when turned and how the hinges squealed and the doorknob rattled. Irons learned too late that a small can of oil was a handy addition to the cat burglars' kit. Every step, every cautious exploration he made deeper inside the cottage seemed to be unnaturally amplified and even his breathing sounded horribly loud. If only it was thundering like last night, with a deluge of rain on the roof to help mask these sounds; but all was still, with just a lonely hoot of an owl from the nearby woods, and the steady 'chunk-chonk-chunk' of a grandfather clock to relieve the profound silence inside.

After what seemed like an age, he'd found the doctor's study and commenced groping around the room and colliding with chairs and jabbing the corner of the desk into a thigh along the way (despite deploying his torch) until he found what he was looking for. It was a risk to put the green shaded reading lamp on, but Irons decided that he would be able to search faster with both hands free and so hopefully be out of there that much quicker. A risk worth taking as he couldn't take much more of the tension winding up inside him like the coiled spring inside the towering grandfather clock in the corner of the study. He just wanted to find that ring and be gone.

And again, Betty had given him good information. There were six little drawers across the rear of the desk and three of these were locked. Irons presumed that it was probable the ring lay in one of those. He was unlikely to find a key, and so the hefty screwdriver proved to be just the tool for the job, offering the leverage needed to spring the locks.

The first drawer was filled with little flat, square boxes, each containing a surprisingly large and heavy gold coin. There were at least twenty of these. Betty had suggested he take some as his reward. He stared in fascination at the coins, turning one or two over in his gloved hands and admiring the glorious patterns formed in the slightly worn and polished gold that had an attractive lustre in the warm light of the reading lamp. They reminded him of the chocolate coins covered in gold foil he used to receive at Christmas as a child, before rationing ended such extravagances. These looked good enough to eat, but there was no doubt they were real.

It might look better if he made it appear as though this was a chance robbery, with some of these coins taken along with the ring? Or would that just reduce the power of the shock Betty wanted to inflict on this nasty old man? These coins were distracting, and he could feel himself becoming confused about why he was really there.

He decided to take just two of the biggest and most exotic-looking examples. It surely made little difference in the grand scheme of things. Not now he was here and guilty of a serious crime – and he might need some cash reserves, because his tenure at Magdalen College School was already hanging by a thread. Turning up dreadfully late the previous night had been a personal disaster. The headmaster had carpeted him ruthlessly that very morning and left him in no doubt that this was both his first and final warning. He could understand why he'd been given the dressing down but wished he could explain that he was trying to help a woman in distress, but that was impossible without confessing to what he was now tasked to do.

Yes, a couple of sovereigns could be a useful insurance policy. He left the draw open and some of the little boxes scattered across the desk before slipping two coins into a pocket, where they immediately clinked with a clear, sharp sound that cut through the stillness of the room. He wasted more time wrapping them in a handkerchief. This tell-tale clink of the coins had proved his undoing.

Irons now leant on the parapet of the bridge that spanned the railway and gulped deep breaths, head hanging, eyes staring at, but not really seeing, the station that lay below, now locked and dark. His heart was banging, his thighs burning from the running and stars swam before his eyes. He couldn't keep running, no matter how much he tried to lose himself in the physicality of the act, and besides, he really did need a plan.

Think! He panted in desperate wracking gulps. You need to find a way out of this mess. He groaned aloud, then leant forward and retched over the side of the bridge, vomiting onto the track.

Why had the stupid old man not just let him run off and have done with it? And how strong he'd been!

Irons slapped the palm of one hand against the brick in frustration, before resting his head against the cool parapet stone, soothing the raw wheal forming on one cheek where Dr Melcombe had swung for him. He'd been caught unawares and sent reeling with a bony punch from the old codger's fist.

He closed his eyes and tried to block out the images that followed, but like a Movietone newsreel, they continued relentlessly; the fists beating on his back, on his chest, the doctor snarling at him in a voice thick with hatred. He'd shouted back, told the doctor to back off and let him go... he would do him no harm, just let him leave, and that would be it.

But this had incensed the old man even more, hurling a paper weight that struck Irons on the flank and yelling that he must 'give it back, give it back you scoundrel!' his face contorted and ugly with rage. Dr Melcombe had body-charged Irons, ramming his bald head into his chest, sending them both backwards across the room until Irons had felt the mantelpiece crash into his shoulder blades. The doctor was like a man possessed, fighting like someone many years younger. What else could he do but fight back?

Irons stood up and looked up into the starry night sky and the cold moon looking down at him, its light illuminating the railway lines below. A barn owl glided past, silent and almost iridescent white, its flat head swivelling like a gun turret to fix a pair of beady eyes upon him as it cruised the night air.

He ran his hands over his face, holding his eyes closed against the penetrating look of this odd bird and wishing he could just shrivel up and disappear. As he slowly regained his breath, he heard a deep regular panting from behind, a sound like the breath of a great beast approaching. He stood still, the hairs rising on his neck and not daring to turn around and face what was coming. But why worry? What did it matter now? He was ruined; finished, washed up and ready to be thrown to the lions, so if the Hounds of Hell were behind him, so what?

Huff, huff, huff. It drew closer and his face was licked by a damp and cloying hot breath, smothering him and working between his fingers pressed to his face. He opened his eyes and for a brief moment could see nothing but a pale mist that completely enveloped his head, gently illuminated by the soft moon light and smelling of damp steel wool. It swirled and caressed his aching head before clearing into smaller drifts and then tiny cloudlets as the sound of a rhythmic metallic clanking from below made sense of it, and he watched as two locomotives coupled together but without a train in tow, gently chuffed their way through the night, travelling stealthily like two black beasts skulking along the line.

He must do the same. He could not stand there and wait for the inevitable. He lowered his hands and stared at them in disgust. It was not the steam from the engines that had made them smell of iron, but the blood on his hands. The blood of Dr Melcombe.

He'd reached for the first thing he could find. The doctor was like a man beyond reason, pounding his fists anywhere he could reach. He'd gone quite mad, like a crazed lunatic. The poker had been the perfect weapon, instantly offering Irons the advantage. He'd not wanted to confront the doctor, let alone attack him even pleading to be allowed to leave. The doctor had attacked first, and caused the first injury – so it was self-defence, surely? There was no intent, just the natural instinct of self-preservation - a court would understand?

He'd struck the doctor on the shoulder, making a sickening crack and forcing a squeal of pain and making old man stagger back, giving Irons the space he needed to wield his weapon. The wounded Melcombe had taken no notice, rushing at him again, swearing furiously that he would kill him. Irons had swung the poker like a cricket bat, hitting the doctor squarely across the chest, then again, scooping him up and sending him sprawling backwards onto the floor. He'd deliberately not aimed for his head. A jury must recognise that he'd tried to use as little force as possible. He'd meant to just put him off, make him calm down and allow enough time to get away. But the doctor had fallen like a sack of potatoes and lain still. He looked dead. And blood had started pooling onto the carpet.

And now here he was on the dark edge of town, sweaty and aching, just a common dirty little criminal on the run. A fugitive with two gold coins jingling in his pocket. He also had a diamond ring in its little box stuffed into his sock, concealed by the broad legs of his Oxford bags. He'd made the swap before the old man had surprised him, so at least he had achieved that goal. But why was he doing this? It was pure insanity. He could hang if the old man was dead, and all because a strange young woman on a train told him to do?

But the ring was genuine. He'd only taken a quick glance, but that had been enough to set the pulse racing. He could see why she wanted it back.

Irons now walked towards town trying to think of a strategy. Could he sneak back into school, get cleaned up and into bed and hope the police did not come knocking in the morning?

He would have to wait long for them to feel his collar. If the doctor was still alive, then he was done for. And besides, he was bruised and badly cut and would struggle to find an explanation for these injuries and his clothes were the same he wore for teaching and now crumpled and blood-stained and he had no others. A teacher's pay did not allow for a fully stocked wardrobe. He was in a pickle.

He should at least drop the ring off as Betty had instructed. But he no longer felt so inclined. He needed to think about self-preservation. She said she'd wait as long as necessary, and might have to wait sometime now, because he needed to get out of town and keep his head down and think of a survival plan.

Irons bent down and stroked his hands through some long damp grass in an attempted to remove the blood, then reached for the comb still wedged in his back pocket and untangled his hair. His hat was gone. He swore. That was incriminating. Things were not looking good. His options were narrowing - stick or twist. Both held little appeal and he was going to lose whatever he did at this rate. But he preferred the idea of getting out of Brackley, and since both railway stations were closed for the night, that left him just the hitch hiker's thumb. The A43 was quiet at the moment, although he usually heard the odd heavily laden eight-wheeler rumbling its way through the town of a night, so he might strike lucky.

Chapter Sixteen

Buckingham Town Station
20th September 1950

'We've got a right fruitcake here!' Sergeant Andrew Giles of the Buckinghamshire County Police chuckled, his rosy cheeks adding to the look of mirth on his rotund face, 'he's as bonkers as a broom.'

'Surely you mean daft as a brush?' Detective sergeant Trinder raised an eyebrow at the odd turn of phrase.

'That's what I said. Completely nuts. Trust me, Sarge, you're going to love this. That's why I asked you over, not because I'm expecting him to try any funny stuff.' He gave the prisoner a sidelong look and spoke the next sentence in a lower tone, as if the man seated just inches away might not hear, 'though it's always as well to have two on this sort of job, just to be on the safe side.' He lifted his voice again, 'No, it's because I knew you'd like to hear this gem of a story!'

Giles yanked the handcuffs linking him to the wrist of Irons, who was staring vacantly at the floor of the railway carriage ignoring the presence of either policeman. His face was grey with tiredness and a look of incomprehension in his eyes as he studied a folded piece of paper in one of his hands as if it were an oracle. Giles' action made his other arm jerk and a limp hand flop on his leg but induced no reaction.

'Oy, you going to entertain us? We've got a bit of time to kill - if you'll pardon the insensitive mention of the operative word. Come on don't go all quiet on me, not now I've invited the sergeant here along 'specially.'

Irons gave Giles a filthy look. 'I'm not a performing monkey.'

'Could have fooled me.' The jovial Giles slapped his blue serge trousered thigh with his free hand and laughed. 'I think you quite fancy yourself as a bit of an entertainer. You should be doing a turn in a variety show.' Giles winked at Trinder who was silently watching the scene unfold from the opposite bench seat. 'Listen, liss-en, you horrible lot... No! Oh...you there - at the back, stop tittering, I want no tittering at my stor-ry, 'cos it's all true! No, it is!' Giles made a decent attempt at emulating Frankie Howerd, the new radio comic now becoming a hit on the Light Programme and inspiring many to copy his distinctive diction. 'Oh, come along now, do tell us the one about the ghost.' He winked at Trinder. 'Tell us how the ghost got you to kill a man.'

'I didn't kill him.'

'Perhaps not, but you tried to. Murder or attempted murder -' Giles sucked air in between his teeth, 'not going to look good either way. He should pull through, but you never know...' He gave a shake of his head in that way builders have when assessing a damp patch on a ceiling, hinting at unimagined complications.

Trinder was watching the prisoner carefully and privately enjoying the sergeant's blustering banter. He and Giles had been friends for years and liked the man's style, though he knew his boss, detective inspector Vignoles, would not be so approving.

Admittedly, the jolly sergeant was a touch loud at times, but even when dealing with the stickier moments a policeman could expect to encounter he usually managed to bring a relaxed approach to the job, reducing the levels of aggression or tension in a situation, finding space for a sympathetic smile or even a joke. It was a technique appropriate to his posting in a quiet county market town and it had made him a much liked and respected pillar of Buckingham society.

The situation today was a perfect example, with Giles maintaining a stream of banter that whilst playfully mocking, was not intended as malicious, even though the man in custody was suspected of breaking and entry and inflicting grievous bodily harm on an elderly man. It was surely preferable to sitting for hours in excruciating silence.

Sergeant Giles had telephoned first thing to see if Trinder could assist with escorting a prisoner on the train from Buckingham to Brackley, where the accused was going to be interrogated further. He would later be taken to Northampton where the county courts were situated. He was sure Trinder would want to accept the invitation.

Detective sergeant John Trinder was with the British Railways Transport Police, one of the small team working in the specialist Detective Department based in Leicester Central station, and part of the extensive Eastern Region. Trinder was still feeling pleased with the recent addition of the word 'Detective' before his title, conferring upon him the same status afforded his peers in the County constabularies and most importantly, with those in Scotland Yard. Added to which, he was also the proud father of a two-month old son, Jimmy. It was with a feeling of considerable indulgence and well-being towards the world that he had taken the call that morning.

Sergeant Giles and he had exchanged pleasantries, traded enquiries about the health of their respective wives and young sons, discussed the lack of sleep that babies induced and the merits of a drop of brandy on a finger as a means to get the baby to sleep soundly; a conversation that caused WPC Lansdowne, bent over a report she was writing on the adjacent desk, to smile and exchange a glance with her colleague WPC Benson. The two women were slowly becoming used to their sergeant's eagerness to share the ups and downs of fatherhood with anyone prepared to listen.

Giles finally cut to the chase. 'You'll find him a fascinating specimen. I realise you're not working the investigation and so it will be purely academic, but I'd enjoy your professional detecting viewpoint.'

'You have me intrigued. What makes him so unusual?'

'He was discovered in the ladies' waiting room at Buckingham station. The night porter forgot to lock the room before he went home - but that's by the by. He was found just after 6am, looking bewildered, in fact he was acting quite odd, staring at some old poster he'd taken off the wall and mumbling and shaking like a leaf as if he'd had a nasty shock. He looked rough, as though someone had given him a pasting. They gave him some sweet tea and tried to find out what was wrong. At first, he didn't want to speak, but eventually when he did open up, all he could do was say that he'd seen a ghost. He repeated it over and over.'

'I didn't see that coming!'

'I told you it was good. Better still, he reckons he's even got a picture of her. Of the ghost! Found it at the station on the wall of the waiting room on some old poster. A young girl who went missing ages ago, back in the war. He just kept pointing at it and saying as it was her. Well, they could make no sense of this and after a while the stationmaster, Mr. Jeffreys decided they needed help. He's a dependable old cove is Jeffreys, and as he and I are acquainted he gave me a bell. Do you know Jeffries?'

'Can't say I do. But please go on with the story.'

'Well, Mr. Jeffreys decided to give yours truly a call and seek my advice, and as luck would have it, he called not long after the balloon went up about a robbery with violence in Turweston. A telex had come through about an elderly man who'd been found by his cleaning woman. He was badly hurt, but at least still breathing. He must have caught the robber in the act and put up a fight. We were put on high alert for likely candidates who might be on the run.'

'I know the telex. We asked all the stations in our patch to keep an eye open for the perpetrator. You think your man is responsible?'

'Open and shut. Cast Iron. The doctor was a collector of rare gold coins, and knock me down with a feather, two were in the pocket of this chap! What's more, the prisoner's got a bruise on his cheek, a cut to his hand and looks rough as Hell. There's no doubt he's guilty. They'll have a watertight case, aided by the fact the doctor he assaulted is recovering in hospital and reckons he can identify the assailant. Furthermore, the scene of crime boys found the prisoner's hat in the house. Nah, what's got us steamed up is his defence. You've never heard anything like it. He's going to plead insanity, and he might just carry it off, an' all.'

'Why, what's he saying?'

'I think you need to hear it from the horse's mouth John, but basically he reckons this ghost put him up to it. Told him to break into the house.' Giles paused for effect, leaving the telephone line to crackle and pop as the silence extended.

'You're pulling my leg?'

'God's honest truth! Swears blind that's how it is.'

'You've got me intrigued all right.'

DS Trinder was holding the fort at the Leicester Central offices whilst his boss DI Vignoles took time off to attend a funeral in his home village, extending this into a weekend visit to his parents. Trinder should perhaps remain at Leicester, ready to deal with any important events that might arise, and could easily send a uniformed PC as escort but looking around the office he saw a full complement of officers, and they were enjoying a period of relative calm with only a light caseload. Everyone was catching up on routine paperwork or dealing with minor incidents of loose cattle on the line and the usual irritating rash of pick pocketing. He could risk a few hours away, and decided to accept the invitation and arranged to take the next train to Brackley Central from where he could walk through the town to the 'bottom station' of Brackley Town and catch the local service to Buckingham.

Trinder was glad he had made the trip. It was a glorious late September day that was both warm and windless. The air was loud with brawling sparrows in the eaves of the pretty station at Buckingham, that glowed with a yellow light on the stonework and so making it look even more like a lodge or gatehouse for the great country house nearby at Stowe.

He was getting hot sitting in the rectangle of sun streaming through the carriage window and enjoying the sensation, a last hurrah for the memory of another summer past. He could hear the sound of muffled shovelling from behind his head and the odd hisses and clanks the crew induced from their engine before departing. The guard blew his whistle and the engine gave a short 'pop' on the whistle in answer, and so they jolted into motion with a series of creaks and groans that put Trinder in mind of a wooden sailing vessel.

Trinder allowed a little smile to himself, wondering if Jimmy was sleeping in the pram in the back yard right now, and if Violet was managing to snatch a few quiet minutes in this pleasant sunshine. He then flipped open his notebook and licked the end of a carefully sharpened pencil and turned his attention back to the captive man seated opposite. He deliberately adopted a more conciliatory tone than Giles, as he was feeling content with the world, and this made him mildly indulgent towards their curious charge – and besides, he was looking forward to hearing his story.

'How about going through what happened, right from the start?'

'I already have.' Irons stared at the dusty carriage floor.

'I appreciate that, but in my experience what someone says in the first hours after arrest is driven more by adrenaline than common sense. It's natural to exaggerate or emphasise things that sound like they might help one's cause, but which don't sound quite so good in the cold light of day. Or warm sun, in this case!' He gave an encouraging smile. 'I'm merely an interested observer, but it would be in your interest to run through the story again and ensure you're comfortable with everything,' he exchanged a knowing look with Giles, who was clearly trying to suppress a laugh.

'What are you suggesting?' asked Irons, who at least looked up and listened to what Trinder said.

'I understand you refer to certain, er, ghostly occurrences, for example? This might not play out too well in court.'

'But it's true! I can't tell a lie, can I?'

'Telling the truth is undoubtedly going to be your best, and perhaps your only, line of defence. I understand you do not deny breaking into the house of...' Trinder looked at Giles.

'Dr Melcombe. A retired gentleman living at Ivy Cottage, Turweston, near Brackley,' Giles replied.

'You assaulted Dr Melcombe once inside his house?'

'It was self-defence! He came at me like a mad thing. I was taken by surprise. He was crazy. Really went for me and I swear would have killed me. He might be old, but he could put up a good fight so I had no choice but to defend myself. I never meant him to get hurt.'

'You've got a blooming' cheek!' Giles dropped his sunny demeanour and glared at Irons. 'You'd just broken into his house in the dead of night and were caught in the process of lifting his coin collection, what did you expect him to do?' Giles shook his head.

'Why were you in Dr Melcombe's house?' Trinder defaulted back to the cautious approach.

Irons did not reply.

'You may as well admit the reason, because you don't deny being there.'

Irons looked crestfallen, as the stark reality of his appalling situation was finally sinking in. Trinder waited. He knew to be patient, and in his own time, the young man would start to open up.

'He looked the wealthy sort. A retired country doctor was likely to have plenty of money I suppose.' Irons was feeling his way forward with his story. 'It was pure chance. He was as good as anyone.' Irons gave a long wearisome sigh. 'I was motivated by nothing more than greed.'

'You first identified Dr Melcombe as a victim, then located his house?'

'Yes, um, no. His house looked promising. I just chose one and went in.'

'But you already knew about his valuable gold coin collection?' Trinder looked sceptical.

'No. I just found them when nosing around.' The last word died on his lips.

'How did you know where to look for the coins?' asked Trinder.

'I struck lucky.'

'Pull the other one! You went straight for the doctor's desk. There's no evidence you rifled through any other cupboards or entered any of the other rooms; sounds like you knew what you were after,' Giles interjected.

Irons looked guilty. 'I don't know...'

'In our considerable experience of house breakings, it rarely happens that a burglar wanders around and chances upon exactly the right series of locked drawers with a few trial explorations first.' Silence. 'You knew what you wanted, so spill the beans! Tell the sergeant,' Giles gave Irons a sly look.

'Someone might have suggested he had them,' Irons mumbled.

'And that someone is?' asked Trinder.

'I'm not sure. I can't remember.'

'Come off it!' Giles snapped, 'that won't wash, that's not what you said at first.'

'I know who she is. That's to say, I thought I did until this morning, but now I don't know what to believe. I'm starting to doubt everything. It's just too strange for words. Stranger than you can imagine.' Irons stared at the floor again and moved his head from side to side, doing a convincing job of looking confused.

'You have an accomplice?' Trinder continued.

'Accomplice? I suppose that's what she was. I'd not thought of her like that,' Irons looked utterly bewildered. Lost.

'Does she have a name?' asked Trinder.

'Betty. Betty Askew.' He spoke the words quietly and looked as if he was about to be sick.

'What exactly is your relationship with miss Askew?' Trinder wrote her name in his notebook, giving Giles a quick look to prevent him from making an ill-timed observation. 'She is a miss, I presume?'

'We met on a train. She was once engaged, but her fiancé was killed. So, no, she is not married.'

'You met her on a train, discussed her marital arrangements and what happened next?' Trinder asked, with a hint of scepticism in his voice.

'Nothing much. We talked for a while and she...' He ran his free hand through his hair. 'Oh God, it sounds so darned foolish. I hardly know her. Truly I don't. We just met by accident and fell into talking. She's a young woman of about 18 or so, though now I can't really say if that is her age or not. How can you tell?' He looked Trinder in the eye and spoke confidently. 'Tell me, how old is a ghost? Do they grow old?'

Trinder and Giles exchanged looks. Irons fell back to staring at the piece of folded paper in his hands that he kept turning over and over in a movement reminiscent of Betty Askew's worrying away at her naked ring finger. 'I suppose I fell in love with her,' Irons gave a queasy smile. ' I lost my senses and acted rashly with a silly notion of helping her. It's foolish – who can fall in love with a spirit?'

'Are you trying to suggest that Betty Askew is a ghost?' Trinder asked.

'It would appear so. And yes, that has come as quite a shock.'

Silence fell in the compartment, as the train rattled and huffed along the single line, threading its way between verdant hedgerows and rolling fields, all very much alive with cows and sheep.

'When did you first meet Miss Askew?' Trinder decided to ignore this statement for the time being and treat this like any other interrogation.

'Sunday, September 3rd. I can remember it exactly, as I was on my way to start at Magdalen College School on the Monday. I'm a teacher. I was a teacher.'

'And how often did you meet?'

'Just three times.'

'And where did you meet?'

'On the train. And always on the last train from Marylebone to Brackley. To be correct, on the last train from Brackley on the final occasion. We only ever met on that train. I tried to look for her in the town, but she eluded me.'

'She must be quite a woman to have such an effect on you in so short a time?' Trinder gave him a sceptical look. 'Did you have sexual relations with her? A quiet train, late at night – it must have been very tempting.'

'Certainly not! I've acted nothing less than honourably towards her. I never tried anything on, not once!' Irons looked offended, although he rubbed an ear lobe with his free hand as he spoke. Trinder suspected this

126

was not the whole truth. 'I must set an example, what with being a teach...'

'You're a card all right. Set an example? Talk about honour? You're heading to be made an example of, that much is for certain.' Giles looked at Irons in disbelief. 'I don't believe you with all your silly talk of ghosts. I think you and your fancy girl are a team; I bet you two have been moving around the country doing this sort of thing a few times; finding folk with stuff of value, robbing them in their homes then taking off somewhere to fence the goods.'

'That's utterly ridiculous!' Irons looked horrified.

'Not as ridiculous as telling us she's a ghost!'

'Where does Miss Askew live?' Trinder kept his voice calm as he changed tack.

'I'm not sure. I asked for her address, but she refused to give it me. I think perhaps Amersham.'

'Why do you think that?'

'That was where I believe she boarded the train, and because something she said implied that she "had to be there," or words to that effect. I got the feeling she did not much like the place.'

'And she was going where?'

'To Brackley. She had to be going there, as that was where the train terminated, and we spoke until shortly before we pulled into the station. On the last occasion she boarded the train at Brackley to go south.'

'Why was she going to Brackley?'

'No idea.'

'To see family? Friends?'

'She didn't say! That's one of the strange things about her. I was never clear in my mind exactly what her circumstances were. She's originally from Brackley - on that point she was clear – and I know she works at Woodford Halse engine shed.

'But you just said she lives in Amersham? That's a devil of a way to travel each day.' Trinder was making notes. 'You've got your story muddled. Try telling us the truth.'

'And I told you she was a puzzle. I'm telling you what I know. I never could got to grips with her circumstances, she was always vague, perhaps deliberately so.' Irons gave an odd smile that unsettled Trinder. 'Maybe ghosts don't worry about time and place in the same way we do? What do you think, sergeant?'

Trinder exchanged another look with Giles who mouthed "fruitcake". Trinder was also starting to wonder if the man was indeed deranged. He decided to get the questioning back on safer ground. 'You walked her home from the station?'

'No.'

'Yet it was dark. Not very chivalrous - for a man of honour.'

'How could I? She just vanished into thin air when we came to the station! Puff! Gone. Ask the stationmaster; he'll back me up. No matter how hard I tried, and no matter that we sat close together in the same compartment, she succeeded with this disappearing act. She eluded me twice - and the station staff got a bit shirty about it.'

'Explain.'

'They denied seeing her! Made me look a proper chump. But that was impossible as it's a small station with hardly any passengers and she's a memorable woman who walked right past them. I don't know why they wanted to make a fool of me. Though it starts to make sense now...when you think about it, I mean, ghosts can probably just walk through walls.' Irons brightened up, 'If you want proof of what I'm saying, why not ask the young porter at Brackley – he's seen her, but on another occasion when I wasn't there. He told me she was a spook; said she was the 'woman in white' that was haunting the railway near the viaduct, and you know what? The funny thing is, she did have a pale mackintosh. That would be why she appeared white.'

'I see.' Trinder frowned and bit his lower lip whilst maintaining a steady gaze at Irons, careful to not encourage this over-wrought and dangerously unstable man, in more of his delusional ranting. However, for all his attempts at maintaining a level of *sang froid*, Trinder felt an unpleasant prickling to his skin. It was only momentary, but the prisoner's words had struck a chord. Despite all logic and reason there was something compelling about how Irons was telling the story. The early part of his testimony rang false, but now he was in full flow, it carried more conviction. But more than that, it touched on something else.

Trinder recalled sitting in the little porter's room beneath the central support of the road bridge spanning the tracks at Brackley Central. It had been just a week ago, listening as the men told him about a mad woman they claimed was haunting the line. She forced some of the trains to slow to a halt, before neatly slipping away into the night and had eluded their best attempts at apprehending her. The men had been certain this was something stranger than a reckless local girl with a death wish. He'd laughed it off as nothing more than a chilling story to tell when sitting with a mug of tea around the fire. But now he was not so sure.

Trinder tentatively wrote "ghost" in his pad, but then drew a line through the word with an impatient flourish and looked back at Irons. 'You are quite determined on this point.'

'I can only tell it as it is.'

Trinder chewed this over for a moment. 'Pleading insanity is not a defence I would recommend.'

'Insanity?'

'You don't seriously expect a jury to consider your testimony of a ghostly apparition? We can hardly haul her up to take the stand, after all.' He smiled. 'They'll think you're barking. But perhaps that is your intention?'

'Of course not.'

'Do you wished to be judged unsound of mind?' Trinder continued. 'Claiming a ghost as your accomplice might just do the trick. Think again, Mr. Irons; you might reckon it the lesser of the two evils to choose a sanatorium over prison, but I would advise you to reconsider. The "treatment" they administer in such places can be extremely harsh and very unpleasant. There are some as say its cruel -' He looked Irons in the eye. '- and the effects are long lasting, far longer than the punishment you would get by pleading self-defence during a foiled housebreaking attempt. Do that with a good lawyer and you could ameliorate your sentence by quite a margin.'

'Here, don't go letting him off the hook!' Giles looked uncomfortable.

'I'm just stating the realities of the legal system.'

'I'm not insane. Foolish and gullible, I agree, but what I'm telling you is the truth. There's no other explanation. I was seduced into doing what I did by the ghost of a dead young woman.'

'Saints preserve us!' Giles rolled his eyes to the carriage roof.

'Miss Askew, either the flesh and blood or spirit version, told you to enter Dr Melcombe's house? Why would she do that?'

'I-I suppose she'd heard something...about his coins? I don't know...' Irons was lying again.

'She cased the joint in advance, or got a tip off?' Trinder asked.

'She said he would be a good target. I can't exactly remember why she knew that.' Irons could feel the little box inside his sock pressed against his ankle and was determined not to mention the ring at any cost. He looked out of the window and clammed up. He was dog tired and his head was aching and filled with images of the doctor's face contorted with anger, of his blood on the carpet - and of Betty waiting in the churchyard.

'Poppycock! You two are in it together. You're just trying to distract us whilst your girl escapes. But you're struggling with your story, it's plain as day. The cracks are starting to show,' Giles shook his head as he was speaking.

'I agree with the sergeant,' added Trinder. 'But I shall humour you for a moment longer and ask you to tell me why are convinced Miss Askew is a ghost. Explain what would be in it for her. The gold coins are going to be of little use if she's not of this world?' Trinder smiled, knowing he had dealt a good hand.

'Betty Askew is the woman on this poster.' Irons unfolded the paper in his hands, Giles allowing him to move his handcuffed hand as he smoothed out a faded poster with numerous pinholes and tears at the corners, handing it to Trinder. 'It was on the wall in the waiting room. Miss Elizabeth Askew, age 19, of Manor Road, Brackley. It says she's an engine cleaner at Woodford Halse shed, which she also told me, taking time to talk about her work and this bunch of women called the 'Dirty Girls Brigade' who are all cleaners there...'

Giles puffed air out of his lips, but Trinder stopped him speaking with a motion of his hand. 'You do know her address, and where she works, and her age? Why did you not say when I asked you earlier?'

'Because I told you only what she communicated to me, everything I knew about her until after the robbery and when I saw this. It was a bloody shock I can tell you. It says here she went missing in 1943. And she's dead now.' Irons sounded convinced on the point.

Trinder looked at the faded poster for some time before speaking. 'This is her? The woman you met on the train?'

'Not a shadow of a doubt.'

The photograph was a pale sepia due to the poor quality paper and years of exposure to light, but the smiling fresh face, the curls of hair and open-necked shirt were still clearly defined, as were the bold black letters above that declared: MISSING, with her name and age below, followed by a short statement about how she had vanished without trace on the 19th April 1943.

'Missing, but that's quite different from being dead.' Trinder was frowning and struggling to make any sense of this odd story. 'Are you reporting that you've found this missing woman?'

'In a manner of speaking, I suppose I am. But do you really think she could reappear after eight years and having not aged at all?'

Trinder squinted at the photograph. 'It's not that long ago and more plausible than your ridiculous ghost story. She would still be young and may not have changed in appearance that much. If you help us find this woman it would work in your favour. You'd win support from her family at the very least.'

'It was her.'

'Then why did you say she lived in Amersham? You've got her address.' Giles was barely managing to keep his voice controlled. 'You're playing silly games with us.'

'No, I told you what she told me, and what I observed for myself... and then, this morning, sitting in that waiting room I saw her face looking down at me, and I've been thinking about it and trying to see how it fits together. You must believe me.'

Trinder and Giles remained silent. Irons spoke with such conviction it forced them to consider the implications.

'There's something else; a taxi driver in Brackley became very angry when I mentioned her name. He gave me a lift to the school and I fell into talking about Betty. I suppose I was desperate to tell someone about her. But he was absolutely furious when I mentioned her name and said where she worked at the Woodford shed. I feared he might punch me! He told me that Betty Askew was dead. He was adamant about it.'

Chapter Seventeen

Dunton Bassett
21st September 1950

All Saints was an austere church, constructed from pale grey limestone stained in places with the ruddy brown of iron, like spots of dried blood. This was stone that could draw in the warmth of the summer sun and appear to glow from within, but in turn could be dour when darkened by rain. The square tower was topped by an elegantly pointed spire visible for miles poking above the yews and other trees surrounding the church; for All Saints was set upon a small hill, one of a series that formed little rolls in the blanket of rich farmland that spread across this part of Leicestershire.

The Reverend Gerard Vignoles was conducting the funeral on the east side, his head bowed over the open prayer book to reveal the circle of sun-browned baldness in his silver-grey hair that gave him an appropriately monkish aspect, gold rimmed half-moon glasses perched at the end of a slightly hawkish nose. The sharp but kindly eyes below the bushy white eyebrows dropping only occasionally to the little book opened in his hands, for he knew the service by heart.

This easy familiarity with the burial service was a cause of private sadness to the reverend in that so many needed him to officiate in this most final of services, but this was also his strength, for he could speak the words with true feeling and not just read them by rote. He was free to lift his eyes and cast them across the family and friends of the deceased gathered around the open grave, making contact with those able to look away from the highly polished coffin in the rectangular hole freshly cut in the graveyard grass. He offered support with this dart of friendly contact; seeking to help the words of comfort and reassurance of a glorious after-life in the embrace of God, ring true and deep.

Today, the service had an extra layer of meaning, for not only was his wife Caroline amongst the mourners, but so were his daughter Gwendoline and son Charles, both accompanied by their partners. This was not a family funeral however, but that of a friend; a friend not only to the Vignoles', but someone much loved by a great many of the folk from the two adjacent villages of Dunton Basset and Ashby Magna.

Young James Hoden - known simply as 'Jimmy' or 'Sunny Jim' - was another victim of every parent's worst nightmare; polio. A horrid disease stalking the country in recent years with a renewed vigour, like a silent, invisible and unbidden killer, though one that sometimes chose to leave its victims crippled until the release of untimely death. Some escaped; touched by the killer's hand but left with manageable scars that allowed a full and long life. But they were the lucky few.

Jimmy had managed to hold out for fourteen years, but his lungs had always threatened to collapse with the promise of suffocating the life from his thin body with the withered leg. It was a sentence unimaginably cruel. His last months had been spent incarcerated in a monstrous 'Iron Lung'; permanently encased from the neck down in a terrifying contraption that unceasingly wheezed and sucked like a broken vacuum cleaner as it forced his chest to rise and fall and command his lungs to inhale the vital oxygen in a relentless torment. It gave him life, but it was a soulless and unnerving machine that squatted on his frail body like a nightmarish metal toad, and which forbade Jimmy meaningful movement, his life reduced to staring at a simple light fitting in the ceiling, feeling the bed sores worsen as his muscles wasted. It had been a release when even this miracle of modern medical science had been unable to keep him going any longer. It was hardly an existence, and one without a future.

Until these last desperate months, Sunny Jim had been a surprisingly active lad with a joyful disposition, ready with a cheery smile and a greeting as he stumped around the two villages on his National Health crutches. He soon became adept at walking long distances, traversing the field paths and bridleways and enjoying the gentle rhythm of the rural community he lived within. But he was to be seen most often with a knapsack containing sandwiches and a bottle of fizzy pop slung across his shoulders and notebooks and pencils stuffed in the pockets of his shorts, heading to and from the railway station. For Jimmy loved the railway and spent the majority of his short life in one of two favoured spots at Ashby Magna, the station that both separated and served, the two neighbouring communities on the busy mainline from London Marylebone to Nottingham Victoria and the north.

Jimmy knew everyone at the little wayside station and was waved and whistled at by engine crew and guards, with packets of gum often tossed from a moving footplate or a Sherbet dip handed over by a kindly guard. The handful of regular commuters often sought Jimmy's view on the punctuality of their expected train, sure in the knowledge that he would be as well informed as the signalman. Come rain or shine, Jimmy was usually there, recording the engine numbers, timing the trains with his grandad's pocket watch and waving at the diners on the crack 'Master Cutler' express that raced through without a pause.

In what turned out to be his last year, he had started taking snap shots whenever he could afford a roll of film from his pocket money, using a camera that was his prized possession. It was a second-hand ex-RAF model, given to him on his 13th birthday by Charles and Anna Vignoles. This now lay upon Jimmy's chest in the coffin, the carefully pasted books of his railway photographs serving as his lasting legacy for the grieving family to cherish.

Sunny Jim was a boy after D.I. Charles Vignoles' heart, and so it was with a mixture of sadness and a desire to offer a final kindness to the young lad, that he now looked at his watch, carefully tracking the passage of the hands. He then met the eyes of his father at the head of the open grave and gave a little nod. It was time.

'We therefore commit his body to the ground: earth to earth, ashes to ashes, dust to dust...' The Revered Vignoles took a small handful of loam and tossed it onto the coffin lid, creating a sound like falling rain as it fell. As he continued the solemn service, Jimmy's mother took a deep breath and followed suit, managing to watch with teary eyes as her husband then did the same, finally turning to bury her head in his black suit.

'...I heard a voice from heaven, saying unto me, Write, From henceforth blessed are the dead which die in the Lord...'

Someone sniffed, a nose was blown; the wind flapped a black dress hem and tossed a couple of leaves into the hole where they spiralled above the coffin, another mourner tossed some grains of soil. Anna gave her husband's arm a gentle squeeze.

'Lord have mercy upon us, Christ have mercy upon us...'

Yes... Vignoles tensed slightly. It was faint, carried on the wind, that odd churning and almost turbine-like sound of a distant steam engine approaching at speed. The constant, rapid-fire beats of the whirring cylinders and panting exhaust blending into a rising and falling note carried across the fields only to echo off the church, entwine in the trees and bounce between the rows of the distinctive slate gravestones or to slip between the holes in the simple cast iron Celtic crosses that were a peculiar feature of some All Saints' grave markers.

As the reverend Vignoles came to the end of the Lord's Prayer and fell silent, there came the whistle. An extenuated wailing like a lonely curlew above windswept moorlands. It stopped, but sounded once again, the powerful roar of the express noisily underpinning the wavering note.

The mourners exchanging teary glances as hands patted backs, arms held others that little bit tighter. Then came the final flourish. After the two heart-rending, keening wails like something from an Irish wake, there followed a ludicrously cheery 'Toot-tooty-toot-toot!' that broke the spell and caused a ripple of spontaneous laughter to erupt, helping release the tension that had become almost palpable.

The timing was impeccable. Sunny Jim's last request had been fulfilled to perfection; a send-off by his favourite locomotive, Leicester Central's big pacific 'Sir Frederick Banbury,' driven by his favourite top link crew and passing at high speed for full effect. As the rattle and roar subsided and the long rake of carriages flew past in a smooth whoosh of wheel on rail, the graveside gathering started to break up into huddles of people, all dressed in black, dark browns and lilacs, in suits or sombre dresses cleaned and pressed especially for the occasion but still bearing a whiff of mothball from the back of the wardrobe.

Vignoles and Anna left his father shaking hands and offering further words of condolence and took the opportunity to slip away. Vignoles had done what he could in arranging the steamy send off, and both he and Anna, together with Gwen and her husband Michael had helped with some of the arrangements for the wake, and they had little more to offer.

The walked down the gravel path from the church and through the metal wicket beside the substantial black and gold painted gates that guarded the impressive entrance to church and rectory, and which had somehow evaded being melted down in the drive for metal for the war effort. Beside these gates there stood a Celtic cross carved from granite that formed the village war memorial, and bearing a surprising number of local names, each picked out in gold leaf. One of the names not included however, was that of Vignoles's younger brother Jack, who had been killed in Spain serving with the International Brigade. The government had not endorsed these anti-Fascist volunteers, and it was a source of some private sadness within the family that his sacrifice was unrecorded on a memorial outside their church.

Pausing for a moment of reflection, they walked down the short but steep hill into the heart of the village, Anna's arm linked through her husband's and Vignoles puffing on a pipe of sweet tobacco, both in that quiet frame of mind that funerals induced.

'Shall we walk to Dunton and back and take a well-earned drink in the Jolly Friar?'

'Splendid idea! And I'd like to call in at the station and see how it went there,' Vignoles agreed. 'It was probably quite a sight with the staff lining the platform.'

'How lovely. But sad that the person who would have most loved to have been there, was not.'

'Perhaps he was - in spirit?'

Anna smiled. 'I hope at least he was aware of the love the village feel for him. We can't ask for much more.' They walked on in silence for a while. 'You know, Charles, I rather like the idea he might come back and haunt the place one day. He could take up his usual spot at the platform end and keep watch on us all, and in the night when it's all quiet and we're lying in our bed in the rectory, we might catch the distant sound of him stumping along the road.'

Vignoles took a puff on his pipe and nodded approvingly. 'I could go with that. Though he might spook the passengers, though I'm sure they'd recognise him as a friendly spirit.'

'A far cry from some of the visitations in that book you gave me!' Anna smiled up at her husband. 'It really is fascinating reading, but unnerving at times.'

'I'm glad you can't put it down.'

'I'm becoming intrigued by all these quite marvellous stories, though I do think we could do with Sunny Jim in the mix to add a friendlier balance. It's noticeable just how nasty most spirits and apparitions are. There are a small number considered benign, but the majority are downright terrifying. I wonder why they always have to be so dangerous, murderous and scarifying?'

'Because they make for a better story?'

'You don't believe in this sort of thing, do you?'

'My inclination is to say no. Delightfully diverting of course, but I suspect the majority are either works of pure fiction invented to fill a winter's evening or based upon events that actually took place, but which have been misinterpreted and or exaggerated over time.'

'You're just such a pragmatist, Charles!'

'It rather comes with my job I'm afraid. It would be very remiss of me to take everything I was told in an investigation on face value and not question it.'

'But you don't completely dismiss the possibility of contact from the other side?'

'No-o, I suppose not,' although he looked unconvinced. 'It would be foolish to presume there was no such thing, especially when I've never had any contact with a ghost, let alone been able to prove or disproved their existence.'

'And you believe in the Holy Ghost.'

'Of course.' Vignoles took a thoughtful puff on his pipe and pondered this apparent contradiction. 'But I'm not sure that's quite the same kind of ghost. Certainly not the sort you have in mind.'

'A force for good rather than bad, but otherwise why so different? Could there not be evil or naughty spirits stalking the world?'

'Ye-es...' Vignoles looked even more unconvinced.

'Perhaps I am getting fanciful, but I can understand how there might be unquiet souls about, doomed to wander the earth or cross the skies forever.'

'What a romantically vivid imagination you have, Anna!'

'You can blame the author of the book for that.'

'All right put me down as mildly agnostic on the issue, though if I ever hear something going bump in the night, I will assume it is an intruder and deal with him accordingly. We have far more to fear from the living than we do from the dead.'

'I shall try to find comfort in that statement.'

An hour later when returning from their walk, they descended the wooden stairway covered by an elongated glasshouse onto the island platform of Ashby Magna station, where Vignoles' attention was immediately taken by a beautifully presented former Great Western Railway locomotive simmering at the platform end, waiting for the right away.

The sunlight brought the oiled depth of the locomotive's deep green colour alive and the bright brass and copper detailing was gleaming in tribute to some serious elbow grease by the cleaners, his eye especially drawn to the curving nameplate that declared in heavily serifed capitals that this was 'Evenley Hall'.

He was asking Anna if she could remember the location of the actual hall it was named after, when the stationmaster approached them. At that moment the engine pulled away with an almost aggressive barking sound, that hurled neat puffs of steam into the air like punctuation marks.

'Fine engine! Looks like Banbury shed must have borrowed her for a few days. When an engine in that shape comes in you want to keep hold of her.' The stationmaster was smiling as he spoke.

'A cracker. Not see her before... Anyway, good to see you, albeit not the cheeriest of circumstances.' The three exchanged the looks one did after a funeral. 'How did it go? Sounded wonderful up at the church.'

'We did the lad proud down here. You should have seen the engine, really bulled up a treat. They'd polished every inch and even put flowers on the buffer beam and wrapped a black crepe ribbon around the smokebox handles.'

'How sweet!' Anna smiled wistfully. 'Engine drivers can be softer at heart than they look.'

'It cuts through everything, doesn't it? Makes you think about what really matters. And footplate men know all about life and death, as theirs is a dangerous job.'

'Quite right. Though thankfully accidents are infrequent on this line -

and long may it stay that way,' Vignoles replied.

'You watched the train come through?' asked Anna.

'Indeed. Everyone formed a line, hats and caps doffed. She was going like the clappers. He was really giving her the gun as they say. She'd be in Rugby before they knew it!'

'Jimmy liked them going fast,' observed Vignoles, and they all smiled fondly.

'Have you time for some tea?'

'Thank you, but we've rather worked up a thirst for pint of 'Tiger' in the 'Friar',' replied Vignoles, Anna nodding in agreement.

'Can't blame you. Wish I could join you. When do go back to Leicester?'

'Tomorrow. We'll call in for a cup of tea before our train,' Anna added.

'Do, please.' The stationmaster grinned as the Vignoles' turned to start the climb back up the steps. 'Oh, wait a moment, I knew there was something else. You must see this! I'll be back in a tick.'

Anna and Vignoles exchanged puzzled glances as the stationmaster sprinted into his office and immediately came back with a carefully folded newspaper in his hand. 'Local rag left on a train. The guard passed it over as he thought I'd want to read the railway story inside. It's quite a surprise!'

Vignoles was eyeing the Buckingham Advertiser with little enthusiasm. 'What on earth could be so interesting in Buckingham? It's on a sorry little branch line. The surprise might be that a train actually ran along it!'

'Ho ho, far more interesting, Charles. You won't guess in a million years, but here; look it over when you have a pint to hand. You might need a drink after that,' and he winked. 'Page two. Tell me what you make of it over tea tomorrow.'

'Thanks. Cheerio!' Vignoles tucked the folder paper under one arm and they climbed the steps.

'Charles, I think you should read this.' Anna was seated on a bench by the window of the pub. 'It is most peculiar, though I'm not sure you are going to like all of it.'

'Oh yes?'

'Dear old John Trinder is involved. With a ghost.'

'A what?' Vignoles had a pint of ale in each hand, the frothy head bubbling over and dripping down the sides and splashing onto the table. 'What has John been up?' Vignoles was mopping up the spilt liquid with beer mats then placed a pint before Anna. 'I might need a fortifying dose of this first.' After swiftly downing a good quarter of his pint he pulled the opened paper across the table and started to read from where Anna was pointing with one of her perfectly manicured fingers.

'Robber's ghostly accomplice sought by police. Is she the long-lost railway girl? The police are hunting for a woman they would like to interview in connection with a robbery that took place on the night of Tuesday 19th in Turweston. There is a mystery at the very heart of this apparently run-of-the-mill crime that has the otherwise sleepy village talking of nothing else and has got the police scratching their heads.' Vignoles paused to roll his eyes at Anna, then continued. *'At first sight this appeared to be just another housebreaking. The criminal was disturbed whilst he hunted through the valuable coin collection of retired doctor Percy Melcombe, 70, of Ivy Cottage, Turweston, just a step across the county border in Northamptonshire. The burglar, Richard Irons, 23, a mathematics teacher at Magdalen College School for Boys, Brackley, assaulted Dr Melcombe and left the poor man unconscious and bleeding.'* Vignoles furrowed his brow. 'A schoolteacher at Magdalen breaking and entering? That does not sound right. *The attack has shocked the usually peaceful community. However, the story takes on a most surprising aspect following the arrest of Irons in Buckingham railway station the following morning. According to Sergeant Trinder of the British Railways Detective Department, the burglar's accomplice in this botched theft was the ghost of a young woman... "They are apparently working as a team", explained Sergeant Trinder.*

'What the blazes?' Vignoles's eyebrows shot up. He turned to his wife. 'I leave the office for a couple of days and the next thing I know my sergeant's talking to the press about goodness knows what nonsense! I've never read such drivel in all my life. Has Trinder completely lost his marbles?' He carried on reading, agog at what might come next. *'Irons has advised the police that the apparition can only be seen on the late Marylebone–Brackley Central train. He claims that the spectral girl told him exactly who to burgle and when.*

'Oh, did she, now?' He drank some more beer and gave Anna a

disbelieving look, she in turn suppressing a laugh behind her own raised glass. *'Irons insists she is the ghostly spirit of a long-missing young woman. He has been cooperative and given us a name and description. We are withholding her name whilst we make further enquiries, as the circumstances are peculiar, added to which, the veracity of the prisoner's statement must be called into question.'* The police would offer no further details about this incredible story leaving us to speculate on what it might mean. 'Thank God for that,' Vignoles exclaimed, relieved. 'At least Trinder appears to have learned something about discretion.' He resumed reading. *'Is there really a ghost riding our railway and encouraging young men to become thieves? Or is the culprit trying to bamboozle the police? The Buckingham Advertiser will be keeping a close eye on developments and is looking forward to witnessing both Irons and his other-worldly lady accomplice when they appear in court. That should be a county session to remember! Dr Melcombe is recuperating in Brackley Cottage Hospital, but he is expected to make a full recovery.* 'Well, that ends the story on a positive note.' He paused for a few seconds, staring into space, then drained the last few inches of beer from his glass and placed it on the table. 'What am I to make of all that?'

'You have to admit it is intriguing? And how strange we were just having a conversation about ghosts not an hour ago!' Anna was smiling, hoping to diffuse her husband's bluster and annoyance. 'It sounds quite exciting and improves a dull old house breaking story no end.'

'I'm glad you think so. Tell you what, you can lend detective sergeant Trinder your book.' He stressed the rank and title with irony, 'perhaps it might help him invent an even better story to fuel this paper's desire for cheap sensationalism. Better still, let's rope in the Shag Dog of Birstall and be done with it!'

Anna looked deadly serious. 'I suspect the dog only frightens off men and is no use for finding women in white.'

'Eh?' Vignoles tossed the paper on the table and stared at Anna, who now gave him a mischievous look, eyes twinkling. 'Oh, yes...' He realised she was pulling his leg. He shook his head, but this time with amused disbelief then tried to drink the last dregs from his glass. 'Ghostly accomplice, my foot.'

'To be fair, John is circumspect on that point. He's just stating the viewpoint of the defendant. And he did withhold her name.'

'True. It could be worse. Another?' Vignoles stood up with his glass in hand and waggled it in the air. 'I could do with one. Let's hope I can keep a lid on it and stop it going national. I'll need more than a drink if the Badger gets wind of it. Can you imagine what that old stick in the mud will do when I tell him we're trying to arrest the spirit of a dead girl! Not that we should be joking about that. If there is one detail in this ludicrous story that grabs me, it is the reference to the missing woman...'

Chapter Eighteen

Brackley
22nd September 1950

'Dr Melcombe, you really must rest. It's not right you are exerting yourself so soon after such a nasty attack. It could set you back and you'll end up staying here longer.'

'Heaven forbid...' he muttered darkly.

'And I'm quite sure neither of us would want that, would we?' Matron Blackthorne was a chubby, buxom, rosy-faced woman with greying hair pulled into a bun, much given to bustle, chatter and fussing – everything a small cottage hospital might want in a matron. However, she had almost met her match in the intractable doctor. 'I think your call can wait until tomorrow at the very least. You have a broken collar and ribs that will only mend by rest, rest and more rest.'

'Nonsense! I'm perfectly fine. They're just light fractures. And since I've been bandaged up like an Egyptian mummy I am hardly likely to fall apart on the walk there and back!' He spat the words out with force, but privately was fighting to conceal the considerable pain in his chest and down one side. 'I'm quite capable of walking down the corridor. Now, if you will just stop your infernal fussing and fetch me my dressing gown, you can point me in the direction of the telephone.'

Matron's mouth formed a narrow line as she fixed her eyes on the swathes of bandages and the livid bruising creeping from beneath them across his sickly skin. 'The doctor gave me strict instructions. You wouldn't want to get me into trouble with the doctor now, would you?'

'I don't give a fig what that drip has to say, and frankly, unless I get to make that call, there will be a darned sight more trouble!' He glared at her.

Matron returned the defiant look. She was used to the odd difficult patient and had learned to develop a thick skin to enable her to let such ill-mannered behaviour slip by like the proverbial water from a duck's back, but even so, doctor Melcombe was particularly irritating. She folded her arms as she delivered her final word. 'I shall allow you five minutes - and not a moment more!' She wagged a finger at the doctor. 'Don't think you are the only one who can kick up a fuss,' and she tossed his dressing gown onto the end of the bed. 'I'll get nurse to help you.'

It took him at least five minutes just to make his way to the matron's little office and shoo the overly attentive nurse away to leave him in peace. He slumped in the wooden round-back chair and took a few laboured breaths, his temples throbbing. Being beaten by fists and struck by a fire poker and cracking ribs on the fire fender had taken a lot out of him, despite what he told matron. He could do with a stiff whiskey, instead, he had to make do with inhaling the ever-present smell of surgical spirit and floor disinfectant.

However, what had really rocked his equilibrium was not the physical assault. The scars he bore would pass and he was not especially disturbed about stumbling on an intruder – no, what had really left him reeling and on the edge of nervous collapse, was the little square of paper he'd found in the top right hand drawer of the desk that had been so crudely forced open. It had perhaps shocked him even more than the actual loss of his precious Cobra's Eye.

He'd finally come around sometime in the early hours of the morning with the thief long gone; a cold draught from the opened front door playing across his face and neck causing him to revive and awaken. The adrenaline had instantly kick-started his battered body, helping him find the strength to crawl across the floor and haul himself to his knees, scrabbling with desperation through the disturbed mess of his desk, not caring for the valuable coins scattered across the green leather surface, which he sent carelessly spinning and cart wheeling across the floor in his desperate panic to see if his secret was safe.

Immediately his worst fear was confirmed; the drawer in question had been forced open, his blurred eyesight clearing sufficiently to detect the fresh pale wound where a screwdriver had damaged the wood. He'd let out a cry of despair realising that the thief had got the ring.

He'd pulled himself up and leant heavily on the desk and stared at the square of cream paper with its enigmatic note. What could it mean? All he could comprehend at that moment were the words The Cobra's Eye, and these words combined with the awful emptiness of the drawer, the very lack of the little ornate box and its precious content made him realise that something truly dreadful had happened, something that went beyond a simple burglary and a cracked rib or two.

Melcombe had made a frantic and futile attempt to search the desk, fighting against the agony of his injuries, his blind fear momentarily cutting through the pain, but he knew it was gone. But worse, it had been taken by someone who knew... Someone had left him a sign that as good as broadcast that they knew about his dark and vile secret.

He had a confused recollection of stumbling and blundering about the room, the little note clenched in one fist, but eventually the effects of concussion and the mental and physical shock of this dreadful night, overwhelmed him, and he slipped back into unconsciousness.

Melcombe still had the note, now crumpled and wrinkled with the force of his grip, and only eased from his hand when the ambulance had come to take him away after his housekeeper had discovered him at about 7.00 that morning. The note had been the first thing he had seen upon opening his eyes in the hospital bed – instantly attracting his attention as if it were a red triangular warning sign on top of a black and white banded post on a sharp bend in a road - forcing him to instantly remember what had happened, and the recollection inducing yet another groan of dismay that had nothing to do with his physical injuries.

The handwritten words were like acid eating him away from the inside in a searing twist of fear, for this could mean only one thing; the ring had been swapped in a deliberate and calculated move. If he was not such a pragmatic, unimaginative sort of man, he might be inclined to think the note was like a voice calling to him from the grave.

But harsh reality was worse than any such wild imaginings. The physical reality of this scrap of paper meant that someone - presumably that young man who had broken into his home - knew about diamond ring how it had come into his possession, even though he would swear blind not a living soul was aware he had it.

'I'm connecting you now, Dr Melcombe,' the operator's voice was clear and crisp, her diction immaculate. He grunted acknowledgment and gripped the receiver hard, the black Bakelite already clammy with his sweat.

'Yes? How might I help?' The voice was confident, the accent home counties underpinned by a richness that suggested a love of cigars and brandy. It was a voice of a man unlikely to be easily flustered. It was everything the doctor needed to hear right now.

'Percy. It's Dr Melcombe.' He was breathing hard.

'I realise that, or else I would not have taken this call at my club.'

'Sorry, but it's important. I cannot speak for long, and we must be circumspect.'

'Of course.'

'I need your help. It's urgent, there's no time to lose.'

'I see.' There was a pregnant pause. 'What has happened this time?' The man's voice betrayed no hint of emotion, remaining as clipped and precise as the operator..

'I've been assaulted, beaten about a bit. I disturbed a burglar in the night and he lashed out at me...'

'Sorry to hear it old man.'

'It's nothing, and that's not why I'm calling.' The doctor was breathing heavily, perspiration on his brow. 'What matters is that I don't think the intruder was just any old house burglar. On the surface it looks like a straight-forward attempt to lift my coin collection.' He paused to stifle a wave of pain. 'The Police will think he was after that, but he took something of far greater value - and this is important - he left something it's place. It was as if he was mocking me.'

'That is most curious, I would agree.'

'He's taken something that absolutely no one knows about - not even yourself.' Dr Melcombe stared at the closed door of the Matron's office, peering through the frosted glass panel to check there was no one outside. 'To do with that particular problem of some years back.' He could feel his breathing quicken, heart pounding. 'This makes me fear our solution to that problem did not go unnoticed – it's the only possible explanation.'

'That's not good, not good at all.' The man cleared his throat. 'Let me get this clear, you are talking about that rather tricky matter in '43?'

'The same.'

'Ah.' He left a heavy pause hanging, as the enormity of the news sank in. 'And what makes you so sure this third party is aware of that event?'

'The message he left is unambiguous.' He felt his hand trembling as he held the handset and a painful tightening around his heart. 'It refers directly to the person in question. I cannot explain over the telephone.' He was gasping for air as he spoke. 'It would be ill-advised.'

'Quite so. And what of the thief? Did he escape after assaulting you and leaving this enigmatic calling card?'

'Yes, but I understand he was apprehended shortly afterwards. He is under arrest. I've been told to expect a visit from the police later today to make a statement.'

'He sounds little more than a rank amateur. Are you quite sure he's such a risk?'

'When I explain the exact circumstances, you will understand why he must be stopped. Dammit, this could jeopardise everything!' He banged the desk with his free hand and immediately felt burning flames of pain scream down his shoulder. 'He could destroy us – do you understand?' Dr Melcombe was failing to control his voice, his apprehension and the physical pain now taking its toll. Beads of sweat forming on his brow and the air rasping through his constricted throat.

'Pull yourself together, man. Going to pieces won't help.' His voice was terse and clipped, and if he shared Dr Melcombe's concerns, then he did an excellent job of concealing it. 'Very well, leave it with me. I will see what can be done with this burglar. Do you know who he is?'

'Richard Irons. A young man working in the town as a teacher.'

'Interesting. I shall make further enquiries. A suitable solution may prove costly, of course.' He left a suitable pause. 'That coin collection might need cashing in old chap.'

'Yes, yes, have them! They're yours, take the lot if you can fix this... Just deal with this man and make sure you get the...' Melcombe stopped.

'Get the what, old man?'

The telephone line crackled as both men fell silent.

'He took some special coins... get them back, that's what I meant.'

'I see.' The clipped voice made it clear the speaker was not fooled. 'Leave it to me. I shall come to speak privately with you as soon as I am able. In the meantime, this is what you will do...'

Chapter Nineteen

Amersham
23rd September 1950

The man coughed quietly to attract attention, then rubbed the end of his nose and twitched his greying moustache, patiently waiting for Jocelyn Liney to look up from The Financial Times.

'Yes?'

'Sorry to disturb you, sir, but we've found something you might want to have a look at.' The man hovered near the open French windows, conscious that he must not step inside and onto the expensive Wilton carpet, something that he had already been warned against, by Mrs Liney.

'What sort of thing? Can't you be more specific?' Liney's thoughts were already drifting back to the lists of share prices and was not in the least bit interested in anything the man had to say. He'd convinced Isabella to allow him to get these chaps in to relocate the stone bird bath and having scored that satisfying victory he was not about to become involved in more gardening unless absolutely forced to. He was paying the man to do the job, and he could jolly well get on and do it.

'It's a sort of box, sir. Buried beneath the bird bath.'

Liney flicked the paper with annoyance. 'It is either a box or it is not. What do you mean by a sort of box? More junk, no doubt. There was enough of the stuff littering the place when I cleared out the border. What makes it worth telling me about?'

'It's wooden and rather good quality. Too nice to be stuck in the ground.'

Liney just raised a quizzical eyebrow but held his silence.

'Shall we lift it, sir?'

'Why not? No bloody use down there.' He put aside his newspaper, folding it noisily and fussily to express his annoyance. Liney stood up, slowly, still feeling the effects of his gardening exertions even after so many days, silently reflecting that his wife may have a point about how cold the room was, as it had left his fingers feeling chilled and his knees stiff. 'I suppose I'd better have a look.' He forced a hint of a smile, remembering how delighted he was to have this man and his mate to do all the work and that he'd best not put the chap's nose out of joint by being unfriendly. 'Maybe it will contain something valuable and offset your fee – ha ha!'

'What is it, Jocelyn?' Isabella entered the room carrying a vase of flowers.

'Apparently they've found something buried beneath the birdbath!'

'Again? Is it more of that women's clothing?'

Liney pulled a sudden look of displeasure, though he hurriedly softened this, and darted a quick look at the workman as though nervous he might react to this revelation. 'Of course not. It's a wooden box, actually. It'll be empty I'm sure.'

'How intriguing?' Isabella put the vase on a crocheted mat protecting a small side table, then brushed her hands together as if to remove some imaginary dust transferred from the brilliantly shiny piece of porcelain. 'It will certainly have to come out as I'm planning a magnolia to go in there.'

The three walked across the immaculate lawn towards the border now partially filled with new plants placed in the recently turned earth. Yet more plants were standing in a neat row awaiting planting, each still in their pots and with little paper tags from the nursery around the stems. A green tarpaulin was spread on the edge of the lawn, upon which lay the birdbath on its side beside the hefty stone base now resting upon two strips of timber to spread the load. A large wooden wheelbarrow holding tools was to hand.

A second workman, dressed in grubby trousers and a cream and brown check shirt with rolled up sleeves was in the freshly dug border, bending over with his hands on his thighs staring intently down a hole. He straightened up as they approached and gave a slight nod to the Lineys, whilst taking a deferential step backwards.

'If you walk on these planks you won't muddy your shoes. There you go... It looks like polished wood. With a carry handle on the top.' The elder of the workmen took his place beside the hole as he was speaking. 'Any idea why it would be there?'

'None at all. The birdbath was in place when we bought the house. Well I never, that is indeed most curious.' Liney looked genuinely puzzled.

'I say, do you think it is one of those time capsule things? It looks awfully good quality and not just a common old packing crate.' Isabella Liney's eyes lit up. 'I've always wanted to know what people put in them. Just imagine!'

'Steady on old girl, that might be raising our hopes a little far, but it's a surprise all right. Well, you'd better haul it up and take a closer look. I just hope it doesn't turn out to be a damp squib after the build-up you've just given it, Isabella.'

The younger of the two men stepped forward without prompting and knelt down, threading a strong piece of cord through the carrying handle before standing upright, wrapping the cord around his wrists and taking a firm grip with both hands and hauling hard. The muscles on his brown forearms bulged as he strained, and then the soil started to give a little, and he made the box jiggle from side to side to release the compacted earth. After a minute of pulling and rocking the box, he was able to lift it free.

The older man caught hold of it beneath the base and held it close to his chest. 'It's not so heavy, though I'd say there's something inside. I'll take it across to the tarp.'

It looked like it might hold a scientific instrument, such as a large microscope or weighing scales. The wood was dark and close grained mahogany with neat brass hinges that had discoloured green, though they looked as though they would polish up bright again. The older workman gave the outside a quick wipe over with a cloth and the soil dropped away cleanly. The sunlight brought the colour of the wood to life, but also revealed an ugly dark stain down one side that badly disfigured it in a series of splashes and smudges. He looked up at Liney, with a questioning expression.

'That's a pity, it rather ruins the box.' Liney wrinkled his nose. 'No doubt that's why it was stuck down a hole.'

'Open it! Come along...' Isabella could not take the suspense any longer.

The man laid the box on its back, so the front could be opened to reveal the contents to all at the same time. As he fiddled with the little key that was still in the lock and had seized during its time beneath ground, a cloud scudded across the sun switching off its cheery and warming rays in an instant.

'Got it. Here we go.' He pulled the door wide.

Isabella's face moved in a fluid slow motion through a series of expressions; from eager excitement into dawning disbelief and finally melting into a mask of terror, with staring eyes, flaring nostrils and lips curling back from a mouth opening wider and wider. Her scream was long and piercing, one awful, blood-curdling sustained note that was finally cut off as her knees inelegantly crumpled and she collapsed onto the lawn, an arm flung wide, the other pressed to her throat.

Nobody moved for what seemed an age, though perhaps no more than a second or two. It was true that in these extreme moments, time did slow to a snail's pace and everything became hyper-real. The scene unfolding before them would remain vivid in the memory as if burned onto the brain and prove impossible to dislodge. Liney was later able to recall, of all the stupid things, an earwig slowly crawling up the side of the box.

How could he be so fascinated by such a mundane insect when the partially decomposed head of a young woman stared out at them. Her empty, rotting eye sockets, sightless, through a matt of pale brown hair, her waxy skin stained with brown blood or eaten away in ugly stomach-turning gashes and wounds, her teeth transformed into vicious points and ugly stumps, the flesh consumed down to the bone around her delicate jaw.

Someone was noisily throwing up their lunch. The stench from the box was appalling. Liney spun away and sought refuge from this nightmarish sight by trying to comfort his wife, cradling her head and feeling her stir in his arms as he knelt beside her. He became aware that his was shoulder was being shaken.

'Do you have a telephone? Mr Liney, sir. Where is the telephone?' The elder workman was ashen, his voice weak and lifeless.

'Er... yes... of course. In the hall... Oh God...' He rocked backwards and forwards on his heels.

'We must call the police.'

Isabella made a loud groan, rolled over on her side and started sobbing, her shoulders heaving. Liney stared at her with an expression of incomprehension, as if he had never seen her before, his face drained of all colour. 'No, wait! Let's not be too hasty.' He stood up and gulped in some air, rubbing his temples with both hands. He tried to not look at the box. 'We need to think about this. What should we do? For the best?' He looked scared.

'Do?' The older workman scowled. 'What do you mean do? There's only one thing to do.' He was jolted out of his own state of shock and recovered some of his previous energy. 'We call the police right this minute and none of us touch anything until they get here, that's what we do!'

'Of course...of course. Yes. Oh dear, but the scandal. I'll be destroyed. Ruined! Have you any idea? Have you any bloody idea what this will do to me!' His shock was presenting itself as anger, just as his wife's was showing as hysterics and the younger workman's with being sick.

'Are you going to make that call Mr Liney, or shall I?'

'I'll do it...' Liney started to move away, his legs feeling like jelly. 'Isabella, pull yourself together and go inside. I want you away from that... thing.'

The older workman stepped in front of Liney, his eyes now suspicious. 'Actually, you take care of your wife, sir. She needs you now. I'll make the call if it's all the same.' His voice suggested that this was not an offer to be refused.

'Let me past!'

The man stepped closer. 'What was that about women's clothing in the garden? Your wife said you'd found some.'

Liney's Adam's apple bobbed, and his cheeks flushed. 'That was nothing, just old rags. I burnt them.'

'A bit of a coincidence?'

'You've got a dammed cheek! You cannot imagine I'm anything to do with...this?' He was shaking, whether from a sense of outrage or shock was unclear.

'I don't know. You burnt women's clothing and now you want to keep this quiet. I don't know what to think about that, and now I'm wondering if there's something else I should be telling the police!'

Chapter Twenty

Leicester Central
25th September 1950

D.I. Vignoles was seated behind his desk, a pipe smouldering in his left hand and feet resting on the fat hot water pipes running beneath his office window that overlooked the station concourse. He had the local newspaper in his hand and another spread open across the mounds of papers and files and other odd items that permanently cluttered his desk, creating a gently rising and dipping paper landscape that could be a contour model of the land near Dunton Bassett. He did not look happy.

'First *The Buckingham Advertiser*; then *The Banbury Cake* and now today's *Leicester Mercury*. The genie is out of the bottle and this silly story is spreading. I've had Mrs Green turn away at least two journalists this morning and the phone has not stopped.' He tapped the paper with his free hand to punctuate his sentence for effect, enhanced by the insistent sound of the telephone ringing, followed by the weary voice of his secretary as she answered it. 'It'll be the nationals next and then we'll really be in hot water.'

'I fear it has rather caught the public imagination,' detective sergeant Trinder looked chastened.

'For goodness' sake, what were you thinking of? Talking to the press about this idiotic rubbish?' Vignoles took a long pull on his pipe and turned his head to eye the embarrassed sergeant.

'It was a slip in concentration. I was assisting sergeant Giles in moving a prisoner, but when we reached Brackley Town this young reporter fellow had obviously got wind of what was going on and asked for a few words as we stepped off the train. He was practically button-holing us. Caught me off guard, I suppose.'

'It's your job as prisoner escort to be on guard,' Vignoles closed his eyes for a few moments as if drawing upon a reserve of patience to face the next part of the confession. 'And then?'

'Giles only mentioned that we had apprehended a thief, but this cub of a reporter slipped in a question about a ghost woman on the train and that rather threw us off balance. It took us by surprise that he already had part of the story. We should have whisked Irons away with a "no comment", but instead I found myself saying something about this being an unlikely angle and requiring further investigation and...'

'In other words, you helped fuel speculation about the more lurid elements of this ridiculous tale.'

'In a manner of speaking.' Trinder winced.

'Did Irons get a chance to say anything?'

'Giles forbade him to say a word, but we could not prevent him nodding in reply to some of the reporters' questions.' Trinder coughed to clear his throat. 'The problem is, Irons said quite a lot at the station before he was arrested.'

Vignoles gave Trinder a long stare, but he knew John was right. There were other avenues for the press to explore if they made the effort to look. 'Do you have any idea what damage this has done? The unnecessary anguish it has caused to the Askew family?' Vignoles spun around so that his feet were beneath the desk and facing Trinder. 'I've had a distraught and frantic Henry Askew on the blower demanding that we tell him exactly where his daughter is. What the blazes was I supposed to say?' Vignoles tossed the paper on top of the other on the desk and jabbed a finger at the grainy image of a young Betty Askew printed on the page. 'The first I heard about her, was when I saw this! Luckily, I bought the paper on the way to work this morning and read the story before I took his call.' Vignoles exhaled as if breathing out his frustration. 'At least I didn't sound like a complete imbecile,' he muttered ruefully.

'Sorry, sir. Her name leaking out was unfortunate. We did not mention her name once and I can only presume that after that first story in the Buckingham paper, other reporters did some digging. One of the station staff at Buckingham might have let the cat out of the bag? The staff found Irons at the station looking distraught clutching that blasted poster declaring that he knew Askew, and that she was a gho...' He stopped, catching Vignoles's look. 'All this was before he was arrested. At that point he was just a crank in need of help and his odd story was soon talk of the station.'

Vignoles sat back in his ancient curved backed wooden chair, tipping it back on creaking springs that allowed such movement. 'Okay,' he waved a hand as if blowing all this away. He spoke softly now. 'I will allow that her name was already in danger of breaking cover before your involvement, but you showed a lack of circumspection in front of the press. They have a job to do and they don't care a jot what upset they might cause by grabbing a headline. Nor do they care about how I'm supposed to explain all this to the Badger.'

'Has he spoken with you?' Trinder winced.

'Not yet. I can only presume the story has not hit the London papers, but it soon will.' Vignoles stopped and fiddled with his pipe for a moment, taking another puff or two, and as he did so, observing Trinder's manful attempts at stifling a yawn. Trinder was tired thanks to a restless night with little Jimmy, and even a rebuke was failing to stop him feeling the effects.

Vignoles suddenly reached across to a bell pull made from a grubby length of rope attached to a brass arm extending through the matchboard panelling that ran along one side of his office, dividing his part from the larger main room his officers shared. He gave the rope a sharp pull, and a bell clanged once on the other side. He'd been promised a proper intercom system for years but the signal and telegraph boys had yet to show any inclination in providing it, and so this crude but simple system continued in use, summoning Mrs Green to his door.

'Two coffees, please Mavis. Make it strong. No, make us a pot; we'll be here some time.'

'I'll have to see if we have enough coffee first. It's been devilish hard to find this last week.'

'Do try your best. Cadge some off the WVS girls if necessary. The poor sergeant here will fall asleep if he doesn't get a dose of caffeine soon!'

Mavis Green rolled her eyes at the idea of asking for this precious commodity from the women running the mobile drinks trolley parked outside their office. 'I'll see what I can do. And you have another six requests for an interview from various nationals and some of the seedier elements of the gutter press – I sent them all packing,' and without waiting for the response she knew was coming, left and closed the door.

'They can all go to blazes!' But Vignoles had reined in his temper and cursed more quietly than he might. 'All right, John, the carpeting is over.

Now let's see what we can do with this muddle. First thing, I cannot see how the Irons burglary has much to do with the Detective Department. It's a constabulary matter. Way off our territory.'

'I understand there is a minor dispute developing about which force should now take on the investigation,' Trinder was cautiously feeling his way into the conversation. 'Irons was arrested in Buckinghamshire, but the crime took place in Northamptonshire and neither force seems eager to follow it through. Irons' testimony suggests he only ever met Miss Askew on the train from London and so both forces are trying to argue that this is actually the crucial link. The railway journey, that is. I think both constabularies would rather like us to take it on.'

'You are joking?' Vignoles raised a hopeful eyebrow, then pulled a face as Trinder confirmed that he was not. 'That's probably because it has the potential to turn tricky with the unhappy parents now on the scene. God knows I'd prefer to avoid walking on egg shells whilst I try to explain how their long-lost daughter is being talked of as a criminal.' Vignoles puffed his cheeks out and exhaled slowly. 'A tough job nobody wants. No, this is just a breaking and entry job that went wrong. There's nothing more to it. All this talk of ghosts, or whatever nonsense, is just smoke and mirrors signifying nothing. Pure Wizard of Oz stuff pitched perfectly to amuse the press, but nothing to concern us.'

'There are some puzzling aspects to the case though,' Trinder was opening his notebook and wondering if this was the time and place to mention how the railway men at Brackley Central had told him about a woman haunting the station area in the past few weeks, and how their description had an uncanny similarity to Irons' description of the woman he met on the train.

'Just as there are at the start of many cases, and surely one of the constabularies can tease those out and make sense of them?' Vignoles was not impressed. 'From what I've read and from what you've told me, they should have this boxed off in no time. Besides, never in a month of Sunday's will Badger give us the go ahead to take this on. Forget about this amateur burglar. However...'

Vignoles paused as Mrs Green entered carrying a tray holding a tall green and brown pottery coffee pot with steam coming from the spout, two mis-matched mugs and a jug of milk. There followed a lot of fuss as the newspapers were gathered up and more space cleared on the desk to accept the tray, prompting a file to drop off the side and spill papers across the wooden floorboards. Eventually some semblance of order was re-established and Mrs Green left, but not before observing that she was planning 'to give this place a proper going over in the coming week.' A statement that sent shivers through Vignoles, who knew that he would be forcibly evicted from his own office for a day and would not be able to find anything until a good few weeks of intensive re-cluttering.

Both policemen settled back in their seats taking sips of the hot and surprisingly strong coffee. 'I don't know how she does it, but this is good,' observed Vignoles.

'I understand your wife may have some bearing on the matter,' Trinder replied. 'Mrs. V can always find a bag of decent coffee beans to pass on to Mavis.' Trinder risked a smile, sensing that the worst of the ticking off was over.

'You're probably right! She can find things to eat and drink no one else can, rationing or not. It's my father in law who tips her the wink about where to look. He has the contacts in the trade, and besides, no self-respecting Italian would serve the wishy-washy muck we usually call coffee in England!

Now, where were we? Ah yes; if we push this Irons fellow to one aside, what is interesting is his claim to have found the missing Elizabeth Askew. I feel duty-bound to follow this up for two reasons. One, I've had her father on the phone, and two, because she was last seen on our railway back in 1943, and apparently she's back on it again now, so that places her firmly within our territory.'

'Good point.'

'Badger will take the bait on this angle. Get Blencowe and the Howerth lad onto it: tell them to dig out her case file. And they can take a look at what the newspapers had to say about her disappearance at the time.'

'Can you recall Askew going missing?' asked Trinder, sipping his coffee. 'I don't remember the case.'

'Vaguely. She went missing and was never heard of again despite some searches and posters put up all over the place and appeals in the newspapers.

Not a word and she just vanished. Sad...' Vignoles waved his hands in the air as if trying to excuse this failing. 'I was not on the case first time around, although I do have a feeling Badger may have been. I think the Northants constabulary were driving the investigation back then, as our department was relatively new and still finding its feet.'

'You could ask the chief super about the case, guv? It might help smooth things over about the newspapers.'

'I shall. But one thing we can be clear about - she's not a ghost, so let's have no further mention of that.' Vignoles peered over the top of his glasses to make the point like a barrister in court, then poured them both some more coffee. It was going down fast.

Trinder was now relieved he had not mentioned the woman on the viaduct, nor the story doing the rounds about "The Seven Whistlers" heard in the night sky by a Woodford loco crew. He cringed at the thought of Vignoles' reaction. 'You think she's his accomplice?'

'It looks that way. A real flesh and blood woman doing a reconnaissance job, finding suitable victims with something worth stealing in their homes and tipping Irons the wink. A young woman is rarely perceived as a threat and could probably wheedle her way into the confidence of an elderly chap living on his own.'

Trinder was nodding thoughtfully. 'That follows. Maybe she worked for Dr. Melcombe for a spell? As a home help?'

'It would be worth interviewing the doctor to find out how she made contact. He might be able to recall when and where he met her, and if she entered his home. We must establish if this woman is the same as the long-lost girl as a matter of urgency. We have a moral duty to determine that point, one way or another. Once we've found her, she can be handed over to face due process of the law, but at least her parents will know she's alive. She worked for the L.N.E.R at Woodford Halse shed, so that makes her one of ours. Part of the railway family.'

'Is it credible this woman is Miss Askew?'

'Why not?' Vignoles shrugged. 'Returning, like the prodigal daughter. The son in the parable was no angel. But let's just hope she has come back, crook or otherwise. At least she would be alive. News of a missing woman always sends a chill to my heart. It rarely ends well, but there's always a first time.'

'Why do you think she disappeared?'

'Why indeed? Vignoles carefully placed his cup on the saucer and looked at the ceiling, watching a spider crawl along the dust furred cable of the pendant ceiling lamp. 'There could be many reasons and one should not assume it was a result of something sinister. Askew was an adult, and...' He searched for an explanation. 'She may have eloped with a man deemed unsuitable by her parents?'

'A lot of our gals took up with Yanks and Canadians over here around that time, and sometimes it was frowned upon? Did you get any idea what her father was like?'

'Hard to say from one strained telephone conversation, but fairly down to earth is my impression. He was tense and brusque, but hardly surprising under the circumstances. We'll speak with both parents in due course. He sounded genuinely worried and upset, but that does not preclude him from having prompted her to run away.'

'An unhappy home life?'

'We should be alert to the possibility. On the other hand, she could have been blasted to atoms by a V1 rocket or something. Were they coming over at that time? No, a bit too early...perhaps a land mine then...no matter.' He looked doubtful. 'But surely someone would have remembered she was in that part of town on such an inauspicious day?'

'Unless... ' Trinder sat upright, looking eager, 'she was somewhere she was not supposed to be.' He held a finger up in the air, using like a conductor might to direct an orchestra, now holding Vignoles back as he tried to think the idea through. 'Maybe Askew deliberately concealed her true whereabouts that day? She slipped away, taking care to cover her tracks because she was having a secret affair, and tragically, ended up as one of those poor unfortunates who got so blasted to bits nobody could identify what was left?'

Vignoles nodded slowly. 'That might work. You see, John, any number of explanations present themselves when you set to thinking about it, and none of them involve the supernatural.'

'Point taken.' Trinder gave a sheepish grin. 'But let's presume for a moment she ran off with a thoroughly unsuitable man and has lived under another name these past years. Are we saying that she's now taken up thieving?'

'People do all manner of things. We've decided that her man was not to her parents' liking,' Vignoles puffed on his pipe and raised an eyebrow, 'so perhaps he's turned out to be a thoroughly bad egg and got her into a life of crime?'

It was now Trinder's turn to look unconvinced. 'But why would she choose to resurface on her home patch? Darned risky, as someone would surely recognise her.'

'That is puzzling, I agree, as indeed is Irons' desire to alert us to her existence. If he'd kept his trap shut, we wouldn't even know she was part of the set up let alone go looking for her. For all we know, she's been working this operation for some time. Did she became over confident? All speculation, so get me some facts. Dig out her file and anything else that might prove useful. I want a copy of Irons' statement and all that you can recall of your conversation with him. We'll interview the felon in due course – not about the burglary, but about her. When

we have something concrete to work on, we'll go and talk to her parents.'

Chapter Twenty-One

Brackley
24th March 1943

'But you simply must come, Betty!' Rosalind Dale's eyes sparkled with excitement as she clasped Askew's hands. 'It's promising to be quite a bash, not like the usual dreary affairs with that terrible old wind-up gramophone and rattling loudspeakers. They've got The Squadronaires performing with a real band, and there's a cold buffet included in the price of the ticket, and as the Yanks are paying for the whole kit and caboodle, it'll be wizard! They always have heaps of food - and top quality too. That alone has to be worth the price of the ticket.'

Askew gave a pained half smile. 'I'm sorry Rosy, but I'm just not in the mood. I've not been in the mood for months. I wonder if I ever will be again.'

'Exactly my point! Look, no one blames you for feeling blue. God knows it's a cruel blow - but you still have the right to live a little. You can't just keep on working all hours and never let your hair down. It's not good for you.'

'Live?' Askew dropped her eyes. 'That's the problem, isn't it? I'm alive and Ray isn't. It just feels so darned unfair! It feels wrong.' Askew looked bitter. 'He was home for just a few precious weeks then forced straight back to that awful desert – and for what? To die. What right do I have to dance and party, when he's lying beneath six foot of sand?' She pulled her hands away from Dale's and pressed a clenched fist to her lips, narrowing her eyes in an effort suppress tears. 'What do I care about it doing me good?'

'Because we care about you. Your parent's care, and I'm quite sure Ray's parents do too. You look tired and exhausted, Betty. You're so thin and down in the dumps. You can't just keep slogging away in the Loco without respite.' She gave an encouraging smile. 'Look, it's just for a few hours, just one evening when you have a chance to dress up and put on a brave face, maybe even to forget about everything for a little while.'

'Forget? Why would I want to do that?' She looked sulky.

Dale smiled sympathetically. 'No one imagines for one second you will really forget Ray, it's just an expression. But you know what I mean; an excuse to leave your worries and cares at the door. They'll still be there the next day I'm sorry to say, so you needn't give yourself such a hard time.'

Askew gave a rueful raise of her eyebrows but looked less tearful whilst listening to her friend.

'Ray would do the same if it were the other way around, I'm sure of it,' Dale continued. 'We all have our cares and there are others have lost loved ones too, but we just have to carry on as best we can. How can any of us function if we spend all day thinking about the suffering in the world and this dammed war - and what might happen to us if a bomb drops?'

Askew sighed deeply, and gave her friend an imploring look, searching for encouragement. 'I suppose I could do with a chance to stop thinking about the war for a while. It makes my head spin so much sometimes.'

'There's nothing wrong with going to a dance with your friends; just for one night. In fact, I think it's our Patriotic duty to stay cheerful and not give in. That horrible Goebbels would like nothing better than to say he'd broken the spirit of the women of Britain, so we jolly well need to show him what's what!'

'I doubt he'll be watching a dance in Brackley town hall.' They both laughed at the absurdity of the idea, and Askew's mood noticeably lightened.

'Perhaps I am exaggerating Betty, but there is something vital, something necessary about not giving in to these blue moods.' Dale took a deep breath, her voice adopting a casual tone, 'I find I can cheer myself up by thinking about all those young American airmen who'll be there...'

Askew raised a carefully plucked eyebrow and gave her friend an arch look, which Dale caught.

'Not like that, silly goose!' She paused for effect, her eyes twinkling with a hint of mischief. 'Well, that depends,' and she giggled. 'I've seen one or two around town who are really quite handsome,' she gave her friend a coquettish look. 'But that's not the reason I'm going to the dance, of course.'

'Are you sure?' Askew gave a wistful smile, as if recalling happier times spent discussing the relative merits of a man in uniform.

'Come to think of it, that's exactly the reason!' They both laughed,

Askew surprising herself in so doing. 'Some of them do look like they've been lifted straight out of school, though!' Dale put a hand over her mouth. 'They look too young to be sent over to fly a dirty big aeroplane to bomb Berlin. And a bit scared to death.'

'Perhaps they are.'

'Probably with good reason.' They exchanged meaningful looks. 'They could be lost a night or so after the dance. Gone forever.' Dale looked thoughtful for a moment. 'Oh dear, and now it is me who's sounding defeatist and gloomy! Seriously, I just think they deserve a couple of hours of harmlessly dancing with the local girls. It seems the least we can do.'

'As long as it is just that!'

'Of course, Betty.' She flicked her hair and gave her friend a coquettish look. 'But if they behave really well, then maybe I could allow just a little kiss on the cheek at the end of the evening. To wish them bon voyage.'

'You can jolly well count me out there, Ros!' But Askew's face had softened, despite her outburst. 'All right, you've persuaded me. I'll do my best. But I can't promise to stay to the end, it might be too much for me.'

'Attagirl! That's the spirit.'

Askew toyed with the diamond ring on her hand. 'So, where do we get tickets? We'd better buy them before I lose my nerve

Chapter Twenty-Two

Leicester Central
26th September 1950

Chief Superintendent John Badger slapped his brown leather gloves on the side of the desk and watched the bluebottle fall dead to the floor. 'That's about the long, tall and the short of it, Vignoles. He's dropped all charges and there's no case to answer.' He gave an almost apologetic shrug. 'Not unless we decide to prosecute the young fool for trespassing in a Ladies waiting room.'

'Which was left unlocked, unlike the general waiting room. He had little choice.'

'Eh? Actually, I was not being completely serious, though between you and me, it sticks in my craw that a common criminal can just walk free. What kind of an example does that set?' Badger twitched his moustache, giving the edge of the desk another swipe as though he were slapping the young man in question.

Vignoles considered this statement. 'If doctor Melcombe is not interested in pressing charges, that is his prerogative.'

'Being whacked about the head has removed his common sense. A ridiculous state of affairs.'

At that moment a locomotive waiting impatiently beside the platform outside let off a jet of steam from the safety valves with a sharp pop, like an over-shaken bottle of champagne releasing the cork. This was followed by a very loud hissing and roaring sound that filled the office through the partially opened window, the sound fizzing about the walls with a sound on the edge of being physically bearable.

'How can you live with that infernal racket?' Badger tried to cover the fact that he'd almost jumped out of his chair by readjusting his position, twisting around and crossing one leg over the other, fingers carefully tweaking a trouser leg, so the fabric did not stretch over his elevated knee. 'So that's it, though frankly I can't say I'm too sorry to see the back of the more crackpot elements of the story. Your job now Vignoles is to ensure the newspapers knock this childish story of a ghost train on the head. I want it killed off.'

'An interesting choice of words, but I agree with you'.

'That makes a change!'

'The trouble is, this sort of lurid nonsense sells papers and the public appear to be lapping it up. I can't do an awful lot to dampen their enthusiasm.' Vignoles brightened up, 'but at least it's boosting ticket sales.'

'Is it now? The traffic department may well clap themselves on the back, but whilst the detective department is being linked to the hunt for some blasted non-existent ghost, it's making us a complete laughing stock. We'll be known as the defective department at this rate.' It was a rare attempt at a witticism by Badger, but Vignoles appreciated it. 'They can sell as many tickets as they like for their little train to nowhere, but cut us out of the picture – and make it snappy!'

Since the newspapers had picked up the story of the "Woman in White haunting the line," there had been a dramatic explosion in the number of people taking the last train to Brackley Central. Monday night had seen the usual hand full of regulars, boosted to a train almost half-full, and the following evening the three carriages were filled to capacity in both directions for the first time since the service had been introduced. The crew had been made to work noticeably harder than usual to lift their train out of Marylebone and when it finally steamed into Brackley, it was to a platform unusually busy with more curious onlookers and a couple of press photographers who dutifully snapped anyone and everyone, including the bemused driver and his fireman. There had been a lot of noise and chatter, much hustling and bustling and much loud complaining there was nowhere to get a cup of tea. After a pause of about twenty-five minutes whilst the engine took on water and reversed around the train, the majority then re-boarded and returned to London. Nobody had seen a ghost.

'I suggest the most effective way to put a stop to this is to find Miss Askew. It works on a number of levels. Find her, and we placate her parents, plus solve a case long grown cold and end this silly story with some positive publicity for our department. We could snatch victory from the jaws of defeat.' Vignoles, although surprised at the news Irons had been set free, was pleased with how everything was working out along the lines he was hoping to follow.

Badger nodded appreciatively. 'That would do the trick.' He placed his gloves on the desk and picked up the poster that Irons had taken from the waiting room wall, his eyes softened, and he fell silent for a moment in contemplation. His voice lacked its usual bark when he spoke. 'Do you think she's still out there?'

'I do.'

Badger stared at the now faded photograph of Elizabeth Askew. 'Then that means she's still alive. And that would fix everything very neatly.' He carefully placed it on the desk. 'Dr Melcombe has dropped charges against that Irons fellow and asked that the investigation be called off. However, there's nothing to prevent us reopening an old case and looking for this young woman; can you justify doing so based on this man's rantings?'

'I've only had the Askew file for one day, but I've read it through and considered the case. The trail is cold, but it strikes me it was never especially hot. I'm convinced not enough energy was expended looking for her back then.'

'There was a war on, resources were stretched to breaking.' Badger sounded defensive. 'It was all hands to the pumps, literally at times. There was so much rail traffic and most of it was war stuff...'

'I remember the time well.'

'Maybe not enough attention was given to the poor lass? But the priority then was the war effort above all else...' Badger made an apologetic shrug.

'Water under the bridge now, sir. However Irons was adamant it was her he met on the train, so that suggests she's out there. It's a major breakthrough in her case. I have a copy of his statement and the notes my sergeant made when escorting him, and Irons is convincing on this point. With your permission, I think we should go on the hunt for her.'

'But can you be sure this Irons isn't just a deluded fantasist? He could have made it all up based on seeing her name and image pinned to the wall,' Badger pointed to the poster. 'From what I've read of his statement, the man knew about as much as is written here.'

'A valid point.' Vignoles nodded agreement. CS Badger had his moments of thinking like the detective he once had been, before aggressively advancing his career up the police hierarchy. 'He's quite able to play games with us, that much is for sure. He's hot headed and even a bit naive, but mentally sound. I'm not sure what to make of his odd claims about Miss Askew, nor what he hopes to achieve by making them, so we must find her as soon as possible and get her side of the story.'

'She could be an impostor? A look-a-like who's taken the girl's identity.'

'That's credible, but either way, the family need to know. They'll be suffering dreadfully thinking their daughter is taking train rides to Brackley and not calling in to see them. We need to give them some sort of answer.'

'Darned right, so make it snappy! I'll give you until the end of the week.'

'That's not long enough; the trail is going to be hard to pick up after so much time.'

'Nonsense, you've only got to follow that idiot Irons as he walks free and he'll take you straight to her. I'd put a bet on it! He strikes me as an incompetent fool. She's his fancy bit, I bet, so he'll soon go running back to her. Anyway, you like all that undercover stuff, so here's your chance to tail him. I'm giving you carte blanche, what d'you say?'

'I also need to speak to the Askews. And to Dr Melcombe, as I need to quiz him about Betty Askew...'

'You'll have to cut the doctor out. He wants nothing more to do with the police.' Badger's attention was now being drawn to the sensuous lines of a bronze statuette depicting a lithe and virtually naked dancing girl. This had resided in Vignoles' office for more years than anyone could remember as an item of unusually attractive lost property that had never been reclaimed. 'He's got his stolen coins back and that's it as far as he's concerned. He was most insistent on the point. You cannot speak with the doctor.'

'But he's crucial. We need to know how Askew tipped Irons off. I think she paid a call on the doctor, or even worked in his home for a while. It's vital we get his testimony in case there's a clue that could lead us to her.'

'Sorry Vignoles, off limits. My hands are tied on that one. So, time to put on dark glasses and a false moustache and get on that young tearaway's tail. You'd better get your skates on, you've only got until Friday.'

Chapter Twenty-Three

Brackley Central
26th September 1950

As the train rumbled south Irons could feel his heart pounding with the same urgent beat of the engine, reminding him of that dreadful sprint from Ivy Cottage in the dead of night. His feeling of apprehension was exponentially increasing the closer the train drew to Brackley.

The last 48 hours had been a living Hell. Or had it been longer? He could barely remember what day it was. It felt like a lifetime since he had been arrested. Day and night were rendered much the same whilst in custody; each hour stretching to breaking point when seated on a hard wooden bench with just a square of barred and filthy window high in the wall that imperfectly differentiated between daylight and the lamp burning on its post outside the cell. His existence had been measured in cups of strong tea offered by burly men in uniform jingling keys and taking turns to peer through that horrid little sliding shutter in the cell door and laughing like cheeky school children at the zoo would at a caged animal. He had indeed become a performing monkey, despite his earlier protestations to sergeant Giles.

Thankfully he was now free, though he felt like a mariner back on shore after a long voyage, with the ground beneath his feet dipping and rising without warning, making him both unsteady and slightly nauseous. It was as though he was intoxicated by this newly regained liberty, and yet he'd drunk just one pint of Sileby Bitter a few hours earlier in an attempt to gather some Dutch courage. One beer had not been enough. He needed the fuzz of inebriation to knock the edges off everything. He slumped into the corner of the compartment and hung his head, thinking gloomy thoughts.

The world that just a few days ago had been normal and ordinary, now appeared alien and dangerous; populated by people who fell silent as he passed, their eyes pursuing him; it was a world filled by pressmen ready to pounce with pencil and notebook, demanding that he tell his story about the ghost on the train. Everyone was a potential threat, from the surly ticket inspector, to the women with their huge wicker shopping baskets in the ticket queue who openly discussed his "being mixed up with a woman who'd run away", to the sly glance from the smart businessman with the sturdy dog on a leather leash on the platform.

Yes, he was free and with no charges pressed, but he was guilty - and everyone knew it. He'd been released through the inexplicable kindness of a doctor he'd repeatedly hit with a fire poker, but he was not absolved of responsibility for his actions nor of the guilt he felt for what he'd done. It almost made him feel worse that the doctor had chosen to take back his property and let him walk. Such generosity of spirit was in stark contrast to his ugly criminal intent.

He'd lost his job of course. Not that he'd dare return to Magdalen College School for a while, but he knew he would be barred for life from teaching without having to suffer the humiliation of facing the headmaster. To go through that ordeal right now would serve no useful purpose other than to crush his spirit even further, and he was not sure he could take much more. In time he would send for the few things in his room, although he was painfully conscious of having little more than the clothes he was wearing.

Irons felt confused and angry. It was his fault for being such a bumbling fool. If he'd just taken more care and not made so much noise...

He ran a hand across his face as though cleansing these thoughts from his mind, just like he used to wipe long division sums from his blackboard with a dampened cloth to reveal a freshly cleaned surface like new tarmac slicked with rain. Waking the doctor was not the point. He should never have listened to Betty and allow himself to be seduced by her tale of woe and loss.

According to Betty, the doctor was an evil, brutish monster. A nasty man who'd taken a valuable diamond ring from her by force. Well, the old fellow had shown a willingness to forgive a heinous crime, and that flew right in the face of her testimony. She'd duped him all right. Pretending to be the poor innocent, whilst wheedling away to get him to do her dirty work. The audacious cheek of it!

And how did a lowly engine cleaner come to own such a diamond unless by devious means? It was laughable to think it was given to her by a humble army private. She'd even got her dates muddled, and the worst of it was, he'd spotted that mistake before he'd committed any crime and yet didn't stop to think. He didn't even challenge her. How could she have been engaged in 1942 and still look like a teen-ager now?

She might be young, but she was nothing more than a confidence trickster, a smooth and dangerous operator able to slip in and out of a railway carriage without being observed. Both he and that pedantic old guard had been looking for a woman walking down the platform in full view, not an agile trickster who might have slipped out of the train onto the running track. Perhaps she'd changed her hat and coat, altered the way she walked and fooled them that way? Music hall illusionists were always pulling such tricks, so why not Betty? One thing was for certain he'd never suspected her of subterfuge for a moment. For all he knew, she'd been close at hand each time, watching and laughing at his antics. It made him angry and embarrassed in equal parts.

He remembered how she was often deliberately vague with her answers and her eyes always so doe-like and constantly on the edge of tears, pulling at his heartstrings in a cynically manipulative manner that he idiotically took, hook line and sinker. Had she not always sought him out in that empty train? Chosen to sit alone with him when she could have had a whole carriage to herself? She even made a point of sitting enticingly close, arousing and encouraging his interest and leaving an enigmatic note that would compel him to stalk the same blasted train until the time and place suited her to reappear and deliver the coup de grace. It was all so bloody obvious.

If that was not bad enough, he'd added ridicule to his ignominy by claiming she was a ghost. What a joke! Irons released a bitter laugh and lit a cigarette, exhaling a deep lungful of acrid smoke, his elbows on his knees and staring at the dusty linoleum on the compartment floor.

His stupid talk of ghosts was pathetic. A long night on the hard bed in a cell had given him a different perspective on events. That DS Trinder had been astute; he was changing his story after having time to think it through. This woman, whoever she really was, had obviously noticed a similarity to the face on that old poster and cleverly exploited it to her own ends. It was a clever touch, a neat twist, in a perverse sort of way and he held a begrudging admiration for how she'd played it out. Someone should put her on the stage. MGM would pounce on acting as good as that.

Irons stared at the burning cigarette in his hands, turning it one way and another to make the smoke curl and loop as it rose towards the carriage ceiling. A slight, ironic smile playing across his face and there was a mean glint in his eye. Yes, but he still had the ring. He held the ace card, and now it was time to play the winning hand.

No one had bothered to frisk him the whole time he was in custody. He didn't look mean enough. It was obvious he was not really the criminal sort and his willingness to confess to the crime and offer up the coins in his pocket and blather on about ghosts and other daft rubbish had been enough for them. The police had just asked him to empty his pockets and left it at that.

He still had it tucked safely down his sock, and this was the only lure he needed. She said she would wait as long as needs be - though neither of them had imagined so much time would pass. Nevertheless, he was sure she'd be there this evening. But she was not going to get everything her way; he'd demand they sell the ring and split the money fifty-fifty. It was perfectly reasonable. She was not walking off with a "thanks a lot" and a thousand or more pounds of diamond in her hand. He'd effectively ruined his career thanks to her, so a split of the winnings was only right as compensation.

Irons felt the train slow, and immediately tensed. The semi-fast stopper was approaching Brackley Central where he would have to run the gauntlet of the staff and their disapproving stares. He would prefer to arrive unseen. He'd timed it, so dusk was encroaching so he might be able to skulk about in the shadows and try to evade being recognised.

He stood up, stubbed the cigarette out on the floor with his shoe and pulled his hat brim low, conscious this same hat until a few hours ago was being readied as evidence against him - a little paper tag bearing a number was still pinned to the inside band like a curious memento.

Lowering the window in the carriage door on its leather strap, Irons leant out to look along the train, watching the fragile clouds of luminescent steam drift from the locomotive cylinders only to be beaten into little cloudlets by the spinning wheels and restless motion of the connecting rods. The train was approaching the station on a series of reverse curves, allowing him a good view of the locomotive and a brief glint of golden light reflected from the polished brass nameplate that he recalled bore the odd name of 'Umseke', until the train swung the other away revealing the blue brick road bridge spanning the tracks and the island platform and its necklace of twinkling lights glimpsed between its arches.

Irons was ready with his hand on the door handle prepared for a speedy disembarkation, but suddenly dipped his head and arm back inside and pressed his back against the vestibule bulkhead. There was a man on the platform in a long trench coat, and Irons didn't like the look of him. Even in that short glimpse of his profile silhouetted by a gas lamp that threw a long shadow across the platform, he knew the man was waiting for his arrival. There was something about his confident stance; the cigarette dangling from his lip, a hand in one trouser pocket that threw his coat open on one side, legs slightly apart. The press! If he were not a hack, Irons would eat his newly returned hat. They had an unerring ability to sniff a story out and clearly this example of the breed had got wind of his return. That was a blow. Nobody must know he was in town and he must not be followed when he went to the churchyard.

Irons frantically looked around trying to think of a solution. The train was almost at a standstill. Irons crouched and kept his head low. He would take a leaf from Betty's little book of tricks and crabbed his way to the far side of the vestibule, reached up and swiftly lowered the window and swung the door open to reveal a view onto a grassy embankment studded with dark bushes with a wooden fence running along the top. He sat on the floor and eased himself over the edge then dropped onto the stony ballast, praying the sound of his feet landing was masked by the passing of a noisy luggage trolley along the platform.

Irons swung the door shut and glanced up and down the line of coaches. The curve of the platform placed him out of sight of the engine crew and the guard should be occupied for the next few minutes. Still keeping low and careful to place a hand on his hat – it had helped incriminate him once too often already – he sprinted to the back end of the train and crouched below the black and white painted edge of the platform, his head close to one of the oval shaped buffers of the last coach. On the platform a couple of wooden boxes were being lifted onto a trolley, whilst a group of school prefect's in their distinctive Magdalen blazers walked towards the stairs, one of whom Irons recognised as Fernyhough minor, from 4B. There were a surprising number of people milling about and he thought he saw a man with a camera and flash reflector mounted on the top. The men from the press were out in force.

The reporter was now striding up and down the platform and smoking aggressively in short, impatient gestures, and Irons allowed himself a satisfied smile that he had at least spoilt this man's evening. No copy dictated down the telephone from the kiosk in the station foyer tonight. He also noticed the stern stationmaster standing sentinel in his office doorway.

It was time for the train to leave and Irons needed to make his next move. He looked back at the embankment, beyond which there stood a sturdy detached brick-built house nestling in a corner between the road and the side of the railway and surrounded by a clutch of verdant fruit trees and flowering bushes. A short run of steps ran from the edge of the railway up to the back garden and Irons guessed this must be the stationmaster's dwelling. The steps were but a few yards away across a length of siding that held a solitary open wagon and masked from view by the train in the station. He heard a call, a door slam and 'Umseke' hissed with anticipation. It was now or never.

He ran as fast as he could, hoping his sprint would beat the famously quick station starts on this line so he could be out of sight before the train cleared the platforms. It felt as though many eyes were boring into the small of his back and he awaited the urgent shout that would betray him, whilst behind him, the train made a great whooshing sound followed by a series of deep barks. The wheels span for a moment until caught by the driver and the tremendous energy was converted into forward motion, followed by more roaring explosions from the chimney. The rhythmic beats grew faster, sending a sulphurous cloud of smoke and steam tumbling over Irons and the steps he was ascending. It was the perfect smokescreen, and he was able to bound to the top and swing open a little wooden gate on a metal spring and step into a dusky garden filled by the scent of engine smoke and roses, hot oily steam and flowering ivy.

The garden was large and filled to bursting with plants. Fruit trees arched above his head and tall bushes flanked the brick path laid in a herringbone pattern and there were rows of vegetables, fruit bushes, a shed, greenhouse and a little square of lawn spanned by a washing line. How the stationmaster's wife must curse the proximity to the railway as she hung out her laundry. He stood still, drawing breath. A blackbird sang loudly in a branch above his head. He could see a warm yellow light from a window.

He adjusted his vision to the rapidly increasing indigo of heavy dusk that was creating darkening shadows between the thick bushes and flower heads. It was the light spilled from an open door that drew his attention, and the pinprick of orange that moved like a glow-worm through the air. He stared more intently and then started as though jolted by electricity as he realised that a pair of eyes were looking back at him through a gap between some hollyhocks and the lower branches of a pear tree.

It was a woman, her dark hair in an unfashionable bun on the back of her head and wearing a dark dress with long sleeves, all of which rendered her virtually invisible. She was standing with one arm across her body, cupping the elbow of her other and a cigarette burning between her fingers. Their eyes met and locked.

'Sorry, you can't come in here.' When she spoke, her voice was not loud, but strong and it carried on the still air. 'This is private land.'

Like a cornered cat, he could think only to flee and instead of apologizing and calmly walking away, he turned and ran blindly to the far end of the path. He felt plant fronds brush against his body and when a twiggy branch of a damson tree caught in his collar, there was the dull thud of fruit falling.

'Hey! Where are you going?'

But Irons was not listening as he scrabbled over a compost heap, releasing the sweet smell of warm moist lawn clippings as he did so, then tumbled over a bramble covered fence, his hands torn with stinging lashes by thorns that snagged at his clothes, causing tears and pulls that were hard to escape.

'What are you up to? Come back!'

He was running down a steep grassy slope towards a rooky wood now loud with the birds at their evening roost and too dark for him to see into its inky interior. The great viaduct embankment was looming ever taller to his right as he drew closer to the mass of trees, his feet slipping and slithering on grass moistened with dew, barely in control of his movements and arms flailing like windmills to keep balance.

Irons guessed he should encounter the Great Ouse on the far side of the wood, and as long as the stationmaster's wife did not raise the alarm, he'd succeeded in getting into a good position to approach St Peter's from the least frequented route. He would lie low and wait for an hour or so, then pass beneath the viaduct and make his way to the church.

He leant on a fence post edging the field to draw breath looking back up towards the station and the house, the distinctive outline of the Scots pines etched black against the vast village of stars turning imperceptibly slow behind, a gentle mauve glowering indicating the proximity of the rising moon. The sound of the train in the distance was echoing faintly and a dog barked. But there was no obvious sign he had caused a rumpus at the station, though he felt it sensible to slip beneath the trees without delay.

But he was not used to this darkly unfamiliar territory. Hampstead Heath or Hyde Park on a sunny day or a walk along a canal path about summed up the limit of his experience of raw nature, and the cover of night had rendered this alien world unappealing. He was grateful for the shelter the wood offered but having to enter it without so much as a torch was alarming, and it was filled by strange noises. There were odd rustlings and the trees made creaking sounds like old joints in limbs, the leaves murmuring and hissing like exhaled breath and then there was that cracking and cawing above his head.

He was not fond of big black birds at the best of times. It was an irrational fear fuelled by childhood stories of witches and goblins, and he could almost imagine the birds were actually laughing at him. It certainly sounded like it. The wood just felt too alive. He knew there was nothing to fear except a twig in the eye, a twisted ankle on a root or a stubbed toe but that did not prevent him feeling anxious. It was as though he were being watched. Whichever way he turned, he felt exposed; caught between the unsettling feeling that someone, something, was observing him from within the dark greenwood or being spotted from the elevated station. He needed to override his fears and step under the trees.

Just as he was about to do so, his attention was caught by a pale shape gliding silently down the embankment, caught in the first tentative beams of the ascending moon's light. It moved swiftly and twisted in the air on fingered wings turning its strange pale face with dark saucer-like eyes and hooked beak towards Irons. It now swooped closer then expertly turned about in a move superior to a fighter plane, and as it did so he was sure he felt the touch of the air pushed his way by the owl's wings. Two flaps, and it accelerated away to follow the line of fencing edging the wood.

Irons was captivated; drawn to those unfathomable eyes. Was this how a little vole felt as it stared in up in the last moments before its life was snatched away? The bird had returned and hovered a few yards from him, its wings scooping the air, holding its head as still as if clamped in a vice with its gaze locked on his. He felt a tremor of deep unease. Did owls attack humans? He could see the curled sharp talons hanging like the undercarriage of an airplane and knew they could do him harm far worse than the stinging cuts from a bramble bush. There was something almost human, and yet so wild and untamed about the little heart-shaped face. He wished it would release him from its penetrating, unblinking grip. The owl flapped a wing and veered to one side and screeched with a sound that seemed to Irons to be full of anguish and pain. Then it flapped stealthily away to the far edge of the trees and out of sight.

Irons now felt an intense sense of foreboding as he trampled along a narrow cut worn down by the feet of others that had travelled the same way. It was ridiculous, but there was actually something about that bird that reminded him of Betty. Something about its pale face and those eyes...

He stumbled onwards, blindly finding his way, holding his arms before his face as protection as he made his way along a footpath that took him to the river. The wood opened out at a bank edged with bull rushes and a vast weeping willow. The black presence of the viaduct dominated the quiet flowing water that held a thin sheet of mist a few feet above its surface. Irons sat on a log in a small clearing that he guessed an angler had made and closed his eyes. He was exhausted and emotionally drained.

But his closed eyelids offered no respite, for his mind was filled by images of Betty's face looking at him in the darkened carriage compartment, eyes growing rounder until they resembled the barn owls, her nose in the twilight gloom sharpening in the half-light into a beak...

Ugh! He opened his eyes with a start, and there was the owl on a fence post on the opposite bank. As he looked, the owl's head swivelled and stared back.

For Christ's sake, it's just an owl. He forced a little snort of mirth. 'Good evening Mr. Owl!' He called across the water. 'Looks like it's just you and me, kid!'

The owl looked back, unblinking.

'Good hunting?' I'm talking to a bloody bird. 'Don't you know it's rude to stare?'

His palms were sweating, and the owl was the source of this sense of unease, as if it held a curious radar system that was sending rays across the mist and water. He found a small stone and threw it, so it hit the water with a loud plop just in front of the bird. It gave an angry screech that was even more unpleasant than the last, before launching into the air with a few effortless wing beats and gliding low and straight across a misty water meadow.

*   *   *   *

Sergeant Trinder finished his cigarette, flipping the butt onto the track and disconsolately walked back into the Stationmaster's office.

'He must have got off at an earlier station.' He pulled a rueful face. 'I knew we should have tailed him onboard the train. Stick like glue to the fellow, that was my suggestion.' He slapped a hand against his leg in frustration.

'I was standing in this doorway the whole time and certain he did not disembark.'

'And I had an excellent view from the porter's lodge. There were others lurking about not intending to travel. You saw that man on the platform?'

'I did. Don't know the fellow, and I don't think he was a local. A gentleman from the press I suppose, and another fellow had a camera.'

'If Irons got wind they were waiting it would explain him baling out early. Did the reporter arrive by an earlier train?'

'No. He went back up the steps a moment ago. He'll have a car,' the stationmaster made a face. 'All paid for on a nice fat expense account, I shouldn't wonder!'

Trinder laughed. 'May I use your telephone?'

'Be my guest. I suppose you'll want to contact the other stations and see if any of them saw him get off?' The stationmaster was standing with his back to the little fire burning in the grate and which was taking the edge off an evening now chilling rapidly.

'Correct. The lack of resources is the problem. If we had the men, we could have someone on the train and at every station.' Trinder heaved a resigned sigh, 'but of course that would be hard to justify, and we were given a strong tip off he was to be on that particular train. We'll find him, just not tonight.' Trinder flipped his coat tails to one side and sat on the corner of the desk, picking up the telephone receiver, but paused before he started to dial. 'I suggested to the boss that we put one of our girls in plain clothes, so she could sit in the same compartment, but he scrubbed the idea. Oh well, I'd better call and give him the bad news!'

*　*　*　*

Irons could hear his feet on the pavement and the rustle of the breeze in the trees - but there was something else. That was the beat of a distant engine working hard behind the sound of his out breathing, but was there another sound lurking underneath, that of an animal panting and the heavy pad of paws – or was that just his pulse banging in his ears?

The moon was unveiled and cast its clear light on the almost glowing form of that dratted owl. It had tailed him all the way along the course of the river and the footpath towards the town. The silver bird skimmed the fields, flashing between the trees and sometimes he thought it had gone, only for it to re-appear on a tree branch or gatepost, ready to turn and observe his approach. It reminded Irons of the menacing taxi that had stalked him through his nightmare. But strange though its presence was, as he neared the houses that demarcated the edge of town and could see the tower of St Peter's close to hand, the owl was no longer his main preoccupation.

Something was following him on foot, but every time he turned about, there was nothing. Not a movement or a sound and yet when he walked on, there it was again, the sound of panting and padding and the tick of beastly claws on stone flags. He resorted to stepping lightly on the ground and holding his breath in order to hear more clearly... Yes, there it was, tick tick tick... It was tailing him and making the hairs on the nape of his neck stand on end.

He span about and the dog stopped. Square in the middle of the road, its beady eyes fastened on his. Irons did not move, but then the dog wagged its tail and swung its head to one side and trotted away up a drive.

Irons exhaled in a long slow breath and leant for a moment on an Alvis he was standing beside to regain some equilibrium. It had been a long and stressful day and he was done in. The dog had slunk off, and it looked as though he was alone with only the car and a few leaves skittering across the street. Looking up he saw he was close to the rear of the church and the constricted entrance of the footpath that ran between two long hedges of dense box reaching above head height that would bring him out beside the main door at the base of the tower. The route was uninviting, and the sharp turn part of the way along rendered the end of this leafy corridor invisible. His lack of enthusiasm for entering this gloomy space was not aided by the poor light cast by a solitary lamp that needed a new gas mantle, as the flame sputtered and burnt with a sickly yellow colour.

With a last look along the road he marched boldly down the path, an elbow rubbing the leaves and releasing the strange scent of box. He softly whistled to help dispel the tension, choosing the lilting Harry Lime theme that had lodged itself in his brain. It felt appropriate however, for it struck him Betty Askew was not so unlike Harry Lime in the film; He was supposed to be dead and buried but was actually alive and well and working an illegal scam. Similarly, was the real Betty dead and he'd met an imposter? Or was she also alive and playing some sinister game for her own ends? Either way, he felt he was an actor in an increasingly unsettling film noir that he wished would soon end.

Despite his valiant whistling he felt hemmed in by these impenetrable hedges and started to run, and again that ominous echo matched the beat of his hurrying feet. He stumbled into the open space before the church door and was thankful the gas lamp on its standard was burning bright. Looking around he saw the dark lines of gravestones like so many irregular teeth each kissed by pale moonlight. Some distance away, a statue of a kneeling figure was praying in the same cold light. But all was silent – and he was alone.

He'd never been one to find well-tended graveyards unsettling, and as nothing appeared to be following him out of the narrow pathway, he relaxed. He was just acting foolishly. If he really was being tailed then it was by the very person he wished to confront, and it was high time they met, face to face. He certainly didn't fear her, if anything, he was relishing the chance to confront Miss Askew and hammer out a deal. But she was nowhere to be seen. Irons started to explore the headstones, trying to read the inscriptions carved on their faces and noting the vases of cut flowers with the colours leached out by sun and rain, the withered potted plants and forlorn unkempt graves lacking even these signs that someone still remembered.

He was trying to identify the resting place of Private Coulson. Askew had given him specific instructions to go there, so that was the obvious place to start. Thinking about the encounter, he stooped down for a moment and extracted the little box containing the ring from his sock and clasped it in his hand. He did not notice the eyes watching him, monitoring his every move.

He was now someway from the path and identified a row of pale headstones that looked newer, one of which was piled high with fresh floral tributes. Another was marked by a short squat tower surmounted by the life-sized kneeling angel he had spotted earlier, her head bowed with hands clasped in prayer carved from white stone. This looked worthy of closer inspection.

He blinked and held his breath. He was sure the angel had just turned its face in his direction. The young woman was carved in sensuous flowing marble that looked convincingly like soft fabric, curly hair and real skin, her hair veiled by what looked like intricate lace, although most of her face was left exposed. It was a masterful piece, but what stopped him in his tracks were her blank sightless eyes now challenging his. He was sure she had been looking down upon the grave, down past her hands pressed flat in prayer. He must be hallucinating through tiredness and an acute lack of food. At that moment the moon slipped behind a cloud and as darkness closed in, he strained to make out her features that struck an unsettling chord.

It was Betty! It was the very likeness of her...it had to be! The shape of her jaw line, of her eyes, her hair... He suddenly felt a rush of anger, all sense of shock instantly replaced by fury; all the frustration, humiliation, fear and regret of the last few days now boiling up inside. She was playing a trick on him. Dressed up like a stone monument so she could observe the dumb mathematics teacher as he left the valuable ring and walked away like a Muggins. Well, he was going to teach her a lesson. He was not going to be spooked by these horror show antics!

He ran forward, all fear stripped away and exhilarated that he had seen through her game of deception, his hand squeezing the ring box so he could feel the pain as the corners of the wooden box dug into his palm to remind him of what was real - and what was not.

As he drew close, the angel moved. Her expression transformed from a beatific half-smile to a look of alarm, then into one of warning. Her white arm lifted and pointed to somewhere above his left shoulder as she loomed above him. The angel's face seemed to contort into an expression of acute fear, her white marble mouth opening in a soundless cry.

Irons was not fooled. She was real flesh and blood dressed up in stage paint for ghoulish effect... and yet... what was that?

The beat of what must be a large dog running hard and breathing heavily was now unmistakable. It was so loud Irons could hear the feet pounding close to his heels and as he tried to turn about, the great head with its fiery eyes and lips drawn back from rows of sharp yellow teeth loomed inches from his face. He saw with awful clarity the dribble of saliva flowing from its jaws, the lolling wet tongue and he smelt the stench of hot foetid breath.

The sharp teeth sank into his throat like pincers, his windpipe offering initial resistance as his knees bent and buckled under the weight of the beast. He was still breathing as he fell, arms frantically scrabbling at the anima locked onto his throat. They landed hard, the force of the impact forcing the dog's teeth through the strong gristle and Irons' last breaths were a hideous whistling, gargling, sucking sound accompanied by a fountain of crimson spraying as if from a hosepipe, his eyes lifted upwards to meet those of the watching angel, the marble of her skin now spattered and streaked by his fresh blood.

A short while later, a smartly-dressed man ran his hand through the grass and pocketed the little wooden box he'd saw fall from Iron's hand, then called his dog away from the corpse, making it obediently walk to heel on a leather leash he fastened to its collar, the dog panting heavily. They calmly continued their evening 'constitutional' as though nothing had happened, he just taking a moment near the iron archway beside the board holding innocuous parish notices, to wipe the dog's jaws and snout free of blood with a cloth and give the beast a hard rub between its ears with his perfectly manicured hands, a flash of expensive watch and a shirt cuff clasped by a titanium link, winking for a moment as he did so.

If anyone did see the man and his dog pass as they strolled quietly along the leafy road lined with fine houses in perfectly maintained gardens, they thought nothing of it. He was a respectable citizen giving his dog a last turn before bed and this unremarkable event passed from their minds. Neither did the drunk staggering down Halse Road pay any attention to the gentleman letting his dog jump onto the back of his car before carefully removing his black coat, folding and laying it on the red leather passenger seat and closing the door, all done in easy and unhurried actions that failed to induce interest or suspicion.

PC Dowd also paid no heed as the same vehicle smoothly changed gear and pulled away. Dowd was unable to recall anything about it, nor bring to mind any suspicious activity that evening during his final circuit of the town before the end of his shift. 'Which was a pity', as D.I. Vignoles gently put it when questioning him the following morning. It was indeed, for this young recruit was about to encounter the most startling and disturbing incident in his short time with the Northampton constabulary. He was not to make such a discovery ever again in what proved to be a long and unspectacular career pounding the beat around a succession of small towns and villages until transferred to a dull desk job in Daventry, from which he was to eventually retire.

Chapter Twenty-Four

The Gorse Hotel, Woodford Halse
September 26th 1950

Whilst Irons was seeking refuge in the woods, a group of friends were enjoying a quiet drink in the Gorse Hotel. This establishment lay in the small hamlet of Hinton-cum-Membris, a part of Woodford Halse in all except in name. The 'Gorsey' sat on the edge of an irregular shaped village green just a short walk from the embankments and bridges carrying the railway that neatly bisected Woodford Halse from Hinton, and which helped preserve the sense of these being two separate places.

The 'Gorsey' was a large black and white timbered construction designed to look older than it was, and whilst it aped a romanticized idea of the Elizabethan era it actually dated from shortly after the opening of the railway at the turn of the last century. It was lavishly appointed with splendidly ornate fireplaces, high ceilings decorated with extravagant plasterwork, a curving staircase and leaded windows just as one might expect in a modest country house. It was divided into a number of bars and saloons and there was a big entertainment space on the first floor that could comfortably hold most of the many railway men and their families who lived and worked in the town. If the sooty 'loco' and the clattering goods yards and busy junction station helped define this as a 'railway town', then the 'Gorsey' had to be included too, for it was the hub of nearly every railway worker's relaxation time.

If someone needed to find driver Boswell or his mate 'Tanky' Burgess; get a message to fireman Robothom; or share a pint with goods clerk Simmons or indeed any number of others, there was a high chance they would be in the Gorsey, and if not, someone propping up the bar would know where they were. This little snug was the place of choice for three friends working for the Eastern Region of British Railways to gather after work and have a quiet drink.

DC Simon Howerth, with his mop of red hair slicked flat after a dash of cold water and the attention of a comb, was returning from the bar with three drinks. Seated beside his friend Eddie Earnshaw on the high-backed bench was signal woman Laura Green, with whom Eddie had been walking out for some months.

'I encountered Gerard Powys Dewhurst today,' observed Eddie with one of those observations out of nowhere that help keep conversation flowing.

'Yeah? Whereabouts?' Simon placed two pints of 'Tiger' and a port and lemon on the little circular table between them and sat down.

'Is he someone important?' asked Laura, innocently.

'Oh aye, very! He's a director on the railway,' Eddie smiled significantly. 'Called in at Woodford, unannounced.'

'You met a director? Gosh, the nobs don't usually have anything to do with the likes of us.' Laura looked surprised.

'He looked a bit rough though.' Eddie winked at Simon. It was clear she had not twigged.

'He'd been drinking?' She sensed there was something going on.

'You could say a bit worse for wear, but after a bit of care and attention, he perked up no end and was given to me and Driver Woodcock to take to Leicester and back! Brilliant fun.'

'You did what?'

The two lads laughed. 'He's a locomotive, Laura,' Simon gave an impish grin. 'One of the 'Director' class, and a bit of a rare bird these days.'

'You little monkey...' She gave Eddie a friendly punch on the arm. 'You had me thinking you were mixing in high circles for a moment.' She pulled a face at him. They were all laughing now. 'I knew the name sounded familiar. Really, I did!'

Laura Green loved the railway; the snorting noisy engines and the colourful cream and red carriages or the impossibly long trains of rumbling coal wagons they hauled; the periods of solitude between in her lonely signal box, punctuated only by the ringing bells of the equipment. Then there were the heavy levers painted in their gay bright colours with polished handles she used to throw the signals and points that kept her figure trim with the exercise. But especially, she loved the people who worked on this vast and complex network. She might not collect locomotive numbers as Eddie and Simon did, and she certainly could not name the years the derby was won by the various racehorses the top-link express engines were named after, as Eddie could, nor indeed trot off the African animals some of the others carried as Simon liked to do, but she could still appreciate the finer points of the workings of a steam engine and the curious mixture of brawn and art needed to operate one efficiently.

'How are things going in the job, Simon?' Laura pointedly changed the subject and took a sip from her port and lemon.

He supped his fresh pint in turn, wiping the froth from his upper lip with the back of his hand before replying. 'Pretty good these last weeks. It was a bit slow for a time as I was doing awfully dull office stuff for simply ages. Making the tea, fetching this, finding that and of course filing, filing and yet more filing. You can't believe the paperwork we get through!'

'I suppose it's all part of the job?' Laura observed. 'You must have to keep records of absolutely everything. It's the same for me in a way; you might think I'm there to set signals and direct traffic through my block section, but I spend most of the time making meticulous records of every movement in a huge ledger or reading through mountains of new instructions for special workings for the week - and then filing these away.'

'Yep, that's about it!' Simon grinned. 'But at last I think the D.I is prepared to let me loose on some real work. Investigative work!' He raised an eyebrow and paused to let this exciting piece of information sink in.

'Excellent,' Eddie nodded approvingly. 'Come on then, what's he got you on?'

'All in good time! I knew it would take a while and the D.I. did warn me I would start right at the bottom.' Simon was clearly enjoying spinning the story out. 'I had to work on menial stuff before I could step up, but that's all right. It's not often one gets a second chance in life, and I have to pay my dues.'

'You landed on your feet, to be honest.' Eddie gave him a serious look.

'I know. After what happened down at Marylebone last year, I could have been properly hung out to dry. I might have ended up in a borstal or even worse...' The three exchanged knowing glances and silently concurred. They remembered all too clearly how Howerth had become drawn into buying and selling counterfeit goods supplied by an especially dangerous and violent gang and how it had cost him his job as a fireman.

'So, come on! What's he got you doing?' Eddie was on tenterhooks. He loved detective work as much as Simon, although since those dramatic events of the previous year he had tried to rein in his investigative tendencies and concentrate on his proper job on the footplate.

'I've been assigned to work with PC Blencowe to look out some old case notes and see what other information we can dig up about the missing woman, Elizabeth Askew.' Simon paused again for effect, his friends looking suitably impressed.

'Not the one the papers are writing about?' Eddie asked. 'Isn't she supposed to be working with another villain on some robberies? I was not sure, as the papers seemed to be muddling this up with weird stuff about a ghost.'

'The same! She left home one morning in April 1943 and was never heard of from that day until now when this chap reckons he saw her on the train to Brackley. They got talking and as a result of something she said, he did a burglary job, which he bungled.'

'She put him up to it?' Laura asked.

'That's what the burglar is claiming - amongst other things.' Simon gave a cheeky grin. 'Now this burglar, one Richard Irons, has given us a very good description and swears blind he's met the missing woman. HE says she even introduced herself and told him her name and everything -'

'Where's the problem?' Eddie gave his friend a curious glance across the top of his pint.

'We can't find her. Not a sight. We've got the railway police, three set of constabularies plus of course her friends and family all on the look-out. Zilch! Nothing. So now we have to wade through the original files and work forwards, trying to make sense of everything we know about her and what might have happened to her on that day, and see if there are any clues to where she is now.'

'Surely this Irons chap must know, even if he says he doesn't?' Eddie asked. 'I reckon he's lying.'

'Now I can't say much, but the department are following that particular lead very closely!' He tapped his nose. 'Not a word to anyone, OK?' The others nodded. 'The guvnor. thinks the same thing as you. Reckons Irons will meet up with this woman soon enough, so it's just a case of waiting for him to lead us to her.'

Laura was listening with a puzzled expression on her face. 'Then it will only be a matter of time before you apprehend her. Why bother digging all the files out?'

Simon raised an eyebrow and deliberately took time to sip his beer. 'Very perceptive. You will have read some of the stranger and oddball theories in the papers I guess, and I can confirm that Irons has stated on record that the woman on the train was actually – wait for it - a ghost! The spirit of Elizabeth Askew.'

'I read something about that, but come off it, this cannot be serious?'

'It's what he claims, Ed.'

'You're working on that railway ghost story that's been in the papers?' Laura clapped her hands together in excitement. 'If ever there was a mystery, that's it. How exciting.'

Eddie took a draught of beer and gave his friend an odd look. 'But what's the real deal? Clearly she's not a ghost...' He opened his arms wide and looked between Simon and Laura with incredulity.

'It is a bit far-fetched.' Simon grinned. 'We're not supposed to mention that part, to be honest. I'd get my head bitten off by the sarge if he heard me.'

'Is it a smoke screen?' Laura asked.

'Could be. The D.I ordered us to drop all references to the ghost angle and I can't blame him, as it is a bit embarrassing for grown policemen to be talking about arresting a spook!' They all laughed. 'We work with facts.' Simon now looked serious, adopting a tone of voice that implied he was already an experienced criminal investigator. 'She disappeared in '43 and not a peep from her until she reappears close to home, at which point she chooses not to get in touch with her family, but to meet a complete stranger and convince him to enter into a bit of breaking and entering. Now the question has to be why would she do that?'

'I can't imagine.' Laura looked flummoxed.

'What did Vignoles have to say? Gosh, do you really work with him every day - talking about the investigation?' asked Eddie, as interested in the way the Detective Department functioned as the case itself.

'Heck, no! I was told to sit at the back and say nothing, and he only spoke to us for a few minutes. Sergeant Trinder deals with us on the whole. He sent Blencowe and me off to the Northampton Constabulary HQ in Northampton to fetch the files and then we got to work in the library looking out newspaper reports from the time. It was jolly exciting to go on an important errand like that, and the county headquarters were fascinating. You know, they have a super canteen...'

'Never mind the canteen, what might be the reason for her odd behaviour?' Laura's eyes were sparkling with interest and she didn't want the conversation to veer off the point. 'You said she encouraged the burglar to commit the crime?'

'That's what he's claiming and gave a full confession, so we have to take it seriously. However, even that part of the story is strange, as all charges have now been dropped against the man and he's been set free!' Simon pulled out a packet of Player's Navy Cut and offered them around.

'Most odd.' Eddie looked stumped, then took a cigarette, eyeing it suspiciously as these were a strong brand.

Simon registered his look. 'All I could get and a rip-off price. Bit rough on the throat.' He sipped some beer. 'The guvnor said we're not interested in the robbery, only in trying to piece together the story of this missing woman – is she or is she not Betty Askew - that's what we must find out. Going back to what you said Laura, even if we do run her to ground in the next day or so, we can't necessarily trust anything she tells us, so that's another reason we need to get more background on her. Now, there are a couple of ideas the inspector shared with us; One is that she ran away from home, deliberately cutting off all ties, and has turned into a criminal during this time. Or two, the poor woman really is still missing – perhaps dead.' They exchanged serious looks. 'If she is dead, then that means someone else is impersonating her – but why?'

'Or...' Eddie added, 'she committed a crime back in '43 and ran off to evade detection and never found the courage to confess to it? She's now forced to live a life of crime, living on the edge of society like Robin Hood...'

'A real-life Maid Marion!' added Laura.

Simon nodded approvingly. 'I like that.'

'Have you found much about her?' Laura asked.

'Not a lot. We've read through the interviews from the time she disappeared. They're mainly friends, work colleagues, mum and dad and not proving a lot of use. We're reviewing the sightings that came in from the public - though there were not many. Sergeant Trinder thinks most of these are rubbish. Blencowe and I were laughing as some of the comments added by the investigating officer at the time are really fruity. There was one telephone call from Carlisle, and the caller was claiming to have seen her, but on the note recording the conversation is written, "A sandwich short of a full picnic. More interested in reporting the loss of his cat Gerald. Worthless!"'

They laughed. 'Another was from someone in Maidenhead who the investigating officer said was "three sheets to the wind and having problems remembering what day of the week it was. Unreliable." But amongst the scraps, was one sighting of someone looking a little like Miss Askew at Amersham station, although the man who was an ARP Warden, couldn't offer much about what she was doing or where she was going. Most interesting, is the testimony of the booking clerk at Brackley Central. However, whilst she clearly remembers Askew leaving, she clearly can't tell us what happened after she left.'

'Askew was last seen on our railway line?' asked Eddie.

'The last confirmed sighting was of her boarding a train heading south, presumably to London, though we can't be sure. She worked here at Woodford as an engine cleaner.' Simon bent down and picked up his ex-Army haversack from the floor at his feet. 'We found these. They must not have been handed out not long after.' He opened a roll of handbills similar to the one Irons had taken from the wall at Buckingham Station, though smaller. He took one from the roll and they positioned their glasses to pin the corners of the curling paper to the table. Betty Askew's young face stared back.

Laura bit her lip. 'I saw the photograph in the paper but it seems more intense like this. More personal.' She looked at the grainy image a while longer. 'I can't see her as a criminal. She looks a nice person and perfectly innocent.'

'Who knows?' Simon shrugged, but he also looked pensive. 'People can change?'

'But is she alive? Whatever she may or may not have done, that's the most important thing.' Laura spoke softly. 'But

why would she not let her family know she's alive?' Laura shook her head. 'It feels quite wrong. But there again, I couldn't imagine in a million years wanting to run away, let alone doing something criminal.'

'How can we help?' Asked Eddie.

'Like I said, Sergeant Trinder wants us to interview those originally spoken to back in 1943. Go back over old ground and all that. Now most are still living around Woodford and they might have something new to offer.' He leant forward conspiratorially. 'They might even let slip they've actually seen Betty Askew in the intervening years.'

'Yes! If she's been lying low and living like Maid Marion, it stands to reason she's been in contact with at least one close friend who might could be in on the deal!' Eddie beamed.

'Exactly. Now you can't be seen to be investigating her disappearance, in fact you should make every effort to not appear that way. We'll put these up around the place to jog memories, and if I slip you the names of her old friends and then if you were to come across any of them in this little village of ours and get talking... they might accidentally drop a clue.'

'Is that likely?' Laura pulled a face.

'Probably not! But that's what real detective work is all about.' Simon replied. 'Asking, and asking again, hoping for that one scrap of information that we can add to another tiny scrap, and the two little pieces when joined together make something more significant.'

'This story is certainly something to talk about over a cuppa and we might just hear something useful.' Eddie nodded as he spoke, already relishing the chance to help.

'Tell me the moment you hear anything, no matter how small.'

Eddie fell silent and looked at Askew's face on the poster. 'I know that officially you can't consider this, but amongst friends having a drink, I don't see as it can do any harm.'

'Consider what?'

'What if this Mr. Irons really did see a ghost?'

'Come off it...'

'There's been all sort of talk of a strange character on the line and odd goings on,' Laura added. 'And now people are going to the station to see that train in the hope of seeing a ghost...'

'This is silly. Nothing to do with the real crime.'

'You said Irons gave a formal statement saying it was so?' Laura dug her heels in. 'I know it's far-fetched, but I makes you wonder.'

'And I did have a very strange experience the other night.' Eddie gave Simon a serious look. 'Near Brackley Central, and it was a woman that you could say looked a bit like her.'

'Getaway?'

Eddie told Simon about the poorly steaming engine, the lost fire iron and the woman on the line. 'And the driver was seriously spooked, and I don't mean shaken up because he nearly ran her down, I mean he was spooked! Crossing himself and talking about the 'Seven Whistlers.''

'The what?'

'Soul birds that fly across the sky warning of death.'

'Right...'

'I know what you're thinking, but engine drivers don't normally talk like that,' added Laura, who had already heard the tale. 'And that's what has spooked me. It has quite put me on edge when working nights. There I am alone in my box with nobody for miles around. Imagine if a ghostly-looking woman was standing on the tracks, just staring back at me! Ooh, it sends shivers down my spine.'

Simon sat there with his mouth open looking at each in turn. 'This is straight up?'

'Honestly, Si, I saw her, and it was just like I said. The lads on the station reckon she's been back a few times as well. So those trippers on the trains are not as stupid as some are making out. Now, I think we need to have a look.'

'Go ghost hunting?' Simon asked.

'What's to lose? We get a bit chilly and stay out late, but we don't have to tell anyone unless we do see her.' Laura shrugged her shoulders. 'I'm game.'

'When do we start?' Simon's smile was wide and eager.

Ten minutes later they had conferred about shift patterns and scribbled some dates and times on a scrap of paper and agreed a strategy. They sat back with newly refreshed drinks exchanging conspiratorial looks.

'We only have a couple of nights over the next ten days. But don't let a whisper of this out to Trinder or Vignoles. They'll kill me - and then I'll have to come back and haunt you!'

'Scout's Honour!'

'I shall look forward to a bit of fieldwork. It will be such a wheeze!' Simon looked content and gave Eddie a cheeky look across the top of the glass. 'Though to be fair, I'm also hoping I get a chance to sit in on some of those interviews with Betty Askew's friends. Not the important ones, but the routine stuff. You see, Trinder might send one of the WPC's to do these, and I'd like to help.'

'I'm sure you would!' Eddie exclaimed.

'What I meant is that it would be good experience. From a detecting point of view.'

'Detecting what, Simon?' Laura asked, a twinkle in her eye. 'Discovering the pleasure of a pretty WPC's company?'

'Or the straightness of her stocking seams...' Eddie winked at Simon over the top of his raised glass and they laughed, happy to take their minds off the ominous presence of the face of Betty Askew still staring up at them in mute silence. 'You got your eye on one?'

'No! Anyway, who said anything about pretty?' Simon tried to look innocent.

'I did,' Laura instantly retorted. 'I've met Benson and Lansdowne don't forget. Both very easy on the eye, do you not agree?'

'I suppose so...' Simon went pink. 'I sit next to them all day.'

'Lucky boy. We'll get you married off yet,' Laura observed.

'What?' He looked at her in mock outrage. 'Not that you two can talk! When are you going to tie the knot?' Simon threw the comment straight back.

'All in good time.' Eddie gave a sheepish look at Laura.

'Some things should not be rushed.' She flashed her eyes at Eddie but shifted her body a fraction closer. 'And besides, we need to save for a lot longer if we're to have any chance of getting a home of our own.'

Eddie blew the air out of his cheeks. 'Too right! On a fireman's pay it's hard to save anything. And there isn't a house or flat to be had around here. I know why those families are squatting in the big empty houses in London.

We might have to join them at this rate.'

'Not on your life! No running water and filthy dirty. Ugh. I bet they're full of rats.' Laura shuddered.

'Some of those squats look really nice. I saw a feature in Picture Post. One family live almost like Royalty in the grandest rooms you've ever seen,' Simon replied.

'No, no and no! And don't encourage him. We just have to be patient a while longer.' She slipped her hand onto the seat cushion between them and Eddie gave it a squeeze, their clasped hands resting against her shapely leg, the curves of which were tantalisingly revealed by the thin fabric of her dress.

Chapter Twenty-Five

Brackley
27th September 1950

The day was bright and cool by the time D.I.Vignoles and D.S.Trinder arrived in Brackley. Thin wisps of mist hung like smoke in the valley and pooled below Helmdon and Brackley viaducts like little clouds fallen too close to earth, however the autumnal sun would burn this away once it had warmed the cold earth - and warmed the colder grave markers in the churchyard of St Peter's.

Vignoles had been awakened hours earlier by the shrill ringing of the telephone on the table in the hall. It had been about four thirty in the morning and he'd stumbled out of bed, reluctant to leave Anna pressed close to him, and who just stirred and turned over, long grown used to these unsociable calls.

It had been short and to the point. There was a body, and he was needed. Vignoles had dressed quickly, well-practised in the art of throwing on clothes in the dark and left Anna a scrawled note telling her not to expect him home until late. He let himself out of the house as quietly as possible and hurried to Belgrave and Birstall Station, his thoughts filled with unsettling images of dead bodies, haunted churchyards and strange slavering Shag dogs stalking the empty lanes of his home town with murderous intent. His footsteps echoed on the deserted streets and for a moment he imagined he was being followed; symptoms of an unease prompted by his dreamy, still half-asleep state and the spare, but potent details given over the telephone about what awaited him.

With a set of keys, he let himself onto the station and used his special authority as part of the Detective Department to arrange a pick up from a goods train heading south. He travelled in the guard's van, collecting an even sleepier Trinder at Woodford Halse along the way. It was a short ride to Brackley and he let Trinder snatch a few minutes dozing whilst seated on one of the hard benches along the side of the van, aware that with a baby in the house his sergeant was suffering from sleep deprivation and needed every opportunity for rest if he was going to be any use to the investigation.

As they approached St Peter's on foot, a fat man in a dark suit was easing himself out of an old Austin Ruby that was made to look even smaller than it already was by his considerable bulk. It was parked behind a black Wolseley 18/85 series 111 police car. His broad moon face beamed as he offered a disconcertingly cheery wave to Vignoles and Trinder before reaching onto the rear seat to retrieve his doctor's bag.

'Fine morning for it, what?' The doctor stopped to take a deep sniff of air. 'Glorious weather, so invigorating, don't you think?' He waited for Vignoles and Trinder to draw close. 'Dr Halliday!' They shook hands. 'I may have had the pleasure before?'

'Indeed. Back in '46,' replied Vignoles as they walked towards the churchyard.

'I remember. I do hope you won't make me climb over more filthy old locomotives this time, ha!'

'Hardly likely here, doctor,' Vignoles answered.

'That was a turning point for me as it turned out. I started to get a taste for the pathology side of things. Sounds a bit ghoulish to a non-professional I imagine, but we chaps understand both the necessity and indeed, the fascination of the task, eh? Anyway, I moved across to doing it full time and am relishing the role.' He grinned, 'So, let's see what horrible delight lies ahead for us this morning!'

Vignoles and Trinder exchanged glances but said nothing.

A uniformed policeman guarding the entrance to the churchyard directed them around the tall box hedges towards a small group standing to one side of the church. There was a hush in the air, broken only by a loud group of starlings noisily hunting for food in the damp grass, their insistent bickering like the thoughtless chatter of young children oblivious to the horror that kept the men talking in hushed voices. As Vignoles approached he was on full alert, taking everything in and deliberately not hurrying, trying to assimilate the crime scene.

The sun cast strong attenuated shadows across the dewy grass and burnished a marble angel a glorious yellow, picking out her delicately sculpted nose and lips and drenching the elegant hands clasped flat and upright in prayer in rich warm tones. This same light made startlingly visible the splatters and rivulets of dried blood staining the stone like a poor experiment in expressionistic modern art. It was immediately obvious to Vignoles that this was a scene of violent death.

One of the men in the group was a police photographer wielding a camera a silver parabolic reflector clamped on a bracket to one side. He was firing shots at something on the ground, the bulbs making little 'pops,' shortly followed by a tinkle as he dropped the spent bulbs into an empty red glass vase placed on a neighbouring memorial slab. The photographer stood in odd positions, his legs sometimes wide or a knee flexed, elbows jutting, and body bent at the waist as he sought to capture every angle of Richard Iron's very dead body.

D.I. Bainbridge of the local constabulary saw the three men approaching and there followed a brief exchange of greetings and half-hearted pleasantries. They had met before, and curiously on the same case that had seen Dr Halliday clamber up the tender of a steam locomotive (at some expense to his suit). Bainbridge was still young, and though now more experienced, Vignoles sensed that Bainbridge looked relieved. He was not going to create barriers, whether or not he felt slighted by a murder investigation on his patch handed over to a virtual outsider. 'Before we start Vignoles, you may wish to read this -' Bainbridge passed a telegram across. 'I got something similar from my own super.'

The few lines confirmed what Vignoles already guessed. The Badger had been busy that morning speaking to his peers in the Bucks, Northants and Oxfordshire forces, and the end result was Vignoles had landed the investigation into the death of Irons and the hunt for Askew.

'Has the potential to cut across too many boundaries, I suppose? I know how hard it can be to manage that, as Brackley lies exactly on the meeting point of three counties and it can be a right pain in the veritable backside if a case strays half a mile to one side or the other,' Bainbridge gave a weak smile. 'Makes sense if the railway pulls everything together and we help out as you see fit.'

Vignoles nodded, then looked at the body. 'That puts the cat among the pigeons in our hunt for Miss Askew.'

Trinder agreed. 'The plot thickens. This alters everything.' He too was now wide-awake and aware this was likely to be an interesting morning ahead. No detective ever liked to see a body nor witness the pain and hurt caused by violent crime, but there was no denying these events usually resulted in the most fascinating and super-charged periods of detective work, and to be part of the lead investigative team was a chance to be grabbed enthusiastically.

'A strange one.' Bainbridge said, 'Looks like a dog ripped his throat out.'

'But I suspect we have not been called here because a mad dog went wild?' Vignoles was holding his unlit pipe, a pre-requisite to some serious thinking.

'There's something quite odd about it.'

'Dear me, what a mess.' The doctor was shaking his head. 'I had better get to work, though I can see life-saving will not be a skill I need to use on the poor fellow.' The doctor's black suit with thin pinstripes served to exaggerate his considerable waistline, whilst conversely making his tiny feet encased in expensive, and impractical, patent black shoes look inadequate to the task of keeping him upright. He bobbed and wavered and looked almost ready to topple over as he peered down at the mangled body. He removed his hat to run a brilliant white handkerchief over his brow. 'So much blood... Dear, dear... rather brings to mind the words of Lady Macbeth, does it not gentlemen?' He replaced his hat, opened his doctor's bag and placed a stethoscope around his neck, finally slipping on a pair of rubber gloves.

Vignoles also took a good look at the body whilst the doctor was chuntering and instantly he could see the most probable cause of death. The man's neck was horribly mangled and torn wide, showing marks that looked like they could have been made by animal teeth. A considerable amount of blood from the severed artery had pooled over the torso and into the grass staining it almost black.

'Do you who he is?' Vignoles sucked on his pipe.

'Irons. Richard Irons, maths master at Magdalen. A formal identification will still be required of course, but we know this fellow.' Bainbridge replied. 'Been warming one our cells these last day or so.'

'The coin thief... and the one person who's seen Betty Askew since 1943.' Trinder looked at the man's face, now horribly contorted into an unpleasant mask of fear or pain but could tell it was unmistakably the same man he'd questioned on the train from Buckingham. 'That's him, for certain.' Trinder looked grim, pacing around the perimeter of the crime scene taking a mental note of everything, a tall PC in an ill-fitting uniform stepping backwards to give him room as he did so.

'That's why I called you chaps over. As you'll be aware, he was set free yesterday with no case to answer – but this queers the pitch. I'm not sure everything was as cut and dried as it first appeared.' He looked at Vignoles. 'I know you lot are trying to find the missing woman he claimed to be working with, so I thought it best you were in on this from the start - and it looks like our bosses agree.'

'Good thinking, I appreciate your actions. Do you think his death has any bearing on the robbery?'

Bainbridge shrugged. 'It's a mighty strange coincidence he's dead less than 24 hours after he was released, and under curious circumstances. Feels darned suspicious to me.'

'Sergeant,' Vignoles looked at Trinder. 'It would appear he evaded you last night.'

'He could have taken a later train? It's a small station and he could not have walked past me and the stationmaster without us noticing.'

'My sergeant was tailing this fellow in the hope he would lead us back to the girl,' explained Vignoles. 'He was a free man and not our target, so we aimed to be discrete. Perhaps we were too much so.' He darted another glance at Trinder, who looked pained. 'So, he did not get off the train that we know he boarded, but he still ended up here. He gave us the slip along the way. But why?'

'We were in plain clothes, so he should not have known he needed to evade us. But if he had got wind we were waiting, why the subterfuge?' Trinder was trying to make the best of the situation.

'Good points, sergeant.' Bainbridge nodded. 'Sounds like a man with something to hide. He was up to something more than house breaking.'

'It is starting to look that way. How did he die?' Vignoles directed the question at the doctor kneeling beside the body and working whilst they talked.

'You are quite correct. I can officially declare the poor fellow dead.'

Halliday gave Vignoles a mildly admonishing look as he spoke. 'Intriguingly, there are a number of ways he could have died, based on this most cursory of inspections.' He looked at both Vignoles and Bainbridge with his beady eyes to ensure he had their full attention. 'Clearly the wound to his throat is the most obvious reason – a completely severed windpipe. Just here, can you see?' He pointed, and the photographer quickly leant forward and snapped the area the doctor was indicating with his podgy forefinger.

'Suffocation – actually, drowning in his own blood. Nice.' He smiled. 'Which brings me on to the considerable amount of blood you can see, some of which is splattered far and wide. This suggests the main artery was also severed and pumped for at least a short while after it was cut, so bleeding to death would have got him, if the drowning didn't. And then –.' he shifted and moved the head to one side. 'He took a severe blow to the back of the head, probably when he fell, and this may have knocked him cold and perhaps spared his suffering. Take your pick gentlemen for now. Until one gets him on the slab and takes a really good and proper look, it would be unwise to be more specific.'

'Time of death?' asked Bainbridge.

'Sometime between 11pm and 1am last night. My PM report will try to be more specific.'

Vignoles took a step closer after acknowledging the doctor's observations and stood with chin resting on his hand studying the corpse. Irons was lying on his back, body twisted as though he had tried to turn around in the moments before he hit the ground. His head was pressed hard against the corner of a monument heavily stained with rapidly browning blood and what looked like a tuft of hair. A scrape of skin stuck to the sharpest angle. One arm was thrown across his chest, red with blood and bearing visible signs of severe trauma, with ugly tears to the skin as though the animal had chewed and worried at it. His other arm was twisted behind his back in a position that only a dead person could maintain.

'A dog did this?' he asked.

'I'd say from the injuries and his position, you are looking for a powerful dog with a very nasty temper.'

'A German shepherd?' Bainbridge asked.

'Or perhaps a Doberman or Wolfhound?' the doctor shrugged his shoulders and started to peel the gloves off. 'The PM will provide a detailed examination of the wounds and I can try to narrow down the exact breed.' The doctor stood up, grunting as he stretched his thin legs, and commenced brushing at his trouser knees and straightening his jacket. 'My immediate concern is rabies. This was a violent assault and dogs do not usually attack in this manner. It's the first time I've seen such wounds.' He was now rinsing his hands in a strong-smelling disinfectant, tipped from a glass bottle taken from his bag.

'A rabid dog, or one trained specifically to kill?' mused Vignoles. 'A Rottweiler for example? Normally placid animals when correctly handled and very obedient to their owner, but highly aggressive if so taught.'

'Could Miss Askew have been responsible?' asked Trinder.

'If she had a nasty dog with her,' the doctor replied. 'A woman is quite capable of training a dog to attack. I can see no obvious signs of direct human involvement, though I offer the usual caveat of waiting for my detailed report on that point.'

'What have you found, sergeant?' Vignoles pointed to near where Trinder was standing.

'There are what could be footprints in the grass. I think Irons came off the path and along this route towards the grave.'

'They are not ours. We noted those marks because the low sun highlighted them and took care to preserve their integrity. PC Dowd has assured me he did not trample his size tens across there either.' The tall constable in question shuffled uneasily, but said nothing, his eyes continually being drawn to the mutilated body in a mixture of fascination and revulsion.

'Dowd, you found the body?' Trinder questioned him.

'Correct, sir. It was just before midnight.' He stood bolt upright in response to the question, with his arms behind his back, staring somewhere above Trinder's shoulder. 'I was finishing my round for the night and took a turn through here – I like to check the church is locked of a night. I almost missed him, but the moon came out and an owl flying low over that hedge drew my eye to the side, and then I saw him.'

Vignoles was kneeling beside the impressions in the grass. 'It is confused and muddled, but I could almost be convinced that two people were here, one of whom would be Irons. Here is a paw print...and another. Quite deep. That implies that a heavy animal bounded past here at speed.' He moved closer to the body, now kneeling on the damp grass with his face just inches from the ground. 'The grass is churned up, probably where Irons was turning to face his assailant and a skid mark made by one of his heels. I'd say the dog was chasing Irons. He ran off the path and towards this grave but was caught about...here. Where presumably he tried to turn about and fend off the attack?'

'The dog got his throat in the first bite. Wallop! His head cracked on that stone and he was done for,' Bainbridge continued the story. 'Pumping blood that poured into his lungs.'

'Sir! I've found some more footprints.' Trinder was peering closely at some impressions at the edge of the gravel path. 'The ground is quite damp and this heel shape is distinctive.'

'There's a pattern on it.' Vignoles joined him and pointed with the stem of his pipe, the low sunlight creating strong shadows that aided their task.

Bainbridge needed no prompting. Having checked that the photographer had completed his task, he removed one of the dead man's shoes and brought it across. He lined it up with the impression, although careful not to let it touch the marks in the damp earth. 'Different shape?'

'Yes. Can you show me the bottom of the heel?'

'Smooth and worn. This was made by a different shoe.' Bainbridge gave a grim smile. 'If a rabid dog is bounding about the place with a death wish, I for one would not be standing nearby watching as it ripped someone's throat out.'

'Most unwise. Though I am not saying the dog is rabid, merely speculating,' the doctor added.

'This might be the impression of the dog owner's shoe.'

'If we can find another impression nearer the body it would be more convincing. As it stands, it could be anyone's and a few days old.' Vignoles was thinking aloud 'Plenty of people pass here.'

'I'll can get the technical lads over to make a plaster cast of all footprints we can find in the vicinity,' Bainbridge suggested, also indicating to the photographer that he should try his best with the camera.

Bainbridge then addressed the constable. 'Guard this site with your life and don't let a soul walk near it! And watch where you stand! I'll send another officer to help. We'll have onlookers down here gawping anytime soon, so you mind you hold them back. Keep the whole churchyard out of bounds until DI Vignoles says otherwise.'

'No sign of a woman's shoe?' Trinder was carefully hunting around like a sniffer dog. 'I'm not getting a sense of Miss Askew being present, although I was wondering if they were planning to meet here.'

'Perhaps he got here first then she saw his body and fled? Was this an unfortunate mad dog attack that through tragic coincidence has been elevated to appear as something more sinister – in which case Bainbridge, I would suggest you get your boys out around town with a marksman to shoot the animal dead on sight. Or was this a deliberate attack by someone using a dog trained to kill? Someone who stood and watched as the dog did its work.'

'I took the liberty of having two men patrol the town in their car looking for a wild dog.' Bainbridge replied. 'Though I favour the latter interpretation.'

Vignoles studied the ground intently. 'I think this was a planned attack. Clever as well, because the real killer, the one with malice aforethought rather than the beast blindly obeying a command, has not touched the body.' Vignoles then fired up his pipe and took a walk across to the blood-stained memorial. 'Quite a mess.'

'Marble is porous, so it will stain terribly. Some water and a splash of Voltas might do the trick, to bleach the stains out.' The Doctor was smoking a cigarette as he spoke. 'This stone angel looks like she's a victim,' he added, pointing with his cigarette at the bowed face with rivulets of blood like tears running from each blind stone eye.

Vignoles took a welcome puff on his pipe and read the inscription.

'Do you know anything about Private Coulson?'

'Can't say I do.' Bainbridge thought for a moment. 'I suppose he could be the son of Richard Coulson who runs the motor garage up Halse way?'

'Sergeant, take a note of the names on all these graves. Just in the immediate vicinity.' Trinder got his notebook out and dutifully started copying the inscriptions.

'Coulson? Where have I heard that name recently?' Vignoles waved this thought away for the moment. 'And why was Irons in this particular place? Why run from the path towards a place that offers no means of escape if being pursued? This perimeter hedge looks impenetrable. If you were being followed you would stand a better chance trying to reach one of the houses on the road. Here, he was concealed, giving his assailant and his dog the perfect location to maul him unobserved.'

Vignoles knelt down and looked at the fresh flowers on Coulson's grave, some spotted with blood on the petals, an effect that looked especially disturbing on the white carnations. There was a bright red dribble down a small card affixed to another bunch of flowers placed in a glass vase. He peered at this, puffing aromatic clouds of Ogden's Redbreast tobacco into the morning air as did so, before reaching forward and detaching the card. He stood up.

'Something interesting?' asked Bainbridge.

'Listen to this; "To the son in law we almost had. Trusting one day you and your darling Betty Boo will be united in Heaven forever. Maud, Henry and Betty – wherever you are."'

'Betty Boo?' Trinder looked up from his writing.

'Henry? Henry and Betty... Could that be Betty Askew?' Vignoles raised an eyebrow.

'Ah hum.' PC Dowd coughed to attract attention. 'Yes, it would, sir. Henry Askew works at the brewery. He knows my father.' PC Ian Dowd fiddled with a sleeve of his uniform jacket as if nervous addressing a detective inspector.

'The same Henry Askew whose daughter went missing in 1943?' Trinder looked surprised.

'That would be correct, sergeant.'

'Hang on, Irons was claiming that Betty Askew put him up to the robbery of doctor Melcombe, and now he's lying dead on the edge of her fiancé's grave,' Bainbridge looked animated.

Vignoles gave a grim smile of satisfaction. 'Now I remember where I heard Private Coulson's name. In Askew's file there was mention she had once been engaged, though her fiancé had died some months before she went missing and so was not thought relevant. It was little more than a footnote.' He stared at the little card for a moment longer, tapping it against the fingers of his hand. 'Right – we need to pool resources and crack on. Bainbridge, can you dig out every scrap of background on Irons – I need friends, family, work associates - the whole kit and caboodle. You know the ropes.'

'Wilco. I can inform his family, and arrange the formal I.D. if you wish?'

'I would appreciate that, as we've got pressing work to do here.' Vignoles needed to keep Bainbridge sweet if they were to work together efficiently. He also needed the more extensive resources of the Constabulary to fall back on. 'We'll need to tease out his movements last night,' he darted a look at Trinder. 'Regular meetings to knot the loose ends together, and we'll crack this. My instinct tells me Irons was killed deliberately, and we need to discover not only why and who's dog did the deed, but why Irons was beside the grave of Betty Askew's long-dead lover at the time. Why did he go to so much trouble to return here, of all places?'

Chapter Twenty-Six

Brackley
27th September 1950

'Have you come to tell us you've found Betty?' Maud Askew's eyes flitted between Vignoles and Trinder with nervous anticipation.

'I regret we have not. May we come in?' Vignoles removed his hat in anticipation of her agreeing to the request. 'We need to ask you a few questions about your daughter's disappearance, and perhaps the doorstep is not the best place.'

'Oh, I see.' Her face instantly lost what little animation it had as she stepped back to open the door wider, indicated they should enter the narrow hall. 'You'd better step in then. The parlour is on the right. My husband is soon to leave for work; he's taking his breakfast in the kitchen. Shall I ask him if he will speak with you?'

'Please do. We called early hoping to catch you both at home.' Vignoles gave her an encouraging smile, as he could see she looked anxious. He knew their visit was unlikely to make her feel better.

The parlour was at the front of the house and the stale air of the closed room smelt damp with a lingering tang of furniture polish. It was unlikely anyone had been in the room for months, possibly since Christmas day, and it felt cold and uninviting. Neither man sat on the uncomfortable-looking wingback chairs standing either side of the unlit grate, nor on the stiff-backed sofa opposite the heavy and old-fashioned mantlepiece of dark wood that supported cheap pottery figures of a boy shepherd and equally young shepherdess, a 1930's art deco clock that ticked loudly, and two massive brass candlesticks. Both men noticed a framed snapshot of a young woman seated in long grass on a sunny day, the curve of a railway viaduct behind being crossed at that moment by a smoking train. Vignoles leaned closer, guessing that this was Betty, and taking a moment to identify the class of locomotive.

Aside from the picture, which caught something of a treasured, special moment in the sunlit countryside, the room was as lifeless as the motionless figurines and the three plaster ducks flying in formation across the loud wallpaper. It was a parlour like so many others across Britain; reserved only for high days and holidays, for christenings, weddings - and funerals. The door would be kept resolutely closed at all other times; the wasted space beyond forever waiting for that occasion deemed special enough to see a fire smoke sulkily up the almost blocked chimney, as over-dressed relatives sat or stood uneasily in a room that felt uncomfortable and unloved.

Mrs Askew had hurried off and they heard a gruff voice asking, 'what was up?' followed by the scrape of a chair on tiles. A man in work clothes appeared at the door, the bib and braces of his dungarees hanging loose at his waist, a mug of steaming tea in his hand.

'Mr. Henry Askew?'

'Who wants to know at this unearthly hour?' His voice was booming, grey eyes narrowed and suspicious. He looked confident and self-assured, filling the doorway with the face of his much shorter wife peering around his bulky frame.

'Detective inspector Charles Vignoles; we spoke the other day on the telephone. I'd like a few minutes of your time, please.'

'I'll make us all some tea...'

'No, thank you, Mrs Askew, I would prefer it if the two of you would answer our questions together.' Vignoles responded quickly, sensing that Mrs Askew was likely to hide in the kitchen.

'Right, so you're the policeman who's going to find our girl?' Henry Askew stepped into the room, making it feel cramped and overly full. 'And have you found her then?'

'I regret that we have not at this moment in time, but I can assure you we are putting every effort into so doing. There are some developments, however, and I need you to answer some questions. I realise this is raking up painful memories, but that cannot be helped.'

'Aye, it is at that! My wife's not been the same since that ridiculous story in the papers. What the Hell's going on? Where is she? Why has she not come to see her family?'

Vignoles spoke carefully, conscious of the anger and frustration in Mr. Askew's voice. 'It was regrettable that you should read about your daughter in the morning papers. It was a most unfortunate example of the press running ahead of events in their desire for a scoop, prompting some hasty and ill-advised speculation...'

'Such as claiming she was dead and come back to haunt us?' Mr. Askew almost spat the words out, his wife making a soft mewing sound like a kitten and fumbled for a handkerchief tucked in the sleeve of her cardigan. She sniffled on and off for the remainder of the interview.

'Can you imagine the hurt that caused?' continued Mr. Askew, who now placed his mug of tea beside the pottery shepherdess, self-conscious even when angry, not to spill the liquid on the spotlessly clean carpet, the fine state of which was further emphasised by its obvious pre-war design.

'I can. But all I can do is try to locate your daughter and discover the truth about what has been going on.'

'She would never just walk out on us. Never!' Maud Askew pulled the handkerchief away from her nose to speak and flopped down on the nearest chair as if her legs were in danger of giving way.

'She was a dutiful daughter. Never gave us any worry. Not until she... Look, something happened to her, inspector. Something -' Henry Askew took a deep breath. 'Something bad'. He threw a glance down at his wife, who buried her face in the handkerchief, eyes screwed closed. 'She'd never turn her back on us, and never get involved in thieving either!' Mr. Askew's voice boomed around the room. 'You can forget that disgusting nonsense for a start.'

'You have had no communication with her since the day she left?' asked Vignoles.

'Nothing. Not a word.' Mr. Askew gulped some tea and paced across the room, taking a deep breath or two as he did so. 'Have a seat, gentlemen.' He stood near the window, mug in hand again, as he looked out onto Manor Road, the detectives ignoring his request. 'I don't believe for one minute that she's been travelling to Brackley and not called to see us. So, what's going on?' He continued to stare out of the window as he addressed them.

'Can I take you back to the time you last saw her? To the morning of 19th April 1943. What was she wearing?' Vignoles had read the file and their statements given at the time, but he wanted to hear if there had been any changes, eight years on.

'She was in her work overalls as she was due up at the shed,' Henry Askew replied.

'I remember she had a white and blue check blouse underneath, and a navy and white polka-dotted scarf about her neck and a turban in mustard yellow covering her hair.' Maud Askew added in a hushed voice. 'The yellow did not suit the ensemble so well, but it was only for work. And a splash of colour was welcome in such a dirty old place.' She sounded apologetic.

Henry Askew's voice whilst still loud now had a softer, dreamier quality. 'Looked good on her though in a funny sort way.' He turned from the window and looked at Vignoles. 'Her working togs. Even though they were as grubby as anything, despite Maud's best efforts with the dolly-peg on washday, she still looked pretty as a picture, didn't she Maud?'

His wife nodded rapidly, handkerchief held to her mouth.

'I'm a working man myself, and there's no shame in my book wearing a worker's uniform.' He looked sideways at Vignoles. 'Of course, she could scrub up as smart as any for a dance or going to the pictures, but it looked right seeing her in overalls.' He managed the trace of a smile at the image in his mind's eye, genuine affection in his voice.

'You work at the brewery?' asked Trinder, pencil at the ready to make notes.

'Hopcroft and Norris's. Worked there since I was 16. Betty used to come along with me as often as she could – you know, Saturday mornings or school holidays. I think that's where she got the love of machines. She used to sit in the engine room with Alan the plant manager. He didn't mind her there as long as she kept out the way whilst he minded the steam engine that powers the brewery. She was happy as Larry down there, and before long was helping out with tinkering with the engine, filling the boiler with water and even taking a turn on the shovel at times.' He smiled at the memory and exchanged another look with his wife. 'Funny. I spent most of my life shovelling barley and malt, but she preferred shovelling coal.' A silence fell that neither detective was eager to break. 'So, like I said she was in her work clothes. Isn't that so, Maud?'

'Yes, of course.' Maud Askew looked at her husband. 'But don't forget she also had a dress with her. The green summery one that she'd been saving up coupons for months, as well as her mackintosh and a sun hat and sunglasses. It was a warm spell of weather, so that must be why she took those.'

'Was it usual for her to take a change of clothes to work?' asked Vignoles.

'Sometimes. If they were going out straight after,' replied Maud Askew. 'Though we only realised she had done so afterwards. I suppose she must have put them all in a bag in the hall and I'd not seen it, what with rushing about filling her snap tin and getting Henry's breakfast on the go.'

'She never told us she was going out that night. I suppose she forgot?' added Mr. Askew, although he looked unconvinced. 'She was on earlies, so I was still in the back kitchen with Maud when she left the house. That's why we didn't notice at the time. The odd thing is, we never did find who she was going out with that evening. All her friends denied any plans to go to the pictures or whatever.'

'But she did not arrive in work, which suggests she had other plans during the day, not just for the evening?' Vignoles countered.

Henry Askew looked as though the wind had been taken from his sails. 'True enough. We've never been able to understand that bit.'

'What colour was her coat?' Trinder asked, sensing the need to change tack.

'Pale cream, sergeant. Good quality.' Maud Askew answered. 'It was Aquascutum. Expensive. It was a touch too big really – too long in the arms - but her aunty Doris passed it on to her. It was still as good as new even though she's bought it back in '39, and what with the war on and all, her aunt thought she should have a really decent coat to go to work in. Though the colour was not good for a railway depot, so Betty usually didn't take it there for fear of ruining it with the coal and oil.' Maud became more animated as she spoke of her daughter.

'Did she take anything else?' Trinder was scribbling furiously.

'What else would she take?' Henry Askew fired back, defensively.

'An overnight bag perhaps?'

An uneasy silence fell and Vignoles sensed an air of tension between the Askews.

'Just things for the one night. It was not really an overnight bag, more a large shopping bag she could put the clothes in with just the barest essentials, nothing more you see,' Maud Askew looked embarrassed. She blew her nose.

'What things?' Trinder looked directly at her.

'Hairbrush, some make up and...' She stumbled over the words, the sense of shame almost palpable. 'A change of underclothes. I-I only discovered exactly what after she didn't come back and was asked to search her room.'

'She was planning to stay the night somewhere?' Trinder asked.

'We had enough of that kind of insinuation at the time! She was not the kind of woman to spend a night with a man, if that is what you are suggesting!' Henry Askew faced Trinder and folded his arms across his chest.

'Perhaps not staying with a man, but with a girlfriend?' Vignoles looked at Maud Askew.

'We have no idea.' She looked up at Vignoles, eyes swimming with tears. 'All her friends swore blind she was not with them, and I believed them. They were just as devastated as we are.'

'Did she have a boyfriend?' Vignoles knew of Betty's engagement, but sensed there was something not being said, something lurking below the surface and reawakened by recent events that was straining to be voiced despite the best efforts of the Askews to conceal it.

'She was engaged to Ray.' Maud Askew gave Vignoles a look that was defiant, despite her reddening eyes and the little handkerchief at her mouth.

'He was killed at El Alamein, was Ray. Brave lad. We owe our freedom to men like him,' Henry Askew gave a grim nod of his head. 'Decent chap. They would have made a nice couple.'

'This is private Raymond Coulson? I understand he was killed some months before Betty went missing?' Trinder was again making careful notes.

'1st November 1942, in El Alamein. General Montgomery mentioned the crew of their armoured car in dispatches.' Mr Askew's voice took on a confident, strident tone. 'They were pushed up deep, right on the front line, observing Rommel's tank movements. Took a direct hit. They didn't have a chance, poor blighters. One of the lads managed to crawl out, but he didn't last long, died the next day.' Henry Askew paused and they all remained silent. 'The date will stick with me forever. Poor Betty took it awful bad. Cut her deep it did. Fair shook us all up. How can we ever forget that morning when Dicky came over with the letter saying how his Raymond was lost in action?' Henry Askew shook his head grimly.

'Betty went missing in April the following year. Had she -' Vignoles deliberately took his time asking the question, observing both parents as he phrased the question, '- been seeing anyone else in between times?'

'No.' Henry looked offended, but Maud stared intently at the carpet and her face started to blotch with pink.

'I can understand that Betty was grieving, but she was also young and full of life and vitality.' The atmosphere in the room grew tangibly tense. 'During those awful years of war, one was forced to become a little numb towards death and loss. Live for the day, and not think about tomorrow. Quite understandable under the circumstances.' Vignoles kept his voice clam and gentle. 'She might have met someone?'

'She was not that sort of girl, inspector!'

'Mrs Askew? Perhaps she confided with you - as her mother?' Vignoles sensed the tension again between the two parents, and he gave her a long stare, willing her to open up. She eventually shook her head and said nothing, but it was even clearer to Vignoles that something was being denied by their silence.

'I realise this is very painful, but we must get to the truth. I wonder if she fell in with a new crowd? She was invited to stay over somewhere with a new girlfriend you had not been introduced to?' Henry Askew made as if to speak, but Vignoles held up a hand and continued. 'Even a decent girl can strike up a friendship with a man, it happens all the time.'

'You think she met another man? You think this man may have done something...' Maud shook her head in denial at the thought.

'It's a possibility. But you must have considered this already? It is vitally important that if you have any information, you tell us.'

'I resent the implication, Inspector. There were some policemen making such allegations at the time and I made sure that particularly offensive line of enquiry was stopped dea...' Henry Askew cut the word off short and looked flustered. 'I was not having it! She was a well brought up girl who went to church every Sunday. You're wrong!'

'Henry,' Maud Askew looked up at her husband, her eyes wide with alarm. 'Please! They're just doing their job. They have to ask, and we have to speak out. Tell it all. For Betty's sake.'

'Quiet woman!'

'No! I won't be. Not any longer. Dear Lord, it's been eight, endless years. I just can't take any more.' She sobbed, 'I can't stand not knowing.' Maud Askew looked imploringly at Vignoles. 'I'd rather you told me what's happened to Betty, even if the truth wounds me more than I can bear. I just need to know where she is!'

'The truth can often hurt in our experience, but in the long run it is always better to know than remain in ignorance. What do you wish to tell us, Mrs Askew?' Vignoles gave a hard glare towards Henry to stop him speaking, before looking back at his wife.

She snivelled for a while and blew her nose, trying to regain some composure, not once looking up from the Art Deco patterned carpet as she did so. The other three remained silent, the clock marking the time relentlessly. 'She was in with a group of girls at the loco shed. They worked together and went out together. They were a good bunch on the whole. Some still drop by at times and one of two send a card at Christmas, which is sweet.'

'Maud, we don't need to be raking all this up...'

'But we do! It has to be said, like the inspector said, for better or worse. Listen, some of the gang were... well, they were a bit bolder and brasher than the others, the older ones anyway. I won't say anything bad about them, but they certainly did know how to "live for the day", as you put it. Our Betty was young and a bit naïve, really. She didn't know so much about the ways of the World.'

'Enough...'

'We must face facts Henry. I sometimes wonder if we tried to protect her too much?' She gave a furtive glance at her husband who was now staring at her in mute disbelief. His wife had never contradicted him or spoken out in such a way before. He appeared to be stunned into silence.

'She became awfully withdrawn after Raymond was killed. Just doing her duty and working all hours, and to be honest, even I thought she should go out and have some fun. You seem surprised Henry?' Her husband looked taken aback. 'Oh, come on, didn't we like to go out for a dance or to see a film when we were younger? Walk in the park and canoodle on a bench until late? What's so wrong about a kiss in the dark?' She stopped and almost looked surprised at her outburst. 'I loved to have a night out with my friends; dancing...' Her face took on a wistful quality for a brief moment. 'And besides, you're glad enough to take a drink in the Red Lion of a Friday or Saturday, Henry -'

'Just a quiet game of dominoes...'

'And no one is begrudging you a bit of a life away from home and work. And away from the torment that poisons every waking moment in this house. No, Inspector, it was not good for her to drive herself so hard and then mope about at home with only her gloomy thoughts for company. And so, eventually, some of the girls did manage to take her out a few times, around March or April I think. It was when the American airmen were coming through the town, I remember that. There were lots of airbases around here in those days and they were coming over in great bus loads.'

'How could we forget?' Henry Askew stared out of the window again, peering hard through the net curtains at the horse drawn milk wagon that had just come to a halt opposite, the muscles on his jaw working as he watched.

'I think she met one. A Yankee, that is. Nothing serious, you understand? Just a dance or two, I suppose.' Maud Askew gave a nervous laugh. 'She was always home on the dot. Always.'

'Do you know who he was?' asked Trinder.

'I don't. She never said, or at least if she did, it was just a Christian name and I really can't remember.'

'Where did they meet?' Vignoles asked.

'At a dance in the town. They held a series of them in the town hall. The USAAF paid everything. They were designed to help the locals and the airmen get to know each other. 'Welcome Dances' they called them, and I really they were for the women in the town to mingle with these young men.'

'More's the pity! I never approved of all that fraternising. Too many lonely young lads getting drunk ... ' Henry Askew shook his head, a balled fist tapping repeatedly on the windowsill.

Vignoles exchanged a glance with Trinder. 'Why was this not reported at the time?'

'There's nothing to report, that's why!' Henry replied. 'They were public dances with lots of people around, and her girlfriends were there too, remember.'

'Henry is right. I'm not sure why I even mentioned it. A couple of evenings at a public dance. That's it.'

'Are you sure you can't help with a name? Perhaps her friends might remember?' Vignoles felt the first twinge of excitement. Here was that little scrap of new information that every investigation needed.

'Sorry.' Maud Askew looked sad, as if she realised she was letting her daughter down by failing to do so.

'Do you know what base the airman she danced with was posted to?'

Both shook their heads, Henry watching the delivery boy ladling milk from a churn into a neighbours' jug.

'She told us nothing about him. That's the truth.' It was Maud who answered.

Vignoles observed them both carefully as he formed the next question. 'Can you think of any connection between your daughter and Richard Irons?'

'Irons? You mean the crazy man on the train? The idiot who thinks Betty is a cat burgling ghost?' Henry Askew spun around and glared at Vignoles in disbelief.

'The same. Are you aware of Betty knowing either Irons, or any of his family, before she went missing?'

'But the papers said he was a Londoner, and a young man. She could never have met him, and besides, he would have been still at school in '43.' Maud looked confused.

'I agree it seems improbable, but perhaps he was evacuated to somewhere nearby?' This suggestion drew a blank. Vignoles shrugged. 'Can you think of any connection, no matter how tenuous? Or a link between Irons and private Coulson?'

'To Ray? How on earth could there be? Why not ask that idiot to his face?' Henry Askew spat the words out. 'I'll gladly wring the bloody man's neck for the hurt he's caused us. I'd beat the living daylights out of him given half the chance.'

'Henry! Don't speak like that.'

Vignoles raised an eyebrow and his expression stopped Henry in his tracks more effectively than Maud Askew's remonstrations. 'I would indeed ask him, but Mr. Irons was found dead earlier this morning under suspicious circumstances. He was lying beside the grave of private Coulson.'

A stunned silence fell. The mantle clock ticked.

'Mr. Askew, where were you between about ten o'clock and two am this morning?' Vignoles asked.

'What? You don't think I...? I don't believe this! Look, what I said just now. I was venting anger at what was in the papers. I didn't mean it! I-I was here, in bed with my wife the whole time.'

'He was. We usually turn in about ten with a cup of cocoa and read in bed. Unless Henry's in the pub, which he wasn't that night. Henry does the crossword and reads the sporting pages. I'm a light sleeper, and Henry was beside me all night. I'd know if he got up.'

'Do you have a dog?' Trinder asked.

Henry looked startled. 'No, I don't!'

'Do you have a friend with one? Perhaps you take it for walks sometimes?' Trinder continued.

'I don't like dogs. I don't hold with any pet.'

'Have you had any contact with Mr. Irons since he was released?' Vignoles continued. 'Did you meet him in town last night?'

'I've never set eyes on the man.'

'You did not meet him and have some kind of disagreement, last night?'

'No, I did not. Maud will back me up.'

'Henry never left the house after he came in at six.'

Her husband suddenly stepped closer to Vignoles and pointed a finger at him. 'Listen, that Irons fella has hurt us badly, but I want him alive and telling us why he thinks he's seen our Betty. I swear I've never met him, let alone killed him. More to the point, instead of wasting your time on this red herring, you should be thinking about the ring. Nobody pays attention to the ring. They didn't back then, and you're not now. Never mind what clothes she had with her, or what bloody pilot she had a dance with or even this school teacher who's got himself killed; you need to think about why she took the ring, together with the wooden box with her that day.' He glared at Vignoles. 'Why did she take that?' His look was challenging.

'Ring?' Vignoles glanced across at Trinder, who indicated he had no idea, with a slight shake of his head.

'It was lovely. A solitaire diamond. A real one.' Maud answered. 'It came complete with a tiny wooden box inlaid with metal –.'

'Copper and brass,' added Henry.

'Yes, copper and brass patterns. A fancy foreign design it was. So pretty. It was Ray's engagement ring for Betty.'

'Worth a small fortune, we reckoned.' Henry Askew added. 'She usually wore it on a chain about her neck to be safe and out of sight. But someone encouraged her to go off with both the ring and the box that morning. That has to be significant.'

'She always kept the box on her dressing table, inspector. It held a little note written by Ray with the date of their engagement on it. It never left there. Never. Well, that is, not until she took it with her that morning of the 19th.' Maud insisted. 'Both the ring and the box, but she left the note behind.'

'Can I see the note please?'

There was a sudden freezing of the atmosphere and an uncomfortable exchange between Mr and Mrs Askew. Henry turned away with a snort of what sounded like disgust, leaving Maud, fiddling nervously with her handkerchief to explain.

'I am afraid you can't. It...went missing. Just vanished a few weeks ago -.'

'You threw it in the bin, silly woman! Not taking care what you were doing.'

'I really don't know... I would never have been so careless. It makes no sense, but it just vanished. It was there one day and gone the next.' She broke down in tears, pressing her handkerchief to her face. When she spoke again it was muffled and almost inaudible. 'It vanished the same day I saw...' She blew her nose.

'You were about to say you saw someone?' Vignoles asked.

'Nothing, nothing!' She shook her head, but her eyes suggested otherwise. 'It has gone and that's it. I must have had a funny turn, not thinking straight. I was not myself that day, probably sickening for something.'

'You can say that again! Unbelievable.' Henry Askew was unsympathetic.

'Perhaps we could look in her room? At her things, if you still have them? We could have another look for the note, just to make sure?'

Maud nodded her head, as Henry fumed in the corner.

Vignoles looked grave as they walked up the narrow staircase. He was rapidly trawling through what he could recall of the case notes and was feeling a mounting sense of frustration that Henry Askew was most probably correct in his assessment of the original investigation. What sounded like a very significant line of enquiry appeared to have been either overlooked or ignored at the time. There was nothing about a valuable diamond ring in the case files.

Chapter Twenty-Seven

Brackley
19th April 1943

Betty Askew walked briskly towards the entrance to the booking hall, the voluminous shopping bag with the long leather straps hooked over a shoulder, bumping into her side. She could see a pale haze of smoke rising from the engine waiting in the station below. This would be the train she usually caught to carry her north to the engine shed at Woodford and knew she had judged the timing to perfection.

She was already dressed in her 'Dirty Girls' Brigade' uniform and looking much as she did every working day. A voice in her head was screaming silently, just catch the train and go to work! Forget this crazy plan, forget about everything and lose yourself in scraping muck off those dirty old engines and joshing and joking with the girls. Carry on as normal!

But the weight of the bag digging rhythmically into her side offered a counter-point; And if you bury your head in the sand in the drying room? What then? If you don't fix this once and for all, what kind of future lies ahead? She pulled a pained expression as once more, for the thousandth time, she contemplated the shame that would surely follow; the contempt of neighbours and townsfolk and even the people she considered friends.

Then what of her mother and father? They would not be able to cope with the shame. It would humiliate them; shatter their world. She'd read that girls like her were sometimes declared mad by their own parents and family doctor and locked away in terrifying institutions far away from anywhere. Hidden from view behind barred windows in ugly buildings behind high walls, where severe white-coated staff pumped these girls full of drugs and gave them electrical shocks that hurt like a penance, and ensured they really were mad before too many years had passed whilst their poor child was sent off for adoption, never to seen or heard of again.

Betty patted the bag that held the change of clothes neatly folded inside. She hoped her hat and dress would not be hopelessly creased beneath her folded mackintosh. She approached the ticket hall which had a great mound of neatly stacked sandbags protecting the entrance on either side and prepared herself for the next stage of her secret journey.

Miss Snowball, one of the ticket clerks, was seated behind the little window as expected, and so, forcing a cheeriness she did not feel, Askew gave a smile and an ostentatious wave whilst trotting past at speed.

'Late!' she mouthed and saw Miss Snowball nod her head vigorously and urge her on towards the impatiently waiting train below with a "shooing" motion of her hands. So far, so good.

Askew clumped rapidly along the wooden bridge in her heavy work boots, deliberately making her steps boom and hopefully reinforcing the idea with Miss Snowball that she had run for - and caught - the train to Woodford. As a holder of a railway travel permit she had no need to buy a ticket and had timed her arrival to give the impression of running and leaping aboard at the last moment. However, Askew slowed near the top of the stairs and crouched low, silently descending a few more steps until she had a narrow view of the platform below. The train guard's torso and legs were visible, washed in pale early morning light that threw a strong shadow onto the grubby maroon carriage side. He was calling 'All aboard! All aboard!'

Askew felt a twinge of guilt. She knew the man, even from this restricted glimpse, and he was a decent elderly fellow best able to serve his country by sticking with the railways and doing his bit to keep them running. He would never knowingly allow a train to depart if someone were rushing to catch it. He'd heard her footsteps and was now pausing in anticipation of someone appearing at the bottom of the steps.

She pulled herself back against the wall and waited, hoping she was out of his sightline. If anyone saw her now crouched on the steps it would be awkward. Moments later she heard his whistle and a friendly shout to someone on the platform, an answering toot from the locomotive and the harsh hiss and bark of the engine.

Askew gave it a few moments, then darted across the open space at the bottom of the steps to the far side of the platform buildings, away from the now rapidly accelerating train. She was in luck; the platform was clear, and she could get to the ladies waiting room unseen.

She must hurry and make the transformation by the time the London train arrived. She had the ladies waiting room and toilets to herself, much as she had expected at this hour. Discovering that her dress had survived being folded, gave her an added lift, and her swift change of clothes had a dramatic effect. Now in the dress with hat and sunglasses, short gloves, best shoes and a bangle about her wrist, it was a very different figure who anxiously sat waiting, fingers toying with the strap of the now considerably heavier bag, weighted down by her work boots and overalls. Her diamond ring still hung from the thin chain about her neck. She could feel it swinging between her breasts when she moved, but she might only wear it on her finger once closer to her destination.

There was the sound of voices outside the waiting room and a rise in those preparatory sounds from signal box and station that presaged the arrival of a stopping train, and so Askew stood up, nervously smoothing her dress once again. She could hear the gentle beat and clank of a locomotive and a rhythmic hiss, suggesting to her well-tuned ear that it was leaking steam from a gland. Askew looked through the glass pane of the door criss-crossed by strips of adhesive tape in diagonals to help reduce the effects of bomb blast just as the filthy black locomotive streaked with dribbles of lime scale and burnt orange on the bottom of the smokebox, clanged slowly to a halt, breathing like an over-heated Pekinese dog. It had pulled in a rake of equally dingy wooden coaches, each stuffed to bursting with passengers and all of whom seemed to be dressed in muted shades of khaki or RAF blue with the occasional flash of white from a sailors cap. It was going to be standing room only.

She stepped out of the waiting room and had just placed a hand on the nearest coach door handle, when she heard a voice close by.

'I thought you were going to work?'

Botheration! What was *she* doing on the platform? Askew felt as though the ground had suddenly given way. She just stared back and could not speak.

'And you've changed?' Miss Snowball stated the obvious.

'I-I have to go to London. On business...' It was lame and unconvincing. 'A private matter, you know? Hush-hush and all that! Rather not say more than absolutely essential.' She desperately tried to keep her voice light, wishing to suggest there was really nothing odd about her actions. 'Look, if you could keep it under your hat?' She offered her enigmatic reply with as much levity as she could muster, then opened the carriage door.

'Gosh, well, mum's the word then!' Miss Snowball gave her an innocent, wide-eyed look. 'Won't breathe a thing, cross my heart and hope to die!' and winked, privately feeling a surge of envy. Miss Snowball understood perfectly; this was quite clearly the preparation for a thrilling, and undoubtedly illicit, liaison with a dashing beau. Miss Askew might had found herself an officer in one of the forces. How exciting. But she would keep her secret safe, and hope that one day she too might have cause to slink off to the big smoke in her best dress for just such a romantic affair. It was like something from the romance novels she loved to read during the quiet times in the booking office.

Chapter Twenty-Eight

Brackley
27th September 1950

'So, Miss Snowball, you are quite clear she was going to London?' Trinder gave her an earnest look.

'Oh yes. At least, it was the London train she boarded, but of course she could have got out anywhere in between. She had a travel permit giving full access, so there was no way of knowing. She did say London, and why would she lie?'

'Because she wished to conceal where she was really going,' Trinder mused. 'How did she seem to you that morning? Agitated, nervous, excited?'

'I hardly saw her, sergeant. She rushed past the window and waved at me and then I heard her tramping over the bridge to catch the down train - or so I thought. What a minx, to fool me like that? She looked exactly as she always did on a workday morning, so I suspected nothing.' Miss Snowball fiddled with the scone that lay half eaten on the plate before her.

'But when you next saw her, she had changed clothes?'

'It was such a surprise! I could hardly believe my eyes. I had to take an urgent message down to the stationmaster because the telephone connection to his office was faulty, so I quickly nipped down to the platform. That's why I was there, you see? Of course, she must have had the change of clothes in her bag, but even so it was like a conjuring trick. Quite startling. I was impressed.'

Trinder could not help but smile at Miss Snowball's innocent excitement in recounting the story. She was as wide-eyed and excited about the event as if it had happened eight days, rather than eight years ago. He paused in his questioning for a moment to take in the staid, and utterly unremarkable interior of the Oak Cottage Café. This poky little establishment sat on the edge of Brackley market square and if he was being uncharitable, the interior and ambience suited the plain and drably dressed woman seated opposite, with her dress the colour of milky coffee and a thin grey cardigan over the top.

Her frowsy clothes did little for her. She was a pale, slightly shapeless woman in her mid-thirties, with eyes just a little too large and prone to staring, and straight hair of indeterminate colour held back by two pale blue plastic clips that made her look girly. Her mouth however was mobile and the upper lip nicely shaped and Trinder found himself thinking that if she ventured to apply lipstick, it could look sensuous. He wondered if being the last person to admit to speaking to Betty Askew on that fateful day was still one of the highlights of this woman's uneventful life. It had already taken a lot of coaxing and one cup of tea and half a scone to get this much of the story out, but he sensed she was actually enjoying the attention. She realised that her testimony was important to the investigation and milking it for all it was worth.

'How did Miss Askew react when you saw her on the platform?'

'Well...' She put a finger upright across her lips to suggest she were concentrating hard, whilst furrowing her brow. Trinder was struck with an image of Miss Snowball as head girl in school asked to stand before class and answer a difficult question. He could imagine her not wishing to appear too clever and so going through the pantomime of looking as though trying to dredge up the answer before responding. Miss Snowball may have no sense of colour and style, but he had little doubt that she was quick. 'I rather think Miss Askew was shocked, sergeant. She looked a little guilty - as if caught doing something she shouldn't.' Her eyes opened even wider. 'You do know what I mean?' She then dropped her chin, and gave him an arch look, hands clasped around the teacup decorated with oak leaves and acorns.

'I think I do.' Trinder smiled indulgently. He was not confident of a startling revelation from this witness, but he was prepared to be patient and take as long as needed, as there just may be something, a little detail that could help. 'Why do you think she was looking guilty?'

'Because she had changed her clothes of course! Now, sergeant, I understand I was the only person who saw her both before and after her amazing transfiguration from worker to lover. I know that because when we talked about it later - once it was known she had gone missing that is - the stationmaster and porters either did not see her at all, or only saw her when dressed up in her best and thought nothing of it. She was got up very nicely and quite obviously not going to work.' Miss Snowball leant forward and both Trinder and constable Howerth, who was seated at the end of the table, involuntarily found themselves doing the same as though they were hatching a plot around the tea things. 'I think she was going to meet a man; I suspected that at the time, and I still think it now.' She gave Trinder and Howerth a knowing look that was hard to interpret as to whether disapproving or envious, nodding her head just slightly to reinforce the point. Trinder glanced at her left hand that was conspicuous in lacking a ring. 'Though I have never said this to anyone before! I don't gossip.'

'She was dressed smartly when you saw her on the platform?' Trinder asked, suspecting that Miss Snowball loved to gossip.

'Yes. Not Sunday best, but most suitable for lunch in a good restaurant.' She gave a surprisingly suggestive look. 'Exactly what one might wear if meeting a man on a hot date.' She raised an eyebrow. 'Though of course, she told me it was "business".' Miss Snowball put a hand to her mouth and giggled. 'What 'business' do you think they were up too! She told me it was "secret" and to keep it quiet, and so I have!' Her mobile mouth took a sudden down turn at the edges. 'When the police asked me about her back then, I told them the bare facts. She had missed her train and took a different one towards London in a change of clothes. One has to speak the truth when the police ask, but I'm really not one for trading in speculation and so thought it wise not to judge or make unnecessary trouble for Miss Askew about her amorous goings on. But there again, I did not realise so much time would pass, and she would still be missing.'

'You thought Miss Askew was having a secret rendezvous?'

'Of course. Her parents are somewhat straight-laced. You see, one gets to know everyone working at the station and can form a pretty good idea of how people are, and I don't see Mr. and Mrs Askew approving. She did not want them knowing, I expect. Can't blame her really. I suppose it is easier keeping them in ignorance than to tell an actual lie. What do you think about that? It's a tasty little moral dilemma.' Trinder remained silent. This was mere speculation, but it was interesting to hear her thoughts. 'I am free of that particular moral tug of war as it happens, sergeant, because both my parents died when I was twelve, so I can meet with any man I like and with no need to act like a femme fatale from a spy thriller!' She gave Trinder a cheeky look across the top of her tea cup before taking a sip, whilst he in turn gave Howerth a sharp glance to stifle what he suspected was going to be a snigger from the young constable.

'Do you have any idea whom she was meeting?' Trinder asked.

'No, and that puzzles me. Let's be frank, I find it hard to imagine she really had a lover in London, but then people are full of surprises. I mean, she's a poor worker in a God-forsaken little town in the middle of nowhere – how would she manage that?' She gave Trinder a challenging look. 'I thought she was meeting someone at the time, but upon reflection, I am not so convinced now. It will sound dreadfully bitchy, but I suspected she wanted me to think she had a man in the big smoke. Though quite why, I cannot say.'

'Are you aware of her seeing anyone locally? This could have been a deception to help hide a liaison closer to home?' Trinder kept his voice flat and unemotional. He needed to keep this woman dealing with facts, not enter into wild speculation. 'We know about her engagement to private Coulson and his subsequent death, but we are interested in the time after Coulson was killed.'

'You want me to spill the beans on her fling with one of those young Americans?' Miss Snowball raised an eyebrow.

'If you have information then it is vitally important you tell us...'

She giggled. 'You are so dreadfully serious, sergeant. I hardly knew her, we just chatted occasionally at the station, so I can't help when it comes to matters of her heart. Sorry.'

'What made you suggest she had been seen with an American serviceman?' Simon Howerth asked. He had spoken his thoughts aloud and surprised himself as much as the others.

Miss Snowball darted a look towards the young constable, who had remained silent until now. 'No reason. It's just what everyone was doing at the time... You must know the phrase, "Over here, over paid and over..."' She looked flustered. 'Well, I'm quite sure you don't need me to complete the line, young man.'

'There were a number of dances in the town around the spring of 1943. Arranged by the U.S. Airforce. Did you attend any of them?' Trinder picked up the thread. 'They must have been quite a pull; an exciting event in a sleepy town such as this?'

'No. I did not.' Miss Snowball stared at the half-eaten scone on her plate.

'I would have thought they would have been hard to resist?'

'I am no dancer, sergeant. I've never mastered the art, and as I rarely take a drink it would have been an uncomfortable and quite tedious evening. A wallflower sitting alone in the corner is nothing to enjoy, believe you me.' She gave a sad little sigh and Trinder sensed an aura of regret envelop her. The spark of perkiness, verging on flirtatiousness that had been visible moments before had evaporated. 'These dances were raucous and noisy affairs with far too much drinking going on and... all manner of other things! I suppose you want to know if I saw Betty at one of these dances?'

'Did you?'

'How could I, sergeant, if I was not there?'

'You speak of the dances as though you experienced them, that's why I asked.' Trinder looked puzzled.

'I did?' Miss Snowball coloured. 'I just imagined that's how they were...from what people told me.' She stopped. It was obviously a lie. In the lengthening silence, Trinder found his eye momentarily taken by a noisy delivery lorry pulling up outside the bay window with "The London Central Meat Co" painted on the side in dark blue letters. Was she on the verge of telling him something significant?

Miss Snowball took a deep gulp of air, gave the young constable a glance that made him shut his mouth rather than speak then faced Trinder. She looked as though she were making her mind up about something and he was prepared to give her time, pleased his young assistant had the intelligence to do the same. 'What I said is not strictly correct. I stood in the town hall doorway with a ticket in my hand, looking in. Can you imagine the scene? It was packed with people and thick with smoke hanging above the dancers and the music was far too loud. An awful racket, just a lot of banging and blaring trumpets. Despite invitations to step inside from a group of loutish young servicemen, I baulked. I confess my nerve failed and I walked away.'

'Did your friends not encourage you?'

Chapter Twenty-Eight

'I was alone.'

A silence fell between them again, enhanced by the noisy lorry suddenly cutting the engine and the blissful end to its noise punctuated only by the sound of teacups being washed in the back kitchen and the low murmur of a couple talking at a table in the corner. 'I find it easier to talk to people when I am behind my glass ticket window.' Miss Snowball spoke with the air of someone confessing a long-held secret. 'I don't find it at all hard talking and getting along with everyone when at work, and even talking to you is surprisingly easy. Even though you are the police. I'm just not very good at these social sorts of events. There, I've said it now. Oh dear, you will think me awfully strange?'

'Not at all.' Trinder smiled indulgently. He sensed this was leading somewhere and wanted to keep her talking. 'You would not have seen Miss Askew at the dance, but perhaps you did on the way there?'

'Not going to the dance. I came a little later, you see? About ten, I think it was. I dithered and delayed before walking down. Silly isn't it?' She gave a wan smile. 'Look, I really don't want to trade in tittle-tattle. I absolutely deplore that sort of carrying on.'

'Indeed. But any information is vital. Anything you say will be dealt with sensitively and as discretely as possible, but I fear the time for circumspection is long past.' Trinder looked serious.

'Of course.' She looked pensive. 'It was during the second of the two dances in town. I don't recall the date, but it was in April. It was a Friday night and you will be able to check this I am sure.'

'Indeed,' Trinder agreed. 'And you saw Miss Askew?'

'I did and she was with a man!' She paused for effect. 'It was late in the evening and a little way from the town hall.' She now spoke in little more than a whisper. 'She was walking arm in arm with him.'

'What time was this?' Simon was making notes in his big open handwriting.

'About 11.30, but after so many years it is hard to be sure. It was a warm evening and I did not hurry home. I was all in a muddle with myself about not going to the dance. One part of me did wish to be there and yet... Anyway, I just wanted to walk around, to settle my thoughts.'

'Where did you see them?' asked Trinder.

'Crossing the humpy-backed bridge near the bottom station. The one over the railway.'

'That's the A41 crossing the L.N.W.R branch from Buckingham to Banbury Merton Street.' Simon chipped in, nodding confidently as he noted this down. Trinder gave him an odd look.

'Very good, constable. They were walking in the direction of Evenley Park, and none too steadily!' She gave a significant look at the two detectives. 'Both looked slightly worse for wear. Walking with arms around each other, and I am not sure who was supporting whom. I find it deplorable how people allow themselves to be rendered almost insensible by drink.'

Trinder was sitting bolt upright. 'Are you absolutely sure it was Miss Askew? There was a blackout and must have been very dark...'

'Quite sure. You cannot blackout a full moon, and young eyes soon adjust to the dark.'

'Eating carrots helps...'

Miss Snowball and Trinder both stared at the constable. He blushed.

'Indeed. And I can pre-empt your next question, sergeant: I have no idea who he was, except that he was American. He was in an airman's uniform, with a cap on the back of his head and had a thin black moustache and I think, slicked down hair. Quite rakish, if perhaps a little young – and on the short side.'

'Your description is excellent and most helpful,' Trinder checked that Howerth was noting it all down.

'I never forget a face. I recall thinking he looked Italian and found that odd.'

'Why?' asked Trinder.

'Because they were the enemy back then, I would have thought that obvious. Although I understand many Americans are actually Italians. Or is it the other way around? Anyway, it stuck in my mind at the time because the last song I heard them blasting out all over the town was 'Chiribiribin'. I always thought this an unpatriotic song whilst our boys were fighting the Italians.'

Trinder smiled. 'The Andrews Sisters with Glenn Miller. "When the moon hangs low in Napoli, there's a handsome gondolier..." I know it well!' He collected 78' records, especially the cuts by the big dance bands, and he gave her an approving look.

'The words were apposite.'

'I can see why you made the connection. Where were they going?'

'I did not follow them! That would be most improper and voyeuristic. But I suppose they were going into the park. There is a footpath at that end of the park and I've heard it is popular of an evening with couples.' She shifted her position in the chair, fiddled with her cardigan for a moment as if privately considering this fact before picking up the remains of the scone, from which she took a large bite. After making short work of this and wiping a crumb from her upper lip and her spirits revived, she grinned at Simon. 'Personally, I think the young Yank was quite in the mood for singing, "Say Si, SI." What do you think, constable?'

Chapter Twenty-Nine

On the Marylebone train
19th April 1950

Betty Askew had expected the train to be crowded. They always were; permanently rammed to bursting with servicemen and women going to places they were forbidden to identify, on trains that took forever as they crawled from one unnamed station to the next, the printed timetable rendered useless. However, there was a distinct advantage living close to the Great Central mainline as this particular route had few junctions and intersections along its run into London, and traversing the pretty, but sparsely populated countryside allowed the trains to keep moving at something like pre-war speeds. It should be a straight run in from now on she reflected. It could be worse.

The men standing shoulder to shoulder in the corridor smoking like chimneys were more than eager to help her squeeze past their kit bags, guns and other bulky equipment, past their hot and pungent bodies pressed unavoidably close, hands gleefully helping her along. These enthusiastic assistants helped her down two carriages until she was finally ensconced in a comfortable corner seat of what had in peacetime been a first class compartment. The young sailor snoozing in that particularly desirable seat had been rudely awakened and invited to give up his place in robustly unambiguous terms by a burly soldier, and so, despite her complaints that this was not necessary she was able to travel in relative comfort.

In truth, she was grateful for the chance to sit quietly, and by pulling her hat brim low she could hide more of her face and close her eyes behind the dark sunglasses. She was aware of the men in the corridor nudging each other and whispering comments they imagined she could not hear, whilst throwing appreciative glances in her direction, but she managed to shut this out.

There was no doubt she cut a memorable figure on her way down the train, but she banked on the passengers being out-of-towners and transported somewhere distant for the war. They would all be far way and it was unlikely any would recognise her and pass word back. Besides, if everything went well she could be home that same evening and no one need suspect a thing. If she had to stay over, then she would need a half-decent story to tell mother and father, and luckily, she had a willing accomplice to provide an alibi. Hopefully it would not come to that and Pearl would not need to say anything. She was young and fit so perhaps it would not knock her sideways too much and she could manage to get home the same day? She groaned silently and felt nauseous at the thought. Please God don't let it be so. Please make everything O.K...

But could she even get him to agree? Pearl had sounded confident when they'd talked last night, but she was only working from the tittle-tattle garnered from the domestics up at the big house. The servants over a period of time had gathered information from snatches of overheard conversations, enough to establish what had happened with Lady Finmere as a result of her clandestine liaisons with her lover at Tingewick Hall. It had been too scandalous a story for tongues not to wag and rumours to spread. And so, according to Pearl, details of the establishment their Lady had visited one weekend were leaked out.

Could she trust what she had been told? Pearl was insistent the information was reliable, and the address scribbled on the back of an envelope was correct. And Pearl had stressed the most important aspect, that the doctor was good; a competent man and not some dangerous back street operator armed with a dirty needle and a pint of gin. It was still a dreadful risk to arrive unannounced, but what else could she do? Telephoning was impossible, not only because the switchboard girls at the local exchange might recognise her voice and overhear everything, but the doctor would surely just put the receiver down, refusing to even speak to this unknown person.

Askew opened her voluminous bag and extracted a small purse. She checked she had her precious ration books, the new ten-bob note taken from her post office account and the handful of coins that represented the sum total of her savings, the coins lying alongside the cap badge Ray had given her last summer. Then, with beating heart, she looked at the little decorative wooden box. She turned it in her hands, taking in every curve and curlicue of the design, running her gloved finger over the edges and recalling how Ray had told her that one of these corners had stuck in his back, and that was how he had discovered the Cobra's Eye. She dearly hoped it would not be necessary to part with this, but she felt the need to take whatever bargaining tools she could muster. It was likely to be expensive, the extortionate cost ensuring absolute discretion.

She had left the note that usually lay inside the box at home. At least this would always be hers; written in Ray's neat handwriting it was perhaps more precious to her than the ring itself. The hard, cold diamond was lovely, but these few inked words were the closest thing she could get to what was left of their love, of their hopes and of their dreams.

Askew put the box away and snapped the purse shut. She'd betrayed his memory in exchange for a drunken romp on the wet grass in Evenley Park. And what about Mancini? What did she think about him? He'd been kind, almost caring in a nervous, fumbling, groping sort of way, and yet what did it all mean? It was little more than a desperate search for comfort and physical contact between two lonely people. She was unlikely to hear from Mancini again, although he'd parted from her in the early hours, his shirt wrongly buttoned up and the combed slickness of his hair tousled into something wilder and unkempt, promising over and over to write, to keep in touch.

But what was the use? Were they intending to become lovers – she did not think so, and besides, they did not have the luxury of time to even consider the idea. Words in a letter in her hands didn't mean he wasn't dead. By the time she read them he could be now more than burnt flesh and broken bones in a field over Germany. Ray was dead, and yet she'd received his last letter a full two weeks after the dreadful telegram, a painful time capsule he'd slipped into an envelope whilst seated on the edge of a narrow camp bed in a khaki coloured tent somewhere in a far distant desert, his sweaty hand causing the ink to smudge one of the words. It had sat unopened on her dressing table for days before she could bring herself to read his words of love and longing from beyond the grave. Perhaps that funny, wise-cracking Yankee rear gunner was already no more...

She didn't want or need another letter like Ray's. She couldn't even start to think if she cared, or even wanted to care, about Mancini. All she wanted was for the war to end and to lie in the comfort of someone's arms and to forget everything...

After taking a few moments to fight back the stinging salty tears, she turned to face the window, and partially concealed from prying eyes, she eased the diamond ring from beneath the neck of her dress and unfastened the chain. Slipping the ring off, she refastened the chain then removed the glove from her left hand and slid the ring into place. The morning sunlight set the stone afire as she held her hand near the grubby window. Askew stared into it, all thoughts of her surroundings momentarily forgotten as she drank in its beauty.

It was lovely, and yet, there was also something almost unsettling about it. Or was that simply because she was aware of its great value? It was not a comfortable ring to live with, at least not for a humble working girl who spent most of her day clambering over steam locomotives, and whenever she did wear it on her finger she felt dreadfully self-conscious. She felt that sensation now, as though she were sitting in the compartment naked and everyone was staring at her, but nobody saying anything; nobody acknowledging the fact, each sharing the lie and that was almost worse - just like the Emperor in his new clothes in that odd story she used to read as a child. One thing she could be sure of, the diamond was now inextricably linked with the violent death of Ray. As she stared into the stone's centre she tried to imagine what his last day may have been like, hardly daring to think about how his life might have ended in that burning tin can in a searing desert. It was nauseating, and all she could really pray for was that the end had been quick.

*　　*　　*　　*

Private Coulson stared through the narrow letterbox-shaped slit, the armoured cover of which was lifted and propped open. It acted like a sun visor but offered no relief to the unbearable heat. It was so hot he hardly knew where blood, skin, metal and the sweltering desert air met. Everything was far too hot, and the air he breathed whilst somehow sustaining him, offered no comfort, just tasting of diesel fuel and unwashed bodies, of stinking feet, overheated rubber tyres, sump oil and the bitter tang of steel. Deep inhalations or gentle sips of air made no difference, and experience told him the best thing to do was to sit as still as possible and try to slip into a semi trance-like state, shutting down his faculties to a level where he could almost forget the acute discomfort of the hard driver's seat, the intense claustrophobia of his position deep in the heart of the vehicle. He must try to ignore the sweat pooling at the base of his spine and his almost complete restriction of movement and vision. Just sit and wait and hope. Wait until captain Anderson told him to fire up the engine and drive, and only then, with a welcome breeze caused by their forward motion and with throttle under foot and the hard steering wheel clamped in his hands could he feel released, able to finally exert some control over his destiny, steering them away from this crushing boredom and into the wide spaces of the desert, bowling along in a deafening roar of engine with the wheels bucking and bouncing beneath him.

But that had been hours ago. He'd followed Anderson's instructions and parked the Humber in a slight depression that hopefully would prevent them being spotted from the ground. Anderson was now scanning the horizon using field glasses fixed to a bizarre periscope attachment that made it look as though he was swivelling a massively elongated pair of very tall and tubular ears, like some grotesque rabbit.

The captain broke the silence every so often, quietly feeding coordinates and cold facts about tank movements down to 'Bounder' Baker on the radio set, in turn repeating everything into the mouthpiece. Occasionally, the radio would crackle, and a distorted and disembodied voice could be heard. Otherwise, they maintained long periods of silence, punctuated by the odd dry cough, a rumbling tummy, a belch or a half-hearted comment that raised a murmured response.

They were men confined and pressed close, locked inside their cramped vehicle, pushed dangerously close to a front line that was now a pitched battle of staggeringly intense ferocity. The danger was palpable, and the usual humour and banter replaced by a quiet edginess.

Coulson stared at the narrow rectangle of sand dune and the equal measure of intense blue sky now increasingly stained by smudges of black oily smoke, and listened to the sounds outside, trying to identify the low murmuring rumble of heavy engines, the squeak and squeal of sand abraded metal on caterpillar tracks, the rapid whump! whump! of guns and the buzzing of aircraft engines. As the hours crept by these sounds grew ominously closer, the constant noise of gunfire prompted one or other of the crew to identify the probable source and type of artillery.

'That's an "88".'

'Yep. Close an' all...'

'There's a battery of them. Keeping up a steady rate.'

'Good guns those 88's. Jerry knows how to make a gun.'

'Worst luck.'

A droning note wavered above the relentless crump and bass boom of shellfire.

'What's that? Hurricane?'

'No, one of theirs.'

'Shit.'

The crump of intense shellfire continued, the buzzing aero engine drifting in and out of earshot.

'Moving away.'

'Thank fuck for that.'

Coulson nodded agreement and spat on to the bonnet, watching the spittle fizz and evaporate.

'Like sitting ducks. Let's hope they've not got much up. If one of them tank busting Fokkers comes over, we're done for. No chance.'

'Quiet down there!' Anderson's voice was not loud, but commanded obedience. The periscope squeaked on its mount as he swivelled it to one side. The radio fizzed with a blast of interference, causing the operator to pull off his headphones and curse, wiggling a damp finger in his ear.

Coulson licked his cracked lips, and for the hundredth time that morning focused his eyes on the little photographs above the windscreen slit. One showed her sunbathing, he was not sure where. It was a picture taken a few years ago, but she had cheekily written on the back that it might "give him something to dream about". She looked happy, and beautiful, and he could admire her lithe limbs and trace the faintest line where her breast was not completely covered by her one-piece suit. It was a lovely image.

And the one of Betty seated in the sun with outstretched legs and one of her favourite trains crossing the viaduct behind. She'd sent these snaps to him in her latest letter, telling him how she'd made prints of each picture they had taken on the Box Brownie in Boots the Chemist even though it had cost her an extortionate price and taken ages to get them done. He stared hard at the little image and tried to imagine himself back there, imagining stepping inside the tiny rectangle of blacks, greys and whites and lie beside her on the rug.

'Can still hear it.' Gunner Harrington's voice was a whisper, his desert booted foot and bare leg close to Coulson's face. 'Like a friggin' wasp.' He fiddled nervously with the breach on the armoured car's gun. It was useless against air attack, but it was all he had. It was their only line of defence; apart from the not especially thick armour plating that encased them. 'It's coming around. I'd swear it is!'

Coulson knew from when he'd taken the hit in the leg last year, that war when it struck, happened too fast to take in, and yet, conversely seemed to unfold in slow motion. It made no sense, and he could never properly explain this contradiction, but that was how it was. Too fast to know anything until it was too late, and yet there was still time to take stock, to see an edited newsreel version of one's life flash by. A final review...

As the aircraft engine screamed into a note that could only instil fear and terror, and as the cannon shells started to rip into the sand, he knew instinctively it was over. He would never get out in time and their vehicle could not protect them from a Focke-Wolf 190. Anderson was yelling 'bale! bale!', knowing their best chance was to lie prone in the sand some distance from the Humber, but even as legs were scrabbling for purchase, arms fighting to move in a space too tight to allow easy movement, unable to disengage from the clutches of gear lever and gun breach and any number of sharp angles, his friends were screaming, and something red was spraying onto the side of his face. There was the horrible sound of metal being wrenched apart, the Humber lifting bodily from the ground, the smell of cordite and burning flesh and petrol in his nostrils and an intense, completely overwhelming searing sensation that made even the desert sun feel cool. He was floating in the air, freed of this life, free of all earthly concerns, flames white hot and golden yellow and some even a searing blue from electrical sparks, all crowding around his head. He fixed his eyes on the little images of Betty that now curled, then cracked, as a bloom of brown appeared on her face from below the emulsion which then bust into a sunflower of flame and peeled apart in layers of slate grey dust.

*   *   *   *

She snapped out of her reverie by meeting the eyes of a young WAAF girl seated opposite. The uniformed woman was reflected by the strong sunlight in the carriage window and she grinned at Askew the moment she realised she'd been caught looking. 'Lucky girl!' The young woman's eyes flashed appreciation.

'I suppose so.' Askew mumbled the reply, not risking her voice cracking.

'Is he far away? Mine's in the Med somewhere. Naval officer. Can't say exactly, of course.' The young woman spoke softly, her voice kind.

'He's very far away. This is all I have now...'

'I know the feeling. A snapshot or two, a few letters, his cap badge and a bunch of memories, that's about the sum of it.' The WAAF gave a rueful smile, full of understanding. 'Not a lot really.'

'Not enough.'

'When will all this end?'

'It already has. For him.'

'My dear, I'm sorry...so sorry.' The WAAF looked genuinely apologetic.

Askew shook her head. No apology needed. Already her interest in the woman opposite was fading, replaced by the overwhelming fear that the price she might have to pay could be as steep as handing over the ring. Was she ready to do that? Not unless there was absolutely no other choice. She looked out of the window, signalling she wished to be left alone with her thoughts, and the WAAF seemed to take the hint.

It was painful being surrounded by so many men in uniform. It made it desperately hard to stop the flood of memories crowding in of the time spent with Ray; of their sunny picnic with he in his army fatigues, and of the woman pilot waving her hand to them lying below on the rug.

All the joshing and joking and banter of the men in the corridor as she had pushed her way through to her seat had reminded her of those even louder, crazier, wild nights at the dances, of the music and endless chatter and everyone acting as though this was their last night on earth, frantically cramming as much enjoyment as they could into a few short hours. It had been a collective madness, with strangers suddenly acting as though they were lovers. Catching the occasional twang of an American accent somewhere along the corridor, Askew felt a dart of remorse and turned her thoughts to Tony Mancini.

Askew pinched the bridge of her nose and held her fingers there, determined not to cry tears of shame or anger or regret for that young man. It surprised her to discover she was thinking about Tony, and wishing she could see him again. Was he even still alive? It seemed improbable. She had long since got over her initial anger about what they had done, realising in the enduring light of day they had both been culpable. She was guilty, just as much as he, and it was too simplistic to curse him for taking advantage. She had agreed to walk out of the dance, and she had agreed to going into the park.

To be brutally honest, she'd wanted him to take her. She'd wanted to lie in the damp grass and lose herself as he pulled her dress aside. She wanted to forget everything in a rush of pure pleasure, set herself free from worry, work, loss and longing and just live, and cry out in a moment of pure bliss when nothing else mattered…

It was the drink of course, and she had too little experience of rum and cola to handle it. God, how that song told the story! Drinking rum and cola whilst working for the Yankee dollar. Well, he'd certainly given her enough presents, so she supposed he deserved something in return. She must have gulped down glasses of the stuff with an abandon that shocked her now. She would never get drunk again. Never. Although as she laid her head against the musty seat cushion, she thought how a stiff brandy might steady her ragged nerves.

Askew caught the reflection of the diamond on in the glass. The ring had started it. Feeling shy and unenthusiastic about going to the dance, she'd made a point of wearing it, signalling loud and clear she was spoken for, that she was unavailable, and hoping and praying that Ray would – through some form of divine communication – realise that he was still in her thoughts every waking moment and understand that this was not a betrayal of his memory.

However, young men far from home and full of beer, and equally full of fear and apprehension, give scant regard to such signals. To Tony

Mancini and his pals it was like a homing beacon; drawing them towards her and the perfect excuse to fire questions from all sides; questions that grew ever more cheeky and bold as their confidence grew and the intake of alcohol increased.

Mancini had been in a group of especially loud and gregarious men, their accents strong and characterful. They swaggered and boasted and threw their money about and the pockets of their well-cut uniforms seemed to be filled with unlimited quantities of scented soap, cigarettes, Hershey bars, precious nylons and all manner of other desirables now impossibly scarce in a country rationed down to the bone.

Askew soon discovered this crowd were from various parts of New York State, and some were of Italian extraction, a heritage betrayed by skin tones noticeably warmer than the typical rain-leached British; Their hair was usually black and worn slicked to a shine with razor sharp partings, with moustaches pencil thin and eyes dark and liquid and full of vitality. They were a bit annoying, and buzzed around like flies and she had been angry the other girls encouraged them.

But these young men were undoubtedly exotic, and it was hard not to be intrigued. They spoke differently, and they quipped and joked at a speed she found hard to follow, but this also made them like something from a movie. Their quick-fire routines reminded her of Abbott and Costello, their witty and flippant repartee was not unlike talking with a Marx brother. It was all so bothering and bewildering, but oddly infectious, and so, encouraged by her friends who seemed to be lapping it up with little concern for where it might lead, she found herself relaxing and actually starting to enjoy the encounter.

'C'mon, babe, how 'bout we take a turn on the dance floor, huh?'

'I-I'm not sure...'

'Say, why not?'

'I think perhaps I had better not...'

'That dress looks like it was made for dancing...'

'I'm happy sitting.'

'Gee miss, but it's mighty remiss of me not to say how sweet you look. You look such a picture in that swell dress I could sit right down an' paint you!'

'I thought you wanted to dance?'

'I thought you'd never ask.' He held out his hand

She averted her eyes to check the hemline of her dress had not ridden up just as the band launched into a raucous rendition of 'Oh Johnny! Oh Johnny!'

'No kiddin' Miss Betty, you look swell and I'd go as far to say it accen-tu-ated those positives, n' what's the point of a positive if ya' don't accentuate it, huh?' He gave a cheeky grin as Askew blushed. 'C'mon, doll, put this guy outta his misery and jitterbug with me. You do know how to jitterbug?'

'I-I'm not sure. I like to dance of course, but this is all so new...'

'Sure you can, babe. Tony's got the moves...'

They danced for a couple of hours. She loved dancing and it had been a regret that she and Ray had only done so on two occasions and then only briefly. He was reluctant to take to the floor because he lacked confidence. A slow lurching sway around a half-deserted floor to a record poorly amplified through tatty speakers was about the best they had managed. But Mancini knew the moves and was only too happy to sweep and swirl her around the floor as best he could in the space available. The jitterbug was a whirl of adrenaline and raw excitement on the back of the driving beat of the live band, the drums pounding and bass strings throbbing, giving her little time to think about anything other than staying on her feet and leaving her hot and flushed when they stopped, and to her surprise, smiling like the Cheshire cat.

As The Squadronaires played 'Little Brown Jug', 'The Beer Barrel Polka', 'Youssel Youssel' and any number of other favourites with the Yankee hosts, they lost themselves in the strong rhythms and their own thrilling proximity, and sometimes his hands strayed across her bottom or brushed the side of her breast. It was excusable now all the couples had become pressed tightly together as more crowded onto the floor, the dancing now reduced to variations on a cramped intimate shuffle, during which it was hard not to be jostled and caressed and feel the hot eager lust of his body pressed hard against hers.

He'd walked her home as part of her equally loud and raucous group loosely formed into 'couples', although everyone was at excessive if slightly drunken pains to make clear that no such relationships had been established. Mary's escort held her tightly around the waist and pecked repeatedly at her neck, but she still maintained a noisy banter that encompassed the group, everyone laughing and giggling as a group and so preventing any attempts to lure one or other of the girls away for a more private encounter, although Pearl's lipstick had still become badly smeared by some enthusiastic snogging.

It was an evening of fun and nothing more. Askew had allowed Mancini a peck on either cheek, gently but firmly resisting his almost desperate plea for one on the lips. But his hands had still given her bottom an unambiguous exploratory squeeze, and as she stifled a cry of outraged complaint he turned and walked away, tipping his cap to the back of his head and waving the fingers of a hand over his shoulder.

'See ya around, doll!'

And despite the best efforts of her rapidly fading will power, she did see him again, at the second dance a week later. If she'd just left it at that and resisted temptation, all would have been well.

The Dirty Girls Brigade had rolled up as a group in even higher spirits than before. The thrill and excitement of the previous encounter had been enhanced by a week of washing with a new block of fragrant soap, enjoying the sugar rush of unrationed bars of sweet chocolate and developing a taste for smoking Lucky Strikes and Camels. With new stockings proudly worn beneath best frocks and extra care lavished on their hair and make-up, they were anticipating an evening as the centre of attention from these young and fit men. Men they discovered, who were both excessively polite and attentive and yet bold and freed by distance and a different culture from the excessive reserve that prevented the British from expressing what they really thought, stifling their interaction with women into awkward, stilted affairs. The Yankees were eager to make it clear they considered the women attractive and exciting and yet were polite to a fault. The air of unreality that seemed to permeate the dancehall made this contrast strangely appealing and acceptable.

Knowing the airmen were due to leave town the next day with no expectation of ever returning, lent the evening an even more reckless and carefree quality, and Askew had been unable to resist its infectious attraction.

She and Mancini had danced with gusto for over an hour, she now feeling more confident of the steps and making the most of the relatively-empty floor in the earlier part of the evening. She had fallen in love with the jitterbug if not with the young airman, unsure of when she might get another chance and wanted to make the most of the opportunity. Mancini was delighted to oblige.

The drinks flowed throughout and the presents he'd brought from the base swelled her hand bag to bursting, Mancini explaining that the base PX store gave him a generous allowance, so she could take it all without feeling bad. As the music took a quieter turn, giving aching feet a chance to rest whilst the pretty vocalist in her tailored army uniform with pencil skirt and cap set at an angle on her blonde curls sang a medley of softer, dreamier Vera Lynn numbers, they fell into talking. Leaning together across a battered card table covered with beer stained baize and a candle stub in a jam jar between them. It was not long before the conversation took on a more serious aspect, the realities of their situation impossible to keep at bay any longer.

'I heard you leave town tomorrow. Is that true?'

'Sure is, doll. Tomorrow, at seven, right on the dot.' He flipped an unlit cigarette into the air, catching it on his lower lip and making Askew smile. 'Two, three, mebbe four days later I'll be on my first run over Germany. Might be my first and my last.'

Askew stared at him as the statement sank in, then screwed her eyes closed for a second, the cigarette smoke that hung thick on the air making them sting. Mancini spread his hands wide, the cigarette now between two fingers. 'I can't fool myself no longer. Heck, I could be dead before the end of the week, and there ain't a whole lot either of us can do about it.'

'No! Don't you have escort fighters and guns to shoot back with?'

'Don't misunderstand me, I'll do my bit, and I plan on taking a few Jerry with me before I check out.' He took a deep swig of beer to ease a drying throat that was threatening to make him cough, his voice now quieter and more thoughtful. 'But I can only tell it like I see it, and things ain't lookin' too rosy right about now.' He popped the cigarette in his mouth, then placed a second beside it, flipping his lighter open and the flame flared between them as he lit each one in turn, Askew's eyes watery in the bright light flickering on their faces. 'See, I'm a tail-end Charlie, Miss Betty. You know what those goons are?' He handed her one of the Lucky Strikes.

She nodded silently, concentrating on inhaling the smoke. She'd heard this moniker, and she'd also heard the stories attached to the least desired position on a bomber plane. 'I think so,' her voice was barely audible.

'It's cos' I'm short, see? It's no job for the taller guys, so guess who gets the short straw, yours truly, little Tony Mancini! Yup, give the little wop the job.' He dropped his voice so low, Askew had to lean closer. 'You know what the percentages are for Charlies? I'm tellin' you, doll, it's worse for the dumb schmuck sitting at the back than the rest of the guys in the crate put together. Hell, we get it in the neck even if they get on home.'

She reached her hand out and grasped his. It was cold and clammy.

'It takes another man to strap me into that Perspex coffin. I can't even get or out on my own. Like a stupid baby, I can't even take a pee without their help. Sorry to be so crude an' all that, but you see what I'm sayin' Miss Betty?' He shook his head, smiling as if the idea was amusing. 'Then, I gotta hope my electric suit stays working or else I freeze to death – or, if the electric gets screwed up, then I fry. I heard it's like death row if the wiring goes nuts. Nice touch, eh?'

'Oh God, no...'

'But that's not all, doll. There's the oxygen line that runs halfway down the old crate that's busy bein' busted up by some Nazi in his Messerschmitt, so I gotta pray it stays in one piece or else I suffocate, and if that weren't enough, they prefer to shoot us up from the rear. So yours truly gets the full and undivided attention of every Goddam fighter over Germany.' He puffed smoke and bit his lower lip for a moment. 'If by some miracle I'm still in the land of the living but we have to bale out...' His eyes met hers, pupils wide and black the tall flame of his lighter reflecting on the glassy surface. 'Yeah, well... There ain't no baling out for a tail end Charlie. There ain't time enough to get me out.' He cut off the flame instantly and it fell dark between them. 'Puff!'

'Please don't say that.'

'Betty, you may be the very last woman I ever look at...'

'I can't bear to hear this...'

'I'd sure like it if...' He swallowed, his Adam's apple bobbing. 'If you'd let me kiss you. Just the once, y'understand? I mean a real kiss, one that counts, so I can take the touch an' feel of a pretty gal's lips with me into that dammed Boeing before I check out. I want to remember the smell of your hair against my face, instead of that stinking rubber mask.' Askew felt her heart almost stop. She hardly dared breathe, raw emotions screaming through her. 'Hell, Betty, I need to confess something, because I figure if I don't do it now it'll be too late: I've never kissed a girl before. Not really kissed, not like they do in the movies with my arms around your neck an'...'

'Shh... Stop. Let's take a walk. I need some quiet. The music is too loud and I've lost the will to dance.' She smiled. It was weak and hid a range of emotions, but it was still a smile. 'Just one kiss then. That's all.'

Chapter Thirty

Brackley Police Station
27th September 1950

'Who has an interest in Richard Irons being dead?' D.I.Bainbridge fired the question at Vignoles as he selected a slice of hot buttered toast from the plate between them. 'And do tuck in - they've been generous with the old roll in the gutter!'

'I'd say suspects are limited.' Vignoles was also munching hungrily, careful to not drip the hot butter Bainbridge was referring to in Army slang. 'Irons claimed he worked with Askew over this house breaking. It is possible, they've worked this before, though his amateurism seems to argue against that. We know is he made a hash job of the burglary and was caught. Perhaps Miss Askew wanted him out of the frame as he'd become a liability?'

'But why? He was let off without charge, so why not be thankful for a close shave and leave it at that? Why would Askew take the risk of being caught for his murder when at best all we can do is implicate her in aiding a house breaking? We've got nothing on her.'

'Beats me. It only makes sense if Irons discovered something else, something important. Perhaps he stumbled on it by accident...and it became imperative Askew kept him quiet.' Vignoles chewed this idea over along with his toast but looked thoroughly sceptical about his own hypothesis.

'Hard to imagine what? He only lifted a couple of gold coins before he was disturbed, but he could have found something else? It would have to be small. Easy to conceal.'

'Perhaps he saw something? He was there to read something, find some vital and valuable information, but once he passed this on, it got him killed?' Both men drank from their mugs of tea as they tried to imagine what could get a man killed by a young woman with a vicious dog. Neither looked inspired.

'What about Henry Askew?' asked Bainbridge after munching on his toast a while longer. 'He had a grievance with Irons.'

'He has to be a suspect,' Vignoles replied. 'His alibi is supported only by his wife and as she shares the same grievance, she is presumably capable of backing him up.' He puffed out his cheeks in a slow exhalation. 'I can imagine Henry Askew and Irons meeting and tempers flaring; perhaps things get out of control and a punch or two being thrown, but I'm struggling with the scenario we discovered. Let's not forget Henry Askew had to find a suitable dog from somewhere for the evening - and that's unlikely.'

'Agreed. And how did he contact Irons to arrange the meeting? It has to have been premeditated, and yet when and how did he do this? And why would Irons agree to see him alone and in a concealed location?' Bainbridge looked crestfallen.

Vignoles took another slice. It had been a long morning and he'd readily agreed to a late 'elevenses' and a chance to review the morning's events in the relative comfort of Brackley Police station on the Banbury Road. The toast was easing his hunger and the melted butter was surprisingly delicious. He was no nearer unlocking the puzzle of this death, but the toast was welcome. 'What do you know of Dr Melcombe?'

'Not much. A retired family GP, who's flown well below our radar. Keeps himself to himself and comfortably off, possibly more than just comfortable, thinking about his collecting hobby,' Bainbridge shrugged his shoulders and took a bite on a blackened edge with a satisfying crunch. 'But he was laid up in hospital when Irons was killed so that puts him out of the picture.'

'I want to know more about the doctor. Why was he so keen to let Irons off the hook? After such a traumatic experience most people want justice, whilst he prefers to jealously guard his privacy above seeing Irons punished. Why?'

'Some people just want a quiet life. Perhaps he thought there was no point in sending Irons to prison?'

'Perhaps. But it is a curious detail and it has to be explored.'

'Agreed. However, if he is just an innocent victim, that rather uses up our meagre stock of suspects.'

'Let's hope my men can find someone more promising.'

Sergeant Trinder together with PC Howerth, who had rushed down from Leicester to lend a hand, had been sent to interview Miss Snowball, the ticket clerk at Brackley Central and the last person to admit seeing Betty Askew in 1943. They were also tasked with speaking to Mr. Hancock the taxi driver, who seemed certain that Betty Askew was dead according to Irons' statement. Vignoles wanted the man to explain himself and he could be called in for more questioning if they deemed it necessary.

One thing was for certain, if this intriguing plot was to be unravelled, then more background information was needed and Vignoles had not wasted time setting further wheels in motion; PC Blencowe together with WPC's Benson and Lansdowne were tasked with tracing any evidence of a valuable solitaire diamond being sold in 1943; with identifying the organising committee of the dances Askew attended and if possible, the identity of the particular squadrons of the USAAF present on those nights. It was a long shot, but they might even hold a list of names of the men who attended. In the next day or so, they were also to speak with all of Betty's friends who had been at the same dances, Trinder having made a note of their names at the end of their interview with the Askews earlier that morning.

Vignoles might be feeling temporarily stumped, but the morning had been filled with activity, and whilst no lead had been uncovered, it was surely only a matter of time before they made a breakthrough. Admittedly, the wild dog hunt organised by Bainbridge had drawn a blank and the house to house visits around the streets surrounding St Peter's had not yielded anything promising, nor had an interview with the distraught vicar and his churchwardens, but it was still only a few hours since the discovery of the body.

However, Bainbridge was proving a useful sounding board. On the face of it, Askew appeared to have done a runner of her own free will, perhaps eloped overseas with an American serviceman. Her valuable ring could have funded their new life, and this lent credibility to the idea. There were problems however, the most obvious of which being that the airmen would have been shipped out of Brackley in 1943 to airbases in the east Midlands or East Anglia – and certainly not home to the States. Both men felt it unlikely she would try to follow him to one of these British airbases. This would be unusual for a young eighteen-year old to do, made harder by the restrictions and hardships of war. And surely someone would have recognised her during the long period of time before her beau was released from action to return home? It was implausible she had remained invisible throughout this time.

'Do you actually think Betty Askew came back from wherever she's been laying low?' asked Bainbridge.

'If so, then where is she? I've had officers and station staff up and down the line on the hunt, and we've had not a glimpse.'

'She just a figment of Iron's imagination?'

'Sergeant Trinder is convinced by Iron's insistence he'd met Askew. He believes Irons was genuinely shocked by that poster in the station waiting room – all of which makes little sense, other than lending credence to the idea the man was going doolally. Irons may have sounded convincing, but he could have been delusional? We cannot discount that idea, as nobody has come forward who saw them together, including two train guards who both insist Irons was alone. I just don't know.' Vignoles looked non-plussed. 'Dammit, Bainbridge I need to find this woman!'

'Assuming she exists.' Bainbridge gave a knowing look.

'I know. When a young woman has not been seen in eight years, the most likely reason, is because she's dead. That grim possibility does nothing to help me understand why Irons was killed!' Vignoles sat back in the battered old chair. He needed a break, something to take them beyond the impasse they were in.

The telephone rang, and Bainbridge answered it, his face changing by degrees through puzzlement into mild shock, then horror and finally into a more professional expression of intense concentration. After a fairly lengthy call, during which he fired off a succession of short questions but in the main listened to an urgent voice at the other end, he replaced the receiver and hung up. He whistled low and long before speaking, raising both eyebrows in an expression of surprise. 'There has been a most intriguing development. A rather disturbing one, and whilst I cannot say how it ties in with the death of Mr. Irons, it will interest you.'

'I heard you mention Dr Melcombe?'

'Correct. That was the Amersham police; there has been a gruesome discovery. It was reported on the afternoon of the 23rd, but only now have they made the connection to Melcombe.' Bainbridge formed his fingers into a steeple as they rested on the desk and tapped his fingertips together for a second or two. 'The severed head a young woman has been discovered in a wooden box buried in the garden of a private dwelling. The house has been identified as previously owned by Dr Melcombe. He once ran his surgery from the premises.'

'Good Lord.' Vignoles put his now empty coffee mug down. 'Any indication how long it has been there?'

'They waited for the PM report to offer guidance, as this date was vital. Dating is proving a challenge, but it could have been put there when the doctor was still in residence. He retired as a GP that summer, moving out in late July 1943.'

Vignoles put his pipe in his mouth and chewed the stem but remained silent. The date was intriguing, and his mind was whirring.

'However,' Bainbridge raised a hand as if to forestall any instant reaction from Vignoles. 'The decomposition rate is affected by being in a well-sealed box plus some other factors, so the best time they can offer is between 6-9 years - not accurate enough to let the current house owners off the hook either - and questions have been raised about them, apparently. It could be a ghastly coincidence and have no relevance, but the connection to our doctor is curious.'

'Almost as curious as Dr Melcombe insisting on dropping charges against a man found dead not far from the cottage hospital in which the good doctor is recuperating. Irons was found dead beside the grave of the soldier who was going to marry the woman who apparently urged Irons to break into the doctor's current residence.' Vignoles was lighting the pipe he had filled whilst Bainbridge was on the telephone, making puffs of aromatic smoke as he spoke. 'If all that were not curious enough, we're looking for a young woman placed on Amersham station. It was not enough to offer any meaningful leads at the time, but now I wonder?'

'We've been asked to make some enquiries about Dr Melcombe. See if he has more of that particular skeleton in his cupboard! Sorry, rather a bad joke.' Bainbridge apologised.

'Just the head was found? That lends a gruesome twist to what is already a dreadful discovery.'

'There are signs of acid burning to the teeth - and lime thrown over the skin.'

'Thereby destroying any chance of dental records helping identify her - presuming she had any – and instantly disfiguring the face in case it was discovered soon after burial. Someone has gone to great lengths to eradicate any identifying features. I suspect if we do find the body, the hands will be missing.'

'Really?'

'Separate all the body parts that aid identification and it makes our job almost impossible. I'm presuming Dr Melcombe is still in the cottage hospital?'

'I believe so. He was in poor shape.'

'It would be useful to keep him there, until tomorrow at least. I want to get down to Amersham immediately, then deal with the doctor when I return.'

'Constable!' Bainbridge stood up and called to the front desk. PC Dowd hurried into the office.

'Sir?'

'Get on to the cottage hospital and confirm that Dr Melcombe is still there, and constable, you know some of the staff there, I understand?'

'My aunt is a nurse, sir.'

'Good. It would serve everyone's best interests for the doctor to remain there until tomorrow or longer. He must *not* leave today, is that understood?'

'Very good, sir.'

'But use discretion. Nobody must know that we've had this conversation.'

'Very well, sir.'

'And make us some more coffee – but put some blasted grounds in this time - this was dishwater!'

Vignoles had been enjoying his pipe and thinking about the latest revelation during the exchange, and as PC Dowd was turning to leave he voiced his thoughts aloud to Bainbridge. 'Depending on where the hands were disposed, there is a remote chance of fingerprints. Where on earth might he have taken two severed hands? He could have thrown them almost anywhere, down a drain or into a river...'

Chapter Thirty

PC Dowd had stopped in his tracks and spun about, jaw dropped.

'What the Devil is it, constable? You look like you've had a fright!' Bainbridge gave Dowd an irritable look.

'Hands? Did you just mention a severed hand, sir?'

'A pair of them, to be precise. Why d'you ask?'

'I must apologise. It's because of all that's happened these last days: what with the body, the wild dog and so much out of the ordinary. Once I'd put the box under the desk it just went clean out of my mind and...'

'Pull yourself together, man! I hardly need remind you D.I Vignoles is in the room, so try not to make us look like a pack of fools. What are you wittering on about?' Bainbridge looked furious.

'Beg your pardon, sir. With permission, if you will allow me to retrieve the box in question it will make more sense. It's underneath that desk, on the floor...'

A few minutes later the three men were looking at the jumble of small bones now laid out on the desk, a variety of expressions on their faces. Bainbridge's was one of controlled fury, and in between darting looks of intense annoyance at the young constable he had taken to sighing loudly or pointedly muttering 'I don't believe this!' at regular intervals. The constable looked mortified, an appropriate expression under the circumstances. He had dug himself deep enough into a hole and could see no way of extricating himself.

Vignoles however, was nodding enthusiastically whilst peering at the bones, occasionally moving them around as he tried to recall his basic grounding in anatomy. If he felt anger or annoyance at Dowd's forgetfulness, he did not show it.

'We need some tests doing of course. These need expert analysis in conjunction with that head, but my instinct suggests we may have stumbled upon another part of that poor woman's body. This is an extraordinary breakthrough, and the timing is fortuitous. I am not sure what we would have made of this discovery a few days ago, but now we have a clear objective: establish if these are from the same body as the head in Amersham, and then establish if these are the remains of... Well, we just need to establish who this was.' Vignoles chose not to make too big a jump and name the woman as Betty Askew, though he knew Bainbridge was thinking the same.

Chapter Thirty-One

Amersham
19th April 1943

Askew stepped off the crowded train, out of the hot fug of cigarettes and sweaty army uniforms, of Brylcreem and cheap perfume and sooty railway carriage onto a narrow rectangle of sun flooding the gap between the shadow cast by the train and the long multi-gabled platform awning with the dog-tooth edging. She took a moment to inhale a few breaths of fresh Buckinghamshire air and enjoy the slight breeze caressing her face.

A wail of wolf whistles aimed in her direction heralded the train's departure, the whistling louder than that blown by the guard on his ACME 'Thunderer', and she bowed her head to send a diagonal band of shadow across her face from her hat brim. She wanted to keep a low profile, but these lads at the carriage windows whistling and blowing kisses were ensuring the opposite. Luckily there appeared to be almost nobody else on the platform and these men were off to far distant postings. The train groaned and squeaked into motion as she gratefully turned her back on the soldiers and walked briskly towards the exit.

She'd run through the drill enough times; walk confidently and look as though you know exactly where you are going, but with head lowered to avoid eye contact. Askew made it across the booking hall vestibule without problem but had to step aside to hold open one of two narrow entrance doors to allow an Air Raid Warden to wheel his bicycle through. His tin helmet was slung from the outside of his shoulder bag, and this bulk forced her to press herself flat to allow him past.

'Thank you, miss. Sorry to be a trouble, miss.' His eyes crinkled at the edges as he smiled, a long brown moustache turning up at the edges. 'Hope I didn't spoil that lovely dress with my dirty old bike?'

'No. You're welcome,' Askew dropped her eyes and instinctively pulled at the brim of her hat, the bracelet at her wrist sliding along her arm as she did so. The action was pointless as the warden had a perfectly clear view of her face.

'You'll need that in this sun. Keep the rays off that pretty little face of yours.' He eyed her appreciatively for a moment, until his expression took on a more serious aspect. 'But that won't be much use if there's a raid. You do have your gas mask?'

Askew had already turned to leave but was still holding the door wide with an extended arm, not wishing to let it swing back and collide with the wardens' bike. 'I-I have it here.' She patted the bulbous bag filled by her work clothes and boots, hoping this would satisfy him. She had long since abandoned the vile smelly mask, keeping it slung on a hook behind her bedroom door just like most others since the Blitz had ended. The threat of poison gas had faded and everyone had grown heartily sick of the things.

The warden gave her a long look, considering whether to challenge her assertion, but then nodded. 'All right, miss. Too many people are slacking these days; but you can't afford to dice with gas! It's for your own protection you know.'

Askew glanced over her shoulder with a little smile. Under other circumstances she would have happily talked for a moment or two to this man who just trying to be helpful, but she desperately didn't want anyone to recognise her. One could not be too careful.

She let a little Morris pass her with crudely painted panels of what looked like white distemper on its wings, then hurried across the open turning space in front of the station building and fell into step behind two young mothers pushing large prams with heavy shopping bags slung from the handles.

Askew had memorized the route after staring for some time at a map book in the W H Smith bookstore in Banbury the previous Saturday afternoon. It looked simple enough on paper. She just had to get her bearings. Along Station Road, but don't go under the railway bridge, instead keep going up to the big road junction to the right and where there should be a parade of shops. A mini convoy of delivery lorries and a depressingly grey 'Austerity' bus with filthy windows trundled across her path in a cloud of exhaust fumes, whilst a horse drawn meat van approached from the opposite direction, the horses' hooves clunking as the heavy metal shoes struck the ground in measured treads.

At the junction she knew not to bother to look for road signs to

Aylesbury or High Wycombe as they'd been taken down long ago to slow the progress of enemy invaders. Instead she must double back on herself down what would be Rectory Hill. This road also dipped under the railway, the abutments of the bridge heavily sandbagged and a small machine gun post created to one side by the Home Guard, although it was presently unmanned. The road followed a gentle descent to the river in the valley bottom and offered a charming glimpse of fields filled with ripening crops and hedgerows studded with trees on the distant valley side.

Askew now walked past a succession of large dwellings set in elegant gardens and backing onto a mass of broadleaved woodland. She should find Dr Melcombe's surgery close by, and if he took his patients from the sort of houses along Rectory Hill, they were going to be wealthy and more than able to pay his medical fees. Askew understood why Peal Cooper had warned her that he was going to expensive.

Dr Melcombe's house was a beautiful rambling Art and Crafts era construction set behind a walled garden and guarded by gracious wooden gates painted duck egg blue. These gates alone must have cost the equivalent of a railway cleaner's wages for a year. The house was all orangey-red brick and dark wooden beams with festoons of hops trailed across the front that were pruned to reveal diamond-paned windows. There were tall barley twist chimneys and a great roof swooping low in a gentle curve to extend over a side extension with an oaken door bearing a bright brass knocker and a polished plaque on the wall beside two windows veiled by startlingly white curtains that covered the lower two thirds of the glass. Askew guessed this was his surgery.

As she stood at the gate, a little car motored up the hill towards her driven by a woman in a nurses' uniform. Perhaps she even worked for the doctor? For some reason this felt like a problem, and Askew rummaged in her handbag and pulled out a compact to check her makeup. As the little car passed Askew gained a clear view of the woman in her blue cape. She made no reaction, and motored on and as the reflection of the car diminished in the circular mirror in her hand, Askew was surprised to discover she had been holding her breath. She flipped the compact closed and steeled her nerves.

All was quiet once inside the gates, the sound of the traffic passing on

Rectory Hill masked by the high perimeter wall and mature trees that rustled in the occasional puff of warm wind. What if he was not at home? She'd not considered that possibility and closed her eyes for a second praying that her journey was not wasted, then approached the door, shoes crunching on the honey coloured gravel. She lifted the huge brass doorknocker in the shape of a fox's head and banged it twice. The sound was heavy and resonant. Only then did she see the little sign made from cream Bakelite with black painted letters screwed to the door frame demanding that she:

Please ring.

Don't hit the fox.

Askew pressed the bell button as well, and as she waited, wondered why the doctor retained the highly polished knocker if not for use? She decided it was affectation, giving the right impression of an expensive country residence. Nothing happened however, and she stood on the step trembling with nerves and uncertain what to do. She jabbed her finger on the bell again, just as a voice boomed from behind the door, 'All right! All right! I can hear you!'

The door was flung wide and a florid face reddened by broken capillaries across the cheeks and a nose edging towards purple stared back at Askew, eyes suspicious behind his horn-rimmed glasses. 'I can hear the bloody bell, there's no need to bang on the blasted door...' He stopped 'And who the hell are you?'

'Dr Melcombe?'

'It's my name on the plaque,' he used his eyes to indicate the polished brass plate to one side. 'It's also my day off. I'm busy.'

Askew tried to make her voice steady. 'Doctor I so urgently need to see you. I've come a long way today... I-I know this is an awful imposition, but it's an emergency, at least I think it is an emerg...'

'Yes, this is an imposition. And you've got a darned cheek banging on my door like this. You need an appointment!' He peered at her, sizing up her clothes and handbag, her makeup, scanning her face. 'Do I know you?' Although still fierce there was a hint of doubt in his voice, eyes narrowing. 'If you do actually have an appointment, you have the date wrong.'

'No. I don't. I-I was given your name. In absolute confidence, you understand. I would never breathe a word to anyone, but I need your help...'

'You're not on my books, are you?' The doctor's eyes looked guarded. 'My God, you can't just roll up here making demands like this. Who gave you my name?'

'I'd rather not say...' Askew clasped her hands in supplication. 'I've been very discreet. Absolutely nobody knows I'm here. Nobody. Please, doctor...'

'What?' He swallowed and licked his lips. 'What are you blabbering on about?' Despite his anger, his voice lacked some of its earlier ferocity and he anxiously scanned the road beyond the entrance gates checking there was no one passing. 'Inside!'

He ushered her into an entrance vestibule that was cool and smelt slightly of surgical spirit and strongly of a great bunch of white lilies in a vase on a low table. He shut the door and stood facing Askew, arms folded across his chest. 'Now let me make this absolutely clear, nobody turns up here unannounced. I'm not some bloody charity for the poor. Who are you? Who sent you?'

'Betty Askew. You won't know me, or my friend Peal. She... she knows someone who's a maid in a big house near Tingewick, and it was this maid who told Pearl that...that the Lady of the house had the same problem I have, and you were kind enough to help.' Askew was burning with embarrassment but blurted it all out. It was said now. All she could do was hope.

'How dare you! You have a bloody cheek to come here and make this kind of appalling allegation. This is an absolute outrage.' But for all his bluster, he looked pale and uncomfortable. 'I am a respectable doctor, with some of the best names in this town on my books. I will not have my name besmirched by ill-formed malicious gossip!' His eyes remained cautious, calculating, continually sizing her up, studying her gloves, shoes and dress; trying to assess this strange thin woman who'd just turned up on his doorstep.

'I've told no one! Pearl would never say a word either, I promise! I have money...'

'Step in here,' Melcombe walked towards an open door and indicated that Askew should enter. It was an elegant office with expensive furniture, including a desk that looked antique and chairs to match. The limed oak floorboards were glossy with polish where not covered by a vast oriental rug. In one corner there was a hand basin and a set of folding screens and a narrow bed with a crisp white sheet. More white lilies scented the room.

He indicated that Askew sit on one of the two Sheraton chairs before his desk whilst he took his place on the other side, a scowl of intense disapproval on his face. He sat in silence for a moment, making Askew squirm. 'Who exactly is Pearl?' He spoke her name as if it were a particularly nasty medical condition.

'Pearl Cooper. She works with me at the loco... that's the Engine shed up at Woodford Halse. She's a loco cleaner, like me.'

'A cleaner in an engine shed? Do you mean to say you clean railway engines?' His voice was dripping with a mixture of contempt and surprise.

'Yes. To help with the war.'

He gave a snort that suggested the war was not a pressing matter in his life.

'Pearl is older than me, and I took her into my confidence. I told no one else. I swear on the Bible I have not breathed a word to anyone, not even to Ros or Susan, but Pearl knows about these things and she once told me how she...' Asked dropped her head and looked at her hands twining and untwining, 'how she had a problem, and got it fixed. I hoped she could help me, and then she mentioned your name.'

The doctor's face was impassive, but Askew noticed a slight tremor in his hands. 'You did not drive here I presume?'

'Of course not. I could never run a car on a cleaners wage.'

'You walked from the station?'

'Yes. But I was discreet. I even changed clothes from my work things into my Sunday best.' Askew tried to look him in the eye.

'You changed your clothes? Why would you do that?'

'I don't want anyone to know I'm here. It's a secret. Really, nobody knows.'

'I see.' He considered that a moment. 'And what exactly is this 'secret'?'

'That I'm pregnant.' She suddenly started to cry. Saying it aloud, the enormity of her situation overwhelmed her, the appalling consequences of what it could mean proved too much to stem the tears. 'It was just one night. He was a rear gunner... He was scared. I could see that, and I was also... and... we'd had a drink or two first. But I'm not like that...'

The doctor sighed heavily and reached for an opened box of paper tissues on the side of his desk, pushing it across towards Askew in an irritable movement. 'Here! Do stop snivelling. You deserve everything you get, and you won't find any sympathy from me, and certainly not by crying. I can't abide all this self-pity and false remorse.'

Askew blew her nose and composed herself.

'Now, you listen to me, young woman, I have a list of patients who are all very respectable people. Decent, intelligent folk who would be quite appalled by your carnal activities, and even more appalled by your scandalous assertion that I would have anything to do with you. We don't hold with this sort of lax moral behaviour around here. And I don't give the time of day to any common or garden shop girl or railway cleaner or whatever you are that feels like turning up like a bolt out of the blue!'

'But Pearl said Lady Finmere came to you when...' Askew stopped, realising she'd made a mistake in repeating the name, but her gaff also floored the doctor. He looked startled, pupils momentarily widening at the mention of Lady Finmere's name and it served to take the wind out of his sails. Silence fell for a few moments.

'I shall pretend I did not hear that. And I suggest you do not mention that fine woman's name ever again. Is that understood?' He leant forward and rested his forearms on the desk. 'I cannot imagine you would wish your name bandied about with no thought for whom might hear it?'

'No doctor. Sorry.' She blew her nose.

He gave a perfunctory nod, then sighed, wearily. 'You are pregnant?'

'I think so. Actually, I'm not sure...'

'How long?'

'A few weeks, seven...'

The doctor nodded again, 'so you won't show. You don't exactly look pregnant I must say.' He put his head to one side, a more curious expression on his face, now more that of the medical professional assessing a patient, than the irritable man disturbed on his day off. 'You've put a lot of effort into coming here. A day off work, I presume?'

'Pearl said she'd book me off sick. I won't be paid of course. It's a hard loss, as we don't earn much.'

'I charge for a consultation, and my fees are beyond the pay of an engine cleaner.'

'I have money!' Askew scrabbled with her large cumbersome bag, hands shaking, finding her purse and opening it. 'Everything I have. It's not so much, but it's every penny...'

Melcombe raised an eyebrow but did not bother to look closely at the opened purse. It was instantly obvious her funds were meagre.

'Please, doctor! I'm desperate... I have my ration books. Take those, I can say I had them stolen.'

'My, you are desperate.' He gave her an impassive stare, though Askew could see he appeared to be weighing something up, trying to make a judgement between options that were equally unappealing. 'Listen, this is all I can do. I shall check you over and tell you for certain yeah or nay. That way, you will at least know. Then you will leave and never come back, and you will not mention this visit to anyone. It never happened.'

'I swear! No-one knows I'm here. Except Pearl...'

'She can keep her trap shut as well.' Melcombe's voice became haughty and heavy with disdain. 'Any doctor with a modicum of humanity would do the same for a young woman in obvious distress, and of course, if I find you are indeed with child, then as a respected pillar of society I shall recommend that you marry the young man in question as quickly as possible and try to live a far more decent life than you've managed so far.'

'But he's been posted away. That's not possible. He might be.... He's a tail-end Charlie. They don't last long.' Askew felt tears welling again, although she was not sure if this was specifically in fear for Mancini or her own situation.

'Perhaps you should have thought of that before you took your knickers off?' His words cut like a knife. 'I think your funds might just run as far as a check-up - and a further word of advice.' He narrowed his eyes, his voice now low and surprisingly menacing, 'I should warn you I don't like the way you came here, and I like even less your implications that I might be prepared to undertake an illegal operation. If I hear you breathe a word about this visit, or anything about any of my patients, I shall press charges. I have excellent legal representation and can wipe the floor of you. Take great care young lady.'

Askew said nothing, just nodded assent.

'Go behind the screen.' He stood up and moved from behind the desk. 'Remove your undergarments and lift you dress, then lie on the bed. My nurse has the day off, so you're going to have to make do with just me. But that's the risk you've chosen to take.' He gave a cool smile that was anything but reassuring as he walked to the sink.

A few minutes later and Askew was struggling to make a small readjustment to her stockings, face burning with shame, hands fumbling as she tried to get a shoe into place that was refusing to behave. Dr Melcombe now sat on the edge of his desk, arms folded looking down at Askew, calmly observing as she tried to put herself in order, almost enjoying her discomfort.

'It would appear your fears were completely unfounded. It was an unnecessary trip – and expense. The God's are clearly smiling on you, as I can assure you are not pregnant.'

'Really? Oh, thank God! Oh, but thank you so much!' She looked up at him, tears welling in her eyes, a broad smile finally lighting up her face, the weeks of apprehension falling away in a moment. 'That is just the very best news. But I missed my period...'

'Nerves, apprehension... It happens all the time. It's not so very unusual.' Melcombe was watching the diamond flash on her finger as he spoke, now sounding distracted. Askew was pressing her hands to her face as she tried to stem the flow of tears. He had not noticed this incredible ring until now, Askew having worn gloves until prior to the examination. His eyes took on a hungry glint behind the lenses of his spectacles. He waved her continued thanks away with a hand. He cared nothing for her or her feelings, nor even for the young, lithe and healthy body he had so recently explored in the most intimate way.

'That really is a very pretty ring you have.'

Askew pulled her hands from her face and instinctively looked at her fingers caught by a shaft of sunlight and making the Cobra's Eye burn bright, but she remained silent, feeling a sudden strong flood of emotion well up; the memories of kissing Ray and lying on the blanket on the grass assaulting her so vividly she could almost smell the grass and his aftershave and hear the drone of a bee on a clover flower...

'It is really astoundingly good for paste. I had no idea they'd got so good at it.'

'But it's a real diamond!' Her face beamed. She was still transported back to that magical stolen moment near Helmdon viaduct. 'I thought the same when Ray gave it to me, I just could not believe it was real and so valuable...' She froze. Had that been a mistake? She was giving too much away. There was something about the look in the doctor's eye she didn't quite like. Askew hurriedly dropped her hand and stood up, smoothing her clothes.

'Impossible! A stone like that would cost a small fortune.'

'Well I-I'm not sure... maybe it's not? My fiancé said it was, but he was just being kind. He wanted to make me feel good.' She gave a nervous laugh. 'I think it is paste, as you say.'

Melcombe reached forward and seized her hand. 'Let me have a closer look. I know something about gem stones.'

'Let go of me!'

'Now let's not be silly. I'm a doctor...' the lenses of his spectacles reflected the pale light flooding the floor, transforming them into two pale moons, his mouth a thin-lipped leer below, his clammy hand gripping her like a clamp. 'I just want a closer look, nothing more my dear.'

'How dare you? Let go of me now!' Askew wrenched her hand free, her strength far more than Melcombe had expected and a consequence of her physically demanding job.

Melcombe gave a little nod, as if her actions confirmed something. 'I cannot imagine how your fiancé came upon such a ring through legitimate means – he probably stole it!' His voice was confident and self-assured, arrogant.

'How dare you!'

Melcombe stared at Askew for a moment, the stillness filled by the sonorous chime of a clock ringing the hour somewhere in the great house. 'Upon reflection, I think the ring will answer perfectly as a fitting payment for services rendered.'

'But you said my money was sufficient? It was just an examination...' Askew darted a hand forward and picked up her purse. 'Take this, please! That was the arrangement...'

'I did say my fees were high, and I do not recall agreeing a specific sum?'

He gave a sneering smile. 'This...' he flicked at the ten-shilling note Askew was proffering, with the back of his fingers in a gesture of smug contempt. 'This is but pin money. No, the ring will do very nicely. I really would like it, my dear.' There was something almost desperate in his voice. 'I do want the ring. Just hand it over, and we are done.'

Chapter Thirty-Two

Woodford Halse
27th September 1950

Whilst Vignoles and Tinder were travelling to Amersham to investigate the discovery in the garden, DC Simon Howerth (much to his delight) was sent back down the line to Woodford to rendezvous with WPC Jane Benson, who had spent the morning tracking down the whereabouts of Betty Askew's work colleagues and friends.

The 'Dirty Girls Brigade' over the intervening years had broken up as a band of engine cleaners, but most of the women had stayed in touch and none had moved far. Conveniently, two were still employed on the railway within the noxious surroundings of the 'loco'.

Mary Bennett had made the grade as a fitter – the last of her sex to stay within what was now an almost exclusively masculine world of the locomotive running shed following the mass dismissals of the women in the years after war ended. Susan Gibson was sewing tarpaulin covers for open wagons in the adjacent wagon shop, having been replaced as a riveter's mate by a surely ex-Marine back from the Far East. It was cooler work, and Gibson no longer suffered the stress of being on the receiving end of a heavy hammer pounded against the red-hot rivets she held in place with massive tongs, but the canvases were still extremely heavy and she looked sinewy and strong, with biceps bulging below the rolled up sleeves of her shirt, her nails cropped short and dirty, her hands calloused and lined by the continual handling of the coarse material.

Both women were now seated on a rickety bench along the outside wall of the running shed, Benson offered the relative comfort of a beaten-up wooden chair, the young constable forced to risk his uniform on an upturned oil barrel and a piece of sacking to prevent the worst of it staining his trousers.

There was soft grey and white ash all over the ground mingled with fragments of coal and clinker, in places this was congealed into sludge or formed opaque pools of spilt oil and water. The air was heavy with coal smoke and a light breeze was whipping little scurries of dust across this dead landscape, lifting the soft ash from the edge of the inspection pit that lay like an open grave beneath the wheels of a big Thompson '01' eight wheeled freight locomotive. From the other side of the blackened brick shed wall a hammer rang out in a sonorous rhythm as one of Bennett's fellow fitters beat seven bells out of something. The hammer bouncing in two lighter strokes after the initial impact, Dong, ding ding... Dong, ding ding...

'How could we forget her going? It was awful. We couldn't understand it. Still can't, really.'

'That's right Mary. It was so out of character. I suppose something dreadful must have happened, not that you want to think like that of course, but you have to be realistic. Have you any news?' Gibson gave Benson an anxious look. 'There has to be a reason for stirring things up after so long.'

'We can't say much at this stage, but there have been developments. I just want you to ask you about the days before she vanished. How Miss Askew seemed to you? Who was the last person to see her?'

Dong, ding ding...

'Last to see her? Now that would be Pearl. God rest her soul.'

'Was she part of the group working here as cleaners?' asked Benson, quickly looking at the list of names she had made in her notebook.

Dong, ding ding... Dong, ding ding... The relentless hammering continued.

'That's right. Peal Cooper. Life and soul of the party she was! She always got us working and laughing together, you know, to help make the working day pass that bit quicker. She could gee us up no matter what.' Bennett stopped, breaking into a fit of coughing, interspersed with attempting to inhale cigarette smoke. 'She's dead now, of course.'

The hammering stopped with accidentally dramatic timing.

'Dead?'

'That's one of the other weird things about it.' Gibson took up the story as Bennett finished coughing. 'Betty goes missing and the very night before, Peal was out on the town in Banbury and got hit by a lorry. Run over on the street due to the blackout. Driver couldn't see her.'

'But Peal was the last of us to spend time with Betty. That's what we reckon anyway,' continued Bennett. 'They went off together straight after work for a drink in the White Hart. I remember that.'

'Was that unusual?' Benson asked, hurriedly trying to readjust to this unexpected discovery.

'Maybe. I mean we quite often had the odd drink after. It's thirsty work in this place, you see. Though mid-week it was usually just a cuppa in one of the cafés, as we've all got to get back and get the supper on the table, then get the laundry ironed and all the mending done. We can't sit around drinking all nights, worst luck! But Betty and Pearl were perhaps not the most likely paring – not without others there too.' Bennett shrugged her shoulders. 'I don't know, but why not? Am I trying to find something that's not there to find? Anyway, next thing we know, we get the news Pearl's been run over.'

'I don't think we clocked Betty was missing until about lunchtime, as it was only then it hit us she was absent. We were so cut up about Pearl, I suppose we just didn't take everything in.' Gibson added.

'I knew Betty had been with her that evening and thought she was at the hospital, or consoling Mickey – that's Pearl's old man. I was thinking maybe she had been with Pearl in Banbury.' Bennett placed a booted foot on a locomotive brake block and rested her elbow on her crooked knee. 'I've often wondered about that.'

'Wondered about what?' asked Benson.

'You know, how the one died and the other vanished at almost the same time. Strange?'

'We believe Askew left Brackley on the morning of 19th April 1943. That might be some time after Pearl Cooper died however. Do you know of a connection between these events?' Benson added.

'No. No connection as I ever heard of,' Gibson shook her head and looked at Bennett who agreed.

'Pearl's death was fully investigated I assume?' Simon Howerth chipped in a question.

Gibson leant back against the grubby brick wall of the shed and gave Howerth a weary look. 'Oh yes. From what I understood the man driving the truck was very shaken up about what happened. Claimed he never saw her until too late. No one doubted his word.'

'It happened all too frequently. The blackout was a menace.' Benson gave what she hoped was a sympathetic look. 'We can follow this up.' She glanced across at Simon, who made a note. 'The last person to speak with Betty, outside of her home, was killed later that night. That is frustrating. Do you have any idea what Betty and Pearl could have been talking about?' Benson knew she was sounding almost desperate.

Bennett drew thoughtfully upon her cigarette and gave Gibson a sidelong glance, as if seeking approval. 'Look, we don't know for sure, and stirring stuff up is not nice. Especially after so long and about someone who's no longer with us, but we've often wondered if Pearl was offering Betty some advice. On the quiet, like.'

'What sort of advice?' Benson was curious.

'Let's say that Pearl was quite a character. Lived her life to the full, and then some!' Bennett laughed and then coughed with the effort. 'Let's just say that she enjoyed the company of men, and not exclusively of Mickey.'

'He was a complete waste of space, anyway.'

'Matter of opinion, but I can't say I had much time for him either. No matter. So she'd... Lord forgive me saying this, she'd gone around the houses. Know what I mean?'

Simon was grinning. Benson, however looked serious.

'I heard Pearl had got herself in the family way. It was a while back now, before the war started. But no thanks to hubby, Ha! She had to get rid, to hide the fact.' Bennett gave Benson a wink. 'On the sly, and we've all heard how bad than can be. Go and see some old biddy living in the back of beyond, and God knows what she'll do to you, ugh!'

The young constable's face changed into one of pain as he considered this image.

'Yeah!' Gibson pointed at him. 'Just you remember that young man when you've got your sweetheart's drawers off!' Bennett and Gibson both laughed raucously, enjoying the look of acute discomfort on his face.

When their mirth and fits of inevitable coughing died down, Bennett continued. 'The point is, she had experience and was willing to share it and help others. I know some of the younger girls asked her about how to avoid getting in the family way. And she was not averse to passing on a few tips about keeping their men happy in bed as well!'

'Especially after she'd had a few glasses of port, Lord bless her!'

'And you think Betty might have spoken with Pearl about something like this?' Benson suggested.

'Betty was young and inexperienced. I'm not sure she and her Ray ever did it. You know?' Gibson gave Simon a cheeky look. 'Keeping herself for the wedding night and all that. A very traditional sort of girl. But she was starting to get into the swing of things a bit more when the Yanks came over. She was seeing one of them. Let's be honest – and don't write this down – we all had our little moments.' Gibson gave Benson a challenging look. 'Don't look at me like that, there was a war on...'

'We're not here to be judgmental, just to establish facts.'

'Were you there when she met the American? We've heard that the 'Dirty Girls Brigade' went to some dances in Brackley as a group.' Simon decided it was time he tried to act the role of constable and regain some composure as he formed the question.

'We were. We had such a time of it, didn't we Sue? Betty was with Tony, I think?'

'Tony Mancini. I'm good with names. I wondered at the time if he had anything to do with her disappearing.'

'And did he?' asked Simon.

'You tell us, young man. You're supposed to be the detectives!' He squirmed. 'Listen, my old man did a bit of asking around at the time, and the poor blighter bought it on his second run over Germany. Raid on Hamburg. Dead and gone before Betty vanished.'

'Not much more than a kid. Loud and full of himself like all of them – but he danced well. Treated her alright, I reckon; gave her lots of presents, but then they all did.'

'That's not all he gave her!' Bennett flipped her cigarette butt away to land on a pool of water where it smoked for a moment. 'Be honest, we were happy to enter into a bit of give and take for a few pairs of nylons, some fags and a good night out!'

'Speak for yourself!' Gibson laughed raucously. 'Anyway, they went to the park together. I know that, as I was there as well behind my own tree...' Gibson put a hand to her mouth. 'Look, you won't go telling everyone all this? Folks don't need to know. Not now. It's history. Most of us have got our lives back to something like normal and settled down. But we liked a man in uniform and our lads were away for years. Men like a girl in uniform for that matter,' Gibson gave Benson a knowing look, glancing across at the DC on the oil drum. 'As I'm sure you've noticed!'

Simon could not resist giving Benson a surreptitious admiring glance, silently agreeing that his colleague suited the black uniform with its silver buttons surprisingly well. Aware of becoming the unwanted focus of attention, Benson fired off another question. 'And Betty, what was she like?'

'She was a sweet thing. Kindly and genuine. She was so cut up over losing her Raymond. Went into a right glump for a month or two. But we snapped her out of it and took her out. I just think she might have got herself a bit carried away and not taken enough care in the heat of the moment. It's just a hunch, but Peal knew everyone and anyone and could sort things out. Perhaps she knew somewhere Betty could go? You know...? I'm only saying, mind – we're as stumped as anyone.'

Chapter Thirty-Three

Amersham
27th September 1950

On the short journey south to Amersham, Vignoles brought Trinder up to date about the discovery of the woman's head and the bones of a hand then questioned his sergeant about his morning's work. Vignoles was satisfied with the progress being made.

'Miss Snowball's account is interesting. She appears to confirm what Askew's parents said, that Betty met a man, and then a month or so afterwards goes missing.'

'And planned to head south, probably towards London, deliberately duping her parents and her friends about her real intentions.' Trinder looked pleased with himself, as he studied the notes PC Howerth had made of their interview with the ticket clerk. 'Looks like she was planning to run away then?'

'Planning on something she wanted to keep quiet.' Vignoles was settled in the corner seat of the compartment, one leg crossed over the over, pipe in full steam. 'We don't know much about this young woman and we need to spend more time trying to understand her. But even with the little we do know, I'm not getting the feeling she's the kind of gal who would do a bunk. Surely she would confide in at least one girl friend about such a momentous decision?'

'But she was going for a clandestine meeting of some description.'

'Yes, John, you're right. It was a rendezvous, and a pre-planned one because she took a few overnight things and her engagement ring complete with the little box - if we choose to believe her parents on that point.'

'And do we?' Trinder asked.

'On balance, I think so. At least in as much as I feel they had nothing to do with her disappearance, though I sense there is something left unsaid, something lurking in that house they don't want to admit. I would like to speak to Mrs Askew without her husband present. I think she knows more than she was willing to say in front of him.'

'She's covering for her husband?'

'I think not. At least as far as the murder of Irons goes, Mr. Askew is no more than a very long odds bet for the killer. But what about the cabbie? Any joy?'

Trinder flipped through his notebook. 'Not a lot. Mr. Hancock is a cocky bugger and thinks he runs the place and has an opinion on everyone and everything. At first I thought we'd really struck the jackpot, but after a while I realised half of what he was saying is just hearsay mixed with arrogant bluster. Teasing out the facts from his fiction won't be easy.'

'Hit me with some facts you think might hold up.'

'His assertion that Miss Askew is dead is not based on his knowing one way or another. It's common belief around town that she's met with a sad end, and he's taken this to be a fact. He's a good friend of Henry Askew. Claims he drove the poor man around in his cab for weeks searching for her. Used all the petrol coupons they could beg, steal or borrow and scoured every village and town asking after her. This part rings true.'

'We can check if we need to. That is why he took Betty's disappearance to heart and reacted badly to Irons claiming he'd met her?'

'That's the feeling I got, sir. It would explain his outburst. Both Dennis Hancock and Henry Askew are long resigned to the fact she's not coming back, and he takes it as an affront to suggest she's riding our railway line and not lying in a shallow grave, despite the fact he wishes she were alive.'

'This gruesome discovery in Amersham just might prove his suspicions correct. Does Hancock have an alibi for the night Irons was killed?'

'He does. I've got the Howerth lad checking it out, but it would appear strong; a fare to collect in Banbury – Brigadier Manton who is a regular, wanted collecting from a dinner engagement. Hancock left Brackley Central at about eleven twenty to drive to Banbury, but on the way back had a blow out in Farthinghoe. Took him a while to change the wheel, then it was over to Sulgrave to drop the Brigadier off. He went straight home after to join his wife.'

Vignoles nodded assent 'I can't see him doing all that and still have time to bump off Irons or even to collect Henry Askew, so he might do the deed. Does the cabbie own a dog?'

'He says his wife has a little Yorkie. I could send Howerth to check the it out?'

'No. We can forget the cabbie as the killer.'

Their train was slowing and came to halt. The window next to Vignoles was filled by the maroon shape of a humming electric loc omotive named Sarah Siddons that made odd little clicking sounds, as if Miss Siddons was clucking her tongue in annoyance at something. The presence of this electrical box of tricks confirmed they were in Amersham, the farthest outreach of the electric Metropolitan line that had given these leafy and distant outreaches of London's suburbia the name of 'Metroland'.

* * * *

'Look here, this is an absolute intrusion into our lives, that's what it is!' Jocelyn Liney's temper had not improved. 'Another bunch of detectives. Why the Hell do we need any more of you, for God's sake?' He squinted at Vignoles, face pale and florid in turns. 'And I have as little to do with British-bloody-Railways as I can; sitting in an over-stuffed train to and from work is my limit, so I really don't see why you of all people are here trampling your clumping great feet over our carpets.'

Vignoles remained impassive during this outburst but observed the expensive carpet in question and the other accoutrements of a conspicuously wealthy lifestyle, the air smelling of elegantly arranged cut flowers in extravagant vases that could be Lalique, and of the Ronuk furniture polish used recently and liberally, by the maid who had answered the door. It was a house that actually smelt of money. Anna and he were unlikely to afford even a sofa like the one he was standing beside, let alone the room it sat within. But there again, they didn't have a dismembered head buried in the garden and a dining table laid out with the charred fragments of a dead woman's life.

'Have you heard of Elizabeth Askew? Betty, to her friends.'

'Never. No idea who she is.'

'Can I ask you and your wife to look at this photograph. Do you recognise her?'

Liney shook his head decisively, 'Sorry, you're asking the wrong man. Never set eyes on her. Here...' He handed the print to his wife who was sitting very stiffly on an upright chair beside the fireplace and staring morosely at the floor. 'Ever seen this funny looking specimen?'

'No. I have not.' Mrs Liney gave the photograph a look that suggested it was dirty and soiled. She refused to touch it. 'This... this outrage, clearly happened before we moved in. It has nothing to do with us.'

Vignoles made a movement with his mouth that implied he might agree. 'Mr Liney, you discovered some items of clothing when you were working in the garden. What were they?'

'Just rubbish. Burnt bits of fabric.'

'A piece of a dress was mentioned in your statement,' Trinder spoke up.

Liney shrugged. 'I suppose so. It was just a bit of green fabric. Was it a dress?'

'It was, you could see the neckline. And an orange bracelet. And a piece of leather strap and a buckle.' Mrs Liney's voice was flat and lifeless. 'I recall I was annoyed they had destroyed a leather bag.'

'They?' Trinder asked.

'They, he, she...I have no idea. Just a turn of phrase.' Mrs Liney looked flustered.

'You burnt these items and threw the metal parts away? Why did you do that?' Trinder continued.

'It was junk! Clogging up the garden. I didn't know they were important, why on earth should I? Do you preserve every little thing you find on the ground in case it might be evidence of a crime you know nothing about?'

Vignoles nodded slightly, it was not an unreasonable observation. 'When the head was discovered, you were initially reluctant to call the police?'

'I was? I don't remember. I was in shock I suppose. My wife had just fainted and was in some distress. I can't say I was feeling exactly chipper myself!' Liney mopped his brow with a handkerchief. 'For Heaven's sake, I was hardly thinking straight. What are you supposed to think when you see something like that?'

'The bird bath was in that location when you bought the house from Doctor Melcombe?' asked Trinder.

'Yes. We'd not touched that border since we moved in.'

'What can you tell us about the doctor? Did you meet him?'.

'Not much. We were taken around the house by the estate agent on a day the doctor was not at home. My solicitor then made the arrangements and I only met the man once, a little later the same month, and then only briefly. He seemed old for his years – that's possibly why he sold up and retired to the country. Failing health or something. He was well spoken and polite. Look, I really think you should be questioning him, not us.'

'And what did the neighbours have to say about the doctor?' Vignoles asked.

Mrs Liney answered. 'We do like to talk, and one gets a sense of how people are perceived, but they didn't say very much. That he lived alone and never married – of course one speculates, but nobody actually knows his private affairs. However, they seemed to quite like him despite being a loner, and all expressed sadness that he retired and left so suddenly. Sold up in a matter of months. It was completely unexpected. I can't see why they felt so kindly towards such a monster. It's disgusting.'

'Did any of your neighbours mention the doctor having a young girlfriend?' Trinder asked.

'No, they did not.' Mrs Liney smoothed her skirt and fiddled with her cardigan.

'You moved during the war,' Vignoles asked Mr. Liney. 'From where - and why?'

'Life did carry on for most of us, you know? The war was a blasted nuisance, but one could still function pretty normally. The house was on the market for a good price and I'd just secured a promotion.' His voice converted his sense of wounded outrage into something approaching smugness. 'So we took the opportunity to take on a place more to our liking. We'd been roughing it in a smaller villa on the edge of town until then.'

'You were not in the services, I understand?' Trinder's look was impassive, but the implied criticism hung in the air.

'Peace or war, someone has to look after the money, sergeant. Wars are expensive and without the likes of us working our guts out balancing the books, I'd like to know who'd pay for it?' Liney parried the observation robustly.

'Some might question if you succeeded? Life is stretched pretty thin even now – for most of us.' Trinder gave a little smile.

'The devaluation of sterling was a measure forced upon us due to circumstances quite outside of our control. If the United States had not reneged on the Lend Lease Agreement then...'

'Thank you. Most helpful.' Vignoles called the sparring to a halt. 'We shall be in touch if we need any further assistance...' Vignoles gave a perfunctory smile that made it clear he expected the couple to leave the room so he and Trinder could inspect the items carefully laid out in readiness of their visit. A uniformed constable held the door open for the Lineys, another stood guard beside the table.

The items had all been recovered by the Buckinghamshire County Police who had done an excellent job of ripping out every shrub and flower from the extensive borders in the once lovely garden, turning it from an elegant oasis of calm filled with colour and loud with insects, into something more akin to the Western Front after a preliminary mortar attack.

'Piece of a ration book. All that's left is the end of an address. This could be "ley" - as in "Brackley"?' Trinder queried.

'Possibly.' Vignoles peered at the scorched paper. 'And this could be a fragment of blue overall. Miss Askew wore overalls like these?'

'Yes. Her father mentioned her wearing them. Pretty standard kit on the railway. Liney said they originally found a bit of green dress as well, and we know she wore green the day she left. Ah, and here's a cap badge.' Trinder picked up the smoke tarnished cap badge and considered it for a moment. 'Was her fiancé a desert rat?'

'Private Coulson?' Vignoles looked across at Trinder held it up. 'That's the 7th Armoured Division insignia, and he was killed in El Alamein. A keepsake? Do you know, the PX stores must have despaired at how many of these were given away by men to their girlfriends - and they all needed replacing pronto, before the next parade.'

'It stacks up. Surely these must be Miss Askew's things. And so that was her - in the box.'

'It is looking that way.' Vignoles sighed wearily. It was not unexpected, but it still felt like he'd been sandbagged. There was a lot of forensic work to be done before they could say for certain, but already Vignoles was anticipating having to break the news to Henry and Maud. 'She had this little badge and the engagement ring with her. Fond memories of her lover, the man she intended to marry. Her new American friend however does not register, at least not from amongst what fragments we have to work with here.'

'There's no sign of the ring.'

'That's significant. Why would a young woman secretly leave home with a light overnight bag and things that reminded her of her long-lost lover?'

'To visit a doctor...' Trinder flipped a blackened penny into the air as if about to call heads or tails.

'Are you thinking what I am?'

Trinder slapped the spinning coin onto his forearm and removed his hand to reveal the head of Queen Victoria. 'She was pregnant. It adds up. She couldn't tell her mum and dad. No chance. They had enough trouble admitting she even had a dance and a cuddle with the airman, so I can't see them taking the idea of her being in the family way too well.'

Vignoles nodded. 'The Askew's would not have coped with that shock. Henry seems very protective towards his daughter. He might have flown off the handle and made a scene - and he likes a drink as well. She might even have been scared of his reaction?'

'She had to keep it secret... and do something about it before they found out?' Trinder turned the penny in his hands, a look of deep concentration on his face. 'Imagine the anxiety she must have been going through? And when she found someone to help her, she took things that really meant something? Memories of the real love of her life, rather than of a drunken indiscretion... It can't have been easy to do what she did.'

Vignoles looked at Trinder, with surprise. 'Yes, John, I think you've read the situation well. Becoming a father seems to have done no harm to your sensibilities.' He moved away from the table and looked around the elegant drawing room with the tall French windows opening on to the recently wrecked garden. 'This is a very fine house. It must be worth, what, a good nine hundred pounds? Even a thousand or more? I've been wondering how a GP became so wealthy, even working in a town like Amersham. It seems surprising.'

'He had an expensive hobby too. Those two coins Irons had in his pocket were worth nearly twenty-five pounds apiece!' Trinder whistled softly. 'He must have been earning extra on the side. Do you think he was onto a little earner, all strictly hush-hush?' Trinder put the old penny down and rubbed his hands together, 'Brr! But is dashed cold in here.'

'I think our doctor ran a side-line in abortions. Discretion, anonymity assured, working under the cover of an eminently respectable country doctor - it could work. Two questions come to mind. How did a working girl in Woodford come to hear about this discreet service? And most importantly, what actually happened between them here?' Vignoles walked looked out of the French windows into the garden. 'You're not wrong, it has to be warmer outside than in here.' He turned around hands plunged in his pockets. 'Perhaps the operation went wrong. Did she die on him? But then why the ghastly mutilation?'

'If the hands found near Brackley viaduct are hers, then I don't understand what's going on. Was she dismembered and spread far and wide?'

'I think you've just answered your question. Such an act reduces the chance of discovery - although it would appear those attempts at concealment have failed.' Vignoles took another look at the room. 'Something very bad happened in this house. I've seen enough, let's get out of here.'

'Gladly. But who has the ring?'

'We need to speak to Doctor Melcombe.'

Chapter Thirty-Four

Amersham
19th April 1943

'How dare you? You can't just demand my engagement ring. It's outrageous.'

'Young lady, what is outrageous is you being here!' He stopped himself, aware his voice was becoming angry. 'It was an emergency, in your mind at least, and I think an emergency situation demands a special fee, don't you?' Dr Melcombe's smile was not warm.

Askew threw the contents of her purse onto the table. 'I am forever grateful for your help, I truly am, and here's all the money I have. Take it, please!'

'I don't think you are in a position to bargain.' The doctor's voice was softer although only through considerable effort on his part. 'Look, you can't need that pretty little thing now, can you? Just think of all the sad memories it will only bring back. And one day when you meet someone else and get married and actually do have children, this ring will just lie in a drawer gathering dust, quite forgotten, unwanted and unloved. Once in a while you will rediscover it, and like a guilty secret it will make you uncomfortable as you recall that other person – now long gone.' His voice was sugary and soothing, cajoling, wheedling away at her. 'I'm sorry, Miss... Gosh, I have quite forgotten your name, how dreadfully impolite. Please, forgive my ill manners and raised voice.' His smile was false. 'And of course, you are still in mild shock after such a state of heightened anxiety.' He took a step closer, eyes attempting to meet hers, but always drawn back to the diamond like a homing beacon. 'It was most insensitive of me to behave in such an uncouth manner when you are feeling so emotional and...'

Askew took a step backwards, dropping her eyes to the floor. 'It's quite all right, I understand. I am also to blame for intruding on your day. But I'm perfectly fine now thank you, doctor. I really do feel revived and in tip-top health and so I would like to leave now. Please take the money – I could send you more. Next month...'

'That will not be necessary. The ring will settle the debt in full.' He held out his hand.

Askew realised the doctor was not going to negotiate. It was one thing to hand over the ring if he had been forced to keep her overnight and perform that dreaded operation, in fact she had almost resigned herself to that possibility, but now after an examination lasting but a few minutes and nothing more needed, he was making an unreasonable demand for payment. This was not fair; she was not going to give it over to satisfy this ugly little man's greed when she was already offering all her hard-earned savings.

Askew grabbed for her mackintosh and handbag, but Melcombe took his chance to pounce as she was bending to lift this. He caught her off guard and whilst her footing was not secure they tussled, his fingers gripping her arms and making her wince as his pale fingers squeezed her flesh. His breath was blowing on her face as they pressed against each other, she trying to free herself from his grip, whilst he in turn was twisting her left hand upwards so the winking stone was that bit closer to his face, the smile of almost childish delight on his face rendered ominous by this brutal aggression. Melcombe looked almost demonic, eyes magnified by the lenses so Askew could actually see two tiny reflections of the Cobra's Eye in his dilated pupils.

They were locked together for just a few moments, Askew's face twisted with the pain and exertion, neither speaking. Just the sound of their breathing and straining against each other and their scuffling feet setting motes of dust dancing in the shaft of sunlight penetrating the room. Askew fought to remain upright, but the doctor's greater weight combined with her heavy boots made the bag swing awkwardly and throw her sideways with a lurch, just at the same moment as one of her feet became trapped behind the leg of a chair - and she toppled.

Free at last from the doctor's grip, she fell just a few feet. It was nothing more. On any other occasion she would have been unceremoniously dumped on the floor to be left looking indignant and embarrassed and no doubt cursing him with words learnt from the enginemen at the loco. But instead she hit her head on the edge of the desk sufficiently hard to render her momentarily unable to react, and in that fraction of a second her skull smacked hard onto the floor with an ugly, sickening crack that instantly twisted Melcombe's guts with the terrifying realisation that this was going to be bad.

Askew lay immobile, her eyelids closed but fluttering slightly. Her legs were almost straight and one of her arms now lay across her brow as though she had slipped into a restful sleep. Her chest rose and fell once, twice, three times and then, from between her slightly parted lips, there was a long slow sigh and she was still. A grandfather clock counted the passing seconds that Betty Askew would never experience as a living being.

Frantically he tried smelling salts; he pounded her chest rhythmically with both hands and blew air into her lungs for long endless minutes at a time. When this failed, in an act of appalling desperation he even slapped her face whilst simultaneously praying and cursing in equal doses and finally beating his fists on the floor with impotent desperation. It was all to no avail, and no matter what techniques he tried, whether expert or simply driven by the waves of intense anger and sickening fear that enveloped him like a blanket of ice, he could not revive her. Elizabeth Askew was dead.

Chapter Thirty-Five

London Marylebone
19th April 1943

Dr Melcombe mopped his brow with a handkerchief before removing his spectacles to give them a wipe, an act he immediately regretted as the now dampened cloth only served to smear the lenses with a fine coat of perspiration. He was agitated, his heart pounding uncomfortably and he was sweating profusely, partially due to anxiety and partially because it was a hot day. He should have worn a lighter suit but he'd deliberately chosen the Harris tweed with the intention of appearing staid and eminently respectable – and quite forgettable. Nobody was likely to remember an elderly man in a dark suit and hat looking like countless others coming and going about the station, although he now feared his florid complexion and shining brow might attract the unwelcome attention of some meddling busy-body with a medical kit slung across their shoulders in a haversack. He had better pull himself together.

Marylebone Station was busy. Every platform occupied by a hissing locomotive at the buffer stops with trains behind of equally filthy coaches, those closest to him in varying shades of soiled teak and looking as though they were assembled not from one of the most beautiful of woods, but from planks of burnt and charred timber rescued from bombsites. The air was acrid with lazily billowing smoke and alive with jets of fiercely escaping steam illuminated by strong diagonals of light scything through the unglazed bars, the glass long since removed for safety in the summer of '39.

Everywhere was noise and activity, with platoons of men in the uniforms of the armed services standing, sitting, talking or shouting and moving mountains of heavy packs and equipment from one place to another in what appeared to the doctor's inexpert eye to be nothing but a hopeless bustle and only to adding to the confusion all about. Orders were barked, doors slammed, whistles blew, women porters trundled trolleys laden with mail sacks, whilst young insolent boys dressed in threadbare clothes with dirty knees and faces hustled to carry luggage 'for a sixpence', keeping step beside overburdened passengers and wheedling away at their resolve with a cupped palm.

If this relentless noise was not enough for Dr Melcombe's fraying nerves, everywhere he looked he was assaulted by enormous posters demanding his attention and exhorting him to do, or not do something for the war effort -

DON'T LEAVE IT TO OTHERS!
Register for Civil Defence Duties!

DON'T ask for bread unless you NEED it!

Keep your children in the country!

It was relentless, and he closed his eyes for a moment to shut out this assault on mind and conscience. Conscience? What was one of those? He took a deep lungful of dirty London air and his face contorted, not with physical pain but mental anguish. Did he have any shred of human decency left in his body?

Know how to behave in an Air Raid Shelter...

The strident demands were everywhere, the giant black letters banging at his forehead, drilling into his frazzled brain.

He opened his eyes and stared at a four-wheeled trolley hauled along the platform by a pretty woman porter. His attention, unlike that of a gang of soldiers close by, was not drawn to her shapely legs with calves defined by honed muscles, nor even by the tunic pulled taut across enticingly heavy breasts as she leant into the effort. He was transfixed instead by the bulk of his wooden trunk sitting square on the trolley deck surrounded by a host of smaller parcels and what looked like a garden spade wrapped in brown paper. The things people sent by train never ceased to amaze him. He snorted, finding something laughably macabre in the realisation that he was surely topping the list of the unexpected – and the abhorrent. A clammy trickle of sweat ran down his spine.

If that young porteress only knew...but enough of this introspection, it was time for action. He could not stand around feeling sorry for himself.

Less Light – Less speed: Look out in the Blackout!

He needed to look out. He had a job to do, and the quicker he completed it, the sooner he could try to push aside this nightmare and seek to eradicate all memory of this awful day. Many a night alone with a bottle of scotch and some self-prescribed sleeping pills might do the trick, but right now he needed to remain calm and unhurried. Less speed...

As the porteress drew close he fell into walking alongside her, leaning heavily upon a walking stick and adopting a limp. He only used this stick when on nature rambles, but felt in need of a prop, both physical and mental. It was also a useful identifier, people would notice the stick and limp if they noticed him at all. He would ditch this as soon as the job was done, and walk upright, thus altering his appearance instantly.

He asked that she wheel his trunk to the portico outside the station, and as they picked their way down the crowded platform exchanged small talk about the fine weather the capital was enjoying. She helped him lift the heavy wooden trunk off the trolley, the slim woman managing her end with ease, whilst he fumbled and almost dropped the other to the ground, his palms greasy and arms suddenly going weak. By the time they had finished, he was panting and looked even more hot and bothered.

'Are you all right, sir? Can I get you a glass of water?'

'No, no don't bother my dear. I'm fine.' He flapped a limp hand towards her. 'Just a little hot.'

'If your quite sure? Can I be of any further assistance?'

'No. But thank you all the same.' Melcombe waved her away impatiently. He could ill afford her to remember him too clearly.

He sat on the trunk to regain his breath, leaning on his stick and eyeing the people standing in groups and loose queues all waiting for the taxis that constantly pulled to a halt in a space reserved between a row of coaches and some chunky army trucks that poured fumes into the hot still air. Despite the headache inducing pollution, he received a lift to his spirits as he realised that the next stage of his plan might prove easier to finesse than he'd feared. He felt inside his jacket pocket to reassure himself the envelope he had put there before leaving home was still there. He looked around for someone suitable to approach.

Three negro soldiers were smoking and talking nearby. All were tall and smartly uniformed, their conversation muted, their laughter noticeably lacking the harshly raucous edge that every so often exploded from the far larger groups of white servicemen keeping some distance from them, as though there was an invisible line chalked on the pavement that neither group might cross.

Dr Melcombe had never met a black man before because they were a rare sight, even in London. It was unlikely Amersham had ever witnessed a man with dark skin. To be honest, he would have steered clear, as he preferred to avoid mixing with these foreign types - whatever their skin colour - but right now he had need of assistance. He needed someone who would be far away before many weeks had elapsed. Preferably someone who may never return to London, and black American solders fitted the bill perfectly.

He stood up and approached the men. 'Excuse me intruding like this, but I was wondering if one or more of you strong fellows could help an old gentleman?'

'We sure can try. What can we do for you, sir?' The nearest soldier gave him a friendly grin. His teeth were perfect, and the doctor was pleasantly surprised.

'I have a heavy trunk.' He indicated it with a hand. 'Full of valuable medical equipment and my reference books. Utterly irreplaceable of course in these difficult times and they need careful handling. I'm a doctor,' he offered by way of an explanation. 'I'm in the process of relocating my practice, so I must place this in storage until I can get moved in and settled.'

'A doctor. We sure need more of your sort right now!' A broad smile followed this observation.

'Ah, well...I'm just a general practitioner, nothing more than that, I'm afraid. I cannot pretend to be of much use on the front line. Now, the problem is, I need to get my trunk a short way across town and into storage - at Broad Street railway station. That's one of the other London stations. The trouble is, I have another pressing engagement to attend out of town and my train departs very soon. It's all terribly awkward and so I was wondering if I could impose myself...'

'You want us to deliver this some place?'

'I would be awfully grateful. If you don't mind helping an old man, that is?'

'Well... We gotta a little time on our hands...'

'You sure, Denzil? We don't exactly know our way about town.' One of the others spoke up, his voice dark and soft.

'It's really not far. Look, I realise this is a dreadful imposition and of course what with the war and everything, you might be suspicious of a chap accosting you like this.' He forced his warmest smile. 'I could be an enemy parachutist stashing equipment aside for an invasion – but my legs are really not up to the jump!' The three soldiers laughed pleasantly. 'No, I really would do it myself, but I just cannot get there and back in ten minutes, so I'm in a bit of a jam...'

'And it looks heavy for an old timer like you to be hunking around!'

'Indeed so.' He made a point of leaning on his stick. 'Those books are rather heavy.' His throat was now parched and his stomach cramping, and he looked convincingly ill.

'You probl'y guessed we're new around here and I can't say as I ever heard about nowhere else 'cept Piccadilly Circus, but you say this Broad Street is easy to find?' The first soldier was speaking.

'Oh yes. Just leave it in the left luggage office. A taxi driver will know the way and only ten- or fifteen-minutes ride. I will see you right for your trouble, of course. How about ten shillings? It really would be awfully kind if you could.'

The three men exchanged knowing glances; it was a tidy sum for little effort. One shrugged, another said, 'why not?'

'We take it to this place, and then what?'

'Ah! Now I thought this problem through and came prepared. I have here a self-addressed envelope complete with a stamp. Just pay for three months storage – I'll give you enough to cover it - and place the little numbered ticket they will give you in here and pop it in a post box. You need do nothing else.'

The first soldier took the proffered envelope and looked at the address. 'Sounds simple.' He shrugged. 'It's a deal.'

One of the others had already secured a cab and had the rear door open. 'C'mon guys, what you waiting on?' Barely noticing the weight, the trunk was lifted by the other two and carefully placed in the back of the vehicle. With a nod and wave to the elderly doctor who was now mopping his brow, they were gone in a trail of oily exhaust.

How long until it was discovered? A week? A month? A Year? The lime and the rubberized coating of the gas cape and the heavy tarpaulin should prevent the worst of the smell. It was possible it could go undiscovered for at least a few months, and by then no one would be able to recall who brought the trunk in. Even if they did, three foreign soldiers long since shipped out to some distant place, were going to be impossible to trace. It should be all right. Just as long as nobody demanded they open the trunk.

He mopped his brow again and walked back into the hurly-burley of the station concourse now glad of the noise and confusion that would swallow him as effectively as any camouflaged uniform in the battlefield, his right hand now seeking for the little wooden box inside his jacket pocket. Dr Melcombe's eyes met those of the porteress who had wheeled the trolley a few minutes earlier, and he realised that she was speaking.

'Feeling better?' She gave a cheery wave, as she dashed past.

'Much!' He realised he was smiling.

Chapter Thirty-Six

Brackley Cottage Hospital
27th September 1950

'I cannot be expected to remember when I took a holiday in 1943. It's quite ridiculous.'

'And it was wartime. Everyone was encouraged to travel as infrequently as possible, so surely it would be a memorable occasion to go to the seaside?' Vignoles asked the questions as Trinder took notes, one standing on each side of the hospital bed.

'Gosh yes! I can recall the week we had at Mablethorpe in '41 as though it were yesterday. The journey took five hours and we stood most of the way, but the sun was cracking the flags when we got there, and the sea was lovely. How could I forget?' added Trinder with exaggerated enthusiasm.

'You might fill your head with frivolous nonsense, sergeant, but I do not. And besides, your argument is flawed: someone could have done this dreadful deed whilst...I was at the shops, or at my club in London, even playing golf or in the dead of night whilst I was sleeping, Heaven forbid! I can assure you I was neither aware nor part of this evil act.'

'Why would someone unknown to you come into your garden to bury such a grisly thing?' Vignoles asked. 'Barely credible, surely?'

'It may seem so, but it is the truth. I cannot start to comprehend it. But it is all a complete waste of time, you are questioning me.'

'Your appointments diary would be a great help. It would confirm the times you were away and help us determine whom you saw around that time – hopefully removing you from the investigation but perhaps giving us some pointers as to who was responsible,' Vignoles continued, his tone helpful and encouraging. 'We feel it must be someone who knew you or your property well.'

'I jolly well hope my name is in the clear now! How dare you besmirch my reputation.' He lowered his voice and spoke carefully. 'You will not be so foolish as to suggest that I am responsible for her death. Do you have any evidence to suggest I am?'

'Part of her body was discovered in your garden...' Trinder observed.

'Your appointments diary?' Vignoles asked patiently.

'I don't have it. I threw everything away with the move.'

'And you really cannot remember your movements that day?' Trinder made a note and sucked air between his teeth. 'Unfortunate.'

'Why did you take early retirement?' Vignoles fired the question from the other side of the bed

'My health was not good. Still isn't, no thanks to that thug and you harassing me. I have a dodgy heart, if you must know.' He waved a hand at a bottle of pills on the bedside cabinet.

'That's not what your neighbours and patients say. They were surprised, even a little disappointed at the way you just upped sticks and left, all in a matter of weeks.'

'What would they know? I kept the exact details private. I don't have to share everything with patients or meddling neighbours. Privacy is everything to me.'

'You live alone?'

'What of it?' Melcombe gave Vignoles a reproving look. 'I never married, but I cannot see that's any of your business.'

'Why were you disposing of a young lady's clothes in your garden?' Trinder asked. 'We found the remains in a bonfire.'

'Nothing to do with me! The chap who bought the place from me must be responsible. He was married, I think.'

'Do you own a set of scales? A rather fine, precision set as might be used for weighing tiny amounts of powder or pills?' Vignoles asked, both detectives keeping the questioning lively, deliberately dancing from one subject to another.

'Of course. Anyone in my profession is likely to have just such a weighing balance.'

'Are yours made by Oertling?'

'Now let me think. It was a very long time ago since I bought them. But, yes, mine are by Oertling. One of the best manufacturers of these instruments – got mine second hand but in perfect condition, but still me cost a week's wages when I was starting up.'

'Where are they now?'

'May I ask where is this leading?'

'Are they still within their carrying box? I would imagine such an expensive item needs careful protection. It could be easily damaged, and during your house move you would wish to take great care...'

'Um... I-I'm not sure actually, I think not. Oddly, I could not find the box when it came to it.' Melcombe appeared genuinely puzzled. 'Look, what on earth is this? I'm tired and need rest. My cracked ribs make it hard to talk. I have no interest in discussing the packaging of some old medical equipment!'

'Of course. But one last thing for now; have you seen this woman?' Vignoles showed Melcombe the photograph used on the missing person posters.

'No.' But Melcombe took a sharp intake of breath, causing him to wince and touch his ribs. 'Never. Sorry, I'm very sore.'

'She didn't visit you recently?'

'What? Why would she do that?' Melcombe's pupils widened and he made his voice crack with pain. He appeared to be having problems with his breathing.

'I wonder if she might have entered your house in advance of the break in. Perhaps she called at the door and you let her in?'

'I've never seen her.' He took a few shallow breaths then shifted his position on the pillows, wincing and his face deathly pale.

'You are quite sure? This photograph was on posters up and down the line, including Amersham, for quite some time.' He unfolded the poster in question. 'Do you not remember seeing this?'

Melcombe's Adam's apple bobbed. 'No. Maybe... I could not say for certain. I can't be expected to remember every person who goes missing. You're grilling me like a common criminal,' he glared at Vignoles, perspiration on his temples. 'If you persist in harassing me like the bloody Gestapo, I shall insist on my lawyer being present.'

'We need to get to bottom of two quite dreadful murders and that entails asking all manner of questions,' Vignoles used his most placatory tone of voice. 'It is unavoidable I am afraid.' The doctor mumbled something and retreated into looking pained. 'We would like to have a look around your cottage.'

Chapter Thirty-Six

'Absolutely not!'

'I can get a warrant because you and your house are a part of what is now a very serious investigation.' Vignoles made an apologetic shrug.

'How so? The robbery was nothing. It's of no consequence.'

'Interesting you should say that.' Vignoles smiled. 'I'm almost inclined to agree with you; Irons made little attempt to take your collection, in fact it appears all rather half-hearted'. Vignoles observed Melcombe carefully. 'Perhaps he was seeking something else? Can you suggest what that might that be?'

Melcombe remained silent, his eyes flicking between the two detectives, but Vignoles noticed that he kept giving the little photograph of Betty Askew surreptitious glances.

'What is the *Cobra's Eye?*' asked Trinder.

Melcombe looked stunned. 'The what?' He coughed and reached for a glass of water on his bedside table and sipped it. 'Sorry, throat's dry.' His voice was forced when he next spoke. 'Do elucidate me sergeant, what is this Cobra thingumybob? Sounds most peculiar.'

'It was mentioned during our enquiries, that's all.' Trinder offered.

'Who told you about it?'

Trinder smiled as if to say, nice try, but hard luck chum.

'You've never heard of the *Cobra's Eye*, and yet are more interested in knowing who mentioned it, than what it is?' Vignoles paused. 'Ah, but then, you already know, don't you?' He was giving Melcombe a hard stare. 'Was Irons interested in it?'

'I have absolutely no idea what you are talking about.'

'Did Irons break in to take it? Or you were going to strike a deal with him, but he reneged and there was a scuffle between you both? Either way, someone got to him later, didn't they?'

'Clutching at straws Inspector. I've never seen that fellow before and as you know, I was laid up in here whilst he met with that most unfortunate end. Cobras and a dead housebreaker: it is quite obvious you have no idea what you are looking for, nor indeed what you are doing here. Now please leave.' Melcombe gave Vignoles a cold, mirthless smile. 'And I suggest you go away and think a bit harder before you return.'

'Oh, I shall. And don't worry, I will be back.

Chapter Thirty-Seven

Belgrave & Birstall, Leicester
27th September 1950

'Take your shoes off and relax, I'll get the tea ready. It won't take long.' Anna put her arms around Vignoles' neck, deftly removing his hat with a manicured hand and holding it behind his back. She planted a warm kiss on his mouth, her curvaceous body flatteringly revealed by a skin-tight turtleneck tucked into a flared skirt with a nipped waist. She pressed herself close. 'A beer?' Cocking her head to one side she observed that he, looked tired. 'It's been a terribly long day I suppose.'

'Long, but productive and intriguing.' He was enjoying feeling her breasts against his chest and ran a hand down the clearly delineated curve of her hip, feeling the corset beneath the fabric, his fingers playfully tracing the fastening of her suspender belt. 'But yes, a beer would be lovely.' He smiled at Anna, now tasting lipstick. 'Am I red?' He turned and glanced in the hall mirror. 'I look like a clown!'

Anna was laughing. 'More like one of those louche variety performers! It's only a smudge. Come along...' and she gently ushered him into their small living room. 'As it's late, I've decided you can have something on a tray. I've got some steak to fry you can have with chips I cut earlier.'

'You actually managed to find steak? Am I dreaming, or have you blown both out ration books for the month?'

'Well, it's horse of course. But it looks good and will taste wonderful. Anyway, you like horse.'

'I do - though I'm the only one who admits to it. There's always an outbreak of horrified moral outrage if I tell the office we've eaten horse!'

'More fool them.'

Despite being a fraction of the size of the large and chilly space inhabited by the Lineys, their room was rendered cosy by curtains of an interestingly patterned material that were now holding back the night, and a small fire taking the edge off any encroaching coolness, offering friendly little clicks and ticks as the coal burned in the grate. The furniture was of the most up-to-date G-plan, suitably austere and inexpensive, yet clean and functional in a way that pleased their sense of design. There was new wallpaper on one wall in a bold design of greys, blacks, pale greens and yellows that had been described as seed heads, but which could be mistaken for splitting atoms, the other walls simply washed with plain, strong colours that matched the atomic fusion of the paper. It was a far cry from his parent's house in Dunton Bassett rectory that was a rambling pile decorated with fussy wallpapers patterned with stripes or flowers and overstuffed with heavy sofas, oppressively dark furniture, long plate racks edging the walls and gilt framed hunting prints. Not only that, but every flat surface was covered in a multitude of trinkets and knick-knacks that his mother Caroline loved to collect, apparently whenever she left the house.

Vignoles turned the on switch of his prized radiogramme in the corner and waited as the valves warmed up, the sound of dance music slowly rising as the radio got up to speed. Listening to Harry Roy's band for a moment or two, and deciding it was to his liking, he slipped his shoes from his aching feet and flopped into one of the armchairs beside the fire and closed his eyes for a few moments. Anna had retreated into the kitchen and he heard the soft clink of a bottle and glass and smiled. It was a reassuringly pleasing sound and a delicious escape from the horrors of looking at the butchered remains of a young woman and the horribly mangled throat of a dead schoolteacher.

Anna returned with glasses and two bottles of Everard's 'Tiger' on a tray that she placed on a low black lacquered oval table. Carefully pouring the beer down the side of the glass, Vignoles detected the first hint of the hoppy scent and enjoyed the sound of the amber liquid flowing into the foam of bubbles now forming on top. He held the full glass high and let the light from a standard lamp shine through the liquid, admiring the clarity and colour in patient anticipation. Anna also lifted her glass and they clinked them together.

'Chin chin!'

'I needed that.' Vignoles nodded appreciatively after a slow and satisfying first taste. 'It's been a funny old day really. Rather short on the funny, actually. It started with a body in the churchyard in Brackley.'

Anna gave him a look.

'I know you would expect bodies in a churchyard, but this was a suspicious death and definitely above ground. If that was not enough to keep us occupied, we were off to see another body – well, part of a body. But we'll gloss over the details, as they are far too ghastly. Now that was buried, but this time in a private garden in Amersham.'

'Ugh! And are these events related?'

'There is a link. And to my surprise, Badger has put me in charge of the investigation – of both investigations until I can be sure they are one and the same. A bit of a surprise really as we're working well off railway territory.'

'Shows he appreciates how good you are.'

'Or that no one else was prepared to take it on. It's a curious case, or cases, crossing different boundaries that will cause all manner of operational headaches.' He gave a little smile at Anna in appreciation of her company and drank more beer. They were silent for a moment or two.

'We have someone in mind as a suspect, but there's still an awful lot of work to do before I can make an arrest. He'd wriggle out with a good lawyer, even with a bad one based on what I have at the moment. I've got the Buckinghamshire boys taking the house in Amersham apart looking for clues, and tomorrow Trinder will get the Northants lot doing the same on the suspect's cottage in Turweston. Our suspect is heavily implicated, but I don't actually have any evidence of him committing either murder. In fact, when it comes to the young man in the churchyard, our best suspect was laid up in hospital at the time!' Vignoles gave Anna an almost apologetic look. 'Pretty lame really.'

'Early days, Charles. It's always like this at the start of a case. You are often telling me nothing makes any sense to start with but slowly, as you discover a bit more and tease the strands out, it comes together.'

Vignoles leant back in the chair. 'You're right. Everything is too raw right now. I need a good night's sleep to think it over and start afresh tomorrow. Hmm, I like this song...'

Sinatra started singing in his wistful late-night voice a song about loneliness, stepping across the rhythm of the band with consummate skill perfectly phrasing the lines.

'He's an incredible singer,' Anna agreed. 'Probably the best', and they listened together for a while. Anna stood up as the song ended, placing her beer on the table. 'I'll get your steak and chips on.' She walked across the room into the hall but reappeared immediately at the door. 'I'm sorry, I forgot. There was a telephone call. I made a note and left it on the telephone table in the hall and just noticed it.'

'Oh yes?'

'A Mrs Askew. She sounded terribly apologetic about telephoning and explained how she'd got the number from the directory as you'd left her one of your calling cards and so had your name and...'

'What did she say?' Vignoles was sitting upright in the armchair, all tiredness forgotten.

'Just that she wanted to speak with you. To explain something - privately.' Anna gave a mischievous look, 'she was most insistent.'

'Then I must call her immediately,' Vignoles stood up. 'This is no laughing matter.'

'Slow down, it can wait. She was explicit that you meet her tomorrow - at work, and not her home. Said not to try in the evening when Henry was at home. Is he her husband?'

'Correct.'

'Anyway, they don't have a telephone and she said she must see you face to face to explain properly. She's at work all day at The Merry Chemist, in Brackley.'

'I know it. What could it be?' He was talking to himself whilst leaning an elbow on the mantelshelf. 'Something about her daughter I suppose....'

'She's the poor thing who went missing? I don't suppose you've found her?'

Vignoles looked pained. 'Possibly. Too early to be absolutely sure, though it looks like bad news.'

'Not the body in Amersham?' Anna winced and Vignoles had no need to say anything. 'How dreadful. Mrs Askew sounded such a sweet lady, and hearing her voice makes it feel all the more real. What will you tell her?'

'I shall call the pathologist first thing and see if they have an identification. I'd rather stand on less shaky ground before I put her through that.' Vignoles was speaking softly. 'It will be a terrible experience for them to see the remains. I've only seen photographs, and that was bad enough.

However, until we have something positive I might play this carefully and only allude to a discovery. Heck, I hate this part of the job, Anna. Trying to judge what to say and not to say for the best, when ultimately there really is no "best".' Vignoles took a deep draught of beer and looked at the flames in the grate. 'I had a suspicion Maud Askew was holding something back. It will be too much to pray that she has found her daughter alive and we can seek an alternative name to pin on the gruesome discovery, but at moments like this I can't help but hope. Of course, I'm just wishing to avoid a painful interview as all I would be doing is transferring the pain onto another family.'

'I'll get you another Tiger.

Chapter Thirty-Eight

Brackley Central
27th September 1950

'My leg is getting cramped.'

'I'm cold.' Eddie Earnshaw was lying on his stomach peering beneath the lowest slat of the wooden fence edging the railway line. In front of them stretched the twin lines crossing the great curving viaduct. Close to his right was a thick telegraph pole that reeked of Creosote mingled with the light tang of oil, wood and a suggestion of flushed toilets wafting from the track, all softened by a stronger odour of grasses and damp loam. 'Any more tea in the can?'

Laura Green stood up gingerly, wiggling her foot to get the blood flowing and retrieved the cream enamelled tea can from her haversack and unscrewed the top. 'Enough for a cup each. And I've two squares of Dairy Milk. I bet you'd like one?'

'Chocolate? Top hole. You kept that quiet!' Eddie rolled over on to his side and even in the dark of the night she could see he was grinning.

'I've been making the bar last all week.' She handed over the lid of the tea can filled with hot sweet tea, then shook out the cold dregs from a spare mug and poured the last of the liquid for herself. She then sat back down on the little square of rug they had laid on the grass and cupped her hands around the mug, gladly absorbing its warmth. 'A cup of tea really helps lift one's spirits!' She took a sip and then securing her mug in a tuft of long grass, unwrapped the chocolate. 'I hope Simon's ok. Any signal from him?'

'Thanks. No...no I can't see a thing.' Eddie looked along the silver rails to the far side of the viaduct where their friend was hunkered down on the steep embankment a little below the sight lines of the station staff and signalman. 'I'll send the "no" signal to him as a test. Just to keep him on his toes.' He clicked on his flashlight and wiggled it from side to side in a pre-arranged signal that indicated "no sign of her". Almost immediately a little pinpoint of light did the same from a spot about a yard below rail level. The torch beam went out and near darkness returned, relieved only by the little station lamps and a faint red stain cast on the shiny rail tops from the oil lamps behind the signal spectacle plates.

'I suppose we can't be too surprised. It's not every day, or night, one sees a ghost. Assuming there really is one,' Green observed. 'What shall we do? Give it another half hour?'

'I think we should wait until the down stopper from Marylebone. It reverses here and that's the one Si reckons she travels on. It has to be our best chance. We can hang on another twenty minutes after, as I arranged for us to get a lift from the newspaper train. But if we miss that, then it's going to be a long cold night.'

'No thank you! I'm game for a while longer, but not all night.'

There was a thin reedy twang and the creak of signal wires tautening followed by the heavy chonk of the arm lifting. A cool green light replaced the red and a tiny bell sounded in the signal box.

'Here comes something...'

They both lay prone side by side on the blanket, hot teas in their hands, the steam brushing their faces. There was a faint whistle and then the measured tread of a slow and heavy train.

Eddie listened a while. 'Heading south. A heavy goods?'

Laura nodded. 'A coal train or perhaps iron ore. I know that sound well because they pass my signal box all day long.' They exchanged looks, enjoying sharing the experience, faces close. 'I bet there's eighty on the back by the sound of it.'

He nodded, reckoning she was better at this than both he and Simon combined. 'She might stop the train! That's what happened to me that time.'

'I'm in two minds about this now.' She bit her lower lip and watched the pale efflorescence bloom like a series of giant white flowers above the station canopy, the black monster snorting and breathing in deep gruff exhalations with its train clanging and banging in a riotous cacophony behind. 'It's one thing to want to see a ghost, quite another to do so.'

'An O2. No wait, I think it's a Western 'ROD'. What a rare cop Laura!' Eddie kept his voice barely above a whisper. 'A Great War survivor. Built for the Railway Operating Division around 1917 up in Gorton. They can pull a whole town, as long as you don't want to go faster than a snail! I can't see the number...is that 3023?'

'Shh...never mind train spotting. Look!' Green was pointing, her outstretched hand quivering with nervous excitement. 'Oh, but quickly, you must signal to Simon!' Her eyes narrowed as she tried to get a better look.

They watched as a slim pale figure of a woman stepped up from the far side of the embankment, moving both smoothly and silently onto the viaduct and oblivious to the thunder of the great train approaching from the other end. She wore a long coat and a hat, her face of the palest skin beneath the brim. She had no fear and stood on the track pointing her arm as though at something over the side of the viaduct parapet.

'Exactly what she did when I saw her!' Eddie exclaimed.

'There's something strange about her...Oh, she's got no hands!'

'That's a full coal train on a down gradient! There's no point in even attempting to try and stop!' He leaped up, sending his lid of tea spinning to land with a clatter on the edge of the permanent way. 'Hey, hey you! Get off the line! Get out the way!' He was waving frantically above his head, but the pale creature stayed rooted to the spot with one foot on either side of a rail, facing certain death.

'I thought we're supposed to just watch...I mean, it can't hurt her. Can it? Oh God, but the train's going to strike her!' Now Laura could not suppress her own natural instincts and was standing, darting a quick glance to the far side of the viaduct where a torch beam was frantically flicking up and down indicating 'YES!' Simon had seen her too.

There was no time to reply as the lumbering train of something like eight hundred tons of unstoppable steel, coal, fire and water ploughed onwards, the crew hanging on the whistle and leaning far out of the almost open cab, quite powerless to do anything. As the train hit the girl there was no sound, nothing but the relentless huff and rumble of the engine. Her slight body could not check the heavy goods train's progress, but this lack of sound was doubly disturbing.

Laura held her hands in front of her face whilst Eddie stared open mouthed. Somehow the engine did not mangle her into a hideous mess beneath the wheels, but the big 2-8-0 freight engine appeared to travel through her, the pale figure melting into the steam leaking profusely from the low-slung cylinders as though she had been vaporized into oily atoms. But immediately this cloud reconstituted, twisting and curling into the shape of a running figure. The young woman was now miraculously running across the tracks, her feet moving soundlessly on the ballast as she came straight towards Eddie and Laura.

She passed so close they could have touched her, yet neither moved and they just watched in mute fascination as she passed, her face a death mask, her eyes filled with a silvery cold light spoke of a deep, pure loneliness that coursed straight into their hearts.

The woman moved smoothly down the embankment side, now tracked by a thin torch beam from afar. Eddie snapped out of his stunned inertia and clicked on his own torch and like searchlights on a German bomber, their two lights traced her pale, now almost luminous shape. She reached the riverbank and stopped, turning her head back from whence she'd come, and despite the gloom and her apparent indifference to them a moment earlier, Eddie and Laura sensed she was trying to engage their attention.

'Look!' Now pointing into the Great Ouse, her arm seemed to be without a hand, but this must have been a trick of the poor light.

Laura clutched Eddie's arm and the torch beam was unsteady in his hand. The woman called again, in a faint sad sound they experienced more than heard, virtually masked by the cacophony of the passing coal train. And then she flowed into the water, appearing to melt into the damp dank mist, their vision further impaired by great cumuli of smoke and steam rolling down from the passing engine.

Chapter Thirty-Nine

Brackley
28th September 1950

'We must leave now, it would be the height of folly to delay a moment longer.' Barnaby Ringham checked his exquisite Cartier wristwatch with a decisive movement. Having done so, he instinctively adjusted the lie of the sleeve of his hand-made suit.

'Yes, yes... but I'm really not sure I'm up to a long haul. I seem to have taken a bit of a setback.' Dr Melcombe was rubbing his heavily strapped torso with painfully slow movements. 'Being grilled by that inspector has knocked me for six, and my neck and ribs are playing up like nobody's business.'

'You look dead beat, but my car is comfortable and I have a travelling rug if you get cold. The Hawker Siddeley 'Hurricane' is a darned fine car and comfortable.' Despite his concerns, Ringham allowed a moment of self-satisfaction. 'I've primed matron. Hopefully she'll keep her trap shut long enough for us to put some miles between us, thanks to a generous donation to the hospital funds. We'll refine our plans once we're under way. Now take this. It's a ticket to Glasgow. We could go on to Rannoch Moor. Scotland's a good place to keep one's head below the firing line.' He slipped Melcombe a small buff envelope with 'British Railways' stamped on the top left corner in red. Ringham then looked around the small private room and wrinkled his nose. 'You have the change of clothes as instructed?'

'Yes. My housekeeper, Mrs MacKendrie fetched them last night. It's the case in the corner.' Melcombe leant heavily on the arms of the one comfortable chair in the room and eased himself upright. Getting into his day clothes had been a lengthy process and he'd needed to sit down after doing so to both tie his shoelaces and regain some composure, aided by the swallowing of a couple of painkillers. 'Policeman plod standing guard over Ivy Cottage was quite obliging and he let her in. But look here, you still have not answered my question.' Melcombe's voice had a whining quality, like a little boy nagging at a parent. 'Have you got it? You must hand it over,

Barnaby. I've got to have it back!'

Ringham ignored his demands, concentrating instead on pulling on a pair of smooth black leather driving gloves with a button fastening on the back. 'Quite right, you're not under caution -' but paused for a fraction of a second for the implied "- yet," before continuing. 'Chop chop!' Ringham picked up the doctor's bottle green leather suitcase with "P.M" blocked in gold letters on the lid, and held the door open for the doctor, who shuffled past. 'The car is parked around the corner, just a short walk away. I'd rather it had been somewhat further, but you sounded all done in on the telephone last night.'

'I'll manage. But the ring...' Melcombe almost hissed the word, his face so close he could smell Ringham's cologne and see a little nick where his solicitor's hand had uncharacteristically slipped when shaving. 'You do have it?'

'All in good time, Percy old boy.' But his wink convinced the recalcitrant doctor to continue walking, implying that he did indeed have the object in question. Ringham had to throw the old man something to pacify him, or he'd just argue the point and refuse to cooperate, and they could ill afford to be overheard discussing such a potent object. Things were in a pretty delicate state and they needed to make their getaway.

The retired doctor's nerves were uncharacteristically frayed however, and he looked but a shadow of the blustering, arrogant fellow who'd bullied matron into letting him telephone Ringham at his West End club. He'd been running on adrenaline at the time, because now he was completely washed out, with every bone and muscle aching and his mind frazzled by a disturbed and sleepless night. His red-rimmed eyes looked like those of a hunted man, restlessly roving about the room and flitting anxiously between the ugly wardrobe in the corner, then over to the window fringed with copper-burnished, rain-sodden Virginia creeper.

Since the moment Vignoles and Trinder had left, he'd hardly slept. As he lay in his narrow hospital bed, restrained by the starched sheets tucked hard under the mattress, he found sleep had abandoned him, jumping at any little noise, and although only small, the building was still a hive of muffled footsteps and murmured conversations, a closing door, the distant cry of a new-born baby. These should have been comforting sounds, the signals that nurses were close at hand and ready to offer help and reassurance, but instead, Melcombe came to dread each new disturbance no matter how soft, fearing they heralded the presence of something unwelcome, something sinister.

The retired doctor had opened his eyes wide from a brief moment of sleep and stared at the door to his room in horror. He had the most intense feeling that she was right outside, now, just standing there, eyes boring through the glossy cream painted wood. Although he'd been dozing he was sure he'd heard her walk along the corridor, her shoes making a soft sigh as they turned on the carpet. It was as though his senses were heightened to an almost painful level of amplification, the blood buzzing in his ears and every tiny sound jangling loud like a warning bell.

His eyes fixed upon the Bakelite knob, convinced that at any moment it would turn, and he had hardly dared breath as the minutes stretched on. What was that? It was her voice... But how could this be? It was impossible, and yet he was sure it was her, but outside on the street below. How could he forget the sound? He tugged angrily at the sheets that were stiff like cardboard and flung them back and driven onwards by a sense of mounting dread, he stumbled across the room, fighting against the pain burning all over his body, and stared down at the pools of light cast on the damp road below. A soft rain was falling, forming halos around the flaring lamps as the leaves of the trees edging the park boiled and stirred in the gathering wind, their branches dipping and rising and throwing moving shadows. But where was she? He opened the metal casement and peered further out, not caring about the drizzle.

A thin, reedy piping sound came from above and he looked up and felt the rain splash on his face and spotting his lenses, but he continued to seek the source of the sound, compelled to look for the soul birds on their tireless migration, but the blanket of rain cloud had blotted out the moon.

Wheep...whee wheep... wee wheep wheep...

Just a few birds on the wing, yet their calls were so mournful and laden with sorrow, cutting through the swish and rustle of windblown leaf, the patter of rain and the distant hoot of a passing train.

I'm so lonely...find me, find me...

Their reedy piping triggered something in his mind and instead the of hearing the call of a curlew or the piping of a duck, it sounded like her voice...

Weep, wee wheep... they will find me...

He banged his fist on the metal window frame. Stuff and nonsense! But who was that? He was shaking now, his body wracked by shivers, from the chilled damp air, and he gripped the windowsill. That pale figure moving along the pavement...in the deep dark shadows by the high wall? No...he almost collapsed with relief. It was just a thin man without a hat taking a walk. How could he have thought it was the young woman? Was he hallucinating? And yet he still had the feeling she was close by, watching him in dreadful proximity.

It was impossible. He knew only too well where her mutilated remains lay, each part deliberately spread far and wide. Though her hands lay closer than he'd planned. That was desperately unfortunate. How he had dithered and delayed on that fateful train ride! The appalling remains, small and slender, wrapped in greaseproof paper like something from the butcher's shop had nagged away at his conscience, and at times he was sure her fingers had tapped lightly on the brown leather attaché case, rapping at the cardboard and leather asking to be released, drawing his eyes and reminding him of what it contained. He had been unable to even look at the packet lying there all day, let alone open the clasps, lift the lid and toss this loathsome cargo away as he knew he must. But the little sounds from within had drawn his attention and finally forced him into action, tossing the loose pencil rolling against the side that had been the innocent explanation of the sound onto the carriage seat in frustrated anger and goading him into grasping the packet and hurling it through the opened window - and about time too. He'd walked for an hour around London from one gloomy weed-strewn bombsite to another, thinking to toss the packet beneath the tumbles of broken beams that looked like a giant's game of Spillikins or drop it down any number of gaping holes into the rubble-filled cellars of these destroyed dwellings, and yet there were always some grubby faced lads larking around or a group of youths stripping salvage and firewood or a homeless figure ranting at the earth seated like a shabby Lear on the skeleton of a baby carriage surrounded by empty bottles and horribly stained bits of rag and blanket. It was impossible to commit the act unseen, as there was always someone watching, walking past, and so many windows looking down on these open spaces. And so finally, in a fit of blind panic and rage he'd tossed the loathsome package from the train window, intending it to drop into a river far below. But it was going dark and he was not sure of his aim. Had he missed? He could not tell, but the shape and length of the viaduct was distinctive and a few weeks later when he'd completed the house purchase in Turweston and was travelling up one evening to finalise some details he realised he'd disposed of her hands in a place as close to his new home as the railway would reach. How could he have been so foolish? Had some unseen force guided his hand?

His fevered imagination was playing tricks on him now, and yet no matter how hard he leant upon his years of medical practice and rational argument, he could not shake off the feeling that she was right there, watching him and he again wondered about what had compelled him to finally act and jettison her hands from the train at such an inauspicious location.

Feeling foolish, he closed the window, latching it closed, eager to shut out the haunting calls of the night birds and then drew the curtains tight together. He lay down, pulling the sheets up to his chin in a childish attempt to find comfort.

What was that? A scratch of a fingernail on wood... Again! She was in the wardrobe! It was certainly capacious enough...she must have slipped in whilst he was looking out of the window.

'Come out! Come on. You won't frighten me. I'm not scared!' His heart was fit to burst, pulse dangerously high, palms sweating profusely. 'You fell. I-I didn't touch you. I just wanted to see your diamond ring that was all... I meant you no harm! Look, it was just an accident. You were not even supposed to be there...' His voice was weak and the words barely audible. 'I wish I'd never set eyes on you, or your cursed diamond!'

Silence.

The catch on the wardrobe door make a little metallic click and the door swung open half an inch with a creak. He stared at the black slit in the gloom and waited. Nothing. Eventually he had found the courage to cross the room and fling the door wide. It was empty of course. He repeatedly tried to secure the catch on the door, closing and opening it. It looked in perfect order, but every time he returned to his bed, it would after a few minutes click open again. He knew the wardrobe was empty, and yet he could not shake off the feeling he was being watched. He wedged a tall chair against the door and the corner of his bed and this prevented the door from opening again.

Melcombe settled for a short time after this, but then the curtains across the bedroom window became the focus for his deteriorating state of mind. The pale light leaking in from outside, sometimes flickered and moved along the floor beside his bed, and he became convinced there was someone outside. Someone or something was flitting silently to and fro past the window, their shadow cast by the street lamp opposite. He tried closing his eyes and ignoring these movements but all he could see when he did this was the face of that young girl in his consulting room lying on her back, her eyes closed, no breath from her lips...

She was tapping on the windowpane. Or was it on the door to his private room? In his mind, he could hear the brass fox-shaped knocker resonating and calling him to the door on that fateful day. Why had she chosen him? Dammit, what ill luck had brought her to his surgery? He didn't deal with working girls; he only ever sorted the problems of the rich and the famous, and only when arranged through Barnaby. He was just given a name (probably false), a day and a time and everything was ordered and organised, all strictly hush-hush and handled by with supreme delicacy and consummate professionalism. Illegal, but they were private patients and they paid handsomely via one of Barney's clever, and complex ruses that ensured nobody would know, least of all the taxman, and it suited everyone just fine. But someone had talked, and his name had slipped out and so this blasted bloody train cleaner had come knocking.

He opened his eyes and stared. But the little hospital was now quiet and peaceful, as it should be. He could hear the clock of St Peter's chiming two. His attention was drawn again to a dark shape sliding across the floor. She seated on the windowsill, hands feeling around frame. He could imagine her face outside looking in, contorted with outrage as she asked him to let her go, let her leave. Why had he not just sent her packing? Idiot, idiot, idiot! He rubbed his eyes and banged his palms on his forehead, but the image of the Askew woman would not leave.

Eventually, driven half mad with torment, he'd forced himself out of bed yet again, adrenaline cutting through the pain and stiffness, and he'd flung the curtains open so they jingled on their brass rings, but all he could see were the complex shapes of a branch bouncing in the wind in front of the gas lamp. He had stood and stared out of the window for a long time, growing colder and colder.

His night terrors had left him drained and now Melcombe gratefully lay back in the front passenger seat and enjoyed the cool smoothness and the intense smell of the ostentatious red leather, trying to relax and let Ringham take control for a while. Barnaby was good at fixing things, just the man when in a tricky situation. He'd worked a minor miracle back then. He'd come to the rescue and hardly missed a beat when confronted with the sight of a dead woman stretched out on the floor. He'd been a rock and dreamed up their plan to dispose of her remains.

Any lasting sense of relief was ruined by a nagging worry about something the inspector had raised, something vital that he needed to thrash out with Barnaby. He was also disturbed by the constant heavy breathing of Ringham's ugly dog.

The Rottweiler panted its reeking breath in noisy huffs like a steam engine, the pale brown and black snout thrust between the front seats, tongue lolling unpleasantly pink to one side of its wet lips. Whenever Melcombe gave it an impatient glance, the dog moved its feet on the rear bench seat as if about to pounce, and fixed its overly-alert eyes on him, an ear flicking. It was unsettling, and then the dog would suddenly close its mouth and the infernal panting would cease, followed by an audible gulp as the dog swallowed more of the excess of salvia accompanied by a roll of its eyes, before starting up the rhythmic panting again. Melcombe was finding it stomach-turning.

'Doesn't that drive you mad?'

'Hades is my faithful companion.' Ringham's gloved hands slid smoothly on the steering wheel in calm, measured movements as he pulled away. 'One gets used to it, I suppose. Annoying you, is he?'

'Yes. And it's breath stinks!'

'His name is Hades. Impolite to call him 'it,' old chap. He might take offence.'

Dr Melcombe shook his head impatiently. 'Can't you make it... make him lie down at least? He can sleep on the back seat like other dogs.'

'Hades likes to watch the road and to keep an eye on things.' Ringham gave the doctor a sly look as he changed gear and the great motor under the long bonnet roared. 'I like him alert to any eventuality.'

Melcombe had to be satisfied with this enigmatic reply and turned to look out of the passenger window at the edge of Brackley town as it melted into a succession of fields and hedgerows and at the Scots pines grouped around the entrance to Brackley Central passing to their right, the parapet of the road bridge they swung across causing the note of the car to change. The doctor caught sight of a steadily chuffing goods' train heading northward, a huge white cumulus of steam hanging in the air and the infernal panting of the dog offering a suitable soundtrack to this fleeting image.

'Where are you taking me? You mentioned Scotland.'

'We have tickets and reservations on the Mid-day Scot. I have a small shooting box on Rannoch Moor and it could be wise to hunker down there and take stock. It's in a darned lonely place and your inspector won't find us in a hurry.' Ringham gave Melcombe a sideways glance as he changed gear. 'But I've not made a final decision on the best plan. Need to have bit of a chin wag and consider options first.'

'Oh yes?' Melcombe glanced back across at his companion and then resumed patting his pockets and peering into his wallet, an action he had commenced soon after the car had pulled away from the Cottage Hospital.

'Need to get a few things straight in my mind,' Ringham smiled and Melcombe caught the sight in the rear-view mirror. He was reminded of the skull on the life-sized skeleton he used to have hanging, as though on a gibbet, in his consulting room. It was cast in a hard cream-coloured plastic and articulated by metal hooks and eyes, and whilst realistic, he always felt the teeth were implausibly perfect and regular. Ringham's teeth had something of the same perfection, enviably free of fillings, but this also gave his smile an unsettling quality, as though he was just too perfect to be true. In many ways Ringham was a true friend, but Melcombe had always retained the thought that he was not completely to be trusted. The man was just too ruthless and efficient to ever allow emotions to stand in the way of looking after number one.

'Then we can start by you handing the ring over. You do have it don't you, Barnaby?' Melcombe retorted, his voice irritable. He was jittery and anxious and had been brooding about the loss of the Cobra's Eye since the moment he had seen that odd note left in its place, the same note that he had scrunched into a little ball in his hand, but which now he could not find, despite the constant searching of his pockets and wallet. 'You did find it? I know Irons took it.'

'I have it. It was easy enough to follow him and choose an opportune moment to retrieve it.'

'But did you have to kill him, for God's sake?' Melcombe spat the words out.

'He was a liability. We couldn't risk him saying any more than he's already blabbed across the papers. They were turning him into a minor sensation. Still, the diamond is quite a beauty.' Ringham raised an eyebrow. 'Clearly you have an eye for quality. I can see why you are so interested.'

Melcombe felt his heart almost miss a beat. 'Hand it over! I must see it at once!'

'I think not. Sorry Percy old boy, but I shall take care of it – for now. You managed to lose it once, and we really can't risk that a second time, can we? And besides, things are a touch dicey at the moment and if you were caught with it on your person, you'd hang without a second's thought, and there'd not be a lot I could do to save you. Far better I hold on to it until we're out of the woods, eh.'

'It's mine! I want it back...'

Hades emitted a low, deep growl, his ears held back.

'Yours?' An eyebrow was raised. 'An interesting interpretation. And how exactly did you come by it?' Ringham gave Melcombe a sideways glance. 'One is coming around to thinking you took it by force from that unfortunate young woman. That does alter the situation, you must admit.'

Melcombe said nothing. The engine rumbled and the dog emitted a similar low note though barely audible as they passed a convoy of three scarlet painted British Road Services articulated lorries, each carrying long sheeted loads of steel from the Corby Steelworks, the sound of their straining motors intruding on their conversation and the car immediately filling with choking exhaust fumes.

'Are you quite sure it was an accident? I have my doubts, frankly. The word "murder" keeps coming to mind.'

'How dare you!' Melcombe's eyes bulged behind his glasses, but he was trembling. 'Murder! How could you imagine it? It- it was an unfortunate piece of bad luck, that's all. Tragic, quite terrible of course, but she fell awkwardly and hit her head. I never touched her.'

'As you said. But I was never fully convinced from the start, but I needed you free of scandal and I couldn't allow an investigation at any cost, so we just brushed it under the carpet, so as to speak. Under the garden ornament, more like!'

The car swept past The Green Man, an old roadside pub set beside fields on the edge of a woody area, the car park packed with exotic and brightly painted motorcars, many in British racing green, though there were others in red, pale blue or even silver, and most bearing white roundels with bold black numbers on their sides. Young men in fur-lined pilot's jackets leant against their vehicles, smoking, drinking and chatting, some revving their engines others tinkering beneath open bonnets. It was the first day of a big race meeting at Silverstone, the racetrack a short distance away down a narrow approach road, and so the racers were gathering good and early at their customary watering hole, the air around them filled with the smell of petrol and loud with burbling exhausts.

Ringham looked past Melcombe at the cars and noticed that his stylish two-seater drew some admiring glances. 'A little more candour would not have gone amiss.'

'I'm very grateful for your help Barnaby. But and I paid you well for services rendered don't forget. I sold four of my finest to raise the necessary funds. My God, Barney, I even parted with an 'Ecu au Soleil' of 1574 and that lovely Genoa 'Quadruple' of 1617!'

Ringham snorted. He was not sounding suitably impressed.

'And don't forget I gave up my practice and moved away.' Melcombe continued his complaint. 'You cannot accuse me of not playing ball, and now to suggest I killed her?'

'But you kept the real reason she died a secret. Naughty.'

'The ring was irrelevant to what happened. She fell awkwardly, as she was leaving...it was just a tragic accident.' Ringham narrowed his eyes and remained silent. 'Look, the ring was no darned use to her by then...why not keep it?' Melcombe was trying to edge himself closer to the passenger door, away from the trails of saliva dripping from the mouth of Hades, who in turn, was staring back with beady eyes and occasionally emitting a sound that Melcombe could feel resonating deep from within the Rottweiler's chest. 'What's does it matter now? What's done is done. God, how I wish I had never set eyes on it. I think that ring is cursed. It brings bad luck, I can sense it.' His voice was weak, he was tiring again and the enormity of the situation was starting to overwhelm him. 'I never said a word, not about her nor about the work I did.'

Ringham was slowing the car and swung it smoothly across the now empty road and into a gravelly lay-by where a black and yellow AA box was set back into the grassy verge, the car's signal indicator ticking loudly and making an orange light flash on the dashboard. There were tall stands of dank trees lining either side of the road edged by a narrow open area of rough scrubby bushes and lank grass holding drifts of recently fallen leaves. They could just detect a faint, distant growl of high-performance engines blazing in short staccato bursts as the men burned scarce and valuable fuel in wasteful dips of the throttle. Though they were a few turns of the road away from The Green Man, it felt still and even strangely quiet in the lay by, with just the gentle drip of water from the night rain plopping from the damp trees. A dank mist was curling around the dense regiments of trunks, weak sun skimming the tops, but barely penetrating the dark interior, lending the scene a mournful quality of soft wet colours and muted sound.

'Is that so?' Ringham twisted in the seat to face Melcombe, square on. 'Before that burglary I might have been inclined to agree old boy. Your discretion was a credit – and you were rewarded accordingly.' He gave Melcombe a steely look. 'The scandal would be incalculable if word got out.' His voice hardened. 'Don't forget, some of those girls are darned well connected; one was minor royalty. It was not our job to comment on their loose morals and apparent inability to take more care in bed. Our job was to fix the situation they got themselves in and keep silent.'

'I know all this. I don't need a bloody lecture thank you!'

'Does no harm to reinforce the point. There could be far-reaching effects. The gutter press would have a field day. One slip up, one leak that you'd helped Lady This or Dowager What's-Her-Name lose an illegitimate child, and you can just imagine the reaction. An absolute rout.'

'Change the record. Nobody has heard a thing from me!'

'You say that, but these last days I've wondered how that idiot Irons knew to enter your house and find the ring? A ring you kept so quiet even I knew nothing about it until you asked me to recover it. Strange, don't you think? And don't fob me off about your beloved coins. He wasn't after those and you know it. You let the cat out of the bag. How else could he know? So I need a name, a time, the place you let your defence down. Its confession time Percy old boy.' Hades now growled with an alarming sense of timing.

'I don't know! He must have stumbled on it by accident.' Melcombe's voice was weak and hoarse and there was perspiration on his brow.

'You're not convincing me. And you look half scared to death. What's got into you? You're acting like you've lost something; you're fidgeting like you've got fleas. What is it?'

Melcombe looked ashen and stopped rootling for the umpteenth time in his tweed jacket pockets. 'Er... There is something, actually. I-I must have dropped it when getting dressed. Look, I think we must go back, we must find it. I rather fear it could be significant.'

Chapter Forty

Brackley
28th September 1950

'The Merry Chemist' was run by a Mrs Merry and Vignoles concluded after only the briefest of encounters, that whilst she may have chosen her husband for all manner of reasons unknown to himself, the fact that she would adopt his appropriately cheerful surname may just have swung the balance. Everything about her radiated a sense of contentment, from her apple-red cheeks creased by an open smile across a rotund face to her broad bare arms folded across a vast bosom encased in a white cotton short-sleeved overcoat and bright floral printed dress that heaved and flowed with her laughter at any opportunity. Even the tight bun of hair held in place by two hair pins that could cause considerable damage if used as a weapon, did nothing to diminish her pleasant demeanour.

Her bright clothes and personality were much needed within the dark and claustrophobic interior of the chemist. The shop was part of a short row that included the Oak Cottage Café and all were ancient structures of local stone with sagging rooflines and dropped window arches. The row was leaning more than standing along one edge of the town square presenting a most decrepit feel to an area dominated by the elegant Christopher Wren styled Town Hall and the collegiate aura of Magdalen College School. The Merry Chemist's window was bowed out and multi-paned, with some of the glass rippled and distorted and so betraying its antiquity, whilst the door requiring a hard shoulder shove to release it from the opening skewed out of true. Inside, the walls were lined from floor to ceiling by dark wooden shelves jam packed with packets and packages new and faded, with bottles both dusty and clean and of glass clear and coloured containing strange liquids identified by rectangular blue edged labels. There were rows of tinctures, oils, lotions and tubes of embrocation, ointments and toothpastes. Curled cardboard adverts for Dreene Shampoo and Calvex Carbolic Compound cluttered the glass topped counter and whole areas of shelving were stacked with medicines and pills and rolls of bandages and emergency slings in sealed packets. It smelt of Fiery Jack and menthol, of dust and brown paper and powerful cough drops. Vignoles wondered if he would live a longer and healthier life just by inhaling this heady mix, but after an exploratory lung full or two, decided he longed for fresh air and his pipe.

Maud Askew, in contrast to Mrs Merry, was looking smaller than he remembered. She appeared somehow diminished in height and character, a slight and shrunken figure in her overcoat and almost overwhelmed by the dark shelves laden with medicinal products. She hovered near a low doorway, but managed a little smile, before dropping her eyes to the floor. After Mrs Merry had cheerfully greeted the two detectives and asked how she might help, Mrs Askew stepped forward and quietly attracted Merry's attention.

'This is the gentleman I said would call this morning. Inspector Vignoles. He's with the police. And this is sergeant...er...'

'Trinder.' He lifted his hat

Vignoles formally introduced himself, showing his warrant card to Mrs. Merry.

'An inspector calls!' Mrs Merry gave a conspiratorial smile, then immediately attempted to look grave. 'You may use the back room. I hope you have news...I can hold the fort here, and take as long as you need Maud.'

Mrs Askew gave Merry a brief look that was hard to interpret, then lifted up a section of the counter and invited them to follow her, but as Trinder passed Merry, she urgently touched his arm and whispered 'She needs you to find her.'

The back room was tiny and Vignoles squeezed himself behind a table that betrayed a lifetime of smoothing by continual scrubbing and shifting a carton of St James' Balm to give him more elbow room whilst Maud Askew perched on a straight-backed chair. Trinder elected to lean against a Welsh dresser crammed with packets and boxes and piles of bills and receipts skewered onto tall metal spikes.

'Would you like some tea?' She held up a teapot encased in a knitted cosy.

'No, thank you. We should not keep you longer than absolutely necessary.' Vignoles had eyed the lethal-looking gas ring in the corner and was pleased to have a valid excuse to prevent the three of them having to shuffle positions and share the space with an open flame. 'You wished to speak with me?'

'I-I want to confess something to you.' She glanced at Trinder.

'Please don't mind my sergeant, but it is better to have two sets of ears in such an investigation. Just talk to me - one to one.' Vignoles tried to be reassuring.

'Yes, of course, I meant no offence.' Trinder gave her a nod that implied none were taken. 'You must take notes and things of course. Write it all down...' She looked flustered and pulled a handkerchief from her sleeve and gave her nose a blow. 'I didn't want to say anything in front of Henry. He would just get upset – not really angry you understand? He's a good man at heart, but he'd take it the wrong way.' She now fiddled with the lid of the teapot. 'He's a practical man. Down to earth, like Betty, really.' She smiled fondly. 'He likes things in black and white does Henry, so he would only tell me to stop talking silly nonsense. There's no room for ambig... ambig-you...'

'Ambiguity?'

'Yes, that's it. No room for any of that in his world.' She smiled sadly. 'I hope you understand. You do need to know this.'

'Any information is vital. Detective work rather depends on facts, demonstrable facts, but we are open minded and willing to listen to anything you have to say...' Vignoles was curious. Was this to be a vital revelation or a wild goose chase? He could not imagine where it was leading.

'That's true...' Mrs Askew looked nonplussed as she considered Vignoles' response. 'You may find what I am about to tell you hard to believe. You might dismiss it and tell me my nerves are frayed, that I need a dose of that Vimaltol.' She pointed to a cardboard box near Trinder's right elbow. 'But I can assure you I am perfectly clear headed and would swear on the bible this happened.'

Vignoles made a gesture with his hands. 'Understood...'

'You will remember that my Henry mentioned a note Betty had in the ring box but which she left behind on her dressing table.'

'And which subsequently went missing.'

'Yes. Well I can tell you when and how it went. I didn't accidentally throw it away. It was far too precious for that to happen.'

'I can appreciate that.'

'But what could I tell Henry? I told you he is not given to things being out of the ordinary.' She dropped the teapot lid on the table and hurriedly replaced it, before folding her arms tight, the hankie balled in one fist. 'Sorry! It's just so upsetting.'

'Why don't you just tell me what happened, and we can see what to make of it?'

'Yes, of course. It was on the 18th. There's no possibility I would forget. I can tell you what time as well. It was 4.30pm, because we have a half-day and I was home by then having queued at the butcher's and got us a bit of brisket for the evening meal and then managed to get a tin of Bird's custard powder. I was nervous the whole time I was queuing because there was the most dreadful storm brewing. It was so close, all sticky and oppressive. It made me feel headachy and I was glad to be home and still out for when the Heaven's opened. Anyway, I had this tin of custard powder and was feeling really pleased with myself as I'd collected some blackberries the evening before, and with a couple of cooking apples I thought to make a nice crumble. I'm only telling you all this because I want you to appreciate that I can remember everything very clearly. Accurately.' She nodded at Trinder who had started making notes but had left his pencil hovering above the page the moment she started discussing her meal options. 'So, there I was in the kitchen with the door open into the hallway having just putting the shopping away and thinking to start making the crumble.' She stopped, dabbing her nose gently and gathering herself for the next stage. Vignoles urged her to get to the point.

'I had my back to the hall, rootling out a suitable dish for the crumble and there I was, head in a cupboard when I got the strangest sensation. I felt so cold it made me shiver all over. I was almost convulsing with the shakes and my teeth had set chattering. When you catch a chill it usually starts with sneezing or your throat, doesn't it?'

Vignoles inclined his head in agreement. Where was this going? He was starting to regret leaving the search of Melcombe's cottage to the constabulary.

'This was more like an icy finger down my spine and such a contrast to the clamminess of the day, it being so oppressive with that storm. I was unable to anything but hug myself to try and stop the shivers. But then I realised someone was looking at me.'

Trinder pulled himself upright and Vignoles took a sharp intake of breath.

'I was staring at the back of the cupboard and I thought, someone's come in and they've left the door open making a draught. But then I thought, they're up to no good, creeping up on me like that, so I picked up the rolling pin and turned around. I'm not having someone come into my house uninvited. I'll give 'em what for!' She nodded to reinforce the point and held Vignoles' attention. 'Jesus, Mary and the Saints preserve me, she was there. Just standing in the doorway as close as the sergeant is to me now. Oh, I nearly died of fright!' She pressed the handkerchief to her mouth, knuckles whitening with the pressure, eyes brimming.

'Who was there?' Vignoles asked.

'Betty! My daughter. Just looking at me.'

Silence fell in the room, allowing the sound of the shop bell to ring softly from behind the closed connecting door.

'Let me get this absolutely clear, you saw your daughter, Betty on the afternoon of the 18th of this month?'

Mrs Askew nodded, keeping the handkerchief tight against her mouth, fighting to keep their emotions under control.

Vignoles leant forward over the table. 'This is extremely significant. But... surely this is wonderful news? You must be so relieved. Whatever difficulties she may have got herself into, the most important thing is that she's...'

'Stop! Stop!' Maud Askew waved a raised hand like a drunken traffic policeman and blew her nose, gulping in air. 'No. She's not alive. It was not the flesh and blood Betty I saw.' She sobbed and clawed for more air as Vignoles and Trinder watched in stunned silence. She regained her composure and after one last sniff, spoke in a quiet if slightly shaky voice. 'It was her spirit, inspector. She was hardly there and at moments she was almost see through, at other moments as clear as you are here...but it was Betty. She came back.' There was a conviction in Maud Askew's voice that could not be ignored.

'I'm sorry?' Vignoles glanced up at Trinder, who had a look of surprise on his face that was almost comical. Vignoles managed to hide any emotion and resorted to the old standby of removing his glasses and polishing them, frowning as he did so. 'You saw the ghost of your daughter standing in the kitchen doorway?'

'I knew you would believe me!' Askew looked as though a burden had suddenly lifted. Her face started to regain some colour and her shoulders visibly relaxed. 'I cannot tell you what comfort I gain from sharing this, and especially as you are the police. That means a lot. She came to see me; to let me know she'd not forgotten us, that we were uppermost in her thoughts.' She gave a strange faraway look. 'At first it upset me, and I was disturbed and frightened. It knocked me sideways. but then you came around asking questions and I knew that something was happening, that things would work out.' Askew made a sad little half smile. 'Something terrible happened to her - I know that now. I think I always thought so, but you don't want to give up hope.'

'No...' Vignoles swallowed with difficulty. Trinder shifted his weight onto another foot.

'She's lost to us in this world, but I know that soon you will find her, find her cold bones and she can be laid to rest. And I can't really ask more than that, not now. You will find her, and we can lie her in the same grave that... that one day I hope we can also lay poor Ray's body in.'

'Perhaps we could take a step back?' Vignoles was reeling. 'You were in the kitchen feeling cold and chilly, you turned around because you sensed someone was there and had left the front door open, and you saw Betty. You are quite sure?'

'I would recognise my own daughter.'

'Of course.' Vignoles was trying to keep his voice level. 'And what did she say?'

'Nothing. Not at first. She just looked at me and I couldn't do anything. I just stared.'

'And then?'

'She showed me something. Her hands were cupped as though she were at the communion rail.' Maud Askew demonstrated the action. 'But in her hands instead of the host was that little note, the one from her dressing table. I saw it as clear as day, then she clasped it tight in one fist and just said, "Forgive me."' Askew dabbed her nose and took a deep breath. 'Now I get a bit confused, what with all the emotion and the shock... but I think I ran towards her, just wanting to hold her, hug her, but she said "No! Please stop!" Oh, and she looked so pained so distressed that I did stop though all of me so wanted to hold her.' She then smiled, a fond, warm affectionate smile that surprised the two detectives. 'She looked me in the eye and said. "I must go. I cannot hold on any longer. I must, but I need this – it will help explain everything. Forgive me! Help me rest..." And then, inspector, she vanished. Just faded away, like steam clears from a window.'

*   *   *   *

'What on earth to make of that?' Vignoles took a long sip of beer and wiped his mouth. 'It's a touch early for a pint, but quite frankly I need something stronger than milky coffee now.' They were seated on one of a number of benches outside the Red Lion, just out of view of The Merry Chemist, as a welcome gap in the clouds allowed the surprisingly strong sunlight to dry the ground around the market place and warm their backs.

'I didn't see that coming,' Trinder agreed. 'It makes you wonder though.' Vignoles eyed his sergeant suspiciously. 'That Irons fellow was adamant he'd met the ghost of Betty and now her own mother is saying the same thing. We have to take her seriously.'

'We cannot dismiss there have been sightings of the woman herself or a look-a-like, but a ghost? Come off it, John!' Vignoles sounded contemptuous and Trinder remained silent whilst they sipped more ale. 'You're saying a ghost took that little note from the girl's bedroom?'

'You heard what the mother said. She was quite convincing.'

'She was, but despite her reassurances to the contrary, she was also emotional and upset. All that's happened these last days has reawakened the loss of her daughter. It could be a mixture of hallucination and guilt for actually losing that piece of paper making her imagine this, by way of an explanation of her own mistake?' Vignoles stared into his beer. 'I don't want to sound hard on her, but being charitable, we still need to overlook the improbable physical difficulties involved for a spirit being to handle a real piece of paper, let alone understand why the ghost of Betty Askew would do that?' A wasp danced around the top of his glass and he flapped at it with a hand. 'OK, let's review we are in the case and see if that helps. We're waiting on a firm i.d. on the head, but early indications from the debris we found in the bonfire and the fact it is the head of a younger woman with the same hair colour, indicate this is likely to be Betty Askew.'

'Agreed.' Trinder nodded, also wafting a wasp away.

'The hand found adjacent to Brackley railway viaduct could well be that of a young woman. We await further analysis but I am not expecting much. There's a limit on what they can they determine from some long-cleaned bones. That they are the hand of a young woman, but no more.'

'There is a possibility they could be Betty's.'

'Based on what? That they were found close to where Dr Melcombe now lives? A coincidence at best. We'd be shot down in flames presenting that as evidence.'

'True...' Trinder looked crestfallen. 'It is more a gut feeling than anything else, but I still think we're on the right track – literally. The railway line links the two locations, and the doctor moved here soon after Betty disappeared, upping sticks in a hurry. Look, what if the hands were thrown out of the window of a moving train? I could imagine he was aiming for the river? It was a decent attempt to conceal body parts that would help identify the body whilst still covered in flesh, but now, picked clean and with no body attached they are virtually impossible to identify with any certainty.' Trinder looked pleased with his hypothesis and drank some ale.

'It's a decent theory. The trouble is that's all it is and all but useless for building a case against him. I think we're right to identify Melcombe as prime suspect in this heinous crime, but so far we don't have a darned thing that will stick.'

'But her head was buried in his garden! In a box that can be clearly linked to him.'

'And his defence will say he was out of the house at the time and knew nothing about it. The box was close to hand and used by whoever committed the crime. Unless the lab boys can find his fingerprints, preferably bloody ones, we may struggle to prove he actually put her in there. It sounds plausible, even probable, but is it enough to convict him of murder? We need something that places his hands on her remains...and we need a body as well. However, we've got the Bucks Constabulary stripping Dr Melcombe's former home down to the floorboards and the Northants chaps doing the same in Ivy Cottage. Let's hope we find the other remains of that poor woman or some clue to her whereabouts. So far we've got nothing more than suspicions...oh drat these wasps!' Vignoles narrowly avoided swallowing one crawling along the top of his glass.

'They're dozy in the autumn.' Trinder was observing a couple at the next table having a similar problem with over-attentive wasps. He shook some coins from his pocket and selected three ha'pennies and laid them in a triangle shape on the table. Vignoles observed with a puzzled expression but said nothing. Trinder continued discussing the case as if nothing had happened. 'We've nothing conclusive to prove he is a killer, and that's why he is not under arrest?'

'And don't forget, he was laid up in hospital when Irons was killed,' Vignoles replied. 'If he was involved, then it was at arm's length. Someone else did the actual deed – someone with a dog.'

'An assassination?'

Vignoles winced. 'Hmm, put like that, it sounds far-fetched, but Melcombe could have paid someone to do it. Or Melcombe has an accomplice, the two working as a team.'

'The man with the vicious dog.' Trinder nodded in agreement. 'What strikes me is that there is always someone else, unknown or unseen lurking nearby.'

'Explain.'

'I went to see 'The Third Man' again last week, I went with Violet. She needed a few of hours rest from looking after the little lad, so Jenny came over to baby sit and we went to the pictures. Only up the road and just for an hour and half or so and a swift drink in The White Hart after. You know the film?'

'Of course, I've also seen it twice!'

Trinder grinned. 'Well, the Joseph Cotton character thinks Harry Lime is dead and is working on that assumption for much of the film, but things only start to make sense once he realises that Lime is actually alive and kicking. Now, until we identify Melcombe's accomplice we can't make a breakthrough here. It's as though this other person is the most important player in this drama. And it's the same with Irons. We've been looking for his accomplice and failing to find her. It's as though there is a third man – or third woman - just outside the frame in both cases.'

Vignoles started to fill his pipe as he considered this observation. He looked intrigued. 'Go on...'

'Don't shoot me down on this, but I think the key is the ghost of Betty Askew. She knows what really happened in Melcombe's surgery, who dismembered her body and where the parts are now concealed, and she – the ghost that is – also convinced Irons to break into the murderer's house and do...something. I don't know what.' Trinder looked apologetic. 'But he was disturbed whilst doing whatever it was, and the plan went wrong.' Trinder held up a hand to stop Vignoles speaking. 'Bear me out. Betty's ghost also went to her parent's house the day of the break in and took something that potentially could incriminate Melcombe. Did she show this to Irons? I'm not sure what happened between them, but she did something that convinced him to turn into a burglar.' He paused and was encouraged by Vignoles' silence. 'It also struck this was a curious detail for Mrs Askew to invent or imagine. So, like Harry Lime has Betty somehow risen from the dead? I don't know...But she's there all right, deep inside this mystery.'

'I cannot disagree with the last part of your argument...'

'I think she gave the note to Irons. Finding both ring and note is vital. The ring is motivation for Melcombe killing Askew. If he is found with it, surely this proves he took it in 1943 when she was at his surgery.'

Vignoles exhaled slowly, blowing air from between his lips so they made a sound. 'Or he bought it from a dealer in the intervening years? But I agree, it suggests he had contact with her and could help our case. Going back to your hypothesis, I appreciate that if Melcombe killed her for the *Cobra's Eye*, he would be shocked to discover something that related directly to this appalling crime appear in his new house. Telling him someone else knows his guilty secret. But how on earth can a shadowy imprint of a long dead person do that?' Vignoles looked stumped. 'Are we saying she's befriending young men travelling on trains whilst carrying pieces of paper?'

Trinder shrugged his shoulders. 'It's like these coins. They drive the wasps away. I cannot explain how or why, all I know is it works.'

'What?' Vignoles drained his glass and stared at Trinder.

'Have you noticed they've all gone? The wasps.'

'That's coincidence!' However, Vignoles noticed the couple were still being pestered at the next table and the woman had even resorted to standing up and waving her arms at an especially intrusive insect in a manner likely to get her stung.

Trinder stood up, walked across to their table and had a brief conversation with them. They looked puzzled, then laughed. The man jingled some coins into his hand and selected three as Trinder returned with an empty jam pot, the last remnant of the scones and cream they'd been eating, with three big wasps crawling over the traces of raspberry jam left inside. He carefully placed this unappetising receptacle inside the triangle of copper coins and sat down. 'Watch!'

'John, if your little experiment works...' A wasp flew into the air, angrily circling like a noisy fighter plane, then flew off on a wobbly flight path. 'I might just countenance your crazy theory.'

Trinder grinned. The other two insects soon followed, and there was a shout from the couple nearby. 'I say? It bally well worked can you believe that? Thanks awfully!' Trinder touched the brim of his hat. 'Remember, only copper coins!'

Vignoles looked flabbergasted. 'It could just be coincidence...'

'I agree. But we are free of them and that's all that matters. My grandmother taught me how to scare wasps like this and it's served me well. Look sir, you always tell me to work on facts, and the fact is this works. I can't tell you how or why, just as I cannot explain the ghost of Betty Askew and won't try to. But the facts of the case suggest that she, though dead, still has an active part to play and I think we need to follow that trail.'

Vignoles was toying with his empty glass, in the act of convincing himself another beer was not a good idea and should return to Ivy Cottage to see how the house search was progressing. 'And how on earth to I tell Badger that?'

'Perhaps keep it under our hats until we get something more definite? We could explore this angle quietly...not shout about it like those adventure seekers on the late train. I admit we could be literally chasing shadows.'

'Low key...yes, that has something to recommend it,' Vignoles shook his head in disbelief. 'Can you find me something tangible? Something physical we can bring to bear against that doctor...'

Their attention was drawn to the sound of a black Wolseley approaching at speed. They saw Bainbridge in the passenger seat uniformed officer wearing a flat cap behind the wheel, both men searching for someone. Bainbridge glanced in their direction and signalled urgently to Vignoles and Trinder as the car swung into the market place, the unlit blue lamp flashing bright as it was struck by a shaft of sunlight.

'Something is wrong,' and both Vignoles and Trinder stood up and walked towards the car that now screeched to a halt. Bainbridge was speaking through the opened window before the car had stopped.

'Troubling news, Vignoles. Melcombe has gone! Checked out a little over half an hour ago with his lawyer. A smooth-talker apparently, who was trying to bribe Matron to say nothing with a ten-shilling note, but she was sufficiently annoyed by his arrogant attitude to call us.'

'She was not to know Melcombe was a murder suspect.' Vignoles looked grim. 'They left by car? Any details?'

'Yes, and that's the better news. A very distinctive vehicle; a two-seater soft top all white Hawker Siddeley Hurricane. Wire wheels and red leather seats.'

'Phew...' Trinder whistled softly. 'Very flash.'

'We have the license plate. It will stand out like a sore thumb.' Bainbridge tried to look optimistic.

'But half an hour's start... Which direction did they go? No matter, they can easily lose themselves and double-back along innumerable country roads.' Vignoles balled a fist and tapped it gently on his palm, thinking hard.

'There's more.' Bainbridge stepped out of the car. 'There was a dog, a big black and tan feller seated on the excuse for a back seat in these sports cars.'

Vignoles and Trinder exchanged looks. 'Interesting. Do we know who the lawyer is?' Vignoles was impatient to get moving but this needed consideration.

'Wait, I think PC Blencowe found a name...' Trinder was flipping through his little black notebook. 'Yes, got it! Mr. Barnaby Ringham. Has a

Belgravia address...' They all exchanged meaningful looks. 'Apparently he's awfully expensive and with a reputation for winning un-winnable cases for the rich and powerful. According to PC Blencowe, anyway.'

'He might prove a powerful ally for Melcombe.' Vignoles observed.

'We have a clear description of this chap from matron and he sounds like the same man. His clothes were immaculate and probably bespoke and has a watch that looked like it cost a fortune.' Bainbridge gave Trinder an approving glance. 'Good work getting a name.'

'Undone by not placing a guard on his room. I slipped up.' Vignoles looked grim. 'I didn't want to appear heavy-handed at this stage and considering his physical condition did not envisage him doing a runner. The hospital could not force him to stay, so the fault lies at my door.'

'Ringham was very persuasive. But look, there's something else you might be able to shed some light on. Melcombe's room was empty his things as you'd expect, except a nurse found this under the bed...' Bainbridge handed Vignoles a tiny ball of paper. It was soft and the paper betrayed signs of excessive handling. The three men gathered around as Vignoles teased it open.

'It's a curious message...' Bainbridge sounded puzzled.

'I could almost believe in coincidences now.' Vignoles allowed a little smile of satisfaction.

'It has to be what was taken from Betty's dressing table! I have the text written in my notebook - just a moment.' The ever-efficient Trinder did more riffling through the pages. 'It was dictated to us by Mrs Askew.'

'The same,' Vignoles was already convinced. 'Written by Private Coulson to go with the engagement ring he presented to Betty.'

Bainbridge peered at the little square of paper again and shook his head. 'You have the advantage on me here.'

'We can confirm its authenticity in a trice.' Trinder nodded his head in the direction of The Merry Chemist.

'Do so! Quickly.' Vignoles took a last look before handing it to his sergeant, who instantly strode off towards the wonky apothecary building. 'Perhaps Irons left this in Ivy Cottage. But could Betty Askew really have given this to him?'

'You've lost me, Inspector.'

'I'll explain later, but right now we need to apprehend Melcombe and Ringham. We must pull out all the stops and find them! As soon as the sergeant returns, would you be good enough to let us have use of your police station? We can mobilize a search operation and I can get word across the railway system to watch out for them boarding a train.'

'But they left by car, remember?' Bainbridge looked puzzled.

'We can hardly set up road blocks as we have no idea in which direction they are headed, it would be futile. But if their car is as eye-catching as you describe then they will have to abandon it sooner or later and choose another mode of transport. My hunch is, they'll park up at a station and take a train and blend in with the other passengers. Either that or they have a bolt hole nearby and will run to ground for a while.' Vignoles was holding his unlit pipe, a sure sign that he was thinking.

'I think you're right. Gosh, we're really up against it now!'

'We shall find them. It's only a matter of time. Their breaking cover has worked to our advantage in some respects. Innocent men don't go on the run.' He watched as Trinder strode purposefully back towards them, the diminutive figure of Maud Askew in the chemist doorway, a hand pressed to her mouth. Mrs Merry joined her, a robust arm encircling Askew's narrow shoulders that were now visibly shaking.

Chapter Forty-One

Brackley Hatch
28th September 1950

'Go back? Out of the question, old boy.'

'It's a tiny thing from inside the box that holds the ring. It would fit perfectly. It just has to be from there. It even names the diamond!'

'It has a name?'

'Yes, the *Cobra's Eye*. When a stone is that valuable there's a penchant for giving it a flamboyant title.'

'*The Star of India...*' Ringham was nodding his head.

'Exactly. The paper is exactly the same size as the box when folded and would have fitted it perfectly. But listen, I'd never seen this before, not until after the robbery that is. This is important! She did not have it in the box or on her person back then. Do you understand what I am saying? It was in place of the ring in the same drawer where I kept it. Irons must have put it there!' Melcombe was starting to sound frantic.

'Are you quite sure?'

'Of course I'm bloody sure!' Melcombe nodded and his frightened expression convinced Ringham.

'What did it say?'

'Just the name of the ring, a date and the initials of Elizabeth Askew and Raymond Coulson. R.C and E.A.'

'Who's he when he's at home?'

'Her fiancé. She told me about him. She claimed he'd given her this ring for their engagement. I was surprised and sceptical and a little insulting about the fellow, but the note confirms it. He was killed in El Alamein.'

'You are remarkably well informed.'

'How do I know?' Melcombe's eyes were wide, his breath coming in short inhalations. Glancing briefly at the dog that had now stopped emitting threatening sounds but was observing both men intently, the doctor leant forward and gripped Ringham's forearm. 'Believe me, there's something very wrong here. Coulson and Askew were both from Brackley!'

'What?'

'I swear I did not know before I moved. What ill fate brought me here? What made me choose this of all the places? I don't want to know anything about her, let alone walk around her home town! I tried to forget everything, to banish her name from my memory. We burnt her stuff and I was glad we did so, and I made a point of not looking at her address or anything that would remind me she was someone's daughter, someone's lover... I just didn't want to know! It was too horrific, too awful to see her as a real living person...'

'Get a grip, man. Calm down and explain - and cut the emotional stuff.' But even Ringham's calm exterior was starting to slip, his voice less forceful, less confident. He was distracted by a number of rooks that had launched themselves into the air from the treetops in a squalling cawing ragged explosion. They circled above the road like vultures looking for carrion. He freed his arm and reached into his suit to extract a silver cigarette case, chased with a monogrammed design on the lid, and flipping it open to reveal a gold interior, extracted two whilst Melcombe continued his story. The doctor's voice was little more than a hoarse mumble.

'I moved to Turweston because it looked like a quiet and respectable sort of village. Filled with well-to-do types and most in retirement, like me. Nobody was going to question my being there, no one ask impertinent questions. The perfect place to keep my head down, maybe do some fishing and live a quiet life...as we agreed.' Melcombe gratefully accepted the proffered cigarette. 'But only then, only after I had given everything up, did I discover that I'm living right in the eye of the storm! Her name was everywhere. Brackley is only a small town and her disappearance was big news. There were posters with her face plastered all over. I've even seen her parents beside the grave of that Coulson fellow. Slowly, I started to hear bits and pieces of the story and to make the connections.' His hand shook that was holding the cigarette. 'It's been a living nightmare, a daily penance. And then a man breaks into my house and not only takes the ring, but he leaves this dammed message. It's a warning! Someone knows everything.'

'Yes...' Ringham's matching silver lighter flared as he held the flame for Melcombe to light his cigarette. 'Yes, that would be most unfortunate.'

'Unfortunate! It's more than unfortunate.' Melcombe wound the window down and puffed a jet of smoke outside. 'Is that all you can say? That Inspector what's-his-name - the one who came visiting? He's rumbled us.'

'What?'

'He's found her. Part of her.' He glared at Ringham. 'But you'll know all about that! He's found her head buried in what was once my back garden. Christ almighty.' Melcombe puffed angrily, making sharp sounds. 'And if that was not bad enough, it was in a box that once held a pair of scales that can be traced right back to me. What were you thinking of? I'm done for.'

'I'd not heard they'd found her...' Ringham was smoking slowly, exhaling through the side of his mouth, eyes narrowed to slits, an elbow resting on the top of the car door, trying to exude an air of supreme confidence. He stared into the misty woods and contemplated this revelation.

'But in the garden? How could you be so bloody stupid. We agreed to take her off site. I trusted you to do that, Barnaby.'

Ringham was silent for a moment, flicking ash on to the ground. He stopped the flashing indicator and the sounds within the car were replaced by the cawing of the wheeling birds, the panting of his dog and the slight burning sound of the two cigarettes as the men pulled hard making the tobacco flare and crackle.

'Sit Hades!' Even Ringham was finding his beast annoying and the powerful dog reluctantly slunk back on the tiny rear bench seat. 'Let me explain. You'd taken the trunk to London, and seeing the taxi convey you to the station with that monstrous cargo was a relief. But I was tired, and starting feel the strain, to be honest. Yes, I can feel it too. There was a lot still to do, all the evidence to burn and that horrible mess to clean up, all the blood to wash and bleach away. I knew we must have the bonfire and get the embers dampened down before nightfall or we'd have the ARP banging on the door.' He sucked on the fag. 'Time was running short.'

'It was a nightmare. But darn it, we did a decent job under the circumstances.' Melcombe was reflective, his energy spent. 'But the woods were so close. A few hundred yards away, no more. You said you'd bury it there...'

'I knew we should remove her from the site, but the most important thing was nobody on your road should suspect a thing. If nobody saw her arrive or suspected she had been there, we could draw a veil across the whole affair. But if we put a foot wrong, we'd be finished. I'd parked the motor some distance away and walked to your house making darned sure nobody saw me, but as soon as you'd gone to the station, the blessed street became a hive of activity; first the baker's van, then the butcher's, although I'm damned if I know what they were selling. Whatever scragg ends of meat he was peddling, it brought your neighbours out, and then, just as I thought it had quietened down, a bunch of Boy Scouts came around with a hand cart collecting junk for a Spitfire fund. I couldn't risk walking out of your house. It only took one person to see me carrying a large box, and we could be in tight spot. I thought it better to bury it in the garden and heave that monstrous birdbath thing on top and get her belongings burnt.' He drew long and hard on his fag. 'I wanted all trace of her destroyed, everything put back in order by the time you returned. By not telling you, it would make it easier for you to live there until you moved away.'

'I suppose I can see that... I just thought her boots and a few non-flammable things were under the birdbath.'

'No, the big stuff went to the boy scouts. I nipped out and left a bundle by the gate whilst they were occupied at another house. I hardly need point out I was especially careful not to be observed. I don't believe they stopped to question why they were there, just gladly hauled the lot away. It was untraceable.'

'At least that makes us equal.' Melcombe's breathing was laboured.

'How so?'

'I concealed the existence of the Cobra's Eye and you lied about what was buried in the back garden.' Melcombe forced a weak smile of triumph. Privately, Melcombe felt an odd surge of relief.

He'd called Ringham immediately after he had realised that Askew was dead. He was desperate for help. He knew he could never hope to conceal this woman's death and remove all trace of her on his own, and so had called 'Mr Fix It,' as Barney Ringham was known to his friends and colleagues. He'd responded immediately and with a chilling coolness that was both a balm to the doctor's frazzled nerves, and yet had also frightened him. Ringham appeared quite unmoved by the situation and able to plan and plot the grisly distribution of her body parts as though planning nothing more taxing than a vicarage tea party. Melcombe had even wondered if this were a task he'd performed before. It was disturbing and set a little alarm bell ringing in his mind.

As they were completing the appalling task of butchering her body, Melcombe had felt the compulsion to do something he'd never fully understood at the time, but which now made more sense. As Ringham left the cold washroom to find the rubberized gas cape they would use to wrap the torso within, the doctor had swiftly deployed a sharp scalpel and sliced off one of the unique monogrammed buttons from Ringham's blazer draped across a chair back. He'd slipped this distinctive and specially commissioned button into a neat slit cut with the same scalpel into the layers of varnished paper pasted on the inside of the trunk, having first smeared it with the blood of the mutilated hunk of meat that once had been a young woman. A little calling card that offered him some protection. It was dreadfully risky to leave any clue that could be traced, but this was his idea of an insurance policy. It placed Ringham right there, incriminated without a shadow of doubt and it might prove useful. It would ensure that his friend would keep on protecting him, continue to keep him safe and do anything to maintain this deadly secret. It was just a case of deciding when he should play his ace and tell Barnaby - if at all.

Ringham knew nothing of Melcombe's thoughts, and nodded, imperceptivity. He might concede the point that they were equal but was not ready to voice it aloud.

Hades suddenly sat upright, pressing his snout to the small rear window, the hackles rising down his back like a ridge of dark trees. A deep growl, throaty and anxious filled the car with an ominous rumble. His front paws shifted in small, rapid movements on the smooth leather, and his big head swung from side to side as he tried to gain a better view.

'What the Devil's got into you?' Ringham twisted in his seat to try and look at his dog that was clearly upset about something outside. The growling was continuing, but now frequently interrupted by a thin whining note that betrayed fear, accompanied by the flashing of the whites of his rolling eyes.

'Stop that!' Ringham thrashed an arm at the dog's haunches, but Hades just redoubled his efforts, pawing frantically at the window and claws scratching at the glass. At that moment the dog realised this was futile and tried to force his big head over the seat, between his master and the door frame, and so out of the opened window. 'What the Hell's got into you? Get down!' Ringham looked flustered and angry.

'Look, there's someone in the woods,' Melcombe pointed, his hand trembling. 'It looks like a young woman in a white...' He was peering through his spectacles, his jaw now gaping. 'No... but that's impossible...' Melcombe wiped a drop of perspiration from his forehead and blinked.

The dog was now forcing his great bulk onto the shoulder of Ringham, the horrible growling and whimpering filling the tiny cockpit.

'Get off me!' Ringham opened the driver's door and both he and the dog spilled out, Ringham almost bundled over such was the frantic urge for Hades to give chase, barking furiously as he powered through the long damp grass at an alarming speed and leaped across a narrow drainage ditch filled with black stagnant water and rotting leaves.

'Come back! Heel!'

Melcombe eased himself out of his seat and painfully waddled around to the driver's side of the Hawker Siddeley. 'You should control him. He's dangerous. God, I never liked that that dog!'

Ringham look worried. 'Come back! Here boy!' He narrowed his eyes as his dog ignored the command. 'He's never done this before...'

They both now started walking in the tracks of the dog, trying to see both beast and the pale figure slipping easily between the dank tree trunks. She was elusive and moved surprisingly quickly. She appeared in one place before vanishing between the many green and grey trunks only to re-appear far away, the whole time the dog's rippling body was bundling noisily through the brown, orange and yellow bracken.

'He might hurt her for God's sake. Call your dog back!' Melcombe's face was florid and flushed but despite his obvious discomfort he lumbered after Ringham in painful lurching strides. Ringham for his part had sensed impending trouble and was now chasing after his dog, drawing away from the slower and obviously ailing doctor.

But the pale woman was able to avoid being mauled with consummate ease. Again and again she reappeared as though by magic, first in one place, then far away in another, forcing Hades to repeatedly change tack as though this was a deliberate teasing game on her part, his great head lifted high and snout sniffing noisily, interspersed by furious machine gun bursts of barking and painful whimpering. The dog's feet pounded on the leaf mould whilst the black birds maintained their cackling high above, but apart from these sounds, the wood felt unnervingly empty of life.

Melcombe stopped, leaning heavily upon a tree, his hat in one hand and head hung low as he gasped for air. He could not carry on and watched Ringham slip out of sight. He had no breath left to call after him. The trampling feet grew quieter and the wood fell still. Not even a squirrel to set a high branch swaying or a nuthatch darting up a trunk. He suddenly felt very alone, an overwhelming sense of emptiness dousing him like a cold shower that made him feel sick at heart. He was shivering and utterly miserable.

How had he come to this? The once respected doctor, a man with nearly £600 in the bank and a lovely cottage paid for in cash. He was a retired gentleman with a raft of investments in his portfolio worth thousands but now, he was standing in a gloomy copse of trees, aching from head to toe, heart painfully pounding in his chest. It was pathetic. And he was frightened.

There was something dangerous in this wood, something silent and elusive and he had the feeling it meant him harm. All he could see were dank trees quietly dripping rainwater onto leaf and floor, but whatever it was, it was close, and sending out darts of pure malice towards him, he could feel it drilling into him, and he was scared.

What was it about that pale figure that had induced him to leave the warmth and security of the car? Why had he not locked himself in and sat tight? Or driven away. For some reason he'd imagined that woman walking in the woods was that poor dead girl. It was verging on madness. And why were they chasing after her? Why couldn't Barney just catch his dumb dog and come back. The dog had dragged them here of course, and yet he sensed Barney was not immune to the spell and he'd been pulled deeper into this unattractive place, as though lured there. Melcombe noticed sadly that his feet were wet and going cold and the bottoms of his trousers were damp. The back of one hand had been scratched by a thorn and was releasing a thin dribble of blood. He watched a drop of scarlet drip onto the yellow leaves.

He pulled himself upright and looked about. He could just see the white of the car and hear a distant whimpering of Hades. Why was that ugly brute so distressed? The sound was almost painful, and Melcombe derived no comfort from knowing they had a powerful dog close to hand to offer protection. But from what? A young woman...

But this was no ordinary woman. He could see the likeness. It had been striking; the light mackintosh, the brown hair and the same style of hat. All night he had sensed her presence, felt her stalking about the cottage hospital, waiting outside his bedroom door, standing near the park wall on the street below, pushing the wardrobe door ajar and peering at him from the inky depths inside, and now here she was luring them into this wood and delaying their escape. Why had Barney pulled over, here of all places, to talk?

There she was beside their car. He stumbled towards her, legs quivering like jelly and almost refusing to work. 'Hey! Hey you!' His voice fell flat and dead as though he were shouting into a pile of surgical lint. 'Wait there!' He was scared, almost sick with apprehension, but he was also angry and tired. Enough of this madness, he wanted to confront her, whoever she was.

She looked up as he drew closer and when her eyes met his it was as though he'd been plunged into a bath of ice. His vision was playing tricks on him, perhaps because he was in such a state, making her appear one moment bright and clear then dull and faint, as though clouds were swiftly crossing the sky and she was first kissed by sunlight then cloaked by deep shadow in rapid succession. He reached the edge of the trees, and the wide verge of grasses that lay between them was a distance of only five or so yards.

There could be no mistake now. He could never forget that slightly funny, freckly face and those pale eyes. He recalled them looking at him, imploring him, he could hear her begging him to let go of her hand, to just take her money.

Askew raised her left hand, the fingers slightly splayed and could see the pale skin stretched taught over the small bones, her ring finger bare. She twisted and turned her hand to make this all the more obvious.

'Go away! Leave me alone!'

She stared back, her bloodless lips parting.

'What do you want from me! Did you send that man into my house?'

Askew raised her other arm, both hands now stretched towards him, reaching out with her fingers that looked so thin and delicate they were more like twigs on a tree in winter. There was no passing traffic on the road. Where were those men in their racing cars and the usual grinding noise of the heavy lorries that thundered past with annoying frequency? Melcombe was transfixed, unable to pull his eyes away from her and praying for a passing car or bus that might break the spell between them. But there was no relief, just the constant cawing of those blasted birds.

He clasped his hands to his heart and let out a cry of pain, eyes bulging in their sockets as her hands slowly dissolved into dust, pouring soundlessly to the ground to leave two vicious red raw stumps pointed accusingly at Melcombe. She laughed soundlessly. He fell forward, his vision now red with a bloody mist, no longer sure what was real or imagined, but he thought her head appeared fade into nothing an appalling headless, handless body was left standing in mute testimony beside the 'Hurricane' two-seater.

'What the Hell's the matter with you? Stop that infernal noise you idiot!'

Ringham was shaking the doctor, and none to gently, trying to pull the now kneeling Melcombe to his feet. 'Shut up!' He slapped the doctor then clamped his mouth closed to stop the hideous wailing he was emitting like a pig being inexpertly stuck in a backyard killing.

Melcombe looked at Ringham in surprise as though he were only just aware he was there. 'It was her. It was her.'

'I've no idea who she was. She ran off and Hades came back.' Ringham clicked his fingers and the dog, tail now between his legs but hackles still ruffled, slunk quietly and obediently through the open door and into the rear of the car. 'Wait there!' He slammed the door shut.

'It was the girl. She's come for us...'

'What are you on about? She disappeared somewhere over the far side of the wood. Who was that beside the car?'

Melcombe started to cough, his hands pressed to his chest. 'Oh...oh...'

'What's wrong? Look, take it easy, deep breaths. There's no one here.' Ringham glanced up and down the eerily empty road, suddenly deeply worried about the state of his colleague. 'Don't do this to me. Pull yourself together man!' But Melcombe keeled over his legs collapsing and mouth and eyes open in a horrible rigor of pain and terror.

'Don't die on me... Not here!' Ringham stared at the crumpled form on the ground and knew it was too late. 'You bloody fool. I don't believe this...' He wiped his brow and closed his eyes for a moment, trying to think. It was his turn to take deep breaths. He opened his eyes again, scanned the area to check that there was nothing approaching and then set to work.

Melcombe was a slim man, and Ringham had kept himself in trim playing tennis as often as he could manage and the occasional fencing lesson, so he found the dead weight easy to drag backwards through the undergrowth and beneath the great stand of trees. The wetness of the long grasses and the slippery clay under foot aided the dragging of the body, but long fingers of wild rose and bramble tore at Ringham's trouser legs and his expensive hand-made brogues struggled for purchase and he had to dig them deep into sticky earth in order to pull the body into deeper cover, releasing a smell of mushrooms and rotting leaves as he did so.

There was no time to properly hide the body, so he just scooped armfuls of dead leaves and piled them over the corpse. It was not a good job, but it just might evade detection for a few hours if he was lucky. He sprinted back to the car, calculating how quickly he could drive to the station. He could hear Hades barking furiously in a yelping frantic noise that made his blood run cold, what had got into the animal?

He stopped dead, face blanching. 'Flats!' He spoke aloud, staring in disbelief at the Hawker Siddeley now sitting low to one side, the tyres completely airless. 'But how? When... it impossible. No, no!'

He ran forward and knelt near the front tyre, eyes working frantically, pupils dilated in shock, trying to ignore the slavering jaws and big paws to his dog pressed to the inside of the glass and the constant barking. He could see the valve had been pulled right out of the tyre and tossed away, ensuring a complete and rapid deflation. These were not accidental punctures, but a deliberate attack. Like pancakes and only one spare. He beat his fist on the mudguard repeatedly, causing Hades to bark even more anxiously.

'Stop! No use flying off the handle and losing one's head.' He spoke aloud, as though to his dog, who was now quiet as though exhausted and sensing something was wrong. Ringham opened the car door. 'Come boy,' he called Hades out, but held him firm by the collar and hitched a strong leather leash retrieved from the glove compartment to this. 'Keep quiet! Time to hitch a lift.'

He looked at his mud-splattered clothes, at the dirty wetness on the knees of his trousers where he had knelt down, at the pulls and small tears from the brambles and his dishevelled shirt and tie. He took a moment to smarten up, then opened the car boot and grabbed a long overcoat lying across their two suitcases and shrugged it on. Once buttoned and belted he looked more like his usual dapper self.

Still a ruddy disgrace, but I might just pass muster.

He hefted his leather case out of the boot and stared unhappily at Melcombe's. He grabbed this as well, slamming the boot lid shut and they started to walk, but after about twenty yards he slung Melcombe's case over a dense blackberry bush and into a thicket of briars, sending the petals of a few last, late flowers falling and launching a group of startled sparrows into the air. After checking the case was not visible, they walked on towards The Green Man.

Chapter Forty-Two

Brackley Hatch
28th September 1950

The AA patrolman was dressed in a neat brown uniform with trousers that flared like jodhpurs tucked into tall brown leather boots beneath a long brown overcoat belted at the waist. He had a peaked cap with a waterproof cover and was carrying a pair of huge gauntlets coloured bright white for their greater part. Trinder thought, uncharitably, that he looked like a Fascist brown shirt but kept this to himself. 'Run through how you found the body again, please'.

'Of course, sergeant. I saw the car in question beside the AA call box. I assumed he was inside and as I had noticed our badge displayed on the radiator grill, I pulled over to offer assistance.' He waved, unnecessarily, at his splendidly shiny yellow and black BSA M21 motorcycle complete with air-smoothed fairing and Cyclopean headlamp like a bold silver eye and the special sidecar that carried his tools and spare parts. This was shaped, ominously, like a coffin and was exactly the right size for an average sized human, the narrow-pointed end facing forwards and a hinged lid along the flat top. Trinder could imagine lifting this to reveal the missing driver laid out with arms folded across his chest.

'There was however no sign of the driver. I checked inside the box of course. I could also see immediately what the problem was. He had been unlucky enough to suffer two flat tyres...' The patrolman now pointed towards the car and Vignoles and Trinder instinctively looked in the same direction. 'Dashed bad luck to lose two tyres in one go, but if he'd run over some broken glass, then it could happen. At first, I supposed he'd walked away for help, although we do always advise out members to remain with their vehicle until assistance arrives.

'I decided to assess what shape his tyres were in and how best to resolve the problem, then motor after him, to advise the gentleman that help was to hand. However, it was then I noticed something odd about the situation, and that was the fact that the tyre valves had been dismantled. Taken apart, in point of fact.'

'Could this be accidental?' asked Bainbridge. 'Is it possible they became dislodged?'

'No, sir. I could imagine one valve failing, for two to do so is pushing it. They've been taken out and the tyres let down deliberately.' They all nodded, his assessment appeared sound. 'I could not immediately find the missing parts of the valves.' The patrolman shrugged, 'I'm not sure why, but I could only guess that he took them out and put them in his pocket, but for what reason I cannot imagine.'

'Or someone threw them away to disable the car?' Vignoles was scanning the weeds and grass at the edge of the layby. 'We'll need a thorough search. I want to know what happened to them.'

Trinder frowned and bit his lower lip whilst making a note. 'They were trying to get away from Brackley – and presumably from us, so why stop here, and why dismantle the tyre valves?'

'Someone was trying to delay their escape? This is no ordinary puncture.' Vignoles was staring at the two flattened tyres as if they might give him an answer.

Trinder turned back to the patrolman. 'Then what did you do?'

'I was puzzled to be honest and stood scratching my head as what to do next, when I noticed all the footprints and the trampling down of the grasses - over there.'

Whilst he was speaking Vignoles was gingerly walking to one side of the visible imprints in the mud at the verge, careful to not step on any of them, with D.I. Bainbridge close at hand and doing likewise. Vignoles was pointing with the stem of his pipe at a number of especially deep and clear impressions and Bainbridge was nodding acknowledgement.

'They looked fresh and like they go to from the car into the woods. I noticed the paw prints and realised that he must have a dog and taken him for a walk whilst waiting for one of our patrols, so I decided to see if I could find them. The route was quite obvious if you take care to observe.' The patrolman pointed at the crushed undergrowth and heel impressions. 'You are the experts of course, but it seems to me that something was dragged along here that really flattened the grass. It's made quite a trail.'

'You have good observation skills.' Trinder gave an approving nod.

'It pays to keep one's eyes open in my job, sir. Anyway, I had not gone far when I saw his feet sticking out of a pile of leaves.'

'Did you approach the body?' Trinder asked.

'I did, but carefully. I immediately got a bad feeling about the situation. Anyone would under the circumstances, and I suspected foul play or something untoward, so I was extra careful not to walk on any footprints around the vicinity. I'm no medical man, but he looked pretty dead to me. I mean, nobody alive lies on their back with their eyes wide open and leaves piled over their face, do they?'

'Good work. We'll need to take a formal statement later.' Trinder closed his notebook and asked the patrolman to wait with his motorbike and sidecar combination in the company of one of Bainbridge's uniformed constables, then joined Vignoles and Bainbridge as they picked their way to one side of the trail and into the woods.

Dr Melcombe looked undeniably dead, dumped on his back with his legs stretched out from beneath an untidy and ineffectual pile of leaves, mud collected around the backs of his shoes and smeared over diamond patterned socks with more mud and twigs and the odd leaf in the turn ups of his trousers; indicating he had been dragged backwards whilst either unconscious or dead. His face was a distressing sight. Perhaps the gusty breeze that set the trees shivering from time to time had done the work, or the hand of the inquisitive patrolman, but some of the damp autumnal leaves had fallen away to reveal his staring, bulging eyes behind glasses that lay at a crooked angle across his nose, a speck of dirt and a few drops of rain from the canopy above spattering the lenses. His mouth was open as though locked in an endless cry of pain. It was a compelling and unnerving sight, as though the doctor was soundlessly screaming at something in the trees above, and all three men at some point quickly glanced upwards to check there really was nobody there.

'I'm loathe to move anything until you can get a photographer here and a doctor to look him over...' Vignoles had his unlit pipe clenched between his teeth. 'But we need to make a rapid assessment, I cannot afford to delay.' He gestured at the corpse. 'This is a poor attempt at concealment. There are footprints, drag marks, a body hastily covered, and a very distinctive car abandoned close by, all of which smacks of blind panic. There's nothing planned or pre-meditated about this.'

'Do you think he was killed?' Trinder was peering at the body. 'No obvious sign of blood...May I?' He reached towards the leaves covering the dead doctor's chest.

'Go ahead. Collar undisturbed and the neck looks unmarked. Could be a heart attack? Or poison going by his expression, though he almost looks like he was scared to death.' Vignoles was watching as Trinder gently cleared the body of leaves.

'No obvious sign of physical attack from what I can see, sir.'

'No dog bites either,' Bainbridge observed.

'Good point.' Vignoles was looking for paw prints in the vicinity as Trinder worked his way around the many pockets on Melcombe's suit.

'I can't see a wound or any blood. Got his wallet...with all the usual stuff inside... and there's a ration book, ID card.' He inspected it. 'Yep, he is indeed our Dr Percy Melcombe. His house keys I suppose?' He jingled them.

'No diamond ring?'

'No, sir. Though I would imagine that was taken.'

'Indeed, the diamond may well have precipitated whatever happened here,' Vignoles agreed. 'Though those flat tyres are bothering me.'

'Oh, but this is interesting.' Trinder stood up and Vignoles and Bainbridge stepped closer. 'A train ticket with a reservation. On the Mid-Day Scot from Rugby to Glasgow - today!'

'Scotland? Can we assume the other man, this Ringham fellow, was also heading north?' Vignoles pointed at the ticket with his pipe. 'I think it possible, it would be a good place to avoid detection for a while.'

'Your hunch was they'd take the train, and by golly we've got him nailed if that's so!' Bainbridge grinned in triumph.

'It's no more than a hunch, but it will serve as a starting point. But what happened here? Two men on the run and one valuable diamond ring. Do they argue and the driver pulls over and they lay into each other? One dies – is he killed or...his health gives way in the struggle? Ringham is forced to hide the body, then discovers the car is immobilised. But who did that, and why?'

'A third party was here?' Bainbridge offered.

'I think so. Did they leave with Ringham?'

'Or kidnap him?' Trinder looked unconvinced by his own suggestion.

'Don't forget Ringham also has a dangerous dog as protection. This could have been an ambush, but perhaps they struck a deal and they've travelled on together.'

'Surely it's too obvious?' Trinder added a note of caution, indicating the train ticket. 'This is a giveaway.'

'Not if he was hoping his attempt at concealment would buy at least enough time to get up north and lose himself in the wilds. It's a strong lead, so we must follow it. Added to which we've put word out to the neighbouring constabularies and the Transport Police are on high alert, so he won't be able to run far - not in this area at least.'

Prior to the patrolman's arrival with his news, they had spent a frantic half an hour, with Trinder, Bainbridge and Vignoles all hitting the telephones and telex machine and Vignoles giving urgent instructions to the stationmaster and signalman at Brackley Central, ensuring the telegraph system was kept hot sending a description of the car and its occupants across the three counties surrounding Brackley and far and wide across the railway. Word was spreading, and even now policemen would be starting to familiarize themselves with the hastily penned pictures of Melcombe, Ringham and their possibly dangerous dog, and no doubt these same policemen were also discussing the style and performance characteristics of the Hawker Siddely 'Hurricane' compared with those of a Jaguar or an Alvis, or any number of other cars, their attention caught by this glamorous vehicle as much as by what crime might lie behind the man hunt. Slowly and surely, the net was spreading.

'It makes sense for him to get as far away as he can, and as quickly as possible. The Scotland express is his best chance. Bainbridge, I need you to take over this crime scene. You know the drill; doctor, photographer, a fingertip search of the site - and get your chaps to work more magic on these footprints. I think plaster casts of these might well match those you took at the church.'

'Wilco. Leave it to me. And we got two good paw prints from St Peter's, so if they match those near the car we're really getting somewhere.'

'Indeed. Now if we could have the use of your driver and car, we need to catch this train. This ticket is a single from Rugby (Midland) to Glasgow. A crack express, with just eight coaches and no standing allowed. The guard will know if he was expecting to collect two gentlemen and a dog at Rugby.' Vignoles looked at this watch. '2.05. We can just make it, but Bainbridge, call Rugby and have the express held until I arrive. They'll be furious but use my name and position and don't take no for an answer!' He pulled a face, 'I'd rather not delay the Mid-day Scot, but we need this man, and trapping him on a train has its advantages.'

'Righty-o.'

'Ringham must have hitched a ride, or was in the mystery person's vehicle,' Trinder observed.

'Looks that way, sergeant. I'll get all our patrol cars and bikes on the roads around Rugby,' Bainbridge added. 'We might just apprehend him before he gets his train.'

'Do so. This is a desperate man in a tight spot. The more visible we can make our presence, the more likely he is to make another mistake. Now we must get going.'

*   *   *   *

Ringham had in his mind that one of the racers would pick them up in something sporty and fast. The driver would be a rich young man or an ex-fighter pilot. Someone daring; a rakish type who would not ask too many difficult questions and yet be up for a mad dash to the station and relishing the chance to put their foot down and do some proper road racing and in return for a crisp bank note slipped from one leather driving glove to another, he could buy their silence, knowing the adrenaline rush had been all the buzz needed. The driver would wink and give him a knowing smile and as he roared away, imagine how the strange, well-bred and expensively dressed hitchhiker was on his way to a thrilling, certainly illicit, rendezvous with a vampish dame.

But instead, Ringham got his worst nightmare.

The little Austin K8 van slowed without Ringham needing to stick a thumb out, nor have the option of waving it past. Painted pink and cream and branded loudly with the name of the paraffin company for whom the driver was delivering, it was a cheerful-looking vehicle that looked as though it might have escaped from the pages of one of Enid Blyton's new Noddy books. The K8 had a flattened front with an elongated silver and black radiator grill and no suggestion of a snout like bonnet whilst the split windscreen curved smoothly into the roofline to suggest speed and modernity. Speed would not be an option however, with its noisy and smoky engine and heavy gear change. But Ringham convinced himself it would suffice, and at least Hades could sit in the back with his suitcase.

The driver had a thick grey moustache and wavy hair of the same colour, a cigarette tucked above one ear alongside an arm of his National Health glasses that balanced on the end of his nose over which he peered at the road, but used to read from the neatly typed sheet of delivery addresses resting on the centre of the steering wheel and clenched in place beneath a thumb.

The driver's window was wound down and he called to Ringham. 'Hello chum got a problem?'

It was to be the first of a ceaseless string of questions, the man apparently unable to take 'no' or a cold, glowering silence for an answer. Ringham regretted accepting the lift the moment they were installed inside, finding himself forced into concocting an ever-deepening series of lies and evasive explanations. He was struggling to find a solution to his predicament, and really did not need this intrusive questioning that only served to remind him how bad things were becoming by the hour.

The driver was desperately eager not only to offer help, but to appreciate Ringham's exact travel plans in order to offer his own advice and assistance.

'Puncture? No problem chum, we can get that fixed up in two shakes of a donkey's tail! I've got a jack in the van. What? Valves gone? Well I never, that's one in a million. Not heard the like of that before, rotten luck. But you know what that is? That's this Austerity for you. You just can't get the same quality any more, it's all shoddy goods nowadays. Hey, but that's a fine motor. What a little beauty! We'll swing over and have a look... What? Oy! Steady on mate, you nearly had us off the flippin' road!' He fought to bring the K8 back onto a straight line. 'You shouldn't go grabbing the wheel like that. Blooming' dangerous that is! All right, all right keep yer hair on...'

They motored on a while in silence, but it couldn't last. 'You can't just leave that car there as someone will nick it. Things are not like they used to be and there's plenty folk around here nowadays that will steal that in a flash. Oh, in a hurry are you, got no time? So, what's the pressing rush? Got a train to catch...right, got it in one! Where you going from? The Midday Scot from Rugby? Phew wee...that's class that is. I can see why you wouldn't want to blow a ticket on that in a hurry. I can get you there in time, no need to worry. Here, we should get to know each other. My name's Graham Rowlands... Pleased to meet you Mr. Jones. We should be a little less formal. Everyone calls me Gray, short for Graham...You're Sam? Sam Jones. I never forget a name or a face, Sam. Good to meet you, chum.

'But look I've been thinking, if I were you I'd get that motor fixed up and somewhere and then go on a later train... To a wedding? Ah ha! Now I understand why you're a bit preoccupied tense, I don't blame you mate, I'm sure I'd be the same in your predicament. So what's your daughter's name? Nice... Where does she live? It's just I've got my aunty Dollie up Glasgow way and I tootle up every so often and I might know the area. Just asking, Sam! All right...all right, but you need to calm down a bit. I can see how you're anxious about not missing that wedding and all, but there's no need to lose your rag, we're well in time.

'No, I don't care what you say, but that car its way too nice to abandon for...how long did you say you're going away? A few days?' He sucked air between his teeth. 'No, listen, I've been thinking this through, I can call my friend Richard; lovely man, salt of the earth is Dicky Coulson. He's got a garage out Halse way, near Brackley. Actually, you must have just driven through it on the way. Well, he's a good mate and I can get him and his mechanic to come along, get the tyres fixed up and then park her up at Rugby station ready for when you come back. He can leave the keys with the stationmaster. It's a big busy station and they'll be able to keep a beady eye on it. Just the cost of the tyres and a drop of petrol, that's all, no problem. Eh? Just being helpful Sam! All right, please yourself.

By heck, that police car is in a rush. Flippin' menace those patrol cars they use nowadays, rushing all over the place like nobody's business. I can remember when they just had bicycles! Ha ha. Eh? No, it can't go any faster, my foot is on the floor already. Look, I'll stop at this phone box and give

Dicky Coulson a call. It won't take a minute and we're still well in time for your train. We've made good progress actually. No, listen Sam, we'll get this sorted out, and then we can get you on your train and you can relax.' The van pulled to a halt and the driver hopped out, leaving the engine running.

The K8 was pulled over beside a red telephone box close to a short bridge over a small culvert overhung by tall rosebay willowherb and enclosed by tall hedges of reddening berries and overarching trees, set between bends in the road in either direction. There was also a telegraph pole and a post box on a short metal post, and the rooftops and smoking chimneys that formed the edge of Rugby could be seen between the trees ahead, whilst the little river meandered its way towards a distant embankment along which a long train of coal wagons pulled by a black locomotive rumbled, illustrating the proximity of the west coast main line.

'Just need to bob into the back, I've got a stack of coins in my jacket pocket hanging in there.'

Ringham mumbled something about letting his dog out before the long train journey, but as he slipped out of the cab he picked up a heavy metal wrench that had been lying on the floor between his feet and felt its weight in his hand.

There was no time to think this through. The van driver knew too much, despite his hasty lies and all that nonsense about a wedding in Glasgow. But it was the mention of the name Coulson that had tipped the balance. Could it be the same family? Brackley was a small town and it was plausible. He was starting to think Melcombe had been right when he'd said the diamond was ill fated, that it was cursed. Nothing was going right, and he felt like he was spinning too many plates and they were starting to fall.

No, this Rowlands man would remember him as clear as day, and he even said he never forgot a face. If the van were stopped on the journey back from Rugby station by that patrol car, the driver would make the connection and the balloon would go up in an instant.

'Sam? What you doing with that?'

He lifted the wrench high and slammed it as hard as he could onto the man's head. It made a stomach-turning noise and Rowlands crumpled like a rag doll into a heap on the van floor, Hades growling in his ominous deep rumble, sensing danger. Ringham tossed the wrench behind him and heard it splash into the water, then roughly hauled the man by his shoulders, taking care to avoid getting the bright scarlet blood on his coat. He huffed and puffed and dragged the body as quickly as he could to the side of the culvert and made him topple over. He could hear traffic approaching and could not risk looking to see how the body had fallen, instead he dashed into the call box and with head bent over and hat brim low, he mimed talking. A couple of cars raced past without slowing and the danger was over. Moments later, he let the clutch out and the little van roared away, leaving a cloud of exhaust hanging in the air.

*   *   *   *

'Princess Alice' was at the head of the train, resplendent in a fresh and shining coat of express blue set off with black and white lining and 'British Railways' in cream san serif letters on the tender sides. The livery evoked something of the magnificent locomotive's previous life, a time before wartime and austerity measures demanded she was stripped of her exotic air-smoothed outer garments and the hidden 'crinolines' that held this in place - not unlike the whale-boned corsetry once worn by the real-life Princess. This covering once removed revealed a leaner, fitter and indeed very nicely proportioned body beneath, and so 'Princess Alice' along with sundry other Duchesses were unceremoniously disrobed, and the brief heady days of streamlining along the west coast line was banished forever.

She had been one of the old London Midland and Scottish Railway's avant-garde streamliners, one of the 'Princess Coronation' class at the cutting edge of locomotive development in the mid '30's. Encased in a metal air-smoothed layer of skilfully hand curved and shaped panels with a bulbous nose that punched the air as she roared through the Westmoreland hills, powered down Shap and scythed her way through the splendid isolation of the Lune Gorge, 'Princess Alice' had been dressed in a glorious pale blue with silver 'speed whiskers' and body stripes, hauling a string of special coaches that continued the livery along their sides in a strikingly beautiful expression of pre-war excitement and pride.

Now, with smoke deflectors like elephant ears on either side of the thick boiler and a curiously flattened 'forehead' before the smoking chimney - a legacy from the streamlining - the engine champed and snorted impatiently at the platform end at Rugby (Midland). The powerful locomotive communicating in a manner no other machine could rival, the impatience of her crew. The two men were of the top link, selected from Camden shed's best, and they were not used to being kept waiting. Even in these difficult years when the railway system was still buckling under years of over use and insufficient maintenance, great efforts were always made to keep the named expresses moving - and to time. It was considered vital the pride of the Midland Region was upheld and the confidence of the wealthy and highly influential passengers that travelled on them was not shaken.

The driver was smartly attired in a white collared shirt and carefully knotted dark maroon tie beneath a clean set of 'blues' that still retained much of their colour, with a cap placed exactly level on his head in a manner that would please a drill sergeant. He was leaning from his cab window, eyes fixed on the guard standing beside the stationmaster in tails and a glossy top hat, both men deep inside the smoking Stygian gloom of the trainshed and rendered as silhouettes by the brighter light from the far end.

There was a brief flash of gold as the stationmaster's pocket watch on its chain was inspected once again and compared with the grand station clock that everyone knew kept perfect time. The fireman, as equally well presented as the driver, was fiddling with the injectors and trying to squeeze a little more water into the furiously hot boiler and so prevent the engine's safety valves from lifting. He was silent, but privately fuming that this unexplained delay might cause him to commit one of the sins of the top link, that of 'blowing off' whilst standing in a station. The sharp noise of the lifting valves would startle the travellers and whilst the jets of steam would loft high into the air, this could dislodge the years of accumulated soot from the front of the filthy-black station roof that spanned the tracks and create an unwelcome shower of dirty water. It was frowned upon, and if his driver gave him the benefit of the doubt, his guard would not let the matter go unmentioned when they finally clocked off in Glasgow.

'Come along...you've checked your watch enough times.' The driver grumbled, his expression imploring the guard to blow his whistle.

'The board's still on. Must be a problem down the line.'

'Mebbe... but then why is the stationmaster and the guard looking like they're expecting someone?' The driver glanced at the signal that held them and along the expanse of criss-crossing silver rails that lay ahead. There was just a smoky 8F class freight engine with a train of box vans waiting to pass through the station, though posing no impediment to their own departure. The station pilot was taking water against the opposite platform side. The driver of this locomotive raised an eyebrow and shrugged, sympathetic, but equally puzzled by the delay.

'Just look at that!' The fireman exclaimed. 'Late comers!'

The driver shook his head in disbelief. 'That takes the biscuit. Just like they always say, it's not what you know, but who you know. Probably pals with one of the directors.'

'They're too lazy to get here on time - but that's the gentry for you, mate. Bring on the revolution!' The fireman agreed although his ire was ameliorated by the hope they would now get under way a fraction before the fizzing valves blew their tops. 'Right away!' The fireman watched the signal lift, then immediately opened the fire doors and hefted his shovel.

The driver lifted a gloved hand in recognition of the urgently waved flag and the overly sharp toot of the whistle. The guard was clearly none too happy about the situation either.

'2.44. I reckon we can make it up by Crewe. Come on old girl, let's get you going...'

A great cloud of grey black smoke lofted into the air, pulsing in time with the roar of the pistons. Whump - shoo, whump – shoo, whump - shoo... With the sanders hissing and steam engulfing the massive driving wheels before shredding beneath the blood and custard coloured coaching stock, the train was soon in motion, offering little resistance to the combination of a powerful engine and the skilful regulator work of its driver. Without a slip on the greasy dampened rails, the Mid-Day Scot was under way and soon roaring north towards Crewe, its final pick up before the long and unstinting race to Carlisle Citadel.

Vignoles and Trinder stood in the vestibule and collectively took a few breaths to regain composure, adjusting hats and straightening ties.

'Phew, that was a dash. Tractor's and horseboxes are not conducive to rapid motoring.'

'They could have moved over,' agreed Trinder.

'Right gents, we followed the instructions to the letter and I am hoping there is a compelling reason for the delay?' The guard gave them both suspicious looks, his voice icily polite. 'No tickets and holding us back seven minutes – I think you owe me an explanation a least.'

'Of course, and my sincere apologies for our late arrival.' Vignoles showed his warrant card and made the introductions. 'Could we step into your compartment? This is not for everyone's ears.'

The guard gave a curt nod, 'This way.'

He had what was little more than a cubicle with a bucket seat and a shelf supporting a pile of timetables and working instructions, a rulebook a red flag and a hand lamp. This was beside a long metal cage that occupied the majority of the brake coach, with just a corridor width of free space to allow passage through to the far end. The cage held piles of parcels and packages, a great number of leather suitcases and trunks and what looking like a small forest of fishing rods and guns in canvas bags or smart leather cases each branded with stencilled monograms, and a brand new Silver Cross pram with a luggage label tied to the handlebars which was now rocking on its springs with the movement of the accelerating train.

Vignoles described the man they were looking for. 'He should have been travelling with one other, but that particular gentleman died before he got here.'

'I presume the man you seek is wanted for questioning?' The guard's initial disapproval had been replaced by a sense of intrigue and a desire to assist this very important member of the Railway Detective Department. He'd heard tell of this Vignoles fellow and the stories were suitably impressive. He would do well to cooperate with the detective inspector.

'Yes, but you must treat the man exactly as you would the other passengers and I should warn you he has the potential to be dangerous. We must not provoke him. Do you believe he is onboard?'

'We were expecting eight on at Rugby, inspector, but I only counted seven, though that would be eight with the dog. Excluding yourselves, of course.'

'A dog?' Trinder asked.

'Correct. Quite normal at this time of year, though mostly people bring spaniels, retrievers and the odd hound. Hunting dogs you see? His was a Rottweiler. I had no time to speak with the owner as he was in a rush to get aboard. He just asked where he could find the dining car and took his dog with him'.

'Can you describe him?' asked Vignoles.

'The man or the dog?'

'Both.'

The description impressively detailed and left Vignoles and Trinder in no doubt that Barnaby Ringham was onboard. 'Good. We shall take a walk to the dining car and assess the lay of the land.' Vignoles was lighting up his pipe. 'Do you have a newspaper or two we could borrow? A quality broadsheet, something that might help make us look more like businessmen and less like coppers.'

'We always hold a stock of The Times and The Daily Telegraph.'

'Excellent. Now, is it usual for passengers to keep their dogs with them, especially in the dining car? I think it might be sensible to separate man from dog.'

'We do tether some in the cage here. It is kept locked, but I am usually on hand to give them water if needed. If he is in the dining car I could respectfully suggest that his beast sits in here whilst he dines? I can be very persuasive.' The guard winked.

'Please do. But take care. Don't push your luck and back down if he rails against the idea.' Vignoles was warming to the man.

*   *   *   *

Ringham was seated at a small table for two next to the vestibule door, wedged at an angle into the comfy armchair beside the window. Hades was lying at his feet and panting in time with the rapid huffing of the roaring engine that was throwing clouds of steam past his window. He had a double of cognac swilling around the balloon glass in his hand, a larger measure of which had already set his throat and stomach glowing. He was tired and leant back in the seat and closed his eyes. So much had happened that day already and still so much to sort out. He was in a tight spot; the trail of muddle and destruction he'd left in his wake was not only uncharacteristic, but potentially lethal. And it was so unlike him.

Fastidious, cautious, careful and calculating – those were the strengths that had seen him make a successful career and swell his bank account thanks to his secret life as the 'man who could,' for the rich and the well-connected. Got an awkward problem? A sticky legal matter that could do with 'smoothing away', with the help of some subtle out of court influence? His methods were less than legal, but it kept things out of the papers. Daughter got herself in the family way with a reprobate who would disgrace the family name? Never mind, dear fellow, I know a man, he's very discreet and utterly reliable, who can sort everything...it will cost, of course, but then what price respectability and one's good name? That wild fling on the Riviera has left longer-lasting consequences than planned? Of course, Barney Ringham completely understands the consequences if one's husband were to discover he had a bastard heir...leave it to me. A short holiday at a discreet address and it call all be forgotten...

Yes, he had a pocket book filled with names and telephone numbers of some pretty darned influential people who had good reason to help him out of this tricky situation. It was just a matter of trying to think how to best play this, whom to call on first. The Commissioner of the Met might not be too bad a place to start, his daughter...

'Excuse me, sir.'

'Sorry.' Ringham blinked, already slightly befuddled by a mixture of cognac and drowsiness. He'd drifted off. The guard was standing beside him leaning slight forwards and speaking in a suitably low and discreet voice. Ringham quickly gathered his wits about him. 'I beg your pardon?'

'Your dog, sir.'

'What's happened?' He looked startled.

'May I suggest we can accommodate him in the guard's compartment? He will have more space there, and we always keep a few blankets on hand for the very purpose, and a bowl of fresh water. He will be in good hands.' The guard smiled obsequiously.

'He's fine here.' He felt Hades lift a head then flop it back down on the floor, also tired after that curious incident in the woods that had precipitated the desperate mess they were now in.

The guard coughed apologetically. 'They will start to serve afternoon tea shortly and we like to invite our customers to leave their hunting dogs, and the like, in the guard's compartment. Only in case a steward was to step on a paw or a tail whilst carrying hot tea, you understand?' He was smiling in that manner that Ringham understood, and indeed often deployed, a look that implied 'I am demanding compliance and offering you a dignified way of doing so.'

Ringham took a deep breath and was about to bawl the man out and tell him to mind his own bloody business, when he stopped and remembered that he would do well to not attract any more attention than necessary. And besides, had not Hades got him into this hole by running off like a possessed animal in the first place? He was fond of the dog, but right this moment he was exhausted, tired by it all. He could feel the energy leeching out of him at an alarming rate and it might be beneficial to let the guard look after Hades for a while. They were to be on this train for another seven hours, so why not let him stretch out and sleep in the van?

'Very well. His name is Hades. Here, take these biscuits.' He dug into the pocket of his jacket and extracted a paper bag. 'They usually keep him happy.' He heard a tail thump on the floor.

'Unusual name, sir.'

'Not when you get to know his character.' Ringham forced a laugh and got his dog to stand up and fastened the short leather lead on his strong collar. Hades flipped his ears up and down and gave the guard an evil look, and yet his nose had smelt a treat and he licked his lips. 'Go along now! Good dog.' Ringham rubbed the dog between its ears and indicated that now might be a good time to deploy a biscuit.

The guard left, with Hades only tugging half-heartedly at the leash, but with sufficient strength to cause the guard to walk quickly. He wanted this dangerous looking animal locked in that cage as fast as possible. Ringham meanwhile leant back in the chair and told himself he should try to resist sleep a while longer. He really ought to get the lay of the land.

Through half closed eyelids he surveyed the other dining car passengers. To his immediate left were an older couple, both well dressed, she with pearls at her neck and a sparkling band to her tiny watch, he in a green and grey tartan suit with leather buttons and patches on the elbows, a cream shirt with a pattern of brown lines, and a huge handlebar moustache.

He wore a monocle. Handy with a 12 bore, no doubt. A deer stalker, or fly fisher? Ringham could certainly imagine him prowling the moors with a gun on his arm. Two businessmen still in overcoats and hats sidled in at that moment and settled diagonally opposite him, just a table away and both ordered coffee, then immediately opened newspapers without speaking another word. Was there a whiff of plain clothes about them? No, they could never be on to him that quickly, surely not? He must not let his imagination run away. After a lot of paper turning and folding the two men settled on doing the crosswords, the older of the two smoking a pipe and resting the folded paper on a knee crossed over the other, his eyes occasionally flicking up and towards him. He was in the man's line of sight, so there was surely no reason to be suspicious.

Ringham jolted awake. Crewe. The train had stopped but he had only just awakened, and he observed as if in a trance the people on the platform. They stared back with looks of envy, taking in the white cloths and little lamps on each table, the coffee pot filling cups, the bottles of wine being uncorked and the white jacketed stewards expertly handling silver platters laden with trays of unrationed delicacies including pots filled to over flowing with strawberry jam, piles of freshly baked scones and stacks of neat triangular sandwiches wastefully served without crusts.

The train started to move, their faces sliding smoothly to one side, to be replaced by a gaggle of over-excited schoolboys in grey shorts and green blazers and caps, running in step with the accelerating train and waving at their top 'kop' of a blue-painted 'namer' steaming towards Scotland.

He had been undecided about changing trains at Crewe, but now the option was taken away and it was non-stop into the dark of night and distant Carlisle, or Carstairs, Motherwell and Glasgow. He clicked his fingers and the steward came to his side. 'I'm ravenous young man, so what can you offer me? No, come to think of it, don't bore me with the menu just bring me something hot – anything, but it must be hot and lashings of it.'

'Very well, sir. Perhaps some soup to start?'

'Whatever you and the chef can rustle up. Oh, and a bottle of burgundy.'

'As you wish, sir. We have a fine selection of onboard today, would you like to choose from the...'

'Just pick up the first bottle you find and bring it to me! I can pay, don't worry about the cost.'

'As you please, sir.'

Those two men were still working on their crosswords. He stole another glance. Whilst he'd been sleeping they'd stowed their coats on the racks above the table and looked slightly less like policemen, or was that just the restorative effect of a nap settling his jangling nerves?

Ringham took out his cigarette case and flipped it open, selected one of the Moritz from inside and lit up. The wine arrived and tasted surprisingly good. He was feeling more relaxed, cocooned in a corner of a warm dining car enveloped in the smell of food drifting in each time a steward passed through to the kitchen car, mingling with that of cigars and even a trace of expensive perfume. It felt strangely secure, a world away from nosy van drivers lying in a foot or two of muddy water and from the body beneath a pile of leaves. It was hard to comprehend all that had happened today, it was as if it was all in a dream, and no longer seemed real or so urgent and pressing. Besides, he was starting to formulate a plan and that always got him back onto a more even keel. He was thinking through a series of telephone calls to make, favours to call in, and overseas travel plans to organise. He had more than sufficient funds in his bank and had taken the precaution of packing his passport. And then of course, there was the ring.

Ah yes, the *Cobra's Eye*. He glanced at the other passengers in the now almost full car and they were all settling down to eating and drinking, including those two gents across the way. The light outside flared into life as the low-lying sun slipped below a thick shelf of cloud and spread a carpet of gold across the land, drenching the interior with its glorious Midas touch.

He slipped his hand into his jacket pocket and checked the little box was still there. It was ridiculous, but he felt a glow of triumph. This was something special. A haul of such value and made all the spicier for being unexpected, and so despite the traumas and problems, he suddenly felt stupidly happy. He almost wanted to laugh out loud.

Catching the steward's eye, he told him that he would be back shortly for his soup and asked which way to the toilet. Once in the vestibule, he dropped the window on one of the doors and leant on the metal frame to smoke and take some cooler air on his face. The swaying motion together with the swish and rush and rapid dum-diddly-dum sound of the train and the constant beat of the engine, were soothing. He wedged the cigarette in his mouth and took the little box from his pocket, flipping it open with a thumbnail then gasped in wonderment. The sun striking across the Cheshire plains set the stone alight and it burned with its strange fire, a beacon of brilliance that at times pierced his retinas with tiny jabs of light.

He was no romantic, but there *was* something about this stone...it was compelling; no wonder Percy had kept it for himself. He couldn't blame the silly fool. He knew Percy had killed her for it. His story was so inane, it was laughable. If it had been him, he'd have had a bit of fun with her first... But it was strange, because the old bugger had always been so reliable. Straight as a die and coldly efficient in his dealings with the women brought to his surgery. Had the diamond turned his head? It made Ringham wonder. It had brought a lot of bad luck.

He changed position to allow more sunlight onto the stone and less sooty smoke into his eyes, the vestibule at times filling with a swirl of pungent exhaust. However, he could not shake off an uncomfortable sensation of dread that tingled like an itch.

'Do you mind telling me where you acquired that, Mr. Ringham?' A hand gripped his shoulder.

He twisted around in the cramped space with some difficulty. The business gent with the hat and silver-framed glasses was now standing very close to him, his tall friend not far behind and blocking the vestibule gangway.

Instantly realising this was trouble, Ringham tried to shrug the man's hand from his shoulder. He jabbed his free arm outward with great force, attempting to bat away the policeman, but as he threw out this arm he caught his other elbow on the metal edge of the window frame and the ripple of searing pain made him lift his hand uselessly in a jerk reaction. Though it took just an instant, he instantly comprehended the appalling consequences of this uncontrolled action. With face contorted in pain, and the plain clothes policeman observing with a comical expression of surprise that seemed frozen like a snapshot in time, he watched in disbelief as the little ring lifted from off the velvet box lining and twisted and turned, flashing as each perfectly formed facet reflected the intense sunlight like a minute spinning Catherine wheel, until it was swept into the powerful current of air and vanished, sent flying to tumble between the tracks and lie lost and unseen to lodge between the stones, or perhaps it bounced and pinged away to land in the brackish water of the drainage ditch that edged the line.

'No-oo!' His voice wailed like a banshee as he elbowed Vignoles viciously with a force borne of desperation and leant dangerously far out of the window, his back buffeted by wind and a stream of dark smoke enveloping him as the fireman shovelled another round on the fire. He stared down the whole length of the train that was now curling around a gentle bend, desperately trying to identify the length of track it must have landed on.

'We must find it!', he shouted as he reached outside for the door handle and turned it, the door swinging open and the vestibule instantly turning cold as the sound of the thundering Stanier pacific swelled and reverberated around the tiny space. The noise and the rush of air, the sulphurous smoke and the telegraph poles pulsing past the gaping doorway, created a terrifying mix and Vignoles stepped backwards for fear of tumbling out, Trinder grabbing him around the waist.

'The cord! Stop the train!' Vignoles had to shout.

Trinder nodded and reached for the red painted chain that applied the brakes. He yanked it with all his might and they both heard the brake shoes come into contact with the wheels. Ringham was now swinging by his arms from the bottom of the window opening, his face turned to one side and pressed hard against the lower panel of the door, legs bicycling uselessly in the air.

'Hold on! Don't let go!' It was hard to get his voice to carry and the sound was pushed back into Vignoles' mouth by the air rushing through the open door. 'We'll haul you in!' Vignoles held on to the doorframe with one hand and braced a leg against the inside of the carriage and was attempting to reach forward and grab hold of Ringham's jacket. 'We're going too fast - you'll kill yourself!'

The train was complaining, juddering and creaking ominously in a truly horrible fashion, the wheels emitting a painful and unrelenting squeal like a thousand fingernails down a blackboard and they could hear glasses rattling furiously in the galley, there was something heavy hitting the floor, raised voices and an opened compartment door slamming violently shut. The engine had changed its note, the driver frantically cutting off steam, but 800 or so tons of train travelling at 70mph just cannot stop at once and must labour under terrible stress for quite sometime before it can even begin to reverse the massive forward momentum.

Vignoles was unsteady on his feet, with the carriage moving in an alarming manner, hunting and pitching dangerously and throwing him from side to side, and his hand was struggling to maintain any grip on the smooth door frame as his own body mass tried to wrench him forward and pitch him headlong onto the sharp ballast stones flashing past the open door in a dizzying blur. He stretched his arm out once more, desperate to grab the man's collar. One last effort...

And then Ringham was gone. One moment he was there, the next nothing; just the door swinging even wider, leaving Vignoles clutching at air. Both he and Trinder heard a cry; an animal yelp of pain, but the train just continued its relentless forward movement as the acrid smell of burning brake blocks filled their nostrils making them sneeze. Vignoles felt his hat fly off his head, there was a breaking of glass, a shuddering and deep groaning of the wooden-bodied coach straining to hold together, a scream or two and calls of enquiry as curious faces appeared in the corridor. A man was shouting to someone to crouch on the floor. Vignoles thought he heard a woman's voice declare - 'we're going to crash, we're going to crash!'

The train finally came to a standstill and an eerie silence fell for a few moments as everyone took stock, patted themselves down in the realisation that they were alive, now checking nothing was broken and appreciating that the Mid-Day Scot had not crashed or rolled over on to its side, and that aside from a few bruised shins, banged foreheads and some broken glasses and spilt tea, the train was apparently undamaged.

Ringham was a fighter, Vignoles had to give him that. Despite two broken ankles and some appalling cuts and bruising, with blood streaming from his shredded hands, elbows and knees, he gamely hauled himself along the track on his hands and knees dragging his feet behind; a grotesque twisted figure in a dark suit leaving a stain of scarlet along the line, scrabbling at the stones and frantically searching for the tiny diamond.

Vignoles stood at the opened door of the carriage and watched him for what felt like an age, such was his slow and excruciating progress. But Ringham was going nowhere despite his manful efforts to the contrary, and Vignoles was shaken from his thoughts after what was probably only a second or two, by a sudden explosion of noise as the passengers all started talking at the same time, as doors and windows were opened, faces peered out to look along corridor onto the railway, questions were asked or shouted in strong voices. A dog was barking furiously. The guard quickly eased Vignoles away from the doorway and dropped down to the track.

'I must protect the rear of the train. Can you look after the injured party? Bring him to the train if at all possible.'

Vignoles nodded assent and commanded Trinder to mobilize the stewards to call the train back into some semblance of order. They must ensure that nobody left the train and seek to quiet everyone down. 'Tell the head steward to give them all a free drink! Brandy's all round! And see if there is a stretcher in the guard's compartment.'

It was now his turn to drop on the tracks and stood there for a moment assessing the situation. The train was stopped on a gentle curve, leaning the slightly to one side due to the camber, the gleaming blue locomotive in the distance releasing little drifts of white steam like a racehorse might after a strenuous steeplechase as a lazy curl of smoke rolled over the open country that surrounded them on all sides. He could see newly ploughed fields with great drifts of lapwings wheeling around and starting to settle down after the disturbance, and there were hedges reddening with berries and trees tinged with gold and reds and the rooftops of the odd farm building. Very pretty, but an ambulance was going to find it hard to gain access.

The driver was standing beside 'Princess Alice', peering into the motion with his gloved hands resting on one of the great connecting rods. There was every chance the engine was damaged as a result of the emergency stop. The huge connecting rods were of the finest forged steel and could handle incredible forces, but even these would twist or buckle after such a sudden enforced stop. They might be here a long time as they awaited recovery of that were so. The fireman was leaning out of the cab and looking anxiously towards Vignoles, who indicated with his arm towards the tiny figure on the track way behind the train. The fireman appeared to understand and quickly dropped to the ground and started walking towards him.

The guard was steadily tramping away from the rear of the train at quite a pace and Vignoles caught a glimpse of signal box roof in the far distance. Salvation. From there they could inform control of the need for a relief engine, if necessary, they could close this section to ensure they would not be struck from behind and alert trains on the up line of their presence. He would be able to call an ambulance and call for uniformed officers to accompany Ringham to hospital, and so start to sort this mess out.

Vignoles looked at Ringham who had now rolled against the outer rail and slumped into a semi-recumbent position. They really needed a stretcher to bring him back to the safety of the train - and a medical kit. Ironically, Ringham needed the attentions of a doctor. The dog was still barking furiously from inside the guard's compartment and Vignoles hoped the beast was securely locked up.

And what of the *Cobra's Eye*? Vignoles decided it could wait. It had brought enough misery already. It would be better to never recover it and just let it lie wherever it had fallen to slowly sink into the ground and be swallowed by the lank grass on the railway verge or work its way between the continually shaken ballast, never to be seen again. Well, there was time to think about that later, as it was going to be a Devil of a job finding it. Right now, the Mid-Day Scot was being held up by a badly injured man on the track and whatever awful crimes he may have committed or been involved in, they could also wait for another time, as Barnaby Ringham needed urgent help.

Chapter Forty-Three

Leicester Central
28th September 1950

The trunk was an ugly beast painted an oily viscous black on the outside, the colour applied liberally and without particular care over the wooden panels and metal strengthening straps, over the sturdy corner braces and even the carrying handles; yet another coat on top of what looked like many previous such finishes over its long and hard life. In places the paint was cracked, blown and mottled as though about to lift away, and the whole trunk was liberally covered in years of grime and what looked like ash and fine brick dust. It also stank rotten as though recently lifted from a sewer.

'What is that smell?' WPC Lucy Lansdowne held her nose and gave DC Blencowe an admonishing look the moment she stepped into the Detective Department office. 'Ugh! Did something die in here?'

'In a manner of speaking, yes.' Blencowe looked grim-faced and did not look up in reaction to her outburst, but instead continued to adjust the fit of the heavy rubber gloves he had just pulled on whilst looking down at the reeking chest, eyeing with trepidation the dreadfully ominous staining on the paper lining that told a silent but not less unappealing tale about the liquefaction of human remains.

DC Simon Howerth had backed away once the lid had been lifted and was frantically wafting a sheet of cardboard to try and dissipate the foul stink that had accumulated inside during the years it had been in Police storage. 'It is grim.' He coughed. 'Could you open the window, please?' He looked a bit green around the gills.

'Gladly!' Lansdowne rushed across the office and hauled the sash window down allowing the noise of the station to enter the room on a draught of cooler air scented with the familiar coal smoke of the busy station. 'What is that thing?' She stood by the window and gave the trunk a suspicious look, immediately aware there was something ominous, almost sinister about it. It was an ugly object and seemed to cast a dark and depressing spell.

Blencowe, having prepared himself for action, looked at the WPC. 'I had it brought here because of something young Howerth here was reading a while back. Wasting his time as usual reading scandal and gossip in a trashy crime magazine.' He gave the lad a wink. 'But for once it actually proved useful as he got me thinking about a cold case, or should that be a cold trunk?' He gave a lame twist to his mouth. 'It was a magazine with a feature about unsolved crimes, including one about the unidentified corpse in a trunk left at Broad Street station. No head and no hands and naked. They couldn't get an identification from the bones and the rotted flesh....'

'Oh don't! Was it in there?' Lansdowne pointed at the ugly black trunk.

Simon nodded and put the cardboard down and started pulling on a pair of gloves that had been lying at his feet. 'That's right. I can't believe Blencowe sent for the evidence so we can have a look. It's awfully exciting! Even if it does pong to high Heaven.' He still looked queasy but was fighting it, determined to play his part in what was his first official act of detective work.

'It played on my mind.' Blencowe continued. 'What peeked me was that I'd not heard of the incident at the time. It was back in '45 they made the discovery, though they had no idea how much earlier it had been sitting there. Could have been weeks or even years, I suppose that was half the problem.' He dropped to his haunches, at one end of the trunk and started to run his fingers along the edges, guiding his eye over every inch, occasionally stopping and looking intently at an imperfection or blemish of which there were many. 'Then there was this business with Miss Askew. You know, with her head and what are probably the bones of her hands discovered but her body still missing, and it set me wondering.'

Lansdowne was still eyeing the trunk with distaste, but she too was managing to replace her natural instinct of revulsion for curiosity. 'You think the corpse found in there could be her?

'A distinct possibility. Sarge reckoned it had to be worth looking at.' Blencowe stopped and looked up at the young detective constable. 'At the risk of this going to your head, I suppose one must thank you for suggesting we trawl the Great Ouse for the bones of the other hand.'

'Yes, why did you think of that?' Lansdowne also looked at the constable. 'It was inspired.'

'I...I just guessed. If one hand was on the steep embankment, perhaps the other had rolled down or was thrown into the river.' He had no intention of confessing his night-time ghost hunting activities. 'I am sure any of you would have thought just the same.'

'I'm sure we would.' Blencowe was eager to rein any sense of over-confidence in the young man and turned back to the trunk. 'The body could have been put in here about the same time. Thinking along those lines, the sergeant had the bones recovered from inside this trunk in 1945, sent over to the lab where the head and hands now are. If it all fits together like a jigsaw as we suspect, then we've at least reunited her - poor lamb.' Blencowe was peering at something on the outside of the lid, but then let it drop down again and shifted his position, so he could look right inside.

'Her parents can lay her to rest at least. All of her.' Lansdowne observed. 'That would be something. Let her rest...'

'What are we looking for exactly?' Simon was concentrating on the outside of the trunk, not yet quite ready to plunge his nose into the stench of decay and mould rising like mist from a swamp.

'I don't know. Most probably there will be nothing. The Met found nothing back then, so why should we now? But I just wondered if they looked hard enough - or if there is some detail that makes more sense now that we suspect Melcombe and Ringham were involved.' Blencowe gave a shrug and started prodding with his finger at the stained brown paper stretched taught across the wooden ribs of the interior. Some of the paper was glossy and smooth as though lacquered at some point, long before the body had been placed inside. 'This finish would have helped stop the liquid running out. Some of this is as tight as a drum skin.'

Lansdowne approached and stood to one side leaning forward, her hands on the top of her thighs and watched them work. 'People always used to line this kind of trunk as it sealed them. More to keep the dust out, rather than to stop anything putrefying from leaking out of course. Ugh, but it is a vile mess down there.'

'I can't find anything on the outside.' Simon looked disappointed. 'I think some of the paper they used beneath the top layer of brown were newspapers and all covered in this Shellac stuff or whatever it is. Do you think if we could date the newspapers they would give us a clue?'

'Apart from telling us what paper the owner liked to read, I can't see that would be much help...' Blencowe was running his gloved hand around one of the bottom corners, feeling each crease and curve. 'Ah, now what's that? A very slight bump underneath the paper. Could be a raised nail or something?' He looked up at Lansdowne, concentration etched on his face as he used his fingers to feel their way inside a tiny, cleanly made slit. It was a cut in the paper so perfectly formed it was all but invisible. 'I'm not sure, but there might be something wedged down there.' He removed his hand and dug into his jacket pocket and pulled out a sturdy penknife. Lansdowne quickly opened this for him, she not wearing thick gloves, and he set to work with the knife blade, stripping away the paper, that was brittle and dry or rotten and soft in turns.

'Should you be doing that to a piece of evidence?' Lansdowne was frowning.

'Ordinarily, no, but to date it's yielded absolutely nothing and serving no useful purpose except taking up space. If there really is something in there and it can lead us to the killer, I reckon it has got to be worth a look? You are my witnesses.' He peeled away another strip of paper and all three took an intake of breath.

'Is that a button?' Asked Lansdowne

Simon picked it up, holding it between his gloved fingers for all to see, turning it slowly in different directions in a movement reminiscent of Betty Askew showing the Cobra's Eye to the Dirty Girl's Brigade in Woodford 'Loco'. 'Silver I reckon, though awfully tarnished. And some letters on the front...'

'A monogram.' Blencowe looked pleased. 'That looks interesting.'

'B and R. - that's British Railways. Can that be right?' Simon was puzzled.

'That's no railway button. Far too elegant and refined.' Blencowe replied.

Lansdowne moved closer to get a better look, careful to not touch it with her ungloved fingers. 'It might have a fingerprint if we're lucky, so handle it carefully, constable. I think I can see a hallmark on the back, and a maker's name. This could prove handy.' She nodded approvingly, her revulsion at the noxious box silently fumigating the room now forgiven. 'I agree, the style and design are way too fancy for British Railways.' She took a sharp intake of breath. 'B and R? I think we know the man who commissioned this, and better still we have him in custody. That's Barnaby Ringham!'

'Got him!' Simon cracked a smile.

'We're a step closer to doing so. If we can prove this is from a piece of his clothing, then that puts him right there when her body was sealed inside, he won't wriggle out of that too easily!' Blencowe looked chuffed.

Chapter Forty-Four

Brackley Central
3rd October 1950

'I think I heard voices!' Anna motioned to her husband, her hand just a blurred pale shape moving through the darkness that enveloped them like a thick blanket. They both fell silent and listened, but distant night birds somewhere far off, a motorbike engine kicked into life in the valley below and the sough of wind in the trees was all they could hear.

'It came from the far side of the railway,' Anna was tilting her head to one side straining to catch any sound.

Vignoles, who had tucked his spectacles into his breast pocket, lifted the heavy ex-Army night vision binoculars and surveyed the opposite side of the main line. The image was a washed out and grainy version of reality rendered in shades of black and white and making anything pale, such as a human face, flare with an almost unearthly radiance, but despite these he could not see anything that suggested there was someone there.

The strange faraway honking like the barking of oddly asthmatic dogs was now mounting in a steady crescendo, with first one calling and others answering in a rapid modulating succession that was almost hypnotic with its complex rhythms that never quite resolved into a repeatable sequence. They both looked up and watched a loose 'v' of great birds etched black against an overarching sky of slightly paler cloud backlit by the dregs of light from an invisible moon.

'The Seven Whistlers...' Anna's voice was hushed.

'Whooper swans.'

'But are they?' There was a flash of her white teeth as she smiled. 'Even you have to admit that there's something in all this. Why sit here otherwise?' Anna was talking softly in short breathy bursts. 'And the signalman was quite adamant about her having been here most nights.'

'True. And some parts of that odd case only made sense if -' Vignoles concentrated on studying an unrelieved mass of black shapelessness to their right. '- if somehow, a long-dead woman managed to take a piece of evidence and move it from one place to another - to our advantage.'

'Exactly. Though I agree with the signalman in that we are too late to see her walk abroad now. And in way I'm glad.'

Vignoles lowered the glasses and gave her a look.

'No really Charles, he was right. Since you reunited her bones and with the promise of a proper burial once the trial of Ringham is over, they've seen nothing of her at the station. She's just vanished. It's because she's at rest now.'

Vignoles grunted and went back to searching the bank. After a short while felt Anna's hand touch his sleeve, her voice an urgent whisper. 'A light! Over there!'

'Got it.' It showed like a white disc flashing three times in rapid succession, then doused moments after. 'There's someone on the far side part way up the cutting towards the Buckingham Road, he's signalling...' Vignoles was speaking softly as he tried to make sense of the thick dark mass of bushes, trees and night sky.

'To his compatriots across the way from us.'

'I've got him in my sights now...' Vignoles shifted position, resting one elbow in a knee as he knelt down partially concealed by a sturdy fence post. 'Moving down the bank, probably coming to join them.' He could just make out a moving blob of black bobbing and ducking; just a murky moving mass that was too grainy for detail like an over-enlarged detail from a photographic print. However, he thought it was a man in black wearing a cap.

'Who are they? Why are they here?' Anna was straining to see anything, but now convinced they were in the presence of others acting suspiciously beside the railway.

'They might well say the same about us.' Vignoles lowered the bins for a moment and darted her a glance. 'I'm not even sure myself why I'm here...'

'I can see him now!'

Vignoles was tracking the man's progress again. 'Youngish, slim build...'

'No, opposite. He's standing up.' She guided Vignoles' arm in the direction and he swung the two barrels of the night vision binoculars onto to the standing figure Anna had spotted. After a moment of adjusting the focus he obtained a clear image, aided by the traces of light spilled from the signal lamps.

'Earnshaw? Edward-blinkin'-Earnshaw!' Vignoles stood up and let the heavy binoculars drop to his chest on their leather strap, whilst ducking through the fence and quickly checking the line was clear, though he could tell by the red warning lights the signals were set at danger. He was not seeking cover now, but boldly striding across the twin running tracks, his booted feet striking the stones with a strong confident sound. 'Hoy there! Stay where you are and don't even think of running!'

'Cripes, we've been rumbled!'

'You have at that, Earnshaw.' Vignoles was soon close enough to see the startled face of the young fireman. 'And what exactly are you doing lurking about... Oh? Two of you?' Vignoles stopped dead in his tracks on the grassy verge of the permanent way. It was now his turn to be taken aback, as the figure of Laura Green dressed in what looked like Land Army jodhpurs and a thick ribbed green sweater rose out of the grass.

'Er, good evening detective inspector.' She tried her best to sound as though this were the most normal place and time to meet.

'It's not quite what you think, sir,' Eddie hurriedly blurted out, however he anxiously looked towards the Buckingham Road bridge and Vignoles catching the movement, did the same. A short distance away a figure was standing observing the meeting.

'Come on! I can see you.' Vignoles beckoned with his arm and the figure reluctantly moved towards them, his steps slow and unwilling. Vignoles ducked under the fence and stood close to Eddie and Laura. 'And what explanation can you give me? No, wait until your friend drags himself here, and then tell me.'

DC Simon Howerth could hardly bare to lift his head, hoping the brim of his cap and the dark of night would somehow protect him from the inevitable carpeting now coming his way. Vignoles however, had lost the ability to speak, just looking at each person in turn and one could almost hear the sound of cogs whirring and mental machinery clunking into place, though that may have been the signal wires and pulleys being activated.

'I think I had better explain, sir.' It was the voice of sergeant Trinder.

'Sergeant?' Vignoles looked stunned. 'How many more of you are hiding here?'

'It really is nothing untoward, it's all quite above board. We...well, that is to say; I...I thought it best we got a result from this line of enquiry before I briefed you on the operational details. Didn't want to waste your time. And we are all working for free, not on overtime, I hasten to add.' Trinder tried his best not to look anxious.

'Operation? You four are...doing...what, exactly?'

'Working undercover, I suppose you might call it a stake out...'

'Surveillance would be more accurate. But under strict instructions to just observe...'

'Making notes! We did so once before and...'

'You will recall the considerable success from dragging the river bed for more bones, well that idea was a result of a similar ghost watching operation, and it has to be low-key because we would only frighten the ghost off if I brought uniformed officers along and posted them beside the line. You see, it has to be this way, sir.'

'Stop! Not all at once.' Vignoles waved his hands. 'Just one at a time! Now sergeant, did I hear mention of ghost watching?'

'Er...yes. I thought...that is, I wanted to see for myself.' Trinder mumbled the words. The others looked shamefaced, like guilty school children each staring at their feet and shuffling uncomfortably.

'I see.' Vignoles paused. 'So, you came here tonight to observe the so-called "woman in white"?'

'Yes.'

'And this is not the first such 'operation'?'

'For myself, it is, but the others have been once before - and with surprising results. They actually saw the woman and she led them to the river. It had to be a sign, a clue...and so it proved. DC Howerth gave us the lead to look in the river as a direct consequence.'

'I see.' Vignoles bit his lower lip.

'May I ask why you have field glasses with you sir?'

'You may not. And have you seen her, sergeant?'

'No. Not yet. It is still early, I suppose. Ah, what brings you here, sir? We did not expect to see you.' Trinder looked apprehensive.

'I... got wind of something unusual. A tip off, so thought I should take a look.' It was Vignoles who now appeared uncomfortable. 'Kitted myself out with suitable gear,' he touched the binoculars by way of example. 'I've been watching your antics with these for a while and with puzzlement...'

'Don't play games with them Charles!' Anna was crossing the railway. 'We came here for the same reason. We wanted to get a glimpse of this celebrated woman in white at Brackley station!' Anna was laughing. 'Why not?' She threw her arms wide and shrugged her shoulders. 'Though we've seen precious little and I don't think we will.' Anna was now part of the group gathered at the side of the line.

'You did believe me about seeing the ghost going into river?' Simon piped up.

'It made sense to search the river below the viaduct,' Vignoles darted the young man a mildly rebuking look, not wishing to concede ground. 'There was logic to the idea.'

'Why do you think we won't see her again, Mrs Vignoles?' asked Laura.

'Because she will soon be given a proper Christian burial. You've reunited her once scattered remains at last, and the awful man who took her life paid the ultimate price for his crime - with his life. The other felon will get his just desserts in due course - with a bit of luck. A wrong has been not exactly righted but ameliorated. She is at peace, and no longer needs to walk the land like a restless soul.'

'Or fly across the sky...' added Eddie, glancing upwards.

Trinder gave Vignoles a look that silently voiced the question, and do you agree with this hypothesis?

'Perhaps we will never fully understand what happened here. There was someone hanging about the line that much is for certain, and maybe it was just a local girl with a reckless desire to play dangerous games, but now perhaps she's seen the error of her ways and given up. Or you really did see the ghost of poor Miss Askew?' Vignoles sounded conciliatory. 'But everything seems quite in order now, and there have been no new sightings reported. Each train that passed since we arrived here did so without being forced to stop, and the station staff and the signalman confirmed this has been the case for some days.'

'I'm chilled to the bone, hungry and desperate for a cup of tea!' Anna spoke up. 'It is high time we all decamped to the station and pressed one of the porters there to get the kettle on. I have a bag with just enough sandwiches and biscuits inside to go around.'

'Same here!' Laura laughed, patting her own black leather railway man's shoulder bag.

'Right, that's agreed then. Back to the station!' Vignoles was glad to change the subject. 'DC Howerth...'

'Sir!'

'It will take us approximately six minutes to reach the station and in that time, you will formulate a wholly convincing reason why the greater part of the Detective Department is tramping along the side of the London mainline in the dead of night that does not involved ghost hunting. And it had better be good,' he added sotto voce.

Chapter Forty-Five

Ashby Magna
27th October 1950

It had been a glorious October day; warm yet with the scent and taste of autumn on the air; that almost palpable feeling the land was winding down in preparation for winter. The sun had just dipped below the line of undulating trees on the horizon leaving a cloudless sky washed pale yellow mellowing through lilac into deep indigo. The platform of Ashby Magna station was now dyed with the tints of this glorious sky, rendering the windows of the little station as rectangles of solid colour.

Charles and Anna were seated on a wooden bench with the station name board forming both the back and tall divider from the twin bench on the opposite side and offering shelter from a light breeze gathering as dusk drew down.

'I hear Private Coulson's remains will be brought back to England.'

'Yes, the War Graves Commission are working with the family to try and achieve this. And I hope they do. There is a considerable cost involved, but the sale of that dratted ring will ease the burden on the family.' He made a wry face. 'I suppose it is the least that cursed diamond can do for both families; to see the two lovers lie together in that grave at St Peter's. It's going to cost a pretty penny to get the monument cleaned up on top, as it was badly stained by that young man's blood. But even so, I find it heartening that the Askew's and Coulson's have agreed the split the money from the sale of the ring between them so something remotely good will come of that unhappiest of diamonds.'

'It will raise a quite a sum when it goes to auction, I should think.'

'It will, Anna. And good riddance! Even if I had the money, I would seriously think twice about buying the Cobra's Eye.'

Anna looked at the tiny diamond on her engagement ring, letting the deepening violet of approaching night and the flare of the gas lamps illuminate its tiny heart. 'I agree. It is an incredible stone, and one's first instinct is to desire it - to covet it. It seems to appeal and encourage the baser aspects of one's nature. Think how it turned that doctor's head. He could never have even worn it, but he still wanted it so badly, desired it so much that Betty lost her life. What a horrible waste of a life.' She gently circled the stone with a fingertip. 'No, it has not brought happiness to anyone, and if anything has just brought sadness, violence, even death and ruined so many lives.' Anna looked along the straight tracks that vanished to a point a long way distant.

'You are right. The British Museum has done a lot of research on the Cobra's Eye, because as with all really special gems, it has a documented history if you know where to look, and it's left quite a trail of sadness in its wake. The Indian prince who first had it set on the gold band as a ring, died of fever together with his young princess, then at one point – sometime towards the end of the last century - it was owned by an antiquities trader in Alexandria. But he was killed – by a British naval shell of all things - leaving his young bride widowed and with the ring travelling in the desert. One supposes she lost it whilst there and Coulson had the misfortune to stumble upon it when serving under Monty.' He gave a mirthless snort of derision. 'It is a perverse fact that the notoriety of the diamond and its chilling link to death, murder and even to a ghost, have done nothing to reduce its value – the complete opposite in fact. It is now being trumpeted as a 'cursed' ring and the value has skyrocketed. Though I supposed this is just our human nature enjoying making connections between completely random events, imagining there is an external force at play when really each stroke of bad luck is unconnected.'

'Are you sure? I wonder...'

Vignoles fell silent, and instead of replying he opened the little hard backed book with the green cover in his hands and flicked through the pages, clearly enjoying the feel of the smooth paper, the smell of printing ink released from pages still fresh and newly bound, approving of the way the book opened perfectly to allow the pages to lie flat. This was a detail he appreciated in his own copy of the same book, his however now showing signs of frequent use and bearing a considerable number of neat red under linings. He looked at the columns of black printed numbers and curious names on the page, reading them as he might read the Apostle's Creed from his 'Book of Common Payer'; a book almost exactly the same size and weight to that now in his hand, and he smiled as he read part of the curious, indeed puzzling, litany of sonorous names -

Colorado
Flamingo
Papyrus
Humorist
Spion Kop
Call Boy
Spearmint
<u>Sir Frederick Banbury</u>
Flying Scotsman
Solario...

The neat underlining of Sir Frederick Banbury in red Biro stood out boldly on the page; a solitary intervention on an otherwise pristine and untouched spread. He now turned to the title page and taking his fountain pen from his jacket pocket, he carefully inscribed a dedication.

To Sunny Jim,
I knew you would want this one in your book. It looked splendid!
Always in our thoughts,
Charles and Anna.

He put his pen away and held the book open to allow the ink to dry. 'It makes no logical sense of course. A bit foolish I suppose.' His voice was oddly gruff. 'Perhaps I should have given the 5/6d to the hospital instead, but...' Vignoles tailed off.

Anna put a gloved hand on his leg and gave it a squeeze. 'It makes perfect sense. And he will thoroughly approve. It is quite the right thing to do. He never came to the station without his loco spotter's book. Not once...'

They looked at each other and stood up. 'Of course, some lucky little lad will no doubt pounce on this first thing tomorrow, but if he gets hours of enjoyment from it, Jim won't mind.' Vignoles weighed the little book in his hand as he spoke.

They walked towards the far end of the island platform, the only people on the station platform. The large dark blue and cream running in board at the far end was planted on two sturdy supports in a small rectangle formed by a low wall holding a little flowerbed. The roses were still blooming and big fat bushes of lavender around the edges released their perfume as they brushed against the out reaching fronds. Anna lit a candle inside a small rectangular lantern that she was carrying and now stood this on the corner of the wall, its light illuminating the purple flower heads. Vignoles then placed the 1950 combined edition of the 'ABC of British Locomotives,' beside it. They stood a moment together and then turned smartly about, Anna slipping her gloved hand through her husband's arm and walked towards the covered steps that up to the road bridge.

'Of course he won't know anything about this. But still nice to pay our own little tribute.' Anna gave her husband a sad smile, eyes swimming.

'All common sense says so...' He squeezed her arm that bit closer to his. 'Don't stop walking and don't turn around, just listen...'

As they walked along the empty platform behind the sound of their own feet, there was the slightly uneven tread of another following behind. A softer, lighter single footstep followed by the sound that just might be that made by two rubber pads like one would expect to find on the end of a pair of National Health issue crutches... step, tock, step, tock...

Anna looked at Charles, hardly daring to breathe and they hesitated for moment, the steps pausing exactly in unison. All was silent. He kissed her, and they moved on, and the little sounds once again kept time offering a suggestion of someone following them.

Step, tock, step, tock...

But neither felt in the least disturbed or unnerved, not a shiver of fear or anxiety. Far from it, they were smiling.

THE END

The Inspector Vignoles Mysteries

'The best of the railway detective novels on the market. The series continues to grow from strength to strength with every new release. First rate.' *Steam Railway*

'A series of books that just keep on getting better. Stephen Done has a fine gift for descriptive writing, and in the space of a few paragraphs vividly brings to life...the smells, the sounds, and the fashions of the day are almost palpable, which together with a clever and unpredictable plot keep the pages turning.' *The Railway Magazine*

Smoke Gets in Your Eyes (1946)

The Murder of Crows (1947)

The Torn Curtain (1948)

The Marylebone Murders (1949)

The Last Train (To Brackley Central) (1950)

New Brighton Rock (1951)

Blood & Custard (1952)

The Mountsorrel Mystery & Other Stories (1953)

Cold Steel Rail (1954)

Coming in 2019: Murder on Broadway (1955)

Available from all UK booksellers and online via Amazon and other suppliers. The GCRly shop in Loughborough Central stocks all titles, as does the Glous Warks Rly, Vale of Rheidol and Severn Valley Railway, all sales actively support the respective heritage railways.

Books direct from the author.

Signed copies are available at £8.99 plus £2.75 p&p (total £11.74).

Please email Stephen.done@gmail.com

Any book suppliers interested in stocking the Inspector Vignoles Mysteries, please get in touch and I can arrange attractive rates.